"The Beast in the Woods" was a folktale native to the Jonesborough area.

It had been hypothesized it was created to keep children from playing where wolves and rattlesnakes roamed. The folktale detailed the story of a backwoods town surrounded by dense forest. Occasionally, the people heard cries coming from the trees. The sounds weren't entirely human or entirely feral, but a wicked combination designed to intrigue and terrify. Not everyone could hear the cries, only those whom the town would later find dead among the pines and willows of inhuman wounds.

Before their deaths, the victims complained of a weeping demon calling to them, sending for them from somewhere hidden in darkness. Eventually, they'd go mad, and no one—not their mothers, fathers, or lovers—could hold them back from running toward the cries, never to be seen alive again.

"Don't go into the woods, Esther," he said.

I'LL
MAKE A
SPECTACLE
OF YOU

Praise for
I'll Make a Spectacle of You

"Steeped in Southern folklore and religious traditions, this gothic debut examines the cost of protection, the strength of belief, and the bloody truth that hides in the past of even the safest of havens. Beatrice Winifred Iker is a phenomenal new voice in horror."

—Kamilah Cole, Lodestar Award finalist and
bestselling author of the Divine Traitors duology

"A compelling blend of Appalachian folklore and dark academia. Iker weaves rootwork and secret societies into a chilling tale that examines the price we're willing to pay for protection—and power. *I'll Make a Spectacle of You* establishes Iker as a smart new voice in horror."

—Alisa Alering, author of *Smothermoss*

"Iker weaves a sinister slow-burn gothic mystery from the strands of family, faith, and the forgotten history of Black Appalachia. Twisty, brooding, and unpredictable—as deliciously creepy as a long walk home through a darkened wood!"

—Bitter Karella, author of *Moonflow*

"Pulsing with tension, Beatrice Winifred Iker's *I'll Make a Spectacle of You* is a chilling, richly layered debut where folklore, academia, and ancestral trauma collide. With the weaving together of horror and history, this story hooks its hold from the very first page as it reminds readers how the past never stays silent for long."

—LaTanya McQueen, author of *When the Reckoning Comes*

"Heart-pounding tension, edge-of-your-seat thrills, and excellent prose; Beatrice Winifred Iker's *I'll Make a Spectacle of You* was a book I just couldn't put down. If you love folk horror and always wonder if the shadows are looking back at you, this is the book for you."

—Kosoko Jackson, *USA Today* bestselling author
of *The Forest Demands Its Due*

"Immersive, inventive, and scary as hell! With impeccable folklore and lush writing, Iker's fresh, insistent voice will remind you of all the reasons you should stay out of the woods."

—Neena Viel, author of *Listen to Your Sister*

"A nuanced and propulsive tale told with great care. Weaving frightening set pieces with such lovingly depicted characters is a tough balancing act; Iker pulls it off flawlessly. Anyone who reads this debut will anxiously await anything this writer does next! I'm talking about me. I am anyone. Add this to your library ASAP!"

—Lamar Giles, author of *The Getaway*

"A mesmerizing debut filled with compelling, complicated characters and steeped in deeply nuanced worldbuilding, *I'll Make a Spectacle of You* will pull you in with exquisite claws from the first breath to the final page. Terrifying, heartbreaking, and unflinchingly honest storytelling. Beatrice Winifred Iker's unparalleled talent dares you not to cancel your weekend plans."

—DaVaun Sanders, author of *Keynan Masters and the Peerless Magic Crew*

I'LL MAKE A SPECTACLE OF YOU

BEATRICE WINIFRED IKER

Run For It
Hachette Book Group
1290 Avenue of the Americas
New York, NY 10104
hachettebookgroup.com

First Edition: November 2025

Run For It is an imprint of Orbit, a division of Hachette Book Group.
The Run For It name and logo are registered trademarks of Hachette Book Group, Inc.

The publisher is not responsible for websites (or their content) that are not owned by the publisher.

The Hachette Speakers Bureau provides a wide range of authors for speaking events. To find out more, go to hachettespeakersbureau.com or email HachetteSpeakers@hbgusa.com.

Run For It books may be purchased in bulk for business, educational, or promotional use. For information, please contact your local bookseller or the Hachette Book Group Special Markets Department at special.markets@hbgusa.com.

Quotes from the King James Bible (2017). Cambridge University Press. (Original work published 1769)

Library of Congress Cataloging-in-Publication Data

Names: Iker, Beatrice Winifred author
Title: I'll make a spectacle of you / Beatrice Winifred Iker.
Other titles: I will make a spectacle of you
Description: First edition. | New York, NY : Run For It, 2025.
Identifiers: LCCN 2025010248 | ISBN 9780316575249 trade paperback | ISBN 9780316575256 ebook
Subjects: LCGFT: Horror fiction | Novels
Classification: LCC PS3609.K46 I45 2025 | DDC 813/.6—dc23/eng/20250402
LC record available at https://lccn.loc.gov/2025010248

ISBNs: 9780316575249 (trade paperback), 9780316575256 (ebook)

Printed in the United States of America

LSC-C

Printing 1, 2025

In association with Electric Postcard Entertainment, Inc.

To DeFord Bailey, Josephine Baker, Ethel B. Beck, James G. Beck, Absalom Boston, Octavia Butler, Will Marion Cook, Henrietta Vinton Davis, Robert S. Duncanson, Nikki Giovanni, Dr. Grant, Prince Hall, Jupiter Hammon, bell hooks, Zora Neale Hurston, Caldonia Fackler Johnson, James Weldon Johnson, Sissieretta Jones, Mary Smith Peake, Tidye Pickett, Charley Pride, Inez Beverly Prosser, Lesley Riddle, Nina Simone, Effie Waller Smith, Louise Stokes, Henry Ossawa Tanner, Robert Robinson Taylor, Edward C. Williams, and William F. Yardley.

You are remembered.

I beseech you therefore, brethren, by the mercies of God, that ye present your bodies a living sacrifice, holy, acceptable unto God, which is your reasonable service. And be not conformed to this world: but be ye transformed by the renewing of your mind, that ye may prove what is that good, and acceptable, and perfect, will of God.

—Romans 12:1–2

I'LL
MAKE A
SPECTACLE
OF YOU

The Beginning

The sun hummed above Zora that lurid June afternoon. It was so bright that she shielded her ten-year-old eyes beneath emerald branches crisscrossing overhead. She sprinted along the golden-lit trail, her beaded braids clacking behind her in air so muggy it had to be gulped. Pine stuck to Zora's pursed lips and then on her tongue when she couldn't lick it away. On an ordinary day, she wouldn't've noticed it. It would be a minor nuisance. But that day, the sweet-laced woodsy sap was an invasion curling down her throat. Her mouth softened, sinking into a frown.

Her older sister, Jasmine, led the way deep into their grandparents' forested Knoxville property like she always had. And as they ran, Zora focused on the textured underside of Jasmine's tennis shoes like *she* always had. But today, something was different.

"Jazz! Hold up!"

Jasmine's stride was unbroken. Her usual gentle smile absent, replaced by scrunched eyebrows folding into a look of stubborn determination. Zora's mouth watered as she passed her favorite honeysuckle bush, where they each plucked blossoms for the sweet nectar hidden within. Jasmine's pace made it impossible for Zora to stop or do anything other than try not to keel over at the burning in her chest. Zora leaned over as she ran and her lungs heaved painfully. She should have been sweltering, but the beads of sweat rolling down her backbone were cold.

Sunrays strained through Zora's hands as she shielded her eyes from the glare. She feared the glow would trick her into taking a wrong turn or tripping over gnarled kudzu vines. Wasn't that what kudzu did? Confused you? Grandpa called it "curly devil" and said it was a powerful addition to any magic. But that power, he warned, ain't always right. Zora was still thinking on that.

The possibility of getting lost and the bright sun notwithstanding, Zora usually loved running. Specifically, she loved running with Jasmine. But her sister had just turned thirteen and had started to love running with Zora less and less. Zora saw it. The way Jasmine had looked down when their grandmother suggested they play outside proved it. Something had changed between them.

The woods around the house were normally a playground. The acres of untouched Tennessee forest hidden on the outskirts of town were the ideal location for exchanging secrets and practicing the basics of conjure. They passed the bright red signs warning intruders they were about to trespass on private property. Zora blinked at the metal triple-stapled by Grandpa two summers before. Then they passed the leather bags of protection amulets, and Zora knew they'd gone too far. These were county woods.

"Please stop, Jazz!"

"Ugh! Fine."

Jasmine's words were incredulous, but she was huffing just as much as Zora. Her narrow shoulders shook as a coughing fit momentarily racked her body. Zora hoped Jasmine would fall over and dirty the sporty dress she wore. Jasmine didn't even wear dresses until a few months ago, and certainly not to play in the woods.

They were silent until Zora could breathe well enough to be angry. "You know we're too far out! Grandma and Grandpa said—"

"Yeah, well, they ain't here," Jasmine huffed again.

Zora glared at how her sister's throat worked to breathe and how her long legs struggled to remain upright. Jasmine adjusted and then readjusted the orange dress that reminded Zora of shiny traffic cones. Jasmine had exhausted herself, and for what? The bubble of suspicion that had been building in Zora's chest since they'd set out from the house burst. Niceties didn't exist in the woods. They never had. That had been one of its beauties—something they'd loved together.

Zora stared Jasmine down. "What did I do to make you hate me?" Spat words lay between them like a furious diary entry spoken aloud. But to Zora, they were more than that. However painful, this moment would forever be etched in her memory, a reminder of the undeniable truth it held.

"Huh?" she asked when Jasmine shrugged away her question. The words swelled, pulsing in Zora's chest before she blurted them out. "Go 'head. What is it? You afraid I'm gonna steal that lil dress? Best believe I wouldn't. It's ugly as sin."

"No, what's ugly is me seein' you in your room *kissin'* the American Girl dolls."

Zora stood stunned as Jasmine's words slapped her across the face. Was it ugly to kiss dolls? Or was it ugly because Zora was kissing them? Heat warmed Zora's cheeks as an emotion thundered through her. She couldn't name it then but knew now it was shame.

"I didn't..." Whispered words drifted off as she registered the smug look in Jasmine's eyes and how her hands sat firmly on her teenage hips, drawing Zora's attention to the subtle but noticeable changes. Jasmine was different. Her once-slender figure had taken on a new, more shapely form. Was this the reason for the burning ache in Zora's chest?

Jasmine had violated Zora's privacy and then used the information she discovered to wound her. She was becoming a new version of herself, someone Zora couldn't understand. A stranger.

It was clearly time to return to their grandparents, but just when Zora lifted her foot to sprint back to their house, she heard it. Voices, deep in the woods, staggered on top of each other. They spoke in a tight cadence. In Zora's childhood mind, her first thought was that they were a singing group, maybe a band or choir. But as their voices grew closer, she heard an anger that surpassed the tones of sister combat. She didn't have a word for it. The closest she could come was rage. Wrath. Some other sin she'd learned in Bible study and verse-to-spell memorization.

"Zora."

Jasmine grabbed Zora's shoulders so tight that Zora yelped in surprise.

"Run, Zora." She'd been out of breath moments before but now inhaled sharply as she glanced over her glaring orange shoulder.

"What? What about y—"

The voices were closer now. So close that Zora could make out a few words.

"Goddess" and "balefire" and "sacrifice."

Zora's body grew tense. Her legs trembled.

"Z—run!"

And Zora did. A mile away, she heard Jasmine's screech, but she kept running back to their grandparents' house and never returned to their woods again.

Chapter One

Jonesborough was heavy. All who entered felt it.

The oldest town in Tennessee had eighteenth-century dust coating the streets. Leaves withered early, desperate to escape life among the whispering sycamores. The wind never blew like it oughta—instead, it lurched around the citizens' spines like lightning cracked across the holler, goading them to lose their way and their wits.

Still, people smiled at you so long as you looked familiar. And kept smiling so long as you smiled back.

The tiny mountain town was a clot of Appalachia's best and worst attributes. Home to Andrew Jackson's restless ghost *and* the country's first HBCU, Bricksbury Mountain College, Jonesborough both shocked visitors and lulled residents with its willful inability to self-actualize.

To Zora Robinson, though, the place wasn't cobblestone streets where Civil War enthusiasts came to argue whether the Union-leaning folk in the area made any difference just up the road in the Battle of Blountville. Nor was it the town where her sister, Jasmine, was finishing her doctorate in biblical studies. No, to Zora, Jonesborough was boundless possibilities. It was a repository of local and global knowledge. It was a pin in the map of her life that would mark the moment everything finally made sense. One day, she'd look back on this place and be grateful for the lessons learned and achievements earned. During lectures and appearances, she'd say, "This was my genesis. Bricksbury Mountain College was to me what Eatonville was to my namesake, Zora Neale Hurston." Or something to that effect.

Bricksbury thought nothing of the Ivies. What were they to the institution with a 99.7 percent graduation rate? What were they to the safest campus, with the fewest employed security officers and lowest instances of crime?

Bricksbury was a feat. A towering display of composed intellect swirled with *just* enough backwoods charm to piss off the uppity city folk. More Black physicists, CEOs, and federal judges graduated from Bricksbury than any other college in the country.

But because Bricksbury thought nothing of the Ivies, Zora's degree in African and African American studies from Dartmouth didn't get her a place there. Nor did her sister—estranged, for all intents, and vocal about *not* wanting Zora to attend the same school—send any letters of recommendation. Made no pleas to the dean of admissions. Not even an email. Zora got into Bricksbury on her own—primarily through her documented research assistance over the last few years. The highly connected professor she assisted taught her the importance of not only what you know but also *who* you know. Dr. Maurice Grant was a formal older man who reminded Zora of her late grandfather—and was the entire reason she was at Bricksbury.

Around ten years old, Zora developed a fascination with the past. She spent years poring over journals, letters, and anything else her grandpa saved from his years as a history teacher. When their parents dropped Zora and her sister off at their grandparents' house on long summer days, Jasmine gardened and gossiped with their grandmother. Zora, three years younger, stayed out of the Knoxville heat and devoured the past with Grandpa. He was delighted to share his passion for local history with Zora, even taking her on "field trips" to places he'd always wanted to take his students, if he could ever have talked the district into funding.

Grandpa gave her more than an understanding of the Clinton 12; he took her to Clinton High School itself. The twenty-minute drive forever altered Zora's life. History was different when you could *see* where one hundred sticks of dynamite had leveled the school building. *Walk* the streets the students had—the Klan had—the media had. It was a roller coaster of emotions from sorrow to rage, and finally, hope—something segregationists never extinguished in the community.

Grandpa took her to the Baptist church that often housed those who fled the burning crosses placed on their lawns by white pastors and their congregants. Zora learned about the people who protected them, including conjurers, whom the church quietly summoned.

Conjurers primarily lived out in the county, as did most of Zora's family before moving to Knoxville. The Robinsons were powerful, backwoods folk, Grandpa had told her, and Clinton was where her family's history intersected with the region's, right at the spot where prayer and magic were woven into Black America.

Zora spent the drive back to her grandparents' house resolved to protect the untold stories—all of them, in full. It was the first time she'd researched what it meant to be a "historian." It was her beginning.

At the same time Zora developed her adolescent interest in history, Jasmine dove pride-first into religion—specifically, their African Methodist Episcopal Zion denomination. However, she'd branched out to biblical studies for her bachelor's, master's, and doctorate. Zora supposed she couldn't really be angry with Jasmine. Well, she could. And was. But she *shouldn't*. She shouldn't blame her sister. They'd both needed something, anything, to cling to that wasn't each other, and that preferably didn't remind them of each other. Zora found purpose and peace in conjure and history books. But Jasmine needed something else to balm her memories of what happened in their grandparents' woods.

Zora's history ambitions led her to Dartmouth, where she braved four New England winters. Afterward, right out of school, she'd spent a few years working tirelessly as an archives technician in her native Knoxville. It was a dream position. The Beck Cultural Exchange Center, headed by Dr. Grant, taught her more of the practical elements of being an archivist, and during those long hours cleaning, repairing, and preserving records in the stacks, she had time to think. Despite her parents' and sister's insistence that a graduate degree in Appalachian studies was a waste of her time, Zora paid them no mind. She was used to being the disappointing younger child.

Zora supposed she should be thankful she didn't grow up indulged due to her spot in the birth order. Jasmine didn't give her a chance. When Zora leaned into Black and Appalachian historical accounts, Jasmine leaned into the Bible. By the time she turned sixteen, Jasmine had ascended to the top of the children's Sunday school leadership board at their home church. Their parents beamed with pride, while Zora grew up invisibly beside them in the pews. Nothing she did—not even awkwardly coming out or failing to hide a pre-prom pre-roll—adequately turned their attention from Jasmine for that long.

When Jasmine left to devote herself to biblical studies at Bricksbury, she was proficient in Biblical Greek and Hebrew and fluent in Latin. Zora's 3.98 GPA and "secular" interests could never compare; she had the pleasure of disappointing their parents both academically *and* religiously, which she decided was just as impressive as it was depressive.

So, Zora was unfazed by their lackluster opinion of her lifelong dedication to folklore. She'd heard it all, as had her therapists, and Zora looked at her acceptance to Bricksbury as two-pronged: proof this was her destined path and an invitation to tell her family to eat shit.

When Zora arrived at Bricksbury, she was determined not to allow her family to take her joy from her anymore. They wouldn't.

They won't, Zora repeated in her mind. This was the program of her dreams. *They wouldn't. They won't. Jasmine wouldn't. Jasmine won't.* Zora repeated the words and kept her eyes on the pebbled path, away from the flaring morning sun. The humidity was enough to distract her from family drama for now. She treaded on stone pavers long cracked and unnaturally angled. The blanched grass creeping through the fractures was scraggly and lifeless. Zora didn't want to look at it, but the sun's brightness glinted painfully every time she looked up. Her eyes already ached. She cleared her throat and slumped her shoulders forward so no one would notice she was holding a leash. Henry Louis, her Rottweiler, strolled beside her. His dark fur was shiny from his welcome-to-your-new-home bath the night before.

The cramped dorm studio would be their place for the next two years, and since dogs were strictly prohibited on campus, Zora had to be clever. Henry Louis's collar sat comfortably around his broad neck as he strolled, the *see me not* mojo bag Zora clasped to it held firmly in place. She snuck a peek every few minutes to ensure it was still there. It wasn't precisely an invisibility spell—she did consider it before ultimately deciding that making Henry Louis invisible to *herself* wasn't ideal—but it rendered the dog less interesting than his surroundings. People would just...look past him. So far, so good.

Zora would get used to walking naturally with the leash, but this first walk had begun with full sun, and she'd been hoping for a rainy, overcast day. If students were busy with umbrellas and avoiding getting their hair wet, they'd be less likely to notice Henry Louis. Instead, Zora marched through the stifling Fisherman Quad, where pollen swarms caused a sneezing fit. When she was done, Henry Louis looked up at her expectantly. His morning walks were his favorite time, and he wouldn't be swayed by anything, least of all the heat. Zora resisted the urge to pet him affectionately behind his ears. Later.

There wasn't a breeze in the heavy September air clinging to her skin. A layer of dampness turned her men's collared shirt into an inescapable swathe. She felt better but more vulnerable as she peeled the linen fabric off. The fresh air offered no reprieve. *At least I look good.* She'd cornrowed her hair that morning and grinned as she felt the ends swish at the dampness on the small of her back. Luckily, she always planned for an outfit change or three. Zora's gray knitted tank was neither too casual nor too formal.

Crimson brick buildings sprouted in imposing clusters around the quad. The massive Gothic-revival edifices looked less like campus buildings and more like mountain mansions. The founders had wanted the school to be a home for the students, many of whom would graduate and then stay on campus to teach and live the rest of their lives.

Zora found a comfortable stride as she passed a group of theater majors doing an impromptu show on the lawn. Henry Louis was too interested in their claps and stomps, so they kept moving lest his jangling collar draw too much attention. The lawn's morning bustle gave Zora the ideal background for agonizing about her thesis proposal, a required part of Bricksbury's application. She'd spent exhaustive hours researching, analyzing, and writing the twenty-page document, and now she awaited her advisor's official verdict. She should be grateful for the calm before drafting, but Zora couldn't relax. The doubts only grew harsher as days passed. Her brain recalled additional sources she could have incorporated and objectives that could have been—*should* have been—better articulated. An inescapable sense of unease enveloped her as her thoughts churned in a murky, unhelpful loop.

Zora knew she needed to get out of her head, though she felt she was not entirely to blame. Her rigorous undergrad program and years spent researching the past taught Zora to look at her work critically and with frequent retroactivity. In theory, the further away you got from your work, the clearer it became. But while true, the maxim impacted her mental health both in and out of college. She hoped to find a better balance at Bricksbury, though she was gravely aware this dream was far-fetched.

Bricksbury was an academic refuge for overachievers and the victory obsessed. With an acceptance rate of less than 4 percent, you had to be consumed with success just to get through the doors. And with her groundbreaking primary-sourced thesis, Zora was gonna fuck success into the next lifetime. She just needed to balance it with regular walks with Henry Louis, meditation, and hopefully, some actual fucking.

Despite her retrospective concerns, Zora stood by her proposal, "The Spiritual History of Affrilachia." It was well researched, with plenty of primary sources she'd unearthed herself. Those were her truest points of pride—the relationships in Knox County *she'd* cultivated and maintained.

Her thesis was strong. There was no need to worry. Besides, this was supposed to be a simple, exploratory walk to ensure Henry Louis's mojo bag worked. And it seemed a success since, despite his undeniable appeal, no one had even glanced his way.

Zora focused on the raucous first-day sounds coming from the windows in the building she passed. They were sharply arched with bright stained glass placed in custom stainless-steel tracks that swung outward—modern fire codes softening into the old world. The building was three stories high, and every window was open, letting the humid air inside. Zora let the morning sunshine and laughter from the open arches wash over her. The air hung motionless, but for a moment, it was too pleasant to complain.

Belatedly, Zora realized her cheeks ached from smiling. She glanced inside a window at random. Her smile sagged, then faded away.

Jasmine.

Zora hadn't spoken to her in three years.

And now here she was. Right in front of her.

Amias Crawfoot
September 1, 1823
Jonesboro, Tennessee
Jonesboro African Baptist Church

Bricksbury Mountain College was born of righteous sacrifice. God demanded it, and Amias delivered, palms bloody and pride dampened. Amias supposed he could've refused God's offer of holy protection. He'd seen fools do more with less. But this was no ambush; Amias had begged for His bargain. He and his sister, Hosanna, had searched frantically for divine protection over their fledgling school. And His word was a lamp unto Amias's feet and a light unto his path.[1] There was nothing for it but to obey Him.

When Amias and Hosanna first thought of Bricksbury Mountain College, they'd meant to nurture curiosity and preserve knowledge.[2] They'd long wanted a haven for Negroes to learn without the fear of racial violence that terrorized the outside world. It was meant to be safe. They'd meant to do many philanthropic things, but they'd never stopped to consider whether they *should* be doing them. They just did. Amias, especially, did far too much. He bloodied his

---

1 Psalm 119:105–106—Thy word is a lamp unto my feet, and a light unto my path. I have sworn, and I will perform it, that I will keep thy righteous judgments.
2 Malachi 2:7—For the priest's lips should keep knowledge, and they should seek the law at his mouth: for he is the messenger of the Lord of hosts.

hands far too many times. And he didn't know it until everyone he'd ever known had died. He had meant well, though.

Hosanna and Amias came from a family of proud Revolutionary soldiers and nurses. Before that, they'd bought their freedom and farmed their acreage within a day's journey to Boston. They were quiet, strong people whose faith in God never wavered but who all wished for idle time to learn. Knowledge was a secret bridge often used to isolate, as they knew well.

Early on, Amias and Hosanna's mother told harrowing nursing stories from the war. They'd given the nurses, especially the Black ones, minimal education, but even that was more than she'd ever gotten at home. Their father and grandfather, newly manumitted, had fought for American independence. Then the heroes returned to seaside Massachusetts with their freed papers clutched to their chests—aware slave catchers rarely caught the person they sought, but they always brought someone back.

It was a heavy thing to realize the war had offered a complicated, frail freedom they'd never have again. And that returning home meant returning to a racial terror that was not frail at all. Even on their successful farm, where the family always had enough to eat, and their mother sent them to school for many years, Amias grew up with taunting from the white children in neighboring towns. "We'll call a catcher on you / Fiddle dee doooo," they'd sing in adolescent soprano. Demons in starched cotton. And not the last demon Amias would see.

Amias and Hosanna battled with the intersection of education, class, and race while watching their elders and the neighboring children. They'd been taught to seek His service, and so spent weeks praying, asking where they would be of best use until He answered. They had meant to honor their parents by ensuring more Negroes could receive education. Though daunting, the siblings migrated from seaside Massachusetts, heading due south, letting God guide them to where they'd be needed most.

But they knew they'd need His protection when they arrived in Jonesboro, long before a Bricksbury brick was laid. Already, there were white abolitionists making homes and noise in the area. The lone Negro church, Jonesboro African Baptist Church, was growing wary of the attention the abolitionists were bringing to them, using the church and their congregants as "examples" of good, God-fearing Negroes. These were similar types of demons to the ones from his childhood in Massachusetts. But instead of using Amias's fear of slave catchers, they somehow hid their white guilt behind additional racism and unearned pride. If not for the damage it caused, he might have been impressed by the extensive emotional loopholes they squeezed themselves in and out of.

Both Bricksbury and Jonesboro needed protection. Amias and Hosanna knew it, but they didn't know how they'd do it without a well-funded army. It was Amias's idea to ask God, if not for an army, then to make him powerful enough to fight one. But God told them to be patient.

They settled in the area. Amias learned the people's needs and used his farming and craftsman skills. His first building was a schoolhouse. It was for all the children and was full on most days the teachers, including Hosanna, could teach. Amias built a few homes, then worked for the church briefly, where he met Elmira. They married less than a year later, and Amias asked God not to give them children on their wedding night. He knew, even then, that marrying Elmira was a social need. People had started asking questions and cocking their heads when he said he was waiting for God to tell him what to do, even though it was the truth. That was when Amias learned to lie well—it was all in the eyes, he learned, after dozens of hours staring at himself in the mirror. His eyes needed to be stiller. Indeed, if he held himself still enough, people stopped asking questions altogether.

When their cousin sent word that the flu had taken both their parents, Amias could wait no longer. Hosanna was wary. "God knows best," she'd said. And she'd probably been right. However, Amias wasn't in the mood for anything contrary to his mission. He wanted Bricksbury. He'd wanted his parents to see the start of it, and now he'd waited too long. God had waited too long.

On a late summer's night, Amias and Hosanna went into the woods behind Jonesboro African Baptist Church. The bubbling creek was peaceful and perfect for grounding themselves in God's light. Together, they asked Him for protection for Bricksbury. God was quiet for some time. They sat with interlocked hands, listening and tuning out the creek beside them and the creatures scattered among the trees. Hours later, God answered. Their sacrifice would need to be great, and it would need to be a life. He would only save a life in the place of another. *Nothing is given freely*, He explained.

Amias and Hosanna looked at each other with wild eyes. Would a bird suffice? A squirrel? They set out with two flintlocks, a musket, and a sharpened hunting knife for backup, eager to only do this once. They still needed to go deeper into the woods before dawn. No one else could know the crimes they were about to commit.

The birds did not suffice; neither did three squirrels and a hare. It wasn't until Amias killed an unsuspecting fox with amber-gold eyes that something took hold of his lungs, squeezing the breath out of him. He fell to the forest floor, grabbing his chest, faintly hearing Hosanna scream in the background. The soil beneath his palms shifted for a moment, swishing back and forth under him. Then it stopped. His heart calmed. His lungs rose and fell like they should. But when he looked past his sister, who'd been cradling his face, worried he'd asked God for too much and was being punished, he saw more amber gold. More foxes, more sacrifices, that God demanded. *A life for a life*, God whispered to Amias, who pointed at the foxes with his bloodied knife and said to Hosanna, "A life for a life."

By morning, they'd killed several more foxes. Amias was having difficulty carrying their corpses. Finally, the soil shifted beneath him once more. Both his and Hosanna's breaths hitched as they felt Him. Tired limbs and sweaty clothes be damned, He was there, giving them the weapon they'd requested. The one they'd killed for. This weapon would protect Jonesboro and Bricksbury from those who would want to harm them. And that was the third time Amias saw a demon.

Chapter Two

Campus noise softened into the background as Zora gaped, numb, in the burning sun while her sister gesticulated at the front of the classroom. Nothing was more important than witnessing this. Practiced hands drifted in time with Jasmine's voice, punctuating and underlining her thoughts. Since her first time teaching a Sunday school class, Jasmine had always been a natural at captivating an audience. Zora remembered asking if she was nervous the Saturday evening before in their shared bedroom, warm comforter up to her chin. Jasmine frowned at Zora as if she'd been asked to question her purpose. Now her—according to the blackboard—Introduction to the Old Testament students/admirers leaned forward in their seats as Zora's sister explained some ancient point or other. They were, as biblical studies students, ironically, enraptured.

Jasmine looked around the room, meeting her students' eyes with a gentle, berry-lipstick smile. A familiar knot swelled in Zora's throat as she held her breath; she, too, was compelled to watch. The shame of their grandparents' woods claimed her lungs. It was a heavy shame. Not the kind that's sweet-talked into submission with comfort food and vision boards. This shame had tainted Zora. It was the weight of knowing she'd abandoned her family.

Knowing she was ten years old at the time and couldn't be held responsible didn't stop Zora from blaming herself. That Jasmine had, in fact, screamed for Zora to leave didn't matter. She couldn't logic her way out of self-blame. At ten, she'd heard voices in their grandparents' woods and knew danger had met them. She knew it. So, why did she run away? Why didn't she stay and help Jasmine or convince Jasmine to leave with her? Questions she and her therapist wished she would stop asking herself.

Fifteen years later, Zora didn't know her sister. Their relationship died in those woods. She stared at the students fawning over Jasmine, spines straight and eyes sparkling. Had her sister ever given Zora as much attention as she was giving them?

Jasmine—*Mrs. Robinson*—massaged her left ear with French ombre nails. No one else would know, but a flat scar was hidden under the glinting kaleidoscope of helix studs and rings. Other scars were scattered across Jasmine's body, but she hid them under an elegant, square-neck dress. The dress's ombre of orange to pale pink and coral gave way to black tights and vintage ankle boots. *Fuck*, she was so…chic. And it looked effortless. You'd think the thin silver rings and helix studs she massaged were decorative, but they were not. They were each a tiny amulet imbued with intention only Jasmine knew, though Zora could guess. She hadn't seen her sister in years, but they shared a childhood trauma only the two of them would understand. It gave Zora more insight into Jasmine than her adoring fans, who might interpret Jasmine's melodic voice and calm eyes as easygoing. But Zora knew better. Jasmine's amulet earrings were probably imbued with clarity, peace, and even uncrossing for good measure.

Of all the intentions, Zora knew one of them had to be protection. The sisters were highly skilled in defensive magic. It was something…the only thing…they could control. Jasmine preferred to use her magical intentions and ancestral prayers on defensive jewelry, makeup, and clothing. Zora gravitated toward spells enhanced by herbs and roots. Either way, the sisters walked the campus with untold passive conjure magic.

"Hi!"

Zora spun around, gasping. A young woman, too bright-eyed for grad school, adjusted her backpack straps and grinned down at Henry Louis. The backpack looked stuck between her damp skin and the thin neon spaghetti straps of her tank top. She barely glanced up at Zora past her long, false lashes when she spoke again. "Is he friendly? Just wanted to ask before I pet him."

Zora plastered on a smile, though her heart pounded, and she licked her stretched lips nervously. "He's very friendly, go ahead!" She looked around frantically for the mojo bag and found it lying in the grass. The *H–L* she'd hand-sewn into the fabric had been soaked in Florida water for three days and currently lay face up in accusation. This was her fault; she'd been distracted by Jasmine. Henry Louis, on the other hand, was thrilled with the sudden attention. His thick tail wagged, and drool had begun to gather in his jowls.

Two more students came over for a canine-based serotonin boost, and Zora hesitated. Hoodoo was long a part of Bricksbury's culture, but that didn't mean every student practiced or was even aware of it. Folklore was rarely believed, even by those who spoke it. They could see the mojo bag and think nothing of it. They could ask Zora what her magical intentions were, giving it no more weight than avoiding ladders or black cats. Or maybe they'd call her a heretical Christian and demand she be burned at the stake...though that might be a fear particular to her psyche.

Zora told herself not to be dramatic as she inconspicuously clipped the mojo bag back onto Henry Louis's collar, noting the chain's broken link. She drank down morning humidity, suddenly overwhelmed by the crowd's noises. Zora put a hand above her pounding chest. Her eyes darted around the packed lawn. She prayed no one else would see them and that she wouldn't pass out, drawing further attention.

The bag replaced, the three students crouched in front of Henry

Louis frowned one after the other, and looked away in different directions. *Thank fuck.* The first one stood and scratched fresh braids; another looked at the hand petting Henry Louis as if he wanted to wash it. Zora didn't wait to see what would happen with the third one. She marched back to her dorm with renewed swiftness. Her "Capricorns Against Chaos" and "Historians Against History Repeating Itself" keychains *clink-clink*ed at her sudden speed. Henry Louis didn't complain, though he did give the three students one last glance before galloping to keep up.

She'd managed the situation, so Zora mentally ran through her itinerary for the day. The practice calmed her. First, she needed to scope out a local apothecary for much-needed herbs. She would not be without an ample stock of rose of Jericho and death flowers, among other necessities. Second, she needed some yoga and a cuddle session with Henry Louis. And lastly, she had to prepare for Conjure Night.

The online flyer was sleek, with glittering gold-and-black letters:

You are graciously invited to Conjure Night,

an evening of herbal bathing games,

moonlit fellowship, and live jazz.

Your attendance is welcome.

Herbal bathing was simple, just touching and identifying an herb by its energy, but it could be intensive if combined with meditation, scrying, or other forms of magic. Zora doubted they'd devote the psychic energy needed to do it with a group of random students. Instead, unfortunately, she'd likely be subjected to Hoodoo games designed for children and newbies. This would allow more participant conversation and foster community but bore Zora with the childlike monotony. Still, she knew, it would be better than the terrible loneliness that was the alternative.

When it came down to it, Zora just hoped to find friends at Conjure Night, others who understood her love of folklore and Hoodoo in particular. Another thing Dartmouth had taught her was that, on college campuses, you're often only as lonely as your will to get out of bed. And Zora wouldn't be lonely again, not like that. Not at Bricksbury.

Preparations for the night meant feeding her protective luck mojo bag, which made the apothecary trip necessary.

"Hey, neighbor!"

Zora froze with her hand wrapped around her doorknob. Why couldn't she have been assigned a normal apartment with an indoor hallway? She'd never had a courtyard door but already hated how open and vulnerable it left her. If Henry Louis's mojo bag had slipped off again . . . she would have a fit. Zora turned to find a short, smiling woman with a mouthful of bright mango in her open doorway, a short distance across the courtyard. She carried two tote bags overflowing with books and loose papers. Jet-black micros were pulled into a ponytail under a wide-brimmed cowboy hat. *Smart.* Zora squinted against harsh sun rays. The woman's braids touched the ground when she leaned over to stop a tabby from escaping. The dress was low-cut enough to show a peek of a tattoo down her sternum—Zora was vaguely able to make out the antennae of some insect, maybe some wings. *Cool.*

"Don't you even think about it, Dr. Ncuti," the woman scolded the cat in a high-pitched, singsongy voice loud enough for Zora to hear. She wagged her finger before kissing the top of his head and locking him inside. "Sorry about that. And, uh . . . he's here low-key."

Zora was happy for a reason to smile at an accomplice in illegal pet harboring. "He looks sweet."

"He's a menace," the woman said, shifting the bags to one hand and fishing her phone out of the pocket of her violet sundress with the other. Her erratic movements caused her thong sandals to smack against the courtyard's brick pavers. The sound echoed against the courtyard's walls, unsettling the birds perched in the beams.

"But hey, he gives me dopamine, and I give him a place to live. Oh, I'm Khadijah."

"Zora. And that sounds like a fair trade." Zora's words cut through the chaos of the flapping birds, but she was only half paying attention. The other half worried how long Henry Louis would stand still without detection. How long the broken clasp would stay intact. How terrible would it be if a Rottweiler magically appeared in front of you where it previously hadn't been. Could it turn into a Shakespearean woman-gone-mad-by-magic sort of thing? Would she break Khadijah's brain?

They stood in the bottleneck of the courtyard. The "Neighborhood," as the school insisted on calling it, was a smattering of two-story buildings surrounding a rectangle of hemlock trees. The trees were fine. That wasn't what irked Zora. Her disdain stemmed from the cluster's misleading label. A true neighborhood was a place where people steadily grew roots, sometimes for generations. A place where folks noticed if you were hurting or sick. No one could cultivate a long-term existence here. The buildings and rooms housed transients. And it wasn't as if anyone besides Khadijah had offered any welcome or hospitality.

But the "Neighborhood" still existed, as did Zora's bitterness. The pine-smelling hemlocks dulled her ire.

"Nice mat. Haint blue, right?"

Khadijah pointed at the doormat Zora'd had for years . . . the one Henry Louis lay on. Her eyes lingered on the mat for a beat longer than Zora was comfortable with. The mat had been a gift from Grandpa, who was particularly superstitious. He believed haint blue should be present all around the outside of one's home, lest evil spirits feel welcome to taunt or interrupt the lives of conjure folk. If Khadijah knew the significance of haint blue...then maybe...

"Yeah, it is," Zora said. How far could she push her luck? The students who stopped to pet Henry Louis were oblivious, but Khadijah seemed less so. Zora's earlier distractions were set aside, and Khadijah's chestnut-brown eyes were alert under that lavender cowboy hat. *Ah.* They were each inspecting the other. Weighing if they should continue or end the conversation. A bead of sweat rolled down between Zora's breasts, and she resisted the impulse to squirm. She was ready for autumn's chill.

"Hey, are you going to Conjure Night?" Khadijah asked. She switched her flooded tote bag from one shoulder to the other and pulled out the flyer Zora had seen online. "Should be a good turnout. Hopefully, I'll see you there."

Zora took the flyer and pretended to read it as Khadijah strutted away, several sheets of paper threatening to escape her bags like Dr. Ncuti in her apartment, which reminded Zora of Henry Louis, who was now adorably sleeping on top of Grandpa's rug.

Khadijah, Zora felt sure, had seen Henry Louis. Which meant that they had quite a bit in common.

Zora's smile faded when her phone pinged.

"Let's get you inside, Henry Louis. I've got a busy day."

Amias Crawfoot
September 1, 1857
Jonesborough, Tennessee
Bricksbury Mountain College—Jonesboro
African Baptist Church

We agreed that you wouldn't come out here and do this," Hosanna whispered behind Amias.

"I agreed to nothing," Amias said.

"This ain't right, you being out here all the time, just staring at each other. Amias? It ain't right, I said. There are students wanting to know when the copies of Jupiter Hammon's last book will arrive. What was it called? Didn't you tell the bookkeeper we needed..."

Amias let his sister talk. Oftentimes, that's all she desired. And it was certainly the extent to which his temper stretched. They stood some distance from the church, facing the demon, and the rocky hills behind it. The surrounding, towering oak trees pulled Amias into a memory of a Bible verse. Oaks were abundant in the Good Book. The first mentioned was in Genesis, where Jacob abandoned his strange gods under an oak.[3] Odd that Amias now bonded with

---

3 Genesis 35:4—And they gave unto Jacob all the strange gods which were in their hand, and all their earrings which were in their ears; and Jacob hid them under the oak which was by Shechem.

the protector sent by God, which lived under the oaks of Jonesboro African Baptist Church.

Hosanna's breath brushed against the back of Amias's shoulders. "Can it even...ya know...see?"

Amias continued ignoring his sister. He wouldn't allow her to ruin this moment, however strange. Sunlight filtered through the shadowy canopy. This was where Amias knew peace. Not in his makeshift office overrun with kind but incessant students. Not among the excited builders who'd gathered to erect Bricksbury's first buildings. Not even in the church, where he'd preached for the first time years ago, and still did occasionally if He called him to spread a message. Nothing was as fulfilling; nothing fed Amias's desperate need for curiosity like the demon gifted by God.

It was quiet save for the sharp chirping above and the bubbling creek. Amias rolled his shoulders, staring into the demon's fiery eyes, and relaxed. It was, for the first time in a long while, safe to relax. He hadn't felt safety in...

Hosanna should be able to scream and dance and sing libations. Instead, Amias heard as twigs softly snapped behind him. She was afraid to come closer to the demon, even though God sent it specifically to protect them. And it had.

Bricksbury Mountain College had been growing and safe for over twenty years. They'd never been bothered by curious abolitionist neighbors or violent out-of-towners. Their students traveled from across the country, and none had been met with resistance or trouble of any kind to or from school. They'd all told Amias how secure they'd felt. The moment they'd gotten the letter with Bricksbury's crest, God filled them with the peace they'd know in Jonesborough. And when they arrived, that peace warmly welcomed them. Many never wanted to leave, and so they stayed on, teaching subsequent generations in the same soft safety they'd grown to rely on.

Sometime later, when night's darkness brought wetter air, thick with honeysuckle, Amias was relieved to find Hosanna gone. *Finally*, he thought as he sat on the ground with a crack of his knees. The night was Amias's favorite time of day because it was easier to see the demon's fiery eyes. And part of him hoped the demon could better see him, too.

To: Dr. Grant
From: Zora Robinson
Date: Tuesday, September 7, 2027 09:17:02 EDT
Subject: RE: Thesis Proposal Rejection

Dear Dr. Grant,

I hope this email finds you well. Thank you for the thoughtful notes on my thesis proposal, "The Spiritual History of Affrilachia." I appreciate your insights on Black Appalachian culture, and yes, I *have* read your collections on the Freedmen's Bureau's original plans for land reform.

Congratulations on your latest *New York Times* best-selling book, *Knoxville's Topography Devil: African American Agriculture Disputes of Postwar Southern Mountain Towns*. No, I wasn't aware you are a personal friend of both Frank X. Walker and Ta-Nehisi Coates. Those must be enlightening relationships.

Regarding my proposal, I was surprised to see it had been rejected, mainly because the provided research indicates the urgent need for oral documentation on the subject. Very few primary sources exist, and the interviewees are consistently elderly, which only stresses the importance of starting research immediately.

As you know, I am passionate about preserving African American Appalachian religious culture and researching the origins of current practices and beliefs. Please reconsider your rejection of my thesis proposal, "The Spiritual History of Affrilachia."

Thank you for your time and consideration.

Regards,
Zora Robinson

———

To: Zora Robinson
From: Dr. Grant
Date: Tuesday, September 7, 2027 09:27:34 EDT
Subject: RE: Thesis Proposal Rejection

Zora,
Please attend my office hours this afternoon or next Tuesday
to discuss further.
—Dr. G.
Sent from my iPhone

Esther Fisherman's Diary
September 1, 1927
Jonesborough, Tennessee
Bricksbury Mountain College—Staff Housing

Dear Diary,

Another school year has commenced, and I once again curse F. Scott Fitzgerald and Josephine Baker in equal measure for legitimizing the inane hairstyle known as "the bob." Fitzgerald's self-important story "Bernice Bobs Her Hair" and Baker's sinful sultriness have poisoned the minds of these college students. Lord, the girls arrive, breastmilk still wet on their lips, and explain to me how "stylish" and "modern" the look is.

"Sloven" is a better word, in my opinion, even, and especially, with a "kiss curl." Of this, I am sure. I would respect it more if their liberation were attained through grim selfishness. They only modify their bodies "in despite of" or "in retaliation to" men. Not for themselves.

Trends are only "modern" to the young, anyway. To the old, they are either an unreasonable inconvenience or superfluous.

Walking around the campus and inside my beloved library, I am aghast by how short these women's hair is. All in the name of displeasing or pleasing a man, depending upon his shattered principles.

Classes have begun. I've enjoyed the steady stream of academic eagerness. Despite their hairstyle choices (and what that might say about their self-worth and understanding of our culture's hair history), they are often overwhelmed by their hunger for knowledge. It is a breath-stealing hunger and a sensation with which I am intimately familiar.

When I was a Bricksbury student in the '70s, I spent a signifi-cant time in the library. Of course, this was ages and marriages and wars ago. The library was a hidden gem, located in the basement of the Jonesboro African Baptist Church. The shelves were only decorated with books, their spines cracked and worn, many adorned with ornate, gilded lettering. Candlelight caused shadows to dance across the room, stretching the shelf's dark mahogany. The floor was similarly covered, with tomes strewn haphazardly as if abandoned in a hurry. But there was no abandonment—only excitement to clutch the next treasure.

Balinese mythologies, early medieval theater, Majapahit mili-tary analysis, and contemporary bridge engineering. Heaven.

I still recall when I couldn't lift a book about Absalom Boston because my hands trembled with excitement. That was how thrilling knowledge was. That was how desperate and relieved I was to be in the presence of so much wisdom. More information and creativity than I thought I could ever know. More lives lived than I could have perceived. It is a sobering thing to be among the infinite.

How is the church building doing up there, abandoned in the woods? Should I visit it? It used to be surrounded by so much life. We sprinted between towering oak trees and read books in soft riverbeds. I am so grateful to have experienced my youth (past sixteen) in Bricksbury's safe bosom. I cannot imagine being anywhere without the mountain air and the books to accompany myself and the students.

Graciously,
Esther Ophelia Fisherman

Chapter Three

The Conjure Shoppe was in the basement of Jonesborough's crumbling historic district. Its square Federal-style building was so old that Andrew Jackson himself probably walked by between devilries. Once neat and coppery, the sun-bleached brick now lay in lopsided rows, threatening to collapse at the very sight of modernity while up the hill, a chorus of construction heralded the rise of luxury "mountain-style" townhouses. Zora made a conscious effort to divert her thoughts from the present-day encroachment.

The shop was halfway down a sunless alley near enough to the train tracks that Zora's teeth rattled as one roared by. She sat staring blankly out her windshield, watching it pass her by like the quiet afternoon she'd planned. After visiting the shop, Zora would have to see Dr. Grant instead of returning to her dorm to chill with Henry Louis until Conjure Night. Should she even still go? Her mind shuffled through her options and the consequences of each one.

She tapped her thumbs against the rubber steering wheel, molten in the unrelenting summer heat. Zora worried about the quietly scathing rejection she'd received for her proposal. The response practically wrote itself in her mind as she typed and sent it before leaving. Dr. Grant responded just ten minutes later. In one sentence, he had rearranged her day, her mood, and potentially her entire life.

Anxiety multiplied within Zora the longer she sat; minutes later, she noticed the sweat gathering on her slippery palms. She rubbed her hands against her taupe linen shorts, willing herself not to spiral further. Rejection was standard in her work; the verdict stung initially, though.

Zora's watch buzzed.

BRICKSBURY CAMPUS SECURITY: Security concern in the Woodlands. Avoid the vicinity. Report suspicious activity to (423) 423-4234. Stay tuned for more information.

The Woodlands were another reason Zora wanted to attend Bricksbury. It was an incredible natural preservation, and the land was rife with untold stories. Before Jonesborough became an abolitionist hub primed for the Underground Railroad, the Woodlands housed a self-sufficient Black conjure community. Zora couldn't prove it, but she suspected it wasn't simply the goodness of white people's hearts that made the town an abolitionist haven. The protective power of the Hoodoo practitioners had much to do with it.

Campus security's text solidified it—Zora would spend the evening outlining a new proposal. Her meeting with Dr. Grant would be fresh in her mind; it was the ideal time to plan a new strategy. She would advocate like hell for minimal changes, but she understood the importance of Dr. Grant's approval. Zora could compromise on some things.

She left the car, considering what she would and would not compromise on.

"Are you good?" a man's baritone asked.

Zora glanced up from her phone as a shop employee unlocked a case of crystals at the front door. His long arms stretched over the blue lace agate as he placed peach selenite palm stones at random. The case's colors, slabs, towers, and bowls might have appeared erratic, but he intentionally laid each stone. He was an artist of organized chaos.

"You've been standing there for like a minute," he continued, curly afro still inside the case as he spoke. He finished fussing with the crystals and carefully locked the glass before turning to Zora expectantly.

Zora frowned, but a slight ache at the ball of her feet told her he could be right. She cleared her throat. "Oh! I'm good. Just..."

"First-week brain fog?" he offered with a gentle smile on his full lips.

They stood below Jonesborough Conjure Shoppe's wide awning, each cringing and covering their ears as a new train rumbled closer. Was he a student? He was older than Zora by a few years, probably just past thirty, with a dark forest-green septum ring against his smooth upper lip. Nina Simone was front and center on his shirt, her mouth open mid-song. The name tag clipped above the lit cigarette in her hand said IMMANUEL; a Brazilian flag pin was directly below that. Under that was a "he/him" pin, then beneath that was a guitar pin with a snake slithering out of the scuffed case. Zora immediately began thinking of songs about snakes, even ranking her top three in no order: "Hiss" by Megan Thee Stallion, "Snakeskin" by Rina Sawayama, and Grandpa's favorite, "The Snakes Crawl at Night" by Charley Pride.

"First-week brain fog," Zora agreed. Her brain had already moved on to the use of snakeskin in conjure, wondering if the shop would be stocked.

"Do you need directions?" Immanuel asked, crossing his toned arms and widening his stance.

He pointed toward her phone like she was using the map and not thinking about rootwork versus conjure versus Hoodoo versus...

"Uh, no, I'm supposed to be here. I just...my thesis advisor..." Zora trailed off, hedging her bets that anyone around her age in Bricksbury would relate to this specific trauma.

Immanuel tsked and put a hand on wide hips. "They're workin' you that hard already? Damn. Mine is at least giving me a couple weeks back before buggin' me about my recital."

Zora nodded at his shirt and row of pins. "Music major?"

Immanuel grinned, flashing bright teeth at Zora. Their cool whiteness was oddly contrasted with his warm brown eyes. She felt suddenly that this encounter was more important than she'd first thought. Now that he'd given her his full attention, Zora better saw how his low jaw set in place as each car passed. He was a bit taller than her, so when his eyes flittered over her, Zora noted how they paused, assessing, for a moment. So quick, she'd think he was just blinking.

"Is everything okay?" Zora asked. She turned around and found nothing out of sorts. People strolled to and from hole-in-the-wall shops and banged-up college-kid cars that didn't look suspicious enough to warrant Immanuel's pause.

"Of course! Everything's fine. Oh, I'm studying jazz composition, by the way. This is my last year. What about you?"

Zora turned back around, having forgotten that she'd asked his major. "Oh! That's so cool. This is my first year in my Appalachian studies program."

Immanuel whistled with a smile. "Damn, now *that's* cool. Well, good luck. I'll pray that your advisor gets their head out their ass and calms the fuck down."

Zora was startled by her laughter and threw her head back along with Immanuel for a moment. She was still grinning as she raised her palm to protect her eyes from the glinting sun.

"I'll take all the prayers I can get." And Zora meant that.

"Hope you find what you're lookin' for. Mallory has a sale on some gemstones this week," he said, chuckling, opening the creaky Conjure Shoppe door for her.

"Thanks," Zora said, already loving downtown Jonesborough.

Mallory must be the shop owner. A shop owner who put gemstones on sale during the first week back at school? Genius.

As Zora entered at the top of a wide staircase, she thought of Henry Louis. He would have hated the grating din of the door's bottom edge dragging against the ground. She hoped he was sleeping lazily on the futon and wished she could join him. The wooden handrails leading downward were buffed so thoroughly that they shone in the dim light, drawing Zora's eyes toward the black carpet. It was spotless.

She hummed along with "Love Like Whiskey," a twangy The War and Treaty song. One of her favorites by them. The ukulele and acoustic guitar cascaded through incense smoke, and Zora couldn't help but rock her shoulders. Good music. It was an excellent sign.

The bricks on the wall flaunted their rich golden-brown color, having been protected by the building's interior. These bricks lasted far longer than their modern kiln-fired counterparts on the gentrified side of town. They were distinct, old enough to have gone in and out of fashion twice in Zora's lifetime, and framed with bold sapphire-blue linen curtains covering pocket windows.

Zora couldn't discern the source of the gentle incense smoke that was halfway between lemongrass and eucalyptus. The faint wisps nudged her shoulders down, relaxing her muscles as she stepped off the black carpet and onto a thick jacquard-patterned behemoth touching all four corners. The wisps were a delicate magic. Zora was impressed that they lightly resisted when she lifted her shoulders, nudging her into a calmer state. Whoever worked here was an impressive conjurer.

There was one light on the ceiling in the far corner above the cash register; aside from that, there were candles on every available surface. They were each contained inside domed glass, which helped throw the flickering flame's light. The result was a well-lit apothecary with organized floating shelves on the walls and neatly marked tables in the center of the room.

"Good mornin'!" someone said as Zora descended the stairs.
"Morning!"

As she approached the herbs on the walls, Zora decided the gentle blanketing scent was definitely eucalyptus. She tapped her foot to the beat as she browsed. Merchandise was ordered alphabetically by folk names rather than scientific ones, which Zora appreciated. She opened her Notes app and began plucking bags off the wall. The thick plastic was smooth and refillable. Zora smiled at the quality.

"I'm Mallory. Did Immanuel come down with ya? No, I don't see him. That boy does *not* listen to me. Anyway, can I help ya, honey?" the same person asked with a thick Appalachian accent.

Zora turned toward the voice. They were shorter than her, with long graying locs that made them look taller. Gold hoops attaching cowrie shells to their hair matched their beige denim overalls. Images of herb sprigs and open books were intricately stitched onto the fabric. Lacy and emerald, their crop top covered toned muscles and completed a look Zora envied. Hot casual was *so* tricky to pull off.

"Zora, and I love your outfit," Zora said, stepping back to appreciate it fully. Even the plain white shoes were embellished with twinkling crystals and stretching black cats. "Incredible attention to detail."

Mallory struck a pose. Layered gold bracelets clinked together and winked as if tethered to the candlelight. "Thank you, thank you. I would tell you that I just threw this together, but actually, this is one of my signature looks."

Zora laughed, her thesis worries momentarily forgotten. She was aware of how relaxed she'd become and that her state was partially manufactured, but Mallory was too pleasant for Zora to care. Was this not the magical version of aromatherapy? Drops of essential oil on light bulbs? "I love the honesty. Is this your place? It's ... wow, it's amazing in here."

"It's my family's." Mallory gazed at the room with pride. Dark green–stained lips parted as they smiled. "Six generations."

Zora gasped in excitement. "*Six* generations? Have y'all always been downtown?"

"We started in the kitchen of my third great-grandmother, Glory Holston. She lived over on Fox Street. We moved here in the early twenties and have been here ever since!"

Zora noted details in Mallory's recounting. Many conjurers and root doctors became prominent after the First World War when there was a sharp increase in demand for both herbal medicine and the skillfully hidden moonshine used in their spells and potions. Still, a downtown storefront, even at the basement level, was impressive for a Black family business.

This was Zora's favorite way to begin an interview—when the interviewee believed they'd given all the information, and yet...

"The twenties? Was this only a conjure shop, or were there live shows, too?"

Mallory's bushy eyebrows shot up. "No one has ever asked that. There was music, yes. Ya know, DeFord Bailey came here to play—before *and* after the Opry."

"Oh my God." Zora involuntarily stepped closer to Mallory, one hand above her heart in disbelief. "Are you serious? The Harmonica Wizard?"

"You know him? Most people my age don't, let alone yours." Their low voice raised to Zora's pitch.

"It's a special interest of mine, and Bailey was such a legend. He and Lesley Riddle, of course. I'm a student at Bricksbury."

"Lemme guess...anthropology?"

Zora smiled. "I'm in Appalachian studies."

"Oh! D'ya know Dr. Grant?"

"Know him? He just rejected my thesis proposal!"

"Yeah, that sounds like him. He's in here all the time. That man goes through Road Opener baths like nobody's business. But anyway, sorry, can I help ya find somethin'?"

"Oh, I've got bethroot. Now I need…sorry, I wrote it down here…do you have death flower and wild succory?"

Mallory's face fell. They didn't blink behind thick golden glasses as their lips turned downward into a frown.

"Did I…say something?" Zora laughed, but she got the sense that absolutely nothing was funny. Maybe Mallory didn't have those herbs, the ones that would strengthen Henry Louis's mojo bag. Zora didn't appreciate the morning's close call and decided to invest in a better metal clasp *and* reinforced magic inside the pouch. She was taking no chances. Henry Louis had nowhere else to live— her parents made that clear when they told her that going back to school for Appalachian studies was a waste of time.

And we'll not be helpin' ya when ya lil spell wears off in front of the dean, an' ya gotta come back to repairin' old pictures, which is what you'll end up doin' anyway, they'd told her. No, her parents would not be helpful at all.

Zora's therapist in New Hampshire was the best part about Dartmouth, and she would always be grateful for his suggestion that Zora adopt a pet upon returning to Knoxville. Henry Louis— named after historian Henry Louis Gates Jr.—was the first time Zora had taken on a responsibility that felt more like a gift. Sure, the cost of pet care was exorbitant, as were the herbs needed to keep Henry Louis under wraps, but they were worth it. The wild succory, aka chicory root, would boost the *unseen* aspects of his mojo bag, and the more expensive death flower, commonly known as yarrow root, would double the general *protection* of both Henry Louis's pouch and the one Zora stitched inside her backpack.

They provided peace of mind.

"You'll be needin' death flower, huh?" Mallory had grown still, like they were preparing for whatever Zora's explanation was. Their shoulders were squared, and they didn't smile but still looked kind and soft. "I'm sure ya understand, but the parent in me has gotta say, these are powerful energies you're workin' with, dearie. Hopin' you're bein' careful."

Zora hesitated. Besides having haint blue rugs and a heroic family conjurer history, Zora's grandparents always reminded her to protect herself first. She was the most important person in her life, and while she would attend Conjure Night to join a community, this community also likely had mojo bags in their backpacks. Hell, they probably shopped at this very store and had their *own* death flower, which could be used in many defensive and offensive spells, depending on the practitioner's intentions.

It was exhilarating to fellowship with other conjurers, but not everyone would have her best interest at heart. Some people, even admittedly Zora, were looking out for themselves. So yes, death flower.

As Zora stood in silence, the eucalyptus incense wafted through the air, swirling around her and settling in her lungs. An acoustic guitar pulsed from hidden speakers, soundtracking her reluctance. Mallory could be an excellent knowledge source, but Zora wouldn't make it a habit of telling strangers about Henry Louis or any other expulsion-possible sins. Still, wasn't Bricksbury the safest college campus in the country? And wasn't Zora armed both supernaturally (mojo hands, five generations of name papers, etc.) and in earthly ways (pepper spray, pocketknife, door security bar, etc.)?

Zora cleared her throat. "Sorry about that. Uh...so, do you have either of them?"

Mallory nodded in understanding, even though there was no way they could understand.

"I get it. Ya don't know me, an' that's fair. But I want ya to know that ya can always come back an' see me. Ya know, whether or not the death flower an' wild succory work, which o' course I have, by the way. This is a *proper* conjure shop, ya know."

Mallory grabbed Zora's hand and looked into her eyes deeper than any family member or lover ever had. Zora's first thought was to protect herself, but there wasn't a hint of ill will in Mallory's infinite brown eyes and thickened accent. Only concern.

"We haven't met, have we? Ya look familiar."

Zora ran her tongue over her lips, a sense of anticipation building within her. Jasmine had to visit this place often—after all, it was the nearest shop to the school. Was this what Zora had signed up for, attending the same school? Would there be no place for her to settle, even temporarily, without the reminder of Jasmine? Without the reminder of a sister half acknowledged?

The Robinson genes were persistent, documented and widely discussed at family reunions and holiday dinners—at least they used to be, back when Zora attended. The Robinsons all had impressively soft jawlines they waggled to burden others with unsolicited opinions. Their plump cheeks and round features gave the illusion of youth, which dissuaded them from any evolution or deviation from their established way of life.

"No, we haven't met."

Mallory didn't look convinced. "Well, this ain't just a store. This is a community, ya hear me?"

"I do," Zora said thickly. *Okay. Here it goes.* "And I am. I mean, I'm being careful with the death flower and everything. I'm only using it for protection. I need...yeah, to protect myself."

Tears burned behind Zora's eyes. She couldn't help it. Suddenly, she realized how alone she'd felt. She'd pushed those feelings aside to achieve her goals and advance her career. But there they were, simmering just below the surface. Existing in insolence.

For years, Zora projected a lack of grief over having a strained and then estranged relationship with her family. She performed normalcy, but Mallory hadn't asked her to perform; they only asked Zora to be. And Zora hadn't expected that on her trip downtown today.

Mallory gathered the death flower and wild succory while Zora collected herself and approached the register with the bags she'd already picked.

"Here's my card," Mallory said after giving Zora her change. "Mallory Holston, ring if ya need me for anythin'. Even just a prayer." They paused, eyes swinging around the quiet room as if hearing something Zora could not. "There's no honor in sufferin' alone, Zora. If not me, call upon Him,[4] at least."

"Thanks, I really appreciate it," Zora said as sincerely as she could.

She hesitated on the grand staircase, casting a final glance at the jarring contrast of the dark rug and the vivid golden wallpaper. Her next stop was Dr. Grant's office. The vibe would be different from this soothing, magical hush. She inhaled the last wafts of eucalyptus, allowing it to relax her spine, and worried it would be the last gentle moment she'd experience at Bricksbury.

---

4 Psalm 50:15—And call upon me in the day of trouble: I will deliver thee, and thou shalt glorify me.

Esther Fisherman's Diary
September 3, 1927
Jonesborough, Tennessee
Bricksbury Mountain College—Staff Housing

Dear Diary,

I've taken on an apprentice for the first time in twenty years, and I haven't stopped smiling since it became official. This was how it was done back when I was learning. "Librarian-ship" degrees, in which my apprentice, Hezekiah, is enrolled, are newer, more superfluous achievements. What does a degree say about trust from one's community? I always taught my apprentices _that_ was the most important aspect about being a librarian. And to have the trust of one's community, one must first know that community. These required activities are done entirely outside of a classroom, and to suggest one must obtain a degree to be a competent librarian is incorrect at best and offensive at worst. It was another way to divide knowledge among the classes.

The knowledgeable librarians under whom I apprenticed would never have made it to Bricksbury, with or without scholarships or patrons. They were taught by their local librarians, who were taught by theirs, and so on. Since apprenticeship has gone out of style, I was surprised by Hezekiah's request. It felt terribly old-fashioned for someone in his early twenties. Later, I'd learn his older aunts and grandmother raised him, and so his query made more sense.

Hezekiah and I first met, obviously, in the library. I have a game I play with students called "duels of data." They tell me what they're studying, and we challenge each other's knowledge of that subject. Although Hezekiah is majoring in librarianship, my favorite program for data duels is French. The students are always shocked to learn that I am fluent in the language and my maiden surname is Toussaint. The duels of data were an opportunity to broaden the students' social minds as much as they were an untraditional way to engage with them.

I'd beaten Hezekiah at one such duel, but instead of marching out of the library with wounded pride or turning the loss into anger against me, he listened intently as we sat on the third floor afterward, sharing a bag of honey crackers (my own recipe). Quickly I learned he has a gentle spirit. I discussed the significance of earning community trust, and he shared his aversion to speaking with strangers—although he noted that talking to me was relatively easy for him. The warmth such a confession left in my heart was immediately damped by the shadow of unease in Hezekiah's deep brown eyes. He wanted so badly to be a librarian. He'd dreamed of handing books to people that made them look at life differently, healed some hidden part of them, or fit the exact needs of their curiosities. It was his purpose, he told me. He could feel it in his bones.

That's when he asked to be my apprentice, offering to work in the library on the days he didn't have classes and on one weekend day. I warned him about his social aversions and that he'd have to face them. Hezekiah looked into my eyes and told me he understood and that while his progress may be slow, he would remain diligent. "I'll be diligent for my dreams," he said. I believed him. Moreso, I connected with him, understanding his desire to be a part of the literature that moves the world. He was a young Esther. Eager, determined, and terrified of failure. He was me before life fed into and withered me.

Because it's been twenty years since my previous apprentice, and it's likely this will be my last, I'm putting forth more effort than in years past. Hezekiah Lee will be my protégé. He has incredible potential and just needs the confidence to turn that potential into reality. I'm excited to watch him on this journey and to be a part of his early experiences as a librarian. I believe this apprenticeship will change both our lives—Hezekiah's and mine.

Graciously,
Esther Ophelia Fisherman

Chapter Four

Zora marched past the stifling Fisherman Quad with a tic in her jaw and mind racing. Bricksbury's academic rigor was an immediate challenge, and she looked forward to rising to—no, conquering—the occasion! She tilted her chin up, making her vulnerable to clouds of pollen, but she didn't care. This was Zora's power pose. It would give her the extra *oomph* of confidence needed for this conversation (rather, debate) with Dr. Grant.

At the very least, he had made clear that despite knowing her, he wouldn't give her special treatment, which Zora appreciated overall.

Dr. Maurice Grant was a renowned historian who was equal parts formal academic and wide-eyed idealist. Despite being in his eighties, he had boundless energy. Every month, he came into Zora's job at the Beck Cultural Exchange Center to teach a public class on various subjects surrounding Black history in the mountain south.

The turnout was consistent since the Beck Cultural Exchange Center was minutes from downtown Knoxville and the University of Tennessee. History, anthropology, music, and even botany students frequented his classes, and the more academic-minded stayed afterward to ask him to sign one of his books or answer a burning question about the significance of banjos on the more extensive Appalachian cultural history or something equally specific.

Part of Zora's job as an archive technician, and the center's least senior employee, was to assist Dr. Grant while he was there. This meant little more than getting him coffee or explaining to him, again, how the printer worked. She didn't mind. This was what she'd expected; she hadn't supposed she'd be given the opportunity to have an ongoing conversation with someone so prestigious.

Still, Dr. Grant always made it a point to talk to Zora. He never made her feel like a faceless, low-level intern, which she was grateful for and was contrary to the horror stories she'd heard about post-degree work. He'd been genuinely interested to hear about her family's history and how it dovetailed with the research she wanted to do. He'd aided her acceptance into Bricksbury, for heaven's sake, which was why this new proposal rejection stung.

And now Zora would have to smile in his face and pretend she didn't feel the sting, as was custom in academia.

Zora passed a humanities building, beaming under the intense sunlight. Its windows were original, turn of the century. While stunning, they did fuck all to keep the chill out in the winter, according to the TikToks Zora had watched late into the night. With a glass of red, she scrolled vlogs of Bricksbury students explaining what life was like on a mountainous HBCU campus. Thanks to them, she'd brought wind-resistant face masks—something the school's website never mentioned.

In her more official research into the school and region, she learned that no administration had ever bothered adding insulation to any building. To their credit, winters in the area were short and dubious, ranging from picturesque flurries to all-out blizzards. Knoxville was a tropical paradise year-round in comparison.

Zora flashed to the glimpse of Jasmine she'd stolen through these windows. The familiar ache grew in her chest at the memory. It was uncanny. There Jasmine was, living her life as if she didn't have a sister at all. As if she had written Zora off as dead. The sorrow in her chest grew until it crawled up her throat and threatened tears. Zora swallowed wildly and tried to focus on her surroundings. *Facts.*

Facts. Facts. Zora could ground herself by spinning through a few in her mind. The . . . the buildings on Bricksbury's campus were historical institutions. They were in . . . good? Or . . . acceptable condition, considering most were over 130 years old, with bricks laid by the sons of freedmen and the local white people who were too poor to let their racism get in the way of a good day's pay.

That was the thing about Appalachia. It wasn't that racism didn't exist; it was that active racism was a luxury reserved for those who could afford it.

Bricksbury was the region's pioneering operation with a well-paid, interracial workforce. The main facade showcased more spire-adorned steeples and noon bell towers than even Fisk University's Jubilee Hall. The massive project lured people from across the tri-state area—Tennessee, Virginia, and North Carolina—and some from as far away as Kansas. Anyone who needed work, anyone who couldn't mind who they rubbed shoulders with, found a job.

Crawfoot Hall, or Craws as students called it, was the building squished behind Hemlock Chapel and the humanities building. It housed the History, Government, and Philosophy Departments. Though it was the youngest building on campus, erected in 1926, Craws still sat wearily on the ground. Towering hemlock trees surrounded it, the roots bucking against the rough bricks for so long that several had abandoned the building. The replacement bricks were too red and too bright. They looked wrong, like globs of shiny newness wrenched inside something too ancient for it ever to understand.

Zora stopped in front of Craws. This was it. Like it or not (she did not?), this was the first of many times she'd have to prove herself on this campus. She needed to explain her case in a way that didn't offend Dr. Grant's ego but made enough of an argument to change his mind. It was a fussy balance, but Zora was willing to play along to maintain it.

Zora inhaled and counted to ten, fifteen, and twenty. While opening the doors, she repeated her plan to make Dr. Grant see reason, if not truth.

———

It was the first week of school, and somehow Crawfoot's elevator was out of service, which Zora wouldn't've even noticed, except the second floor of Crawfoot Hall was bustling with a crowd vying for space on the U-shaped staircase. The parallel flights were packed two deep on each stair, and Zora was worryingly far from both the landing that connected the flights and the other staircase on the building's opposite side. She stood, hand on hip, the other hand flicking her wrist back and forth, antsy as she checked her watch. Zora was early. She was always early. That had been her thing, even when her nagging annoyed her parents and sister; even when she learned it was probably a trauma response or symptom of something more, she didn't try to stop. She went harder. Early was on time, and on time was late. It was page one in the convoluted "Black Excellence" handbook and the second page of the Capricorn handbook, following a full page devoted to the slow edging of delayed gratification.

"Are ya all right?" the man beside her asked in a gentle Southern drawl. He wore a baby-pink crop top that matched his twin beauty-mark cheek piercings. "Should clear up in a second, honeypie. First week's always the hardest on account o' no one knowin' where the fuck they're goin'."

Zora hadn't noticed she'd twisted the toe of her shoe into the hardwood floor. She righted her leg and gave as soft a smile as she could manage. It wasn't helping that her backpack straps were digging into her shoulders. No rearranging of the padded nylon relieved it.

"I'm okay, thanks!"

Regrettably, Zora was *not* okay, and she made as much clear when she gave up her place in line and headed for the other flight of stairs, which surely must be less crowded. The eternal optimist on her shoulder dreamed that the elevator on that end might have been fixed already. This was swiftly debunked.

Her shoulders ached more when she sighed heavily, jostling the backpack's contents. But she couldn't help it as she joined another impossibly long line for the stairs. Her watch told her she'd been standing in Crawfoot Hall for over half an hour. The fluorescent lights above her flickered in an erratic rhythm and seemed to blink even faster when Zora's eyes lingered on them. It was as if they were trying to dissuade her. Zora's eyes darted around the sweltering hallway at the fidgeting and apprehensive faces of the others. Did they feel trapped, too?

A shadow flittered beside her. A group of people dressed in orange, three or four of them, moved as one. They positioned themselves just a foot away from the wall, then contorted their bodies in an unnatural bend until their backs curved and touched the flyers for tech assistance and an emergency Caribbean Otaku meeting. It had to have been painful, but oddly, that was what made the crude pose. Zora was entranced, unable to tear her eyes away.

Their identical orange tank tops were pulled tight against their sweaty bodies as they shimmied, eyes cast upward at the drop ceiling. Zora shivered as she heard the low humming emanating from their throats angled high.

A tall woman came into view. She introduced herself as Eliza Deadbody, snapping at the downbeat of the group's hums. Zora realized she'd been too caught up in the group's bizarre entrance to see that it was an *entrance*. Zora stood on her toes and looked down both directions of the long, packed hallway. It was impressive the group had even found the room to accost their fellow students with this prideful display in the worst location possible. Bravo.

The woman wore a black tank top but the same matching orange shorts as the others. Where the troupe's low humming had doubled in volume, Eliza's voice sharpened. Tinny and high-pitched— breathy. "Welcome to Bricksbury's third pop-up theater event. This piece is called 'Sacrifice.'"

The group against the wall hummed louder, suddenly stomping and disrupting the crowd. Zora wasn't the only one watching. Most others stood, half wanting to watch and half wishing they'd never walked into the building. Zora was on the fence until Eliza spoke once more; this time, her eyes landed on Zora's. Their mutual brown-eyed stare...lingered. "Sacrifice" wasn't a remarkably calming word to bounce around in Zora's head, but it did so anyway. Followed by "offering," then "surrender."

Alarms blared in Zora's thoughts as the line for the stairs finally started moving.

Danger, something inside her declared. Zora didn't question it.

Esther Fisherman's Diary
September 5, 1927
Jonesborough, Tennessee
Bricksbury Mountain College—Staff Housing

My second husband's daughter, Annie-Jean, wrote to me that her father was in failing health. Nicholas wishes to see me, lest he meet God without resolving our differences. I've always enjoyed Annie-Jean. And though I never attempted to replace her mother, she was the only one of Nicholas's children I would've adopted. She was too soft and precious for that household—her father and siblings were the same. They had disquieting souls. Having departed myself before she turned ten, I hoped she also took her leave at the first opportunity.

I wrote back explaining to Annie-Jean how she could humorously portray my refusal to see her father, though I hoped she would have her own approach. She was always so creative. Part of me wanted to write to her all these years, but so much time has passed.

I forget about time until it's gone.

Time seems to move differently at Bricksbury. It doesn't, I'm sure. I'm sure. I'm sure. But, there's a stillness in the air, a slowing of the rivers, that fogs everything else. Somehow, everything and nothing exists inside Bricksbury at once.

The students possess an extraordinary ability to navigate this time, or at least, that's how it appears. Every semester, they enter with wide-eyed enthusiasm and depart with even grander aspirations—and I've lived lifetimes by the holidays. I have the privilege of witnessing their growth, their process of intellectual transformation, and the way they courageously confront their mistakes. Yet, my blurry consciousness misplaces faces, professors, and whether I've gone to church. At first, it was frustrating. Then, months later, it was concerning. But Annie-Jean's letter arrived, and although I thought hours had passed, I've just confirmed with the post office that I received it two days ago.

These are not ramblings, though you already know that, diary. These are accounts, in case my memory is further altered? Degraded? I'm unsure, and that opaqueness rests heavily in my chest as I write this.

I do know, however, that Nicholas shouldn't worry about our "differences" being unresolved—he will not see me again. For he will not see heaven.

Graciously,
Esther Ophelia Fisherman

Chapter Five

"Thank you for coming in, Zora," Dr. Grant grumbled above a disheveled desk.

"Of course. Thank you for seeing me so quickly."

She sat across from him with a tight smile, concerned about her late arrival, which wasn't actually late since his office hours were still in effect for another hour. But Zora was having a difficult time getting the theater troupe's humming out of her head. She kept seeing the painful way they arched their backs. The way Eliza Deadbody looked into her eyes with cool sureness. *That's over*, she told herself. What mattered now was Dr. Grant and rescuing her thesis.

The armchair Zora sat in was plush, and so deeply cushioned she worried about getting out of it when it was time to leave. She subtly shifted but couldn't find comfort in the soft depths.

Dr. Grant hadn't noticed her awkwardness. He hadn't looked up when she opened the door, nor when he invited her to sit and asked if she wanted some "tea or chocolates or something." Zora wasn't offended. She delighted in finally seeing Dr. Grant's chaotic office at his beloved Bricksbury. Even under the circumstances, Zora could take a moment to witness this. To be grateful she'd made it, even if she'd have to fight to keep it.

His spindly arms flipped papers over randomly while he read them, set them aside, and then reread them with a frown. His desk was oversized to accommodate long legs that still peeked out at Zora from underneath the scratched wood. His sweater's harsh brightness reminded her of the sun. The yellow glare made Zora blink behind her glasses and subtly angle her body toward his wall of accolades.

As the air conditioner in the corner rattled, Zora instinctively reached for the jacket that was usually wrapped around her waist, but she had thought it would be too casual for today's mission and had left it behind. There *were* notes of chocolate in the chilly air, and Zora noted for later that he had a sweet tooth. She should've known Dr. Grant would have the one room with a working, frigid AC. The word "tenure" flashed across Zora's mind.

"Okay." He laughed and finally stood, holding out a wrinkled hand for Zora to shake. "Sorry, once I get goin' on somethin', it's best not to stop, or I'm liable to lose my place! Zora Robinson. It's fantastic to see you. And congratulations, again, on that insight-ful speech you gave at the Southern Black Historical Convention in June."

His smile barely reached his eyes.

"Thank..." Zora frowned...Was he trolling her? Referring to the email where she'd said the same thing in reverse? "Thank you," she settled on saying.

"I wrote down some notes, actually," he said, opening a drawer to his left. "Tell me if I have this right: 'Deconstructing the Centuries-Long Respectability Politics Plaguing the Black Church.'"

Zora struck a little pose in her seat. "That's the one. D'ya want an autograph?"

Dr. Grant chuckled, apparently satisfied with Zora's prodding. Did he think she'd be ashamed of her work? She'd spent months on that speech and had enough religious trauma from a childhood of shame and repression to write *five* speeches. *Ten, fifteen!* She could write one entirely on how her turn-of-the-century home church only recently allowed women to wear pants. And another discussing how it wasn't as if Zora would ever get permission from the bishops to marry a woman on church property; they'd publicly refused anyone who had ever asked. So, what was she supposed to do? Hope for eternal singleness? Get married elsewhere and bring her wife to a church who refused to house their love? Hell no. Zora had plenty to say in her head. The work was in editing all her queer rage down into succinct points.

"So, tell me, how is Bricksbury Mountain College farin' for our newest Knoxville native?"

Zora couldn't stop the smile that spread across her face. "So far, so good. I'm hoping to join some groups, maybe mark my territory on a desk in the library."

"Smart." Dr. Grant's brown eyes sparkled. "From what I hear, desk space is a cutthroat business."

Zora laughed.

Dr. Grant gazed into the distance. Perhaps a long-ago library memory called to him. Zora gave him time. After a couple of years spent working with Dr. Grant at the Beck Cultural Exchange Center and hearing all about the communal intellectual atmosphere of Bricksbury, Zora was suddenly overwhelmed by gratitude. She'd worked her fucking ass off to get here. The Southern Black Historical Convention's acceptance of her speech had been essential to her application. "Had you been to the library before now?" he finally asked. "It's one of my favorite places on campus—in Jonesborough, even. I'll have to find someone to show you around."

Zora swallowed as a familiar knot tightened in her chest. She hadn't told Dr. Grant her sister went to Bricksbury. The two had long been estranged, so it didn't make sense. Jasmine had moved on with her life. She was married now, not that Zora had witnessed the event. That'd been the final nail in their estrangement. Jasmine and Ngozi met as undergrads at Bricksbury and had been together for a decade. Although Jasmine and Zora hadn't been close since they were young girls, and had grown further apart as they aged, Zora was still devastated to learn she wasn't invited to their London wedding.

Three years ago, she received a text from her sister, who had long given up on calling Zora because of her unpredictable (i.e., constant) overtime hours.

Jasmine: Ngozi proposed. I hope you will be happy for me. I've prayed about this, and I want us to be in a better place, but I can't have the energy of my day diverted from its purpose. God bless, and I hope you return to church full-time, where you belong.
Zora: Fuck. You.

Ngozi Okafor (Zora only knew Jasmine had kept her surname after a long, late-night social media stalking session) had become Zora's sibling-in-law, and she'd only met them twice: at each of Jasmine's graduations.

Jasmine's bachelor's degree ceremony was cordial. At that time, Zora kept up with the family, so they could make idle small talk. Jasmine's master's degree conference was an entirely different story. Zora had just gone no-contact with her parents after the last time they'd belittled her and her work. She'd gripped on to the last thread of sisterly obligation and attended graduation, planning to skip the hotel rooftop party afterward to save awkwardness; instead, her mother cornered her in the bathroom after the ceremony and told her that *freezing your family out is the dumbest way to avoid accountability that I've ever heard of.* After that, Zora was in a sour mood and acknowledged Ngozi with only a curt hello as they passed each other in the hallway. She didn't think about it then, but that brusqueness plagued her for months after. Sometimes, in her darkest, truest moments, Zora knew she was a soul haunted.

Given all the sisterly fighting, and ultra-religious parents who favored their eldest, bringing Jasmine into the conversation would muddle the professional relationship with Dr. Grant, which, while rewarding, already had vast power imbalances. Zora wanted to keep her personal and professional lives entirely separate. It made her more comfortable. Being at Bricksbury and seeing Jasmine, even in passing, already tested the bounds of Zora's prideful discipline.

Still, if she didn't mention the connection, and it became known to Dr. Grant later, wouldn't that invite more inquiry than Zora wanted? A lie of omission was a lie nonetheless. She decided to keep it brief. "Yes...well, my grandpa graduated in the eighties, so I've been back a few times for alumni stuff before he passed. Then my sister, Jasmine Robinson, graduated and now works here. She's in the Religious Studies Department." Zora spoke quickly, hoping he wouldn't cling to any particular thing she said.

Dr. Grant straightened in his seat. Was he excited to learn more about his academic mentee, or was this just more of the same—a continuation of everyone's exceeding interest in whatever Jasmine was doing? Would Dr. Grant look up Jasmine's Old Testament research and wash his hands of Zora's more complicated relationship with Christianity? Would he, like everyone else, prefer her?

"Jasmine Robinson? Honestly, I'm unfamiliar with the religious studies faculty. Tedious folk. Though I know they've been doing some fascinating research on the underground layout of ancient tabernacles. Has Jasmine been teaching long?"

Zora worked to keep her voice from cracking. "This is her second semester, I believe. Uh, we aren't close."

The amused spark left Dr. Grant's eyes, and he looked at Zora with sudden seriousness, finally seeming to pick up on her discomfort. He nodded his head and intertwined his fingers above his chaotic desk.

"You're in one of my classes this semester, right?" he asked, glancing down at his computer, but not attempting to look up the information.

"Yes, Rural Health Projects. First thing in the morning," Zora said.

Dr. Grant abruptly turned to gawk down at his calendar on the nearby side table. "Is it really? How early?"

"Uh…"

He flipped the page of his oversized monthly calendar with beige coffee stains seeping through less and less as he thumbed. "Eight in the morning? Every week? Now, how in the world did Hadiyya set me up with this? I don't remember agreeing…"

Zora glanced down at her watch, unnerved as the lull in conversation had her mind return to Eliza Deadbody and her strange troupe of performers. They'd moved in shuffling unison, all while Eliza worked the crowd. Her high-pitched voice flirted with sounding angelic before veering sharply to cruel and otherworldly, then back again. It was a shrill cycle. Zora wrapped her arms around herself as a shiver ran through her at the memory.

Offering. Surrender. Sacrifice.

"Okay, let's get down to business, Zora."

Zora jumped and cleared her throat to cover her surprise.

"Yes, I'm happy to discuss my thesis proposal," Zora began, pitching her voice an octave lower than usual. "As you know, the region is—"

"I'm gonna stop ya right there." He laughed, putting his hands above his rounded afro in surrender. "You look ready for a fight, but I promise ya, I enjoyed your proposal."

Zora blinked. "You enjoyed the proposal you rejected?" This was a bit too cutting, even for a semi-familiar colleague, and Zora regretted the words even as they spilled off her tongue. "What I mean is—"

He smirked again, and now Zora *was* ready for a fight. Was he mocking her? Had she been wrong this entire time? Had he never taken her seriously? She bit her lip to stop herself from saying something else she'd regret.

"I want more," he said.

"More?"

"Yes, spiritual history is far too broad a topic at this level."

At this level was professor-speak for *I think you're a fucking idiot.*

"I believe you'll find, in my research, the urgent need for cultural and heritage preservation in the community on this exact topic, Dr. Grant." Zora spoke slowly to catch herself mid-word if an attitude crept in, justified or not.

Dr. Grant nodded and crossed his arms, so each hand gripped a slender, neon-yellow bicep. "I don't disagree with you, but I'm pushing you to be more specific than 'spiritual history.' Which spiritualities? What practices? What beliefs? There are and were so many in this region. It would be a disservice to your cause of cultural and heritage preservation if you do not narrow your scope and dig in deeper with one or two spiritualities rather than the dozens that have existed in all Black Appalachian communities between the revolution and now."

Zora paused to rub the goose bumps on her naked forearm. She hadn't prepared for that line of argument. The cinnamon brown of his eyes narrowed once more at his desk; they were too antsy, too hooded to be still or calm. Instead, hungry, they turned with his body, roaming the built-in shelves.

"Here," he said, finally plucking a book from inside a box in the shape of the famous peaks of the Blue Ridge Mountains. He gently ran his hand down the spine, closing his eyes as if the graying leather binding whispered to him. His pause was so heavy that it felt like reverence. After a moment, he handed it to her and said, "Now, take your time. What are your thoughts on this?"

Zora's years in the stacks kicked into gear when she touched the book. She first noted the heavy weight as she bounced the volume tenderly in her palm. The stitched leather must've been expensive, but there weren't many pages between bindings. Immediately, she knew the book's owner cared more for quality than quantity.

Was the leather's slight aroma of birch oil what Dr. Grant had been smelling? Its checked pattern told her this was diced leather. It could've been bound in the 1830s or '40s, which she only knew because bookbinding was one of her hyperfixations in undergrad. She'd researched the various methods while listening to gospel music or any of her favorite audiobooks. (Basically, Rebekah Weatherspoon and Christina C. Jones on a loop.) It was impossible not to see the distinctively curved way the bookbinder sewed the gatherings together. This was a notable tome.

Zora gasped when she noticed an intricate fore-edge painting. The top half showed a cloudless sky with a flock of birds soaring away from the blazing orange sun, while the bottom half showcased death. Below the baby-blue sky lay a softly painted slaughtered lamb. It was far from the first fore-edge painting Zora had ever seen, but something was curious about it. The brushstrokes were on an irregular angle, creating an uneven, colorful texture. Zora's eyes moved along the painting, past the lamb, which lay at the entrance to a forest of...

"Are those weeping willows?" she whispered, unsure if she was talking to Dr. Grant or herself. But Zora didn't look up from her inspection, and Dr. Grant didn't interrupt. He seemed to know she was talking through her thoughts.

The lamb's blood poured out of its body to create a flowing river around the trees, which disappeared in the distance. As lambs were used throughout history to indicate innocence, and this lamb was violently killed, Zora was comfortable saying this fore-edge painting served as a warning. Her curiosity was piqued as she opened the cover.

The book was initially blank. The first writing was in tight cursive on the leather's backside. *The Diary of Esther Fisherman.* Then, in smaller letters, the subtitle read, *Esther's belief in the beast in the woods, and her unholy domain, endures.*

"Who is Esther Fisherman?" Zora finally looked up to find Dr. Grant reading his own book, but she was too lost in thoughts of birch oil and slaughtered lambs to care. "That name sounds kinda familiar."

He didn't look up from his book. "Esther Ophelia Fisherman was a librarian at Bricksbury from sometime before the Slaveholders' Rebellion till the late twenties. She lived on campus all those years and didn't have much family, so when she died, her possessions became university property."

It'd been a couple of months since Zora left her job in Knoxville and had last seen Dr. Grant. She'd forgotten his refusal to call the Civil War anything other than the Slaveholders' Rebellion. Zora thought it must be his favorite tangent. According to him, it was *not only a more accurate name but also what it was called at the time.* And *A historian's job is* accurate *preservation*, he'd lectured.

"Fisherman," Zora said, mind searching. "As in the Esther Fisherman Quad?"

He half nodded. "Named for her. She was beloved. Helped pioneer library science, too." Finally, he set down his book and fixed Zora with an even stare. "Are you familiar with that phrase, 'the beast in the woods'?"

"No, should I be?" Zora's mind pivoted once more to consider historically accurate metaphors for "beast" across history. All the beasts she could recall referred either to men or vague humanoid figures serving as symbols of men's horror.

He sighed, and a look of genuine disappointment softened his face. "Honestly, I'd hoped you would be, as a rootworker."

Zora's frown deepened. No one knew about her practice or her power, except Jasmine. Zora's first thought was of Henry Louis and his mojo bag. Should she deny it? How safe was it to discuss this? "I...didn't put that in my proposal."

"Oh, you certainly did," he said, laughing more gently than before. "Don't get me wrong, it's entirely possible your extensive knowledge of conjure was learned in one of Dartmouth's undergrad programs, but..."

He lifted her proposal, which he'd printed and had covered in far more annotations than he'd given her in his terse rejection.

"This is too passionate of a defense for something you aren't actively practicing, don't you think?"

Okay, so you agree it's a passionate defense?

"My degree was the summation of years of immersive research, Dr. Grant." Zora paused occasionally because she couldn't stop an attitude from creeping into her tone. "I find it hard to believe you'd discount it like—"

"I apologize," he said, in the least apologetic tone possible, "but you must agree that to divorce your practice from your research, as you tried and failed to do in this proposal, cannot be to your benefit. You have a unique perspective that makes this research even more compelling."

"If I were a rootworker, wouldn't that be a conflict of interest? Wouldn't it nullify my findings, my conclusions?"

"Trust your gut, but if you can maintain broad objectivity, I'll allow some specific subjectivity; in this case, if using your practice can help this proposal, I suggest going down that path. Even just to see where it leads you."

Zora nodded, astonished. "I—I appreciate that."

He gestured to the volume in her hand. "I found that in the library's Rare Books Room over the summer. It was wedged between some rather unremarkable tomes."

"You *took* this from the library?" Zora wasn't judging; on the contrary, it was nice to see Dr. Grant show some nontraditional tendencies.

Instead of answering, Dr. Grant said, "I've encountered the 'beast in the woods' motif multiple times since coming to Bricksbury in the eighties. It's part of a larger legend or folktale, I don't know which. It's always been on the periphery of my work, though I've never had time to investigate it further." He leaned back and put his hands behind his head. "There is history there, a story. One that hasn't ever been documented from what I can see."

Zora had heard enough. Esther and the beast in the woods called to her. Dr. Grant was right—she had a unique insight into her research topics.

Besides, this was unexplored ground. This was the chance to make history. Maybe she *should* lean into it, especially if she could tie this to conjure somehow.

"I'll do it," she said firmly.

Dr. Grant looked at his watch but remained in his seat. "Do you have any other questions before I let you go?"

Zora's eyes danced around the room, searching for anything that would activate a thoughtful question. Out of the multipaned window, Zora could see a group of unfamiliar men. They appeared too mature to be freshmen, but everyone at Bricksbury looked older than their actual age. It was their eyes. Already tired from the constant studying, anxiety, and self-imposed deadlines.

She studied their letter-embroidered tennis shoes and straight backs. They must be in one of the Greek societies. Rush was soon, though she was too out of the loop to know any specifics.

There. An idea.

"You mentioned wanting me to dig deeper and uncover more specific religions and practices. To that point"—Zora licked her lips, confused, as something inside told her she was making an irreversible mistake—"what do you know about Bricksbury societies?"

A look of surprise crossed Dr. Grant's face, but he quickly recovered. "Can you be more specific? Academic? Political? Hell, I even think they just started an esports league, though I don't think that's what you're gettin' at."

Zora laughed. "Um, yeah, I'm referring to ones connected to... Hoodoo?"

Dr. Grant sat back in his seat and considered Zora. "Now you're askin' some good questions."

They shared a smirk, and Zora was glad. Even if the rejection was a pain in the ass, she had to believe Dr. Grant valued all the work she'd done in her past and the drive she'd had to get into Bricksbury in the first place and knew she was destined for more.

"When it comes to societies, all Bricksbury's are old. The youngest one, I believe, is... Phi Beta Sigma? Did it come before or after Omega Psi Phi?"

Zora opened her mouth like she knew the answer, but she most certainly didn't. Still, those were facts easily googled. She pivoted to a juicier topic.

"Those are the younger ones. Which ones are older?"

He nodded, pulled out a notecard with writing on it, put it down, and searched his desk until he found a fresh sheet of paper. "I'm gonna send you to someone who'll know more than me."

"A society member?" Zora held her breath, knowing it was unlikely at best and impossible at worse that he would have those kinds of connections and freely give them to her.

Dr. Grant shook his head. "I want you to think bigger than Bricksbury. Let's send ya down to Jonesborough African American Historical Society. Try to go sometime in the next couple weeks because I'd like a follow-up meeting to review everything before the month is out. Sound good?"

Zora took the paper and stood. "Thank you, Dr. Grant."

"Use your rootwork practice to endear yourself to your inter-viewees. You'll have it in common with many people around here, including your first appointment, who will be waiting for you across campus."

Zora swallowed, though her throat had gone dry. The scratchy feeling brought on a ragged cough.

"What," she finally said. "What are you talking about?"

"There are Bricksbury alumni with a rich and, more importantly to you, local family history. They agreed to speak with you this afternoon since they'd be on campus anyway for Conjure Night. Was that one of the groups you wanted to know about?"

Half of Zora was impressed; the other half was concerned by how well he'd read her.

"You've got one hour to prepare. You'll interview your sub-ject on the way to Conjure Night. Be at the south entrance to the Woodlands."

Annoyance quickly turned to awe for Zora. Canvassing was her favorite form of interview. She loved observing people's faces and body language during discussions. So much was lost in the region's oral histories. This would be an opportunity to further her research and contribute to the documented folklore. A thrill raced through her body at the thought. Still, something nagged at her.

"What if I hadn't come to your office hours today?"

He'd been inching toward the door, but Dr. Grant paused at Zora's question. He looked at her with downturned lips as if she'd offended him.

"Had you not shown up rarin' for a fight within three hours of that email, you never would've gotten into Bricksbury, Ms. Robinson."

Esther Fisherman's Diary
September 13, 1927
Jonesborough, Tennessee
Bricksbury Mountain College—Staff Housing

Dear Diary,

If I told the other librarians what I overheard the president and vice president saying last night, they would call me a loon. They would tell me I was tired/batty/fanciful and that I was too old to be laboring long hours among the university shelves.

To my face, one of them, invariably Patricia, would suggest that I take a walk near running water or in the eyeline of a wealthy and affection-starved gentleman. When I turned my back, they would suggest an asylum or whatever they've renamed a place for the aged. Moreover, as I near seventy-three, I'm not entirely sure they'd be incorrect. Despite it all, I know what I heard. I know it.

President Williams mentioned the recent deaths. One was a student, and the other an assistant working in the Music Department. It grieves me to say I was happy to hear the men speak of the deaths. I was pleased because no one else would even hear of them.

I spoke to Mrs. Tubbard, Dr. Vaughn, Dr. Jones, and Mr. Ellington about the police being up in the woods every night for the last week. They each gave me a little, reassuring smile as if I'd just told them I'd experienced an inconvenience rather than feared an evil had made a home at Bricksbury.

The specific thing that set this diary entry into action was the vice president mentioning that the bodies were found in Hosanna's Crypt, a place I've never heard of but must reference Hosanna Crawfoot, the cofounder of Bricksbury, now long dead. I wouldn't know where to start if the president hadn't hidden a book from the Occultism section in his pocket before leaving.

I again spied on the president and vice president after hours in the library. To catch them, I switched shifts for the past week with Patricia, who was thrilled to have evenings off to frolic however young people do these days.

As I organized and reorganized books in the Religion section, the men spoke softly in the stacks two rows away. President Williams said he'd been out to Hosanna's Crypt and would ensure no students went that far into the woods again. His voice shook as he described ghastly scenes in the "old church."

Meanwhile, the vice president praised him for his bravery, as he apparently had decided against going into the woods himself after a menacing conversation with his wife (who I can account is not an easy woman).

By then, I had heard and seen all I could from my safe perch in the library. It was time for Mohammad to come to the mountain, as Mama used to say. At sunrise this past Saturday, I left a note (and a last will and testament) on my kitchen table detailing where I was going and why, in the likely scenario that I should encounter someone with terrible intentions in the woods. I brought with me a sheathed blade, chloroform, and my Bible. Weapons for the only violence of which I'm aware.

I set off from the staff housing so early that the biting mountain air burned the tops of my cheeks. Although I'd put on several layers, it was as if I were marching naked to my doom. The campus was deathly still, far too quiet. And yet I trudged on. I imagined myself a womanly Hannibal, which is to say, a woman.

When I arrived at the entrance to the woods, though, I was stopped. Not by police, whose cars and ungodly noise I would've noticed. No, I was stopped by three deans, though I couldn't say what they were deans of. I'd seen the young men around campus and recognized them, and they recognized me, which helped underplay my intentions (I stated I often go on morning walks, which wasn't the least factual but had the advantage of being plausible).

They were kind but firm in relaying that I wasn't to go into the woods for my walks any longer and to find a new place. Perhaps, they prodded, I would be happier walking indoors so as not to catch a chill since winter was nearly upon us anyway. Although they used my advanced age to emphasize their point, they did so in a way that didn't offend me. Considering how I've heard students and administration talking in their regurgitated slang, I'd call that a victory.

What wasn't a victory was the fact that I couldn't go into the woods, and my long walk was all for naught. I returned to my room and, half-relieved, half-anxious, slept for much of the weekend.

Yesterday, Monday, I decided to change tactics. My coworkers didn't/couldn't care when I mentioned the disappearances, but when asked how I'd spent the weekend, Dr. Jones was concerned to learn I'd gone for a morning walk in the woods.

"What made you do that?" he asked, incredulous. "I didn't know you walked for leisure."

This was ridiculous of him to say for several reasons, not the least of which was that he knew nothing of import about me at all, so his surprise at my actions was annoyingly melodramatic. But still, I was in pursuit of information he might've had. So, I lied through clenched teeth. I told him I often spent time there reading scripture, which he smiled at gently because that better fit his picture of me. He asked why I didn't read in the newly completed Hemlock Chapel, built beside the library, and offered to formally introduce me to the pastor, his personal friend.

As I inwardly yawned at this grueling back-and-forth, eventually Dr. Jones got to his point about why I shouldn't be reading scripture—or anything for that matter—in the wild. He'd asked if I'd heard of the folktale "The Beast in the Woods" and then explained when I said I hadn't.

"The Beast in the Woods" was a folktale native to the Jonesborough area. It had been hypothesized it was created to keep children from playing where wolves and rattlesnakes roamed. The folktale detailed the story of a backwoods town surrounded by dense forest. Occasionally, the people heard cries coming from the trees. The sounds weren't entirely human or entirely feral, but a wicked combination designed to intrigue and terrify. Not everyone could hear the cries, only those whom the town would later find dead among the pines and willows of inhuman wounds.

Before their deaths, the victims complained of a weeping demon calling to them, sending for them from somewhere hidden in darkness. Eventually, they'd go mad, and no one—not their mothers, fathers, or lovers—could hold them back from running toward the cries, never to be seen alive again.

"Don't go into the woods, Esther," he said.

I was silent for a minute while absorbing this information.

Then I asked why he was still so concerned about the woods if this was a fictional story—and a cloud passed over his eyes. I saw it! A misty haze almost too thin to make out (I wouldn't've without my cheaters) fully crossed from one side of his eyeball to the other.

He breathed in slowly, then looked at me and asked how my weekend had been.

Upon further thought, I realized that attempting to enter the woods was woefully hasty of me. There's something happening here that I do not fully understand.

But know this, diary: I will understand it, so help me God.

Graciously,
Esther Ophelia Fisherman

Chapter Six

It took Zora fifteen minutes to haul ass back to her dorm and another twenty to take Henry Louis to relieve himself and assuage his separation anxiety with treats and cuddles.

She took a ten-minute shower and listened to one of her favorite podcasts, *The Read*. She'd followed the hosts for over a decade, laughing at their cutting commentary on Black culture and entertainment. Other times, she cried with them, relieved and pained they suffered from fears and anxieties similar to her own.

Zora's showers were often short. They were squished between overtime work, dissociative memory holes, and practicing conjure. However brief the shower was, it did wonders for her concentration. She laughed along with Kid Fury and dressed quickly. There was no time for makeup, only a quick once-over with body lotion, facial moisturizer, and her homemade citronella bug spray.

Zora flew out the door and headed for the Woodlands' south entrance. It was dusk, the end of the day, yet an electrifying energy sparked on campus. With classes finished, there was no restraint in people's laughter. They weren't memorizing theories or calculations. They weren't late for a quiz. People walked with a smooth nonchalance that could only be achieved at the end of a long day.

Even Zora walked lighter on the stone pavers.

She read the pictures she'd taken of Esther Fisherman's diary on her phone as she walked. She needed to research the fascinating woman more, but Esther had already taught Zora something.

"The Beast in the Woods" was a folktale that kept children from playing in Jonesborough's woods, Esther wrote.

It was a standard origin for this kind of story; the Beast was created as the antagonist to ensure children stayed away. But what caught Zora's attention most was that people were *drawn* to the woods, whether by design or for punishment for their sins, by a sound only they could hear. That sounded less like a fictional antagonist and more like an actual spirit. One with bad intentions. This was the very point where her academic interests and personal understanding of the supernatural intersected.

Don't go into the woods, Esther. Don't go into the woods.

The librarian had been cautioned. Now the words repeated in Zora's mind; an eerie lullaby. Perhaps they were reused from an old story or song. Or, possibly, they were an earnest warning. Zora knew which she preferred as she stepped off Bricksbury's manicured lawn onto the woods' south entrance path. A few people were in front of and behind her, but Zora was too absorbed in Esther's words to look up. Still, it was nice to be surrounded by others. Their presence calmed Zora. The crowd seemed to be moving toward Conjure Night, although they'd be early. She couldn't say much, though; Zora would be early to her own death if it meant avoiding the anxiety of feeling rushed.

Zora took a deep breath as she reached behind her, ensuring that her trusty bear spray was securely clipped to her backpack. She stepped into the dense woods looming ahead. Her jeans were tucked snugly into her thickest socks, a shield against the elements. Still, she couldn't prevent intrusive thoughts about the lurking ticks, each one a potential carrier of Lyme disease. Zora considered giving herself another layer of citronella bug spray but decided she'd wait until she reached her destination.

During her thesis research, she illegally canvassed old neighborhoods with the bear spray in her backpack. It was necessary after a particularly heinous Bichon Frisé didn't blink at regular pepper spray. The jeans idea she got from her sophomore year roommate, who hiked in the White Mountains (too easy) with her parents every—single—weekend. And in any weather condition. Apparently, it was meant to prevent tick bites.

Zora didn't know how this stopped ticks from burrowing between her sock and shoe, but she crammed that thought aside. It was something she couldn't control.

"Zora!" someone's throaty voice shouted from Zora's extreme left through the trees.

Zora stalled. Someone collided with her. She stumbled forward, gasping.

"Sorry, I didn't know you were right behind me," she apologized.

"You're good." The person didn't even look back at Zora, just kept trekking along.

Zora moved off to the side of the trail and caught her breath, inhaling the musk of damp soil and decaying foliage. She squinted at the trees. The sun's light crept through branches, casting slender yellow-gold streaks across rough bark. There was nothing there. More importantly, there was no *one* there. And therefore, no one could've yelled at her.

She swallowed. *Get a fucking grip.* She wanted—no, needed—to keep her mind on what was real and within her command. An interview, a way to deepen and, honestly, to save her thesis.

It had been dusk when she'd left Henry Louis with a frozen peanut-butter-filled bone, and now the light sky had darkened into a coppery color. Fireflies blinked in the air, though the overhead canvas of leaves didn't allow Zora to see much of anything. The humidity oozed into her lungs. Each breath demanded her attention. Her mind kept returning to the librarian—the lullaby. *Don't go into the woods, Esther. Don't go into the woods.*

Zora tipped her neck backward and squinted at a sign. Cracked, pale wood leaned backward against thick brush. It looked exhausted by time.

BRICKSBURY MOUNTAIN COLLEGE WOODLANDS

THIS 300-ACRE TRACT WAS ONCE THE WOODLOT OF JONESBORO AFRICAN BAPTIST CHURCH (C. 1796). IT WILL BE LEFT UNDISTURBED FOR PRESENT AND FUTURE GENERATIONS. REMAIN ON THE PATH.

Zora had a terrible feeling that "left undisturbed" meant "wild animals every-fucking-where." But she wouldn't be moved from her plan. None of the others on the trail looked worried, plus she had the bear spray and the mojo bag in her backpack. She'd been in too much of a hurry to feed it, but it would be strong enough until the next quarter moon. She was at the entrance to the woods; now, where was her subject?

"Zora?"

Zora looked up to find Mallory Holston, owner of Jonesborough Conjure Shoppe, off to the side of the trail. Their fingers drummed impatiently on their backpack straps. Their locs were pulled into a high bun, but they'd kept their green lipstick and overalls.

"Mallory?" Zora couldn't believe her eyes. "*You're* the local conjurer Dr. Grant sent me to interview?"

Mallory rolled their eyes. "It's just like him not even to tell ya who you're meetin'. Anyway, let's get to it, honey. I'm workin' at Conjure Night. You are comin' to that, right?"

They didn't wait for Zora's response before ducking into a grassy clearing. Zora followed, immediately recognizing Immanuel and his moisturized afro from the store. He wore the same light-wash jeans and Nina Simone T-shirt as that morning, though he'd changed into hiking boots, which was more forward-thinking than Zora had been. Beside him, Zora's cowboy-hat-wearing neighbor across the courtyard, Khadijah, carried an instrument case. Its long neck suggested it could be a guitar, or maybe a violin? What was bigger than a violin? A viola?

Khadijah's white cowboy hat had a curled brim, and she'd traded in her violet sundress from earlier for frayed denim shorts and a faded red baseball shirt with "Diamondbacks" written in bold across her chest. The snug shirt matched her mysterious, bright red instrument case. She was close enough in the clearing that Zora saw the look of recognition when their eyes met—and the soft smile after. *Oh, fuck.* Zora matched her casual smile—she was in no rush—then, maintaining eye contact, she added a quick upward nod. She *would* rush if Khadijah wanted. The two stood, smiling momentarily from many yards away. *Oh, fuck yes.* Zora turned and pretended not to see when a chuckling Immanuel playfully slapped Khadijah's arm.

It had been far too long since Zora had shared a knowing smile with a woman and longer since she'd given more than an acknowledging smile back. Her vibrators got the job done; they always had, but Zora had seen Khadijah's smile and had already fantasized about ways she could make her smile more. Zora was a single grad student living on campus. She was thrilled to start acting like it.

Her smile slipped away as she shifted her gaze from Khadijah, her eyes wandering to the others gathered in the clearing. A paranoid part of Zora worried Eliza Deadbody would be standing somewhere in the back, fiery eyes focused on Zora and the word "sacrifice" echoing from her mouth. But luckily, the crowd was chill. And devoid of Eliza. Their cheerful chatter lifted Zora's mood...until she saw what they were doing. Two people in matching dark overall denim shoved poles with curved ends into the ground. *Scythes?* On closer inspection, they were long metal shepherd's hooks. Zora's focus, though, returned to Mallory as they offered her a mini can of Coke from a cooler. Zora said no, but Mallory looked determined.

"If you're diabetic, you should take it. Won't be eatin' for a lil while."

Zora took the can, seeing that this was becoming a point of contention. Her eyes flitted back to Khadijah and Immanuel for a moment. They'd begun stabbing the ground with the shepherd's hooks, their faces scrunched. Immanuel worked at Mallory's shop. Did Khadijah also work there?

Zora began with a more pressing question. "Did you know we'd meet later when I saw you this morning? In your shop?"

"Child! D'ya think that man gives me that much of a heads-up? If he weren't my best customer, he'd get more of my lip than he already does. Anyway, I got the call as soon as ya left."

Zora pulled up her Notes app. Did Dr. Grant plan their interview on a whim? It was a strange coincidence that he set up a meeting between her and someone she'd already met that morning.

"Let's get going," Zora said. "Dr. Grant said your family—"

Mallory cut her off. "Tell me about your thesis. The one Dr. Grant rejected." They sat carefully with crossed legs atop the blue plastic cooler lid, only occasionally shouting instructions to the others on opening the folding tables and laying out the yoga mats.

Zora cleared her throat, ready to discuss her research. "It was called 'The Spiritual History of Affrilachia.' And he rejected it for sure, but it wasn't for the reason I thought. He knows how important Jonesborough is, and the rich history of rootworkers here, but he wants..." She trailed off.

"He wants it done his way, I'd wager," Mallory said under their breath. "Hope he's not givin' you too much of a hard time. We need more of *us* researchin' the area. People don't think Black folk live up here in Appalachia. An' ya know they go outta their way to erase us. Someone's gotta keep an' tell our stories."

Zora smiled. "That's my plan. So, now I'm narrowing my thesis topic. As you know from earlier, I'm a rootworker. My practice involves working with many herbs, roots, and other plants. With that in mind, I wanted to ask about you and your family's history in Jonesborough and Bricksbury, where conjure and rootwork are so openly displayed."

Mallory looked deep into the trees as a memory tugged at them. "Ya know, my father didn't even want me to go to Bricksbury. I only came here for my doctorate after he died."

"Really? Why?"

"It's a long story."

"Well, I'm here to listen. It's kinda my job."

Mallory laughed. "Right, okay, where do I start? When I was sendin' out college applications in...oh Lawd, I won't even tell ya the year. My daddy had to sign off on each of 'em 'cause he was payin' for it. I didn't argue. I wanted to get outta the house, ya know? I sent applications to every college south of the Mason–Dixon and east of the Mississippi—those were his initial rules. But the rules changed when it came to Bricksbury."

"Yo, Mallory, are we supposed—"

"Young man," Mallory began, eyebrows wagging with humor, "I *know* you didn't come over here an' interrupt my ongoin' conversation."

Immanuel had been yards away, shouting. Now he sighed and calmly walked up to Mallory.

"My bad," he said, grinning and out of breath. He glanced at Zora, then back at Khadijah, mischief sparkling in his warm eyes. "Sorry I interrupted you."

Mallory patted his hand affectionately, silently accepting his apology for them *and* Zora.

"This is Zora," Mallory formally introduced them, oblivious to Zora's blushing. "Zora, this is Immanuel, who will continue to work at my shop only so long as he doesn't piss me off an' uses common manners."

Immanuel scratched the back of his head. "There are ants all over the cinnamon brooms. What do you want us to do with them? Oh, and while I have you, one of the freshies broke a crystal case down the trail. Also, your drummer is late."

Mallory pinched the bridge of their nose and sighed. Immanuel and Zora exchanged a repressed-smile look. He'd switched out his forest-green septum ring for a burnt-orange one.

"Which case?" Mallory finally asked.

Zora took a moment to breathe in the honeysuckle while Immanuel explained. He seemed cool, as did Khadijah.

I'm gonna try to be his friend, Zora told herself. *No, I will be his friend. Well, I mean, not against his will, but it's time to put myself out there. With him, platonically. With Khadijah, maybe something more.* She groaned inwardly. Why was making friends as an adult so cringe? And dating—super cringe. Or maybe she was the one who was cringe in the end.

A few early students had arrived for Conjure Night, interrupting Zora's thoughts. They laid towels and blankets on the ground, which Zora had *not* thought of. Others, including Immanuel, carried in multiple sofas—wingback leather monstrosities that took four people to carry. *This monthly Conjure Night must cost Bricksbury a fortune.*

"Anyway," Mallory said when they were alone again. "Daddy refused to let me apply, even though, as ya know, it's one of the most prestigious schools in the country, HBCU or not. Growin' up, there were rumors. Everyone knew them. Rumblings about mysterious happenings on the campus. Disappearances. So, the school always felt…forbidding. But still, it has, to this day, the best botany program in the country, so I was gonna suck it up an'…ironically, considerin' our current location, never go into the woods."

Zora looked up from typing. *Don't go into the woods, Esther. Don't go—* The way the phrases had echoed through her mind… she'd chalked it up to her academic anxiety getting to her. Mallory's words, though, were something real.

Never go into the woods. And yet, here she was.

Something else made Zora frown. Disappearances on campus? It was highly unlikely. Any crime or crime-adjacent happening was unlikely at Bricksbury. Everyone knew that. Then Zora's mind turned again to Esther Fisherman. She'd written about missing students. Unlike Mallory's father, she'd been certain about it, and she wasn't going off rumors. Zora would've added his concerns to the growing collection of Appalachia superstitions, but she'd already heard about this one at home—well, at her grandparents' home. Grandpa was a distinguished alumnus of Bricksbury who took great pride in his alma mater, yet never once graced the campus with his presence after graduation. Whenever Zora or Jasmine would ask about it, Grandma alluded to an incident but always skirted the details. Zora had never paid it much mind, but now wished she'd been more curious.

"Rumors?" Zora tried to keep her voice neutral. "I was unaware."

Mallory nodded. "Bricksbury's dirty little secret." They pulled out a pack of cigarettes, looked at the students trickling in, and returned the pack to their pocket. "The bodies were always found in the woods. Anyway, my father refused to pay for my application, an' after several heated back-an'-forths between him, my mother, an' me, he finally admitted that he studied for a single semester at Bricksbury in the twenties. It was when a series of folks vanished. My father was a librarian, ya know. An' Bricksbury's library is…I mean, you've seen it."

"I have, it's beautiful."

Mallory frowned. "Shoooot, beautiful? *Beautiful?* It's four floors of extravagance. Rare paintings, priceless chandeliers, invaluable volumes in the rarest editions. Their Botany Library collection is actually five comprehensive, noncirculatin' research libraries." Mallory stood, eyes glazed over as they walked through their memories. "It's the single most important collection of botanical manuscripts, field notes, an' correspondences in the country. An' Daddy knew that! I begged an' begged. Sorry, where was I?"

Zora smiled to let them know that feeling their feelings around her was okay. The sun was lowering on the horizon, leaving thick evening humidity. Zora lightly rolled her neck inside her collar, feeling, then ignoring her sticky skin. She waited for Mallory to sit and cross their legs again before speaking.

"You were saying your father spent a semester at Bricksbury during the disappearances?"

"Ah. Yes, there were several. One was a sweet elderly librarian Daddy was close to. Her goin' missin' was the ultimate reason he left."

Zora shivered in dusk's pale light. "Did he mention the librarian's name?"

"Honey, this was over thirty years ago. Maybe Emily or Eleanor or somethin' like that. Anyway, anyway, it scared him bad. But Daddy said the strangest part of it wasn't what happened. It was that people...people didn't notice. Or maybe they didn't care. He didn't know which. But no one ever talked about any of it. Never even mentioned it. Students, faculty, staff, hell, even Jonesborough residents, all 'walked round like ghosts,' he said."

Zora hung on Mallory's words until, at that moment, a woman rounded the corner. She strode with purpose into the clearing, wearing a brownish-orange sleeveless shirt the same color as tiger's-eye. Jasmine. Zora didn't see any protective gemstones among Jasmine's multiple piercings, but one could be hidden on her person, like Zora's mojo bag. And her bear spray.

Mallory nodded. "Not literally," they said, "but dead in the eyes. Daddy insisted it was some other rootworker's magic that made people turn their cheeks away from the sufferin'."

Zora pried her eyes off her sister long enough to glance back at Mallory. "And why would they do that?"

Mallory shrugged. "I suppose...to make sure that whoever was doin' it got away with it."

Amias Crawfoot
September 1, 1877
Jonesborough, Tennessee
Bricksbury Mountain College—The Woodlands

The Klan entered Jonesborough, no warning before their heavy hoofbeats. They terrorized the countryside, leaving bruised men and bleeding mothers screaming on packed dirt, stampeding over one another in their attempts to escape the horror; they writhed around like nests of crimson serpents across the ground, intent on swallowing one another. But the white men never stayed. The Klan didn't just attack towns—they crashed through them in under an hour, using the element of surprise and wielding His cross in a terrifying, unholy manner. Unbeknownst to them, the Son of the Living God would soon declare Jonesborough His.

Amias was having breakfast in his room, planning to visit the demon in the woods later that day. It'd been weeks, but Amias's knees didn't bend as well as they used to. Even walking from his rooms to his office in the newly erected Mary Smith Peake building took great effort and, oftentimes, assistance. He delighted in the warmth of the golden-brown bread, perfectly complemented by a cool spread of seedy blackberry jam. The tranquility was shattered as the door burst open. Hosanna stood in the doorway, her tear-streaked face and disheveled appearance wordlessly wounding Amias. The Klan's intentions had next been set on Bricksbury.

Amias left his sister sitting in his favorite armchair, cradling a sturdy teacup filled with amber whiskey. Agony had claimed her, and anger him.

Amias met the minister and the nurses. He'd missed the assault, and as he interviewed those who witnessed it, he noticed a peculiarity with their eyes. The longer he stared, the more certain he became—their souls were irrevocably burdened. Their reddened eyes were furiously marred. Amias shook with his inability to protect that which he loved. He knew there was nothing he wouldn't do at that moment. There was no pain he wouldn't endure or inflict on others to prevent this from happening again.

The Klan had plundered Amias's home, where he and Hosanna birthed and mothered a sanctuary. Why did He require this? Could the demon not prevent this? Warn them?

Two students, Wilhelmina Anderson and David Matthews, were killed in the attack. Wilhelmina was a band student who played the banjo and violin. David would have graduated in weeks with his philosophy degree. Their instructors told Amias that they each had bright futures. Wilhelmina was grounded and studious, whereas David was lively and passionate. They were two bright stars—two who could no longer shine.

Amias's knee and many other joints ached, but at nightfall, he made his way to the woods, knowing it'd take him a while to reach his destination. Hosanna was in better shape. She'd be able to get to the church quicker and quieter (with less cracking bones as she walked). But Hosanna was still lost in her agony. Despite all the work she'd done and the sacrifices she'd made for the school's safety. He'd seen grief in many people that day, but it was his elderly sister's crying that undid Amias. It was her pain he couldn't look away from for fear of forgetting the moment he'd become a failure. Amias never ran from his shame. He often ran toward it.

He had waited until the moon was visible in the sky and most students had gone to their rooms. They didn't linger outside the doors or along the tree-lined walkways like usual. They weren't shouting their laughter or anger or homesickness. The students had gone to bed. Bricksbury was their haven, yet they'd been faced with exactly what Amias had feared most. It simply could not be. He wouldn't allow it. Had he and Hosanna not sacrificed? They spent their whole lives both outworking their prospective marriages and, therefore, sacrificing their love in the end.

When Hosanna's husband divorced her, it had been a quiet scandal on campus but a great sadness for her. When Amias's wife left a note on his desk saying she'd never be back, he was relieved. He hoped she'd find someone who cared about her more than he did. Someone who didn't dream of demons.

"Are you here?" Amias croaked in the darkness.

He was still on the beaten trail and could just make out Bricksbury's newly installed oil streetlamps. They fluttered in the still air in a wrong sort of way Amias couldn't explain. When he turned away from their stuttering lights, he faced the demon's fiery eyes. Amias gasped and nearly dropped his cane, wincing as a sharp pain radiated down his leg. The demon's translucent skin reached out quickly, steadying the curved wood and keeping him upright. It didn't speak, it never had, but it lingered closer to Amias until he straightened his back again.

"Thank you," Amias said, hearing the shock in his voice. "I... thank you."

It was the closest they'd ever been, and Amias couldn't think straight as his senses were overwhelmed with sweet honeysuckle and damp grass that crawled through his nostrils and then down to coat his throat. Did all demons smell like this? Like a clawing wind?

The demon wasn't human-looking, though it had four sheer limbs. Years ago, Amias decided it was the color of fog. It could hide in plain sight anywhere in the woods, especially at night. Though, interestingly, only if it closed its eyes, otherwise people would see their God-given fire. Sometimes, Amias thought he'd seen it on campus, but he was never sure. Fog was like that.

Now, with grief heavy in his chest, Amias gaped at the demon. The only thing on its smooth head were twin flames inside square eyes. Amias dreamed of those squares. Was God sending him messages in the shape, the fire's existence, or the fire's amber-gold color: the same color as the foxes sacrificed for the demon? The color of tiger's-eye. Was *this* the hidden message? Or was Amias insane? He'd accept either answer so long as it was The Answer.

They stood together for several long minutes before Amias remembered why he'd gone on this unlikely nighttime woodland stroll. Before he spoke, he paused, knowing his relationship with the demon was about to change, whatever happened. The sadness immediately after this realization was heavy. He waded through it.

"Where were you?" he asked, now remembering Hosanna in his chair. She still hadn't left.

The demon didn't move.

"I said, where were you? People...students were killed today. Now, where were you?"

The demon didn't move, but still, Amias felt the damp grass sag in his throat. As if God Himself was dissuading him from speaking. Amias quieted. This wasn't going well.

"Okay, let's...get up to the church," he said, walking several steps, then glancing back at the still fog. "We'll ask Him what to do."

Finally, the demon moved.

———

3:17 a.m.

"Dear God, I come humbly before you," Amias whispered on his knees.

The demon walked Amias to the church and then waited, as it must, outside. He tried not to think about whether it was still there and focused instead on the grief in his heart. But it was difficult.

"We need you. Please send me a more powerful protector."

Amias bowed before the pulpit, body smeared with freely given blood. One candle was lit. Strips of raw leather lay wet beside Amias, waiting should the Lord call him to draw blood again. Just as Jesus gave His life, so must His children.[5] So must Amias, especially.

8:40 a.m.

"Dear God, I come humbly before you," Amias whispered on his knees.

Soreness and then numbness overtook the lower half of his body, so he leaned perilously back and forth, allowing the blood in his body to rest in one place before moving to another. The blood across his back was still wet, though some of it had hardened uncomfortably. He didn't try to get up. This was part of the upcoming sacrifice, he knew.

"Hosanna needs you. The students need you. Jonesborough needs you. We need to be fully protected, God. I will do anything you ask. Anything to protect them, please, please, O Lord, hear my cries."

---

5 Romans 12:1–2—I beseech you therefore, brethren, by the mercies of God, that ye present your bodies a living sacrifice, holy, acceptable unto God, which is your reasonable sacrifice. And be not conformed to this world: but be ye transformed by the renewing of your mind, that ye may prove what is that good, and acceptable, and perfect, will of God.

5:03 p.m.

Amias's body curled painfully above his knees again. God allowed
him to exit the church to relieve himself for the first time. He did
not see the demon. It must be a sign of favor. He was getting closer
to the newer, mightier protection, closer, closer, closer.

11:19 p.m.

"Dear God, I come humbly before you," Amias whispered on his
knees. And finally, He answered. There was no number of foxes,
mules, or other creatures to satisfy a stronger protection. He needed
more from Amias: a human life.

"Amias!"

Startled, Amias fell over. The hardwood floors were unforgiv-
ing, digging into his bruised and bloodied skin. His open wounds
brushed the floor briefly, and he yelped in pain. His limbs were
too stiff to move afterward, so he lay still while Hosanna stood
above him. Her soft wrinkles, usually in motion due to her incessant talking, were still. She looked at Amias like he was a different person than the one who'd left her with the teacup of whiskey.
He was.

Minutes passed in silence as Hosanna took in the scene in the
church. Amias lay still, allowing his surroundings to tell the story
for him.

When she spoke, it was in a strangled whisper, as if the words
were stuck in her throat like the damp grass and honeysuckle had in
Amias's earlier.

"You hand-stitched a whip, Amias?"

He heard the pain in her tired voice. She'd already hiked to the
church, which had taken him longer than it probably took her, but
he hadn't arrived to his sibling in a pool of her own blood.

"I thought I might need it one day," he said, grinning, proud of himself for thinking ahead a few years ago.

"This..." Hosanna began.

"Vengeance is mine; I will repay, saith the Lord."[6]

"You fool," she whispered, eyes cutting. "How does that chapter end? Huh?"

"Do you want to know what He said?" Amias asked, ignoring her as usual.

"Be not overcome of evil, but overcome evil with good.[7] Is that what you've been up here doing, Amias? Overcoming evil with good? Or have you been merging good and evil for so long now you'd lay with them both?"

Amias swallowed. He bit back anger, and denials, and the unfairness of God sending him an evil he wasn't supposed to consume. Didn't He know Amias's heart? His desperation for connection, for splintered authenticity cracked open by cravings and longing that ached? His sister could never understand—in truth, Amias feared he was all haunted hunger.

"Do you want to know what He said?" Amias repeated.

"No."

"What?" Amias lifted his head to stare up at her in shock.

"Let's get you cleaned up, Amias," Hosanna said, urgency in her voice. "We'll need a nurse to look at you until Dr. Wallingford gets back tomorrow—"

"Hosanna!" Amias screamed at the floor, watching as his blood rippled gently against his breath. "He requires a sacrifice. One of us must die."

Finally, Hosanna sat in a nearby pew.

---

6 Romans 12:19—Dearly beloved, avenge not yourselves, but rather give place unto wrath: for it is written, Vengeance is mine; I will repay, saith the Lord.

7 Romans 12:21—Be not overcome of evil, but overcome evil with good.

"Foxes won't do, He said. The sacrifice must be human this time," Amias said as he slowly sat up, slipped in his blood, then sat up once more.

"Human," Hosanna echoed.

Amias nodded. He sat quietly with his sister, letting the knowledge of what they must do sink in. It had been so long since their childhood in seaside Massachusetts. He'd almost forgotten the initial reason they started Bricksbury. It was the preservation of knowledge. But that preserve needed protection if it was meant to survive in America. Would they really do anything for Bricksbury? For Jonesborough?

He stood suddenly, a Godly strength aiding him in his swiftness. *Forgive me*, he thought as he brought his hunting knife from his pocket. He considered slicing his throat right there. It was fitting. He'd fall in his sacrificial blood, and Hosanna and Bricksbury would be gifted more protection. It was fitting. It was what God probably wanted him to do, and what he should have done, but Amias wanted to live.

———

Hosanna lay in the darkness, moaning incessantly against the stone floors. Death awaited her.

"O my God,
I am ashamed and blush
to lift up my face to thee."

"How could you do this to me?" she fiercely whispered in the darkness. She'd finished quoting scripture and turned her voice from deferential to furious. "This can't be happening. You're only in my mind. This isn't happening. Only in my mind. This can't b—"

"Does playing pretend like a child make you feel better?" Amias asked coldly.

"We are both too old even to exist."

"Indeed, but as you know, God can subdue all things."

"He can't hide the rot in your heart."

"Nor in yours."

"Amias, it's 1877. Bricksbury is built. The Slaveholders' Rebellion is done. War's over. Yet here you are, still fightin'."

"You think because they freed the enslaved, they freed the people?"

"Well... at least we ain't—"

"What? In the fields? In the kitchens?" He sighed. "God's war will never cease."

There was silence between them. They listened to the sounds of the woods outside the church. Birds. Rustling leaves. After a moment the strangled cry of a fox sounded from the trees. Amias laughed, and while it was a kind sound, new madness overran the edges. He giggled, whispered nonsense to himself, and giggled more.

"You gotta die," he said eventually, somberness wilting his hysteria. "God has decreed so. It must be fed. Then, and only then, will Jonesborough and Bricksbury be safe."

"Only then?"

"Only. Then."

"This is what you've been doing? In the woods, in the church. All those years of isolation. You've been talking to Him."

"Yes. I'm sorry, sister. But yes."

"One day, you will die, Amias. You are wicked, and *the wicked shall be turned into hell*,"[8] Hosanna said, not somber but certain.

"Sister, there must be a first sacrifice to herald what is to come. I am sorry, but it's my duty."

---

8 Psalms 9:17—The wicked shall be turned into hell, and all the nations that forget God.

Amias felt the gritty handle of his hunting knife as he crouched with his crying sister. He held her hand and whispered the words that she'd carry with her forever.

"I beseech you therefore, brethren, by the mercies of God,
that ye present your bodies a living sacrifice, holy,
acceptable unto God,
which is your reasonable service."

When the knife entered her body, Hosanna screamed, the church doors flew open, and Amias was wrong once more. Demons were not bound by the confines of the church. They could enter where— and whom—they pleased.

Chapter Seven

Despite her best efforts, Zora couldn't stop staring at her sister. Jasmine seemed aware of this because she reached out a hand to stop Ngozi behind an overhanging oak, positioning them under a drooping branch with dark acorns and long, furry catkins. For long seconds, they only existed against shifting shadows. Although she took out her phone, Jasmine didn't look down at it. She only clutched the golden-yellow rectangle and nervously whispered while licking her lips. Ngozi looked up, squinting behind thin designer frames. They wore a casually chic pear-green babydoll dress and cushioned sandals. A strange choice for a hike, unlike Immanuel's boots. Even from across the field, Zora made out their neatly stitched gladiators. When they spied Zora, Ngozi's sharp jawline fell into a frown. *Not promising.*

Zora slowed her breathing, wielding these seconds to collect herself. After all this time, holy fuck, here Jasmine was, her sister, as sophisticated as ever. She wore the kind of muted casual clothing that hung in any teaching assistant's closet. The soft pleats on Jasmine's peplum top shot down her body toward her simple dark-wash jeans and beige tennis shoes. The shoes twisted into the ground when Zora looked at them. *I'm not the only nervous one.*

Zora rubbed at the black button-down collared men's dress shirt she'd chosen for the night. It was her go-to for casual professional events. The quick-dry fabric was breathable but too formal. Her toes squirmed inside the Birkenstock sneakers she'd bought as a present for her twenty-fourth birthday last January. She'd reasoned that they were a sensible luxury at the post-holidays sale.

Compared to Jasmine, Zora wasn't going to Conjure Night but to some sorta Conjure Gala for Chronically Overdressed Studs. There was nothing to be done about it now. Zora's gaze drifted to Jasmine's amulet helix studs, where she was certain multiple protection spells must lie. Seeing her here, among the trees like this, reminded Zora of the past, back when they loved racing around the backwoods—together. Back when the woods were just the woods and not the place where their child selves had been met with evil. They'd loved spending hours outside.

Plucking sweet honeysuckle, memorizing root oil meanings, running, running, running.

Jasmine's gaze ticked over to Zora, and the sisters stared at each other, silent. Zora clenched her hands into fists. Her eyes burned with approaching tears. Jasmine knew her sister was here. Yet she had no interest in contact or even a civil word. Zora knew this, had known it for a long time. So why did it pierce her heart like a blade?

Warm evening air brushed against Zora's cheeks. She barely felt it. She was fixated on Jasmine. Determined to pick at the scab she'd sworn had healed years ago. She marched toward them.

"Hi, Zora." Ngozi spoke first as Zora approached, likely so Jasmine wouldn't have to. "Congratulations on your speech over the summer. Saw it online—it was so good! I loved your point connecting Prince Hall Freemasonry with the church's—"

Zora could barely hear Ngozi over her hammering heart. She was done with pleasantries. "How was your *wedding*, Jasmine?"

Jasmine glared up at Zora, amber-brown eyes livid. "This is not the place or the time," she spat.

"You're right," Zora said, lowering her voice. She put a hand up between her and Ngozi, wordlessly telling her sibling-in-law not to intervene. "What would be a better time for you? Let's schedule brunch. Or, better yet, how about you text me at three in the morning, then block me so your cowardly ass doesn't have to face me?"

Jasmine lowered her eyes. *Ah. At least there's some shame in there somewhere*, Zora thought. *It's the least you could do.*

Jasmine was a coward. She'd watched when Zora came out at age eleven, and their parents had taken it... poorly. She'd seen how they'd treated her differently, insisting it was a phase and that God would help her see the light. Jasmine never once defended Zora. Instead, she'd waited until arriving at Bricksbury. From the safety of the campus, Jasmine came out and eventually introduced Ngozi to the family. By then, their parents' homophobia had dulled into passivity.

Zora had felt the brunt of it, while Jasmine had observed.

"We'll obviously see each other around," Zora said, lifting her voice to conceal how dark her mood had become, "so let's just stay out of each other's way."

There was less than a foot of space, yet an immense chasm of loss between them. Two cowards cosplaying as sisters. She gave Jasmine a long, blank look before turning back toward the center of the clearing. As she walked away, Zora realized that she had thrown away reason somewhere along the line. She'd hoped that if she just put herself in Jasmine's way, they'd end up sharing some part of their lives together. Bricksbury and this academic piece at least. And what about conjure? It was, after all, the essence of who they were. They'd grown up practicing together; it was an intrinsic piece of their family history. It should be something they shared—not just because they were sisters but because family veneration was a core tenet of Hoodoo.

Zora had spent hours of her life at her ancestor altar, cleaning it, feeding it, and talking with those who came before. Jasmine should've been there. She should've. Instead, she was anywhere else. And there was always somewhere else.

Amias Crawfoot
September 1, 1877
Jonesborough, Tennessee
Bricksbury Mountain College—Jonesboro
African Baptist Church

The bright light shone so harshly that Amias covered his eyes and ducked beneath a pew. Crouching and crying, he rocked himself, seeking comfort but knowing he deserved none. The slits down his back, self-inflicted, didn't matter. Neither did the blood the demon splattered across the church floorboards. The blood Amias had spilled. The pain pulsing across his skin didn't matter. He'd killed his sister. For Bricksbury and Jonesborough, he killed her. For God's bargain. He'd saved them all.

Then the demon consumed her. And the energy was blinding.

Then the merge's brightness had turned from ghost white to headstone gray, one shade away from the storm clouds that would chase him until he died for his sins. *Oh God.*

Looking back, it had to end this way. It was obvious. Why hadn't he seen it? It was like he'd dreamed of it before, and now that it'd come true, his mind refused to grasp the slippery truth. He'd thought more than once about somehow joining the demon in the woods. He'd spent his life at Bricksbury, building and maintaining staffing and housing for how many years…? Had he wasted his time, or was He raising Amias and Hosanna, preparing them for decades for this moment?

They could never *both* live, could they?

"Five," Hosanna whispered minutes later. Her soft voice croaked across the church's shadows, flimsy and stumbling.

Amias shut his eyes tight. *No.* She was gone. He'd done it himself.

"Five."

He shuddered. Whatever she was now, he wasn't ready to see it. Would they look as one? Would Hosanna's body be withered away, replaced by the demon's foggy skin? Perhaps that would be a mercy. Seeing his sister and knowing it wasn't her would be too much. Surely, He wouldn't ask that of Amias. Surely, Amias had done everything asked of him and more. Surely.

He opened his eyes and was met with his sister's chestnut-brown ones for a moment before they flashed to amber gold and were overtaken by the demon's fire. She stood and held out her hand, waiting patiently for Amias to take it. He leaned over the pew, and the pain across his back stole his breath. He glanced over to find Hosanna looking curiously back at him. Her skin was still the same rich brown color, and she wore her pale blue dress, though it was soaked with blood. She looked the same except for her eyes, which never left his. In fact, they followed him as he straightened to survey the nave.

"Are you...?" Amias finally spoke, though he wasn't sure how to finish his sentence.

"Five lives," Hosanna said, finally looking away, out a stained-glass window. "For Bricksbury."

Amias swallowed, sweeping his eyes up to the altar. He'd prayed to God for this. And now he'd have to ensure the next lives taken weren't the ones he'd meant to protect.

Chapter Eight

The air in the Woodlands clung to Zora in a warm shroud, stickier than she had anticipated. A heated argument with Jasmine, for the first time in years, hadn't helped cool her down. Zora wiped the dampness from the back of her neck, feeling the weight of the humidity settle around her. With a swift motion, she gathered her braids into a high bun, securing them tightly to keep her hair off her wet skin. There was a difference between being cute and being foolish.

"Hey, neighbor!" Khadijah walked up with an easy smile. The silver studs across the curved brim of her cowboy hat twinkled at Zora, just as Khadijah's eyes did. "Glad you could make it."

Zora cleared her throat, suddenly noticing the crickets chirping nearby. Their mellow droll was a welcomed distraction. She angled herself so she wouldn't have to see Jasmine and Ngozi. Her watch told her there were only a few minutes until the start of Conjure Night. *Get it together, get it the fuck together.* She scolded herself. Her stomach was still clenched, and she'd just begun loosening her fist. Zora had told herself Jasmine wouldn't interfere with her life at Bricksbury, and she damn well meant it.

"Oh, hey." Zora cleared her throat for the second time. "Yeah, thought I'd drop by and see how it was. Do you come here every month?"

"I try. Conjure Night has been a lifesaver. It's nice to talk about

Hoodoo without folks gettin' all weird, ya know? Anyway, you just moved in, right? Grad school or working or both?"

"Grad school. I'm here for my Appalachian studies degree. You?"

"I came here for my master's in jazz studies, got a side hustle stock replenishing at a local business."

Khadijah led them farther into the clearing. She cast a fleeting glance over her shoulder, back toward Zora's older sister. Worry creased Khadijah's arched brow. Did they know each other? Zora felt a story there, woven into the fabric of the moment, an unspoken connection that made the air around them feel even heavier.

There were more bracelets on Khadijah's hands than earrings in Jasmine's ears. These were normal-looking, but Zora was at Conjure Night. She had to assume any jewelry could be used for magical purposes. Khadijah wore several bangles—gold, which Zora knew was used to attract prosperity and wealth; a three-tone metal bangle, which was usually reserved for protection; and a twisted copper one that was meant to attract love and, to Zora's interest, sweetness.

If Khadijah's plan had been to distract Zora, her mission had been accomplished. The rattle of her bracelets snapped her out of her smoldering anger, anchoring her firmly in the moment. Metal... Zora's eyes wandered over the dozen shepherd's hooks stuck in the ground. How much metal was in this uphill clearing? It felt like a strange contrast with nature. Like people just couldn't help but bring their *stuff* into places—even ones not meant for them—no matter how far from their own habitats they were.

Khadijah's sudden tsk was so sharp it felt personal, even to Zora.

"Were you talking to Jasmine Robinson? You don't have her for a class, do you? She's here with her spouse at every meeting. Brings the vibes down whenever someone gets a Bible verse wrong. She's always correcting everyone like she knows every fucking thing."

Zora laughed, suddenly disarmed by Khadijah's perspective on her sister. She'd always thought everyone loved Jasmine. Had her sister finally met someone unswayed by her charm and academic prowess?

"Jasmine is...uh, my sister," Zora admitted.

She observed Khadijah's expression, anticipating the look of awe that typically followed. However, Khadijah didn't seem impressed. Confusion briefly crossed her face, followed by unmistakable pity. Had she noted that Jasmine never mentioned a sister and deduced their fraught relationship? Or was Zora simply projecting?

"Damn" was all Khadijah said.

Zora gave a half-hearted laugh. "To your point about her bringing the vibes down, we aren't close."

Khadijah bit her full lip, looking uncertain whether to push for more information or not. Zora swallowed, unsure how to ease the awkwardness. This was *not* how she wanted this conversation to go. She looked back over at Jasmine, but she and Ngozi were gone. In their place beneath the oak, Mallory whispered furiously with four men, all taller than them. Each one had his hands in pockets and eyes cast downward in shame.

"Wonder what's going on over there?" Zora said quietly, leaving Khadijah a subtle opening. Maybe she could learn something about Mallory, who was a potentially significant source for her thesis, from a third party.

Khadijah followed Zora's line of sight. A second passed. Then two. *Oh God.* Zora's heart beat furiously. Her mind was dizzy with the directions it'd gone in in the last hour. Was Khadijah about to say something important? Something that could change the trajectory of her research?

"Oh." Khadijah laughed. "That's my boss."

"Your boss?" Zora asked. She used her thumb to point behind her, despite not knowing where Immanuel was in the clearing. "You're Immanuel's coworker?"

Khadijah took a step back. "You know Immanuel?"

"I hope you aren't cursing my name." Immanuel strolled up with the evening's last sunrays casting shadows under his slender, pointed chin.

A woman walked beside Immanuel, keeping her gaze mostly on her phone, which had a tarot card case—the Tower. Zora thought it was bold, considering it symbolized sudden trauma and its lasting impacts. She looked around the clearing to see if the others had tarot card phone cases—maybe it was a Bricksbury conjure community thing—but there wasn't a pattern to the other cases she saw. There were just as many black-and-white stripes as starry skies and smoldering candles.

Khadijah's frown grew as she spoke to the woman on the phone. "Hey, Shawna. Um, Immanuel? Y'all know each other?"

Shawna and Immanuel brought with them the strong scent of weed. Zora suddenly pined for her stash, which sat sealed in a duffel bag under her bed.

"She came to the shop earlier," Immanuel said. He smiled widely at Zora, his dark brown eyes gleaming. "I'm still prayin' your advisor calms down, ya know."

"And I still appreciate the effort," Zora said with a smile. Her shoulders began relaxing and she was glad to notice her neck had cooled considerably.

Khadijah cleared her throat. "Well, did you know Zora is an Appalachian studies major? We might have an Old Timer's Music class with her." Khadijah paused and turned to Zora. "Shawna is studying ethnomusicology. Immanuel's like me, he's a jazz studies major."

Zora remembered the guitar pin below his Brazilian flag pin.

"Have you taken Music and Community yet?" Shawna spoke to Zora for the first time since walking over.

Shawna's soft makeup had begun to succumb to the oppressive heat, making her cool, ashy-brown complexion appear marred and weary. Zora gazed at the shadows creeping across her features. Shawna's powdered brows arched at the prospect of sharing a class with

Zora, a fellow soul wanting connection? Conjure Night was becoming promising, a welcome reprieve from the disastrous encounter with Jasmine and the haze of awkwardness still clinging to Zora.

"No, not till next year," Zora said.

"That's too bad, I'm taking the winter course."

There's a winter course?

"Y'know." Immanuel tilted his head as he looked at Zora. "You look familiar. Is this your first year?"

Zora swallowed. Mallory had asked the same thing that morning in the apothecary. Being Jasmine's sister was a scourge she could not outrun.

"My last name is Robinson. You might know my sister, Jasmine. She's a religious studies TA. And from what I gather"—Zora glanced at a worried-looking Khadijah—"she's usually at these Conjure Night meetings?"

Immanuel blinked repeatedly. Each time he opened his cedar-brown eyes, they looked at a different part of Zora, who began fidgeting under the scrutiny. She preferred Shawna, who had become disinterested in Zora and returned to her phone.

"Yeah, that makes sense. Wow, Jasmine's sister? She didn't say she had one."

Zora fell silent. She immediately wanted to melt into the warm forest earth.

"How much older—" Immanuel began.

"Did you know Immanuel is almost done with his degree?" Khadijah smoothly cut Immanuel off, her honeyed voice higher and sweeter than natural. "He's also getting a certificate. What's the certificate in, Immanuel?"

Immanuel frowned but followed his friend's lead in conversation. He couldn't miss the desperate look on Zora's face, silently urging him to stop discussing Jasmine. She was grateful to Khadijah, who was trying to spare Zora further discomfort.

"My certificate's in Music Business Law and Policy," Immanuel said proudly.

Zora noticed his chest did puff a bit at the declaration. It made her smile. Khadijah rolled her eyes, framed with thick liner, and pinned Zora with an exasperated look. "Quincy Jones over here." Immanuel scoffed. "Instrumentalists used to be worshipped, ya know. But these days? I have to look out for myself. Gonna make serious money. Record industry's full of sharks. I'm just—"

"Learning how to swim with 'em," Khadijah jutted in. She stretched her arms and pointed her oversized top bun at the sofas in the back of the clearing, where instrument cases were strewn across lush grass, including her bright red one. "Meanwhile, you're playing on furniture your broke ass wishes you could afford."

Immanuel threw his head back and hollered his laughter. "Damn, can't argue with you there."

"You playing at homecoming?" Khadijah asked.

"Briefly," Immanuel confirmed, turning his attention back to Zora. "Are you plannin' on being there?"

"Well...yeah," Zora lied through her teeth. "I mean, I'll definitely be there."

Zora hadn't planned on going to homecoming. As a rule, she didn't attend sporting events since earplugs never dampened the storm of noise well enough. But for Immanuel and Khadijah, oh, Zora would make an exception. This was a clear opportunity to make friends, and maybe more, and in the least cringy way possible.

Mallory loudly cleared their throat. The attendants formed a circle around Mallory, and Zora followed their lead. Five imposing leather trunks sat before them, their studded tops flung wide open like giant clamshells revealing hidden treasures. Inside, two neat rows of wooden boxes awaited. Zora trailed after Khadijah and Immanuel, her heart racing as she pretended she knew what the hell was going on.

Chapter Nine

W elcome to Conjure Night," Mallory began, a hushed tone replacing their usual bold demeanor. "I thank the ancestors all y'all could make it tonight. First, we'll play an herbal bathing game." They gestured toward the boxes at their feet. Mallory picked one up and presented it to the clearing. "Inside, you'll find various herbs, roots, and such. Each has a unique energy you'll be asked to identify. Afterward, we'll have fellowship with live music and refreshments."

Zora paid little attention to Mallory's words. She'd been doing herbal bathing games in her grandparents' backyard since preadolescence. Instead, she focused on Mallory's body language. They glanced around the shadowy clearing, a calmness smoothing the fine lines between their eyebrows. Zora tracked who Mallory kept eye contact with. These could be other powerful conjurers or at least persons of interest. She might want to talk to them over the course of her research.

"There's no better place to fellowship with one another than under the stars. I see some of y'all brought towels an' such, which is fine. We have sofas an' chairs, too. I also see some barefoot folk, which is your prerogative, but I'd advise against it in these woods. Now, you can leave anytime, so long as you do so quietly. If I hear a cell phone go off, I swear to the Son of God Himself, I will—"

"I'm glad you decided to come," Khadijah whispered to Zora as she swatted away a lightning bug.

Zora smiled. Jasmine and Ngozi had left the clearing. Typical. Part of her was disappointed, the other part felt like she could finally breathe.

"Me too." Zora's words carried a weight of seriousness that exceeded her intention; even she could hear it in the dropped tone. Mallory cleared their throat. "Everyone, grab a box, find a seat, an' get ya'selves comfortable."

"Yo!" Immanuel waved to another group on the other side of the clearing. He turned back and smiled knowingly at Zora, then Khadijah. "Y'all have fun!" His voice trailed off, rising at the end until he sang a high note and left, grabbing Shawna along the way.

There was a beat of awkwardness before Zora and Khadijah burst out in laughter.

"So, he's your bestie, huh?" Zora guessed. "He's not subtle."

Khadijah looked over at her friend with emotion suddenly thick in her voice. "Yeah, we've been through a lot. Taught at the same charter school in Austin and quit around the same time, too."

"And now you're in grad school together," Zora continued.

She observed Khadijah closely, who, in turn, kept her gaze fixed on Immanuel as he moved across the crowded expanse of trampled green grass. The lamps peppered across the clearing cast long shadows across the faces of others nearby. Eventually, Immanuel settled into his spot a few paces away, creating a sense of seclusion even while remaining within earshot.

"Yeah, now we're in school together," Khadijah said, turning a lovely smile on Zora.

Zora followed Mallory's instructions and picked up one of the boxes that lay in front of them. She settled on an unclaimed armchair, knowing Immanuel would still be sneaking peeks at her, as he'd done since learning she was Jasmine's sister. Soon the whole campus would probably know.

"So, uh, sorry I said that about your sister," Khadijah whispered.

"No worries." Zora waved the apology away. "It was funny—and accurate."

"She's a regular at Mallory's store," Khadijah explained. "I know she and her spouse teach, but in different departments; she uses a lot of peace amulets…I bet she misses you."

"What makes you think that?" Zora frowned at Khadijah. If Jasmine was using peace amulets, it *would* indicate that her life was lacking contentment. But that couldn't be true, could it? She'd gotten everything she'd ever wanted, and charmed everyone—save Khadijah—along the way.

"Look, I'm not asking for details; I'm just saying that whatever happened, it must be tough for both of you, especially now that you're at the same school."

Zora could only speak for herself, but she found it hard to believe Jasmine faced challenges as difficult as hers. Moreover, on campus, Jasmine was not alone. She had Ngozi and her devoted students. Regardless of any complicated feelings Jasmine might experience, she was still better off than Zora. The concept of solitude was foreign to her. Zora's loneliness, combined with guilt, shame, anger, and Mommy *and* Daddy issues festered within the few romantic relationships she had managed to maintain. They were passionate yet short-lived. For although Zora desperately wanted love and intimacy, she was never fully present enough to give herself to a girl-friend. Part of Zora was always trapped, terrified of the past.

Still, she was finally at Bricksbury, with promises to herself that she'd put herself out there more. So, she hoped to make some changes on the romance front. Soon. If not immediately.

Zora's soft seat was positioned near one of the shepherd's hooks she had noticed earlier. It was now adorned with a braided rope connected to a dark red vintage lampshade. The fringe dangling from the shade remained perfectly still, the evening's air heavy with no breeze to stir the leaves. The lamps were tasteful, with intricate circular designs woven into the thick fabric. Zora felt like they had been pulled from another time to grace her generation with their presence.

She sat with Khadijah in comfortable silence until Mallory cleared their throat, and the whispers around the clearing stopped.

"Herbal bathin' is all about emotion. Leave logic somewhere else. The bottles are marked—I will tell ya when to open them. You can touch the herb or just the space around it, sensin' the energy. Again, this is all about feelin'. It's about what?"

"Feeling," the clearing said together.

"Bottle number one! Whoever can guess the correct folk name first wins a fifty-dollar gift card to Jonesborough Conjure Shoppe an' a customized Conjure Night hoodie, to be delivered within the month," Mallory said to a round of cheers.

The lamps gave off dampened, ruddy light, just enough to see in front of you. Zora inhaled and did what Mallory said. Although the game was basic and intended for novice conjurers, understanding the mechanics was essential and going through the process was soothing. Feeling, she reminded herself, could be calming, especially if it didn't involve her sister.

The round box fit nicely in Zora's lap and was smooth against her fingers. Plush filling sat on the bottom, protecting three square glass bottles. The cold squares each contained an herb or root. Zora gawked at the quality. For some naive reason, she'd thought cheap materials would be used since this event was for college kids.

The root half filling bottle number one was dried and cut into chips. Zora opened the glass to inspect it further, but she was already sure. The bright chestnut-colored pieces were pulsing and warm. They carried the steady protective energy of beggar's-buttons. She was familiar with it. Several chips lay in the mojo bag in her backpack. Was it strange that Bricksbury's Conjure Night *also* used this root tonight? No, it was a fairly common root.

The others in the clearing were frowning, trying to discern the root's identity. Zora could speak up. It would draw unwanted attention, but she also didn't want to be shy. She looked over to Khadijah, who was frowning down at the herb.

"Beggar's-buttons!" Zora shouted above the chatter. She put on a bold smile so everyone would see her confidence as they turned to her. But another, louder voice rose as Zora's fell.

"Burdock root!" Immanuel hollered nearby.

Mallory chuckled. "You're both right. But I asked for the folk name, which is—beggar's-buttons."

Immanuel frowned briefly as Shawna, along with Khadijah, snickered lightly. "Dammit, Zora," he said playfully.

Zora shrugged nonchalantly, sharing his smile. This felt...good.

"Bottle two!" Mallory shouted next.

"Hey," Khadijah whispered, "great job."

Zora's cheeks heated as she blushed. "Thanks."

The herb in the second bottle was thin and leafy. Tiny pale green shards crumbled at her touch. The plant's name came rushing to her and lay fragmented on Zora's tongue. Shutting her eyes didn't help. All she felt was lukewarm *protection*; all she saw in her mind was the aura's dull orange color. Zora had to push herself harder. She opened her eyes and peered down at it, sure what to do next. She pressed the herb to the bottom of the bottle, forcibly exploring its energy and insisting on its compliance with her invasion.

Ah. There you are.

As Zora opened her mouth to say Folo, the flaky shards in her hand warmed quickly. Too quickly. Acid swelled in Zora's belly, and she instinctively started swallowing to prevent vomit from crawling up her throat. This couldn't be happening. *No. No. No. No. No. No.* The aura had been a faint orange in Zora's mind, but now, in front of everyone, it grew brighter until it looked like Zora held a single flame in her palm.

"Holy shit," Khadijah whispered.

Zora's jaw trembled. She looked up to find everyone in the clearing staring at her. The raucous laughter and lighthearted guesswork of the game faded into silence. Gazes pressed against Zora's clammy skin. She forcefully licked her lips and swallowed hard, determined to keep the bile in her stomach from erupting.

Someone nearby took out their phone, mouth gaping. Immanuel launched himself at them and smacked the device out of a startled undergrad's hand. He scooped up the phone and tucked it into his pocket, standing tall with his arms crossed, eyes locked on the onlookers as Mallory approached Zora. Shawna and several others rose to their knees, prepared to step in if necessary. It felt... organized?

"Got a lil carried away, huh, kid?" Mallory spoke gently as they crouched in front of Zora's armchair.

Zora resisted the urge to say, *I'm not a kid.* They were her feelings, but even thinking the words sounded juvenile and contrary to their meaning.

"I'm sorry," Zora whispered the only non-swear words spiraling in her mind.

Mallory's bushy eyebrows drew together, and they grabbed Zora's free hand.

"Never apologize for having power, Zora. Certainly not for using it, ya hear me?"

"Yes." It seemed Zora was always destined to be awed by Mallory's casual wisdom.

They whispered gruffly, "Now, look at my hands and breathe with me."

Mallory didn't speak again. They used their fingers to count from zero to ten and back. Zora hiccupped but otherwise followed instructions, allowing her heartbeat to slow and her jaw to unclench. By the third cycle, the herb's aura had fizzled to an amber glint before fading away.

Zora smiled, and Mallory smiled with her.

"So, what's the herb?" Mallory asked, breaking the clearing's silence.

"Folo?" Zora asked.

Mallory raised an eyebrow.

Zora cleared her throat, her smile widening. "Folo, I'm certain."

Mallory patted Zora's knee before ensuring Immanuel returned the phone and apologized to the teary undergrad, whom Zora thought got more than they bargained for tonight. They didn't look like a practitioner. They'd been shocked to see Zora's magic. On the other hand, Immanuel, Shawna, and Mallory had quickly jumped into action. It was as if . . . Could they have anticipated it?

Mallory cleared their throat. "All right, last one. Bottle three! Everyone, focus!"

Zora's cheeks heated. Everyone was staring at her. Mallory yelled once more, and finally, the crowd returned their attention to the game. Zora, meanwhile, thought it best to sit this last round out.

It was so dark that Zora depended on the fireflies and the nearby lampshade's light to see anything. She was about to reach for the water bottle outside her backpack when she stopped. Zora knew what the third herb was. She withdrew her hand from her backpack and frowned as she considered why Bricksbury would have High John, one of the most potent herbs in conjure, at a casual meeting.

"High John!" Khadijah shouted above the others.

Zora looked over at her with renewed interest.

"Yes, that's right," Mallory said, clapping, though they were the only one.

"Dammit!" Immanuel said. He glared at the box in his lap in accusation.

"No one wins," Mallory said.

There were groans from the audience.

"Which is fine," Mallory calmly said as if they'd expected agitation. "It's fine because the purpose of Conjure Night is what?"

"Fellowship," grumbled a few.

I really am late to this.

Mallory looked down at the crowd of adults as if they were teens. Like they were their children. "Exactly. Band, you're up!"

"You're staying, right?" Khadijah asked as she rushed to her feet. Her black micros cascaded across her body while shadows flitted across her face, making her appear to be moving in multiple, conflicting directions at once. She was lovely and she'd wanted Zora to stay. Zora rewarded her with a genuine smile.

"Wouldn't miss it." *Is that too casual? How will she know I want her to sit on my face?* "I'm looking forward to seeing you play."

"Thanks. I'll be the one slamming on the banjo."

"You play the banjo?" Zora blinked. She had never met a banjo player younger than seventy. During her canvassing, the elderly players she encountered often lamented how little the instrument was played these days. They would be amazed to see it being played at a gathering in the woods in Bricksbury.

"I play a lotta things," Khadijah said with a wink before heading over to the band.

Zora's smile widened as she sipped the can of Coke from Mallory's blue cooler. She sighed as it burned down her throat. Now, she figured, was a good time to ready herself for people-watching and note-taking. Zora stepped back to observe as the others gathered in familiar groups. She settled in a natural curve in the tree line, pretending to look down at her phone. *Just like Jasmine did earlier.*

As Immanuel and Khadijah were chatting and adjusting their instruments, they glanced in her direction. Zora decided it was time to take notes. She could look at Khadijah all night long, and just might, but she should at least get some work done while she was there. After all, she was missing out on quality time with Henry Louis and watching his namesake on *Finding Your Roots*.

Conjure Night Attendees:

- *Mallory, Immanuel, and Shawna jumped into action when my magic got outta control—Khadijah looked shocked, like I scared her.*
- *Immanuel can move from group to group but gets bored like he did when correctly guessing my program concentration.*
- *Shawna tried to hug Khadijah, but she sidestepped Shawna in a very cool/funny way. Shawna handled it well but looked hurt. Ex-friends? Exes?*
- *Immanuel and Mallory know each other well and have been talking all night, possibly related?*
- *I think Khadijah keeps looking over at me. Is this good?*

Skittering sounds behind her caught Zora's attention, and she turned to face the woods. A prickly feeling snaked across her skin. Zora shivered as she stared into the untouched forest, blinking with lightning bugs. They sparkled and danced in the heavy blackness. She eyed nothing strange but felt a presence upon her like a cloying mist before a thunderstorm. It saw her. Knew her? Or maybe she was hallucinating. Still, Zora couldn't help but feel what she didn't want to believe. Something was there. She *had* heard it shout her name.

"Hey," Mallory said with a sudden, gentle hand on Zora's shoulder.

Zora screamed. Despite her efforts to present herself as normal, she turned the heads of every person in the unfortunate cleanup crew. Some were wrapping the sofas in tufted quilts, preparing to carry them back down the trail. Others were taking down the simple wooden platform stage where the musicians had played. Khadijah, Immanuel, and Shawna were directly parallel to Zora, standing stock-still, cinnamon brooms and garbage bags in hand. They were the only ones left.

How much time had passed while Zora stared into the woods?

Mallory, their makeup undisturbed by the soppy wet air, gave her an exasperated look. "I think it's 'bout time for ya to go home, honey."

Zora licked her lips. "Of course, yeah. And thanks for answering my questions earlier."

"Mm-hmm. Be careful gettin' home. Stay on the path."

"I..." Zora glanced back at the blinking forest. "I will."

The trail was lined with shepherd's hook lampposts whose dull light was minimally helpful. The presence Zora had felt was gone, replaced by crickets' shrill chirping and the scritch-scratch of clawed animals scurrying across the forest floor.

"Zora!"

Zora stifled another scream, only letting out a muffled sound as Khadijah approached. She was out of breath.

"Sorry, I—I just wanted to say, again, that I'm glad you came."

Did she run after me?

"Me too." Zora's voice wasn't convincing. "I'll...definitely be back next month!"

"Hopefully, I'll see you around the courtyard before then," Khadijah said softy.

Zora looked into Khadijah's eyes, happy to see their mirroring grins. She let a beat pass before reaching out and grabbing her warm hand. They both sighed. It was like they'd both been waiting for it, a quick touch, all night.

"Good night, Khadijah," Zora said, her voice softer than it was before.

"Good night, Zora." Khadijah smiled.

Zora waited until Khadijah was out of sight and the chorus of crickets had resumed before she finally let herself say it. "Holy fuck." *Did that really just happen?*

The longer she stood there in giddy disbelief, the more the crickets reminded her of the solitary walk back to her dorm with their increasingly sharp chirps. Finally she listened to them and continued on home, the memory of Khadijah's smile and the soft touch of her hand making it easier to move through the dark woods—at least at first. After a few minutes of spirited and confident strides, Zora could have sworn she heard a steady crunching of leaves somewhere behind her, unsettlingly timed with her own steps. Frowning, she paused to look over her shoulder.

"Khadijah?" she called out, even as all her instincts aggressively asserted that it was someone else. Zora started walking a hell of a lot faster after that, and unfortunately, so did whoever was following her. Every time she stopped to pay better attention, the other sound—human footsteps? An animal?—ceased as well. A terrible seed of fear sprouted to life in Zora's chest as she realized that she wasn't going to outpace her stalker.

A low hooting sound suddenly pierced the air from farther up the trail, causing Zora to realize that she wasn't alone with whatever was sneaking around in the shadows of the woods. A barn owl sat perched atop an arched iron lamppost, its pale beak disappearing behind white feathers that were fine and stiff. Heart-shaped and motionless, its ghostly face gave way to a spotted chest and long legs, with talons that Zora couldn't see but knew were there. As she watched, the owl turned its head sideways and shuffled across the iron in apparent curiosity at something among the trees behind her.

Zora turned with a sharp gasp to check the direction she'd come from once again, still unable to see anything of...wait. Her eyes squinted as they caught a strange flutter of tiny orange-and-red lights that burned in the deepest darkness of the forest. It was as if a pair of candles floated, though it must have been the reflective eyes of some nocturnal animal, if the eyes were filled with glowing embers. Right as she thought of the word "embers," something in the air changed around Zora, filling her nostrils with the horrid smell of burning paper and sweet, meaty decomposition.

Absolutely not. This was as much as she was willing to witness before making herself some serious protection. She hurriedly ripped her mojo bag out from its stitched encasement in her backpack. The cool leather sack from the vintage shop in Knoxville still smelled of smoke and musk, a comforting counter to the horrible odor that had risen along with the unsettling embers. The mojo bag warmed in Zora's palms, ready for her spell.

Zora pointedly ignored the owl as it started flapping its wings in animalistic excitement, keeping her eyes closed as she cleared her throat. Spells were best spoken aloud, and if there was ever a time to go all out, it was now. Accordingly, she repeated herself twice. *"Though I walk in the midst of trouble, thou wilt revive me: Thou shalt stretch forth thine hand against the wrath of mine enemies, and thy right hand shall save me."*[9]

Ancestors, please protect my steps from evil.

Then Zora waited, allowing the patience she'd been working on in her free time to take root. She acknowledged her anxiety and breathed, a little more relieved with every inhale. She found strength in the darkness of her closed eyes, a coping mechanism she'd learned in overnight study sessions. It was the most straightforward lesson she'd ever learned, the one she'd continue practicing in grad school and when she inevitably became an award-winning historian.

There. She felt a pull forward and opened her eyes. No more embers in the darkness. No more smell. It was the same dark trail, but the mojo bag in her palm had warmed to near burning. Her spell had been successful, but it wouldn't hold forever. She needed to get the fuck home.

The walk back to her apartment felt longer than the one coming in, but when the time finally came, she was profoundly grateful to step off the trail and onto the pavement. A few students were fumbling across the lawn back to their rooms. Zora kept her chin up and her ears alert. The mojo bag was still warm. Zora stayed vigilant until her front door was closed behind her and the lock was secure.

---

9 Psalm 138:7—Though I walk in the midst of trouble, thou wilt revive me: thou shalt stretch forth thine hand against the wrath of mine enemies, and thy right hand shall save me.

Amias Crawfoot
September 3, 1927
Jonesborough, Tennessee
Bricksbury Mountain College—Edward C.
Williams Library

He had staved off the Beast's demands over a period of fifty years. Though Bricksbury remained safe—out of reach of the Klan and others who'd want to do harm—Amias had never known such pain. His sister was with him, and yet not. Her movements were strange, animal, but with an unnatural bent. She'd contort around a tree, peering at the sun, her head tilted to a peculiar angle. Her new eyes had given her a sparkling sort of vision. She knew things, could see things, that he couldn't. Things she kept from him. He could feel it.

There were years of silence. Then a period of anger, then a time where Amias truly feared for his life. She'd come out of the woods at night to stand above his bed singing scripture to him. Was she truly haunting him, or had guilt overrun his senses? How long would she blame him? How long would he blame himself? And did God blame him, or was He too busy ensuring Amias's continued immortality?

People had searched for a way to cheat death all throughout history. They wanted to remain young and soft. They wanted sweetness forever. Amias had never asked for such a gift, which was why he received it. But God didn't just hand out sweetness for nothing. First, apparently, one must kill for it.

Before the fifty years arrived, Amias contemplated how the right type of sacrifice could be identified. First, it had to be someone from the community. *A life for a life* only mattered if the life sacrificed was valued as highly as the lives being saved. Although Amias would have preferred to seize any hitchhiker within a twenty-mile radius, God was too clever for that. The sacrifice had to mean something.

It had to hurt.

The obvious answer was the parishioners at Jonesboro African Baptist Church, but the building had been abandoned for years. Fifty years, in fact. Amias couldn't allow another student to enter that place. It'd been so peaceful and holy until he'd turned it into a filthy waystation for sacrifice.

So the first thing Amias did after leaving the church, still shivering from the sight of Hosanna's fiery new eyes, was create a policy that made the surrounding area off-limits. Eventually, fewer and fewer students would make the hike as their memories of the church waned. Because the campus was grieving and in shock after the Klan attack, no one even questioned it. They'd probably thought he was being cautious—and he was. Hosanna was not the same woman, and he couldn't guarantee a thing except that she could never return. He'd told her as much, and she'd just stared at him blankly before turning back to the woods. That was where she belonged now.

The second thing Amias did after leaving the church was fake his sister's death. He told the others she'd been sick with the flu and, in her confusion, had stumbled out of her rooms, wandering into the woods never to be seen again. This presented an unexpected opportunity to satiate the Beast's hunger via the numerous waves of search party members who were bent on finding Hosanna as time continued to pass. Some searched the woods and surrounding towns for days, others for weeks at a time. Even Hosanna's longtime assistant searched for her body once a month for decades. These were not some random hitchhikers; they were subjects whose deep-seated dedication to Hosanna made them the perfect subjects for consumption. It wasn't the only acceptable criteria, but the more personal connection made the fire in her eyes glow a little brighter.

During the Beast's hungriest times, some of the party members were said to report a strange smell, something between burning and rot, before they disappeared. Others were seen standing on the trail, staring blankly ahead, unresponsive to initial attempts to bring their focus back to the present. Everyone assumed those specific individuals who never showed up again had simply given up with the search and moved on with their lives.

At first, Amias thought the sacrifice of his mortal life was a provocation. A scheme made to ensure he'd live forever in the purgatory of pain and loss, the hell of regret. Then he'd watched Hosanna thwart attacks against the school. For years when Jim Crow turned from an affront to a system of laws, Hosanna sliced through flesh that was soured by hatred, popping tendons and crushing bones as though they were nothing more than eggshells. She absorbed blows and bullets with foggy skin that only became less opaque the more she killed and maimed. By the turn of the century, Hosanna had turned into something completely translucent, save her fiery eyes.

Hosanna wasn't Hosanna anymore. Each life she ended twisted and turned her into an amalgamation that wasn't entirely demonic or human. She still wore the pale blue dress from that fateful day in the church, but that was the only thing that hadn't changed about her.

After Amias's "death," which he orchestrated in the '80s, he spent long years wandering the woods, yearning for lives he could've lived had he done things differently. What sort of man could he have been had he tried to love Elmira or value Hosanna more? Now all he had was existence. And even then, he had not finished paying his price to the Beast.

The newly named Edward C. Williams Library was a stunning feat Amias couldn't've, and wouldn't've, dreamed for Bricksbury. When he and Hosanna had originally traveled down from Massachusetts, they'd meant to build something more permanent than flimsy schoolhouses, but nothing as sizable as the multimillion-dollar, offensively grand library.

The president who succeeded Amias, Dr. Mercer Williams, took the school in a decidedly flashier direction. Was he a doctor of a subject or a doctor of glamouring his subjects? Amias had his suspicions. There were more crystals on the chandelier in the library's foyer than on the entire campus during Amias's natural life. It was shimmering excess.

Still, Amias didn't go to the library to scorn its decorations or reread its books, but rather to see a specific librarian.

She'd worked in the library since Amias had lived a natural life, before Hosanna had sought him out in the church and everything changed. Even then, he'd thought fondly of Esther, with her expansive knowledge of multiple subjects and propensity to challenge students.

He found himself amused by her "duels of data," a simple game where they took turns asking facts about the student's degree program until one answered incorrectly. Young people believed their fresh taste of knowledge propelled them forward in life but never considered the power of wisdom; this was always the students' downfall. They'd begin the duels of data with pride widening their grins, but by the end they were irrevocably changed.

And like most librarians, Esther wouldn't boast about her victories for long, instead lovingly taking the student and their wounded pride for a snack on the upper floor. They'd chat for a while, though Amias had never gotten close enough to hear exactly what they said.

He was careful to never be seen and had improved at evading detection over time. There were still a few on campus, Esther included, who might recognize him.

Eventually, the student and Esther would descend the stairs with her warm, sturdy laughter leading the way. Esther always found the book they'd need to beat her the next time they played the game, and the student always took the book. While wounded at first, they always left heartened, and that was what impressed Amias the most. Knowledge was a bridge, as his Revolutionary parents and grandparents knew well. It could heal or harm. Esther Fisherman was a living personification of Amias's dreams; she was the best of Bricksbury.

One such student, a librarianship student named Hezekiah Lee, was so moved by Esther's kindness that he even went as far as to ask to be her mentee. Esther was humbled; Amias was enraged. He couldn't explain it, but he didn't want someone else taking up Esther's time. Amias couldn't have it, so naturally, Hezekiah was the first student marked for sacrifice when it came time to feed the Beast again.

Chapter Ten

As showers went, Zora's that night was the longest one she'd had in recent memory. A green-gray eucalyptus branch dangled from the showerhead. Its minty scent blended well with her orange-and-cedarwood body wash. She took the scent into her lungs with long, deep breaths, forcing the memory of the horrible smell in the woods further away with each one.

Zora closed her eyes and allowed steaming water to bathe away the sweat that had dampened her clothes and salted her tongue. She stood until she couldn't see embers flashing in the forest's blackness. Until she couldn't hear the thunder of her fearful heart. Then until the water was too cold to stand.

Henry Louis's tail wagged as she exited the shower and pulled on her pajamas. She checked that the security bar was still lodged under her door handle before sitting cross-legged on the too-thin navy-blue futon.

Zora absentmindedly picked at loose strands on the upholstery cover with one hand and pet Henry Louis with the other. She let her mind settle. There was a whole slew of possible explanations as to what had happened out there in the woods, and few pointed to someone trying to terrorize Zora personally. There was a lot of history in those woods, a lot of stored energy that could manifest in different ways, especially to someone so in touch with her rootworking skills. Still, what might have happened if she hadn't had her mojo bag ready to go? Zora bit her lip as she contemplated before deciding that it didn't matter. She was safe now, thanks to her own capabilities. It comforted Zora to be reminded that she could take care of herself.

With one last sigh that purged all remaining worries about the eerie embers in the night, she told Henry Louis all about her day, which had been far longer and more complicated than planned. Henry Louis looked up at her as she spoke, and his gentle eyes pulled a smile from the depths of her thoughts. His heavy paws across her legs further grounded her.

"What else does Mallory know?" Zora whispered in the silence.

The more she thought about her new acquaintances from Conjure Night, the more she realized that it was time for some internet stalking. She'd learn more about Mallory, but first...

She found her neighbor across the courtyard, Khadijah, listed at a jazz ensemble performance on Bricksbury's website:

Khadijah Marquez
Jazz Piano, Violin, Banjo
Master's in Music in Jazz Studies
Las Cruces, New Mexico

"Hmm. New Mexico," Zora said. "Do they wear a lot of cowboy hats in New Mexico versus other states?" She googled the question, then the town, but couldn't find a definitive answer.

Zora quickly found Khadijah Marquez's social media accounts. Khadijah was a consistent poster to her public account of tens of thousands of followers. Zora noted there might be private and/or secret accounts. She utilized six dummy accounts herself to circumvent subscription services and confuse anyone who noticed her lurking.

Khadijah was a selfie connoisseur; her grid was manicured and sepia toned, full of photos of herself holding tabbed book pages, bedazzled cowboy boots, and a tabby kitten in various costumes, including the bloodied dead cat from *Pet Sematary* for Halloween and a vampire for an Octavia Butler silent reading club.

Zora scrolled through the pictures for a few minutes, then clicked on videos. She was captivated by how Khadijah talked about books. In one reel, she compared an N. K. Jemisin novel to a four-leaf clover inside a picture frame set on fire. Another was a three-minute-long clip from a larger video essay titled "What Nikki Giovanni and bell hooks Had Right, and What They Had Frighteningly Right."

Immanuel's face flashed across Zora's screen, and she paused, scrolling. He sat on a stool, instructing a student while simultaneously playing the guitar, which wasn't especially interesting. She needed to learn more. He wasn't tagged, but she clicked on a commenter's profile and found another Immanuel picture where he, again, wasn't tagged. Zora frowned and licked her dry lips. She followed another commenter, but Immanuel wasn't anywhere on this person's competitive chess champion profile. No digital footprint of significance.

Damn. Quite a feat. And purposeful, to be sure, excluding himself so thoroughly from the possibility of discovery.

Henry Louis shifted in Zora's lap, and she checked the time. It was nearing midnight, so she gave him an apologetic scratch behind the ears before getting up. She found the bag from Mallory's shop thrown to the left of the front door. Zora'd been in such a hurry after seeing Dr. Grant that she didn't even have time to use the herbs she'd left campus for. The trip to Jonesborough Conjure Shoppe felt like it happened weeks ago, not hours.

The bags sat on her laminate kitchen counter while she boiled water. Beside them, Jensen McRae's alto lilted from a pocket-sized speaker. Zora hummed along to "Massachusetts," a longing song of remembrance, tapping her feet to the build of the second bridge. She sank into the rhythm of praying over the herbs while the boiling water rested.

Zora thanked God and her ancestors for keeping her safe in Jonesborough. There were dangers they stopped before she was even aware of them, and others they cut off at her spell's request—like what happened in the woods earlier. She asked the ancestors to boost the herbs she sprinkled inside Henry Louis's mojo bag, her own, and the filled water bottle. They each warmed slightly, and Zora felt a calming presence in the room. They were here, helping her to protect and bless her space.

She prayed over the herbs once more before bringing them around the room to the *protection from evil* amulet pouches and, below them, the *sound dampening* ones. The leather warmed at her touch, welcoming its food. The twine from which it hung stretched and shrank, cling-clanging the attached cowrie shells.

When she felt the amulet's enhanced strength, her shoulders loosened. Zora took a moment to appreciate the magic she'd woven across her home. It pulsed along the hardwood floors, up the walls, and replayed on a loop on the honey-colored wood-planked ceiling.

The generous twelve-foot beams had dark splotches and stains from decades past. She supposed she couldn't complain about it in a room so spacious. As she snuggled into her covers, her eyes fell to the scratches upon the mahogany headboard. The deep grooves were harsh against her fingertips, jagged from roughness.

Zora exhaled loudly and looked again at the security bar under her door handle.

"I survived my first day at Bricksbury, Henry Louis. Even got some work done. See you in the morning."

He didn't awaken from his spot on the futon. Zora took this as a sign to finally go to bed, which she did after adjusting the air conditioner rattling beside her in the window. Her bed was pressed up against the drywall that reeked of white paint; she was too tired to care or worry about fumes.

Before she was overtaken by sleep, Esther Fisherman and her warning was the last thing on her mind. The diary's words were simple, but they'd shaken Zora.

Don't go into the woods, Esther. Don't go into the woods.

Against her body's wishes and all sense, Zora sat up in bed. She sighed. The diary was calling her, and as much as she'd tried, she couldn't let herself completely forget about what she saw and felt in the woods. She needed to know more.

Esther Fisherman's Diary
September 17, 1927
Jonesborough, Tennessee
Bricksbury Mountain College—Staff Housing

Dear Diary,

I must stay. I must stay. I must stay.

The president and vice president came for their nightly collusions, and I crept closer than usual. I was one row away, pretending to shelve books, and I heard them clearer than before. Of course, they didn't notice me, or perhaps they did and wrote me off as a silly woman, or an innocuous elder, or any other variations of witless misogyny in which men feast.

Sadly, there wasn't any talk of Hosanna's Crypt. I was hoping to learn more from them since I'm sure they are responsible for the rotating guard of male school officials at the entrance to the woods. I watch them daily from the library's top floor on my break. They laugh with cigarettes in their mouths (and possibly blood on their hands, if not literally, conspiratorially) and turn away anyone who comes near. They'd been given strict instructions. Not even beloved band members or sinewy secretaries could dissuade them.

What are they keeping secret? What lives in those woods? And why do I feel its macabre presence stalking me around campus? Sometimes, I feel I'm being watched. Surveilled. It can't be a coincidence that since I wholeheartedly began my investigation into the president and vice president, chills sprinkle down my arms whenever I open a door. I'm serious. Any door. Even my private bathroom. It's as if someone is always there, one step ahead, waiting for me to catch up. Waiting to catch me? It's making me behave like I'm mad, stretching my neck around corners, determined to outwit them before they capture me.

I got off track. Apologies.

I found a disturbing book in the library after the men left. They'd been picking at its lock all night, and before that, they had brought it back after stealing it days prior. I'd been waiting for them to bring it back. Oh. I shouldn't say "them" when only one of them stole LIBRARY PROPERTY, no doubt for nefarious reasons, which ought to be sacred on such an esteemed campus with a distinguished staff who have—

I got off track again. Apologies.

The lock on the disturbing book couldn't be opened in the short time I had between when they'd left and when the lights needed to be turned out. And I wouldn't steal from the library—I'm not a heathen. So, I hid it behind the desk, under Patricia's wool jacket, and picked it up the following day. The book's weight increased as I climbed the stairs to a quiet spot on the fourth floor. With each step, it grew heavier, or maybe I was lighter? I'm unsure which.

But that wasn't what made the book disturbing. I would've preferred if that had been what'd made up its malevolent energy. That would be better, I'm sure. Instead, my stomach twisted at the sight of this book because of its impossible title, <u>The Living Crypt: How Conjure and Sacrifice Shaped Nineteenth-Century</u>

<u>Jonesborough.</u> Impossible because the book was made of goatskin, far softer and less expensive than calfskin, and useless for the roughhousing of a college campus. I know of and have cleaned the only four goatskin books in Bricksbury's library, and they're kept behind glass.

This book was from the library, and yet wasn't. It shouldn't be here, yet it looked familiar when I caught the president's paws on it. I swore I'd seen that exact shade of fragile gray combined with the dark gold stitching. This would be a collector's item, something we'd keep on display if only to showcase Bricksbury's prominence. And yet, and yet, and yet.

I am not well-versed in the art of thieving and thus didn't know how to open a lock. And, diary, this is where things get even more disturbing. This is where I considered going home and abandoning the book and my entire investigation. But as I constantly remind myself, no one else is even searching for the truth. Everyone else—on the inside—has died.

I talk to students and my coworkers daily, but they aren't behind their own eyes, especially whenever I try to inquire about anything having to do with the woods. The only person who understands that something is going on is Hezekiah, shown by his constant asking after me and if I'm all right. He's clearly noticed that something is festering within me, but I refuse to expose him to the danger, refuse to do anything that encourages him away from continuing to build the foundation of the future he so badly craves. So I encourage his focus away from the dark circles beneath my eyes to instead land on the things that will give him the experience he needs to thrive as a librarian. This is not something for him to take on.

No. I must be the one to complete this journey. Otherwise, there will be more victims. Someone may well kill us all and be the only one left to tell the story.

I must stay. I must stay. I must stay.

———

The lock opened for me. I was holding the book, wishing I could understand why it was there and why the president stole it. I felt the book must possess some information that could aid in my fight against this evil. And as my mind raced, the lock sprang open.

I jumped up, frightened for myself and what it could mean. Frightened that whoever or whatever had been following me was watching, waiting for me to obtain this information so they could use it against me. Seconds passed, and I calmed. I hummed a song I'd learned as a girl in church back in Asheville. After a few minutes, I sat back down. This was greater than me. This was an investigation I needed to take seriously.

I spent my entire free day in the library, which I hadn't done since before I had children. I'd missed when rows of books were rows of books instead of numbers and themes and organizational patterns prescribed by that semester's head of library. For one day, I was just a reader.

The book contained multiple disconnected legends about a "Beast in the woods." In some stories, the Beast was a protagonist, watching over the townsfolk and warning them when danger approached. In others, it was a danger. In one of the shorter stories, the Beast was called upon to keep (racial? territorial? secular?) violence out. In a longer one, it was the personification of bigotry and narrow-mindedness.

Even after a full day of reading and absorbing, I know there's still much to learn. There is a reason why the lock opened for me.

There is a reason why it felt heavier, and I felt lighter as I carried it. I'm connected to this book and its stories. And, diary, I will find out how.

I must stay. I must stay. I must stay.

Graciously,
Esther Ophelia Fisherman

Chapter Eleven

Emphatically, the Edward C. Williams Library was Zora's favorite place on campus. It was a shame it'd taken her a week of classes to drudge up the energy to visit. Mallory had been right; it was pure extravagance. First constructed in 1907, then redone after a fire in 1927, it was the second to last building erected before the "Neighborhood" and was by far the most expensive. *An Exhaustive History of Bricksbury Mountain College: Mysteries Unearthed*, which Zora had read three times, explained that at the turn of the century, the administration enjoyed contributions from progressive politicians and clergy members suffering from self-righteous white guilt and a lack of Black public support.

Bricksbury's president at the time, Dr. Mercer Williams, was charismatic and wealthy, making him a force in Black culture. He was in his early twenties and enjoyed the company of many. All genders waxed poetic about his good looks and easygoing personality, and he was a known friend of Sissieretta Jones and Will Marion Cook, among other vaudevillian and classical performers.

Everyone knew you needed Mercer Williams to vouch for you if you wanted to make it. Saloon owners and railroad executives piled money into his...er, Bricksbury's, lap. This was a way to appease public scrutiny of their immense wealth.

Dr. Williams brought in Black artisans and craftsmen from Halifax to Havana. The library's historic lobby boasted an elaborate sculpted ceiling measuring fifty feet high. The trim featured leaves on tiny hemlock branches alternating Bricksbury's traditional gold, silver, and crimson colors. The lobby's chandelier had ten bronze arms, hurricane lamps, and a brass crown. It was estimated to have 8,500 crystals and weighed two thousand pounds. It was a feat. A deliciously ostentatious feat.

Zora knew of four floors aboveground, and at least one below— the latter was today's destination. The Rare Books Room was for students/faculty/staff and appointment only, a drastic change from the Rauner Special Collections Library at Dartmouth, which was open to the public and wasn't staffed enough to handle checking-in appointments. But at Bricksbury? Where groundbreaking research was expected, not congratulated? Library staff wearing crimson shirts outnumbered the students.

Zora lowered her gaze from the library's twinkling chandelier and finished the rest of her Darjeeling tea. The subtly sweet caffeine sat warm in the botanical-inspired tumbler gifted by Victoria, a former fuck buddy/coworker. She had been inspired to open a plant nursery after a year of intense questions aimed at Zora's vast knowledge of herbs and roots. As Zora reflected on the deep connection she had with Victoria, memories of their intertwined lives and bodies filled her mind. The scenes rapidly shifted to a still image of Khadijah smiling from across the clearing before Conjure Night. Zora grinned at the memory.

As she headed up a flight of worn carpeted stairs toward the reference desk, Zora didn't think about Victoria—she thought about Esther Fisherman and her fascinating, if frightening, diary. Zora had spent the last week poring over the book, entranced by Esther's recounting of Bricksbury's early days and her insistence on Bricksbury's dark presence.

Esther had been following the president and vice president, who met at night in the library. She hoped they'd discuss something called Hosanna's Crypt, but they didn't. Esther had tried to go into the woods, but school officials banned and blocked it. Afterward, Esther felt a presence when she looked at the woods, just like Zora had that night last week. Esther had felt like she was being watched—first there, by the woods, and later inside her apartment, in staff housing, and at work in the library. The same library where Esther found a locked book with stories connected to the "Beast in the Woods" legend.

With her heart racing, Zora was hungry to uncover more. She tasted the culmination of her dreams on the diary's faded leather binding. Folktales and legends had always fascinated her. She loved learning how Black storytellers—mothers, midwives, reverends, educators—wove intricate stories that danced between religion, culture, and community. But Esther's words were something else; they were a hidden history. And Zora had the shining opportunity to bring it into the light.

By the time she'd gotten to the top of the stairs, Zora was out of breath and sat at the closest empty table. She pulled out Esther Fisherman's diary and was again struck by how brightly rendered the blood pouring from the lamb was on the fore-edge painting. The book was in immaculate condition.

Zora swallowed loudly at the page that opened to her. She knew the words well.

Don't go into the woods, Esther.

Don't go into the woods.

Zora didn't want to sit with the dark feeling the phrase brought up, so she approached the reference desk.

"Hi, good afternoon. How are you?" she asked the attendant.

"Mm-hmm…I'm fine, baby."

The middle-aged woman kept staring at her bright computer screen as she typed. She sat primly in a leather computer chair with a bulky blanket over her lap. Her name tag said MRS. YVONNE REDMOND.

"What can I help you with?"

Mrs. Redmond didn't grace Zora with a glance as she spoke, but nothing would stop Zora today.

"My name is Zora Robinson. I have permission to go down to the Rare Books Room."

"Permission." Mrs. Redmond frowned. Her acrylics ended their *tap-tap-tapping*. Dark amber eyes glared, suspicious, behind beaded eyeglasses.

"Yes, ma'am." Zora looked down at the computer, unsure if she was already typing in Zora's name or if she should spell it. "Dr. Grant said—"

Mrs. Redmond's slick bob swayed as she shook her head and sucked her teeth. "How many times...Lawd h'mercy...how many times do I have to tell him, you can't just decide to go to the Rare Books Room whenever the hell you feel like it."

She stood with her blanket fisted in her hands yet spoke so softly that Zora found herself leaning over the desk to hear her better. She quickly leaned back again. The heat in Mrs. Redmond's voice terrified Zora more than a little. Dr. Grant had clearly pushed his luck too many times. Zora could tell Mrs. Redmond wasn't the person to try that with.

"This is a library. There are rules. I don't give a damn if he's a world-renowned historian or my own fuckin' mother. An' now he's gon' start sendin' fifty 'leven students round here? No. *HELL* no. You go to Dr. Grant an' tell him—"

"Dr. Grant set it up, but he emailed me the confirmation. I have it here." Zora pulled up her emails and searched frantically before the prickly anger radiating off Mrs. Redmond somehow pierced her skin.

Zora scrolled faster. Then, certain she'd passed it, she scrolled back up.

"Sorry," she said with a weak laugh and inward curse.

Mrs. Redmond didn't smile back.

"I got this, Mrs. Redmond." A familiar-looking man rushed forward, not so inconspicuously tucking his phone into his pocket as he ran. His name tag read LAMONT. "My bad, my bad, I'm here," he said.

Mrs. Redmond's eyes slid to Lamont's for a moment, then she turned sharply and left, heels tapping as she went.

"Sorry." Lamont turned to Zora, panic in his warm brown eyes and a Georgia accent so deep it was soothing. "She's on one today, an' liable to kill me. 'Course this time was my fault, not Jabari's. He's the other librarian assistant an' is more late than I am, but it's somehow never his fault. An' to make it worse? He's from *Austin.*"

Lamont tsked and lifted his eyes to appeal to the heavens for mercy. By the time he was done, Zora's tension had eased, thoroughly distracted. She opened her mouth to speak at the same time Lamont did. They both... paused. There was a beat of silence before they both burst into laughter at the awkwardness of it all.

"Sorry, I ramble when I'm rushed," Lamont spoke quickly.

Zora waved away his concern as she racked her brain, trying to pinpoint where she knew him from. The university's website, maybe? Lord knew she'd online stalked this library for months before her arrival, and was a frequent visitor to its virtual tour.

"How can I help you?"

Zora had forgotten where she was. "Oh, I have an email confirmation saying I can go to the Rare Books Room. One second."

Lamont groaned, scratching his thick beard. "Yeah, Mrs. Redmond is in a mood today. You don't need that to go down there. What's your name? I'll look ya up."

"Zora Robinson, and damn she played me."

Lamont scoffed. "Yeah, she's like that. One time, she lied to a group of law professors, claimin' that we had moved the legal encyclopedias. She watched with a smile on her face as they frantically searched the top floors for *three* hours. Eventually, one of them thought to check their usual location. Afterward, she admitted to me that she hates lawyers."

Faced with a situation like this, Zora would normally tell a self-deprecating joke. But something about Lamont short-circuited that impulse. She laughed so hard she forgot, momentarily, that she was in a library. He dramatically shushed her, then began typing. He stopped abruptly and looked back up at her. "You're Zora Robinson? As in, 'Deconstructin' the Centuries-Long Respectability Politics Plaguin' the Black Church'?"

Zora frowned and tried to smile at the same time.

"You've heard of it?" she asked. Did she sound too incredulous? Her research *was* important, especially in a place like this. "I mean...yes. That's me."

"I was there!" Lamont beamed. "At your lecture."

He reached out to shake Zora's hand, enveloping her in a sharp saffron scent that warmed into cedar and sultry amber the longer Zora smelled it. She leaned forward into the intense spice, happily falling into the lull of conversation. Lamont was able to raise his voice in excitement without raising his voice in volume, which must be a talent specific to librarians, even librarian assistants. She held on to his words as he spoke again, but part of Zora wanted badly to ask what fragrance he wore.

"I was so geeked when I was invited as a social media critic. The convention had a section for content creators. Honey, my nose was *bleedin'* up there, but I loved what you said about growin' up queer in the church." He lowered his voice and released Zora's hand, but his scent held on to her. "When I started transitionin', my home church...they kicked me out. So, anyway, it was nice to have my experience validated, although I'm sorry you had such a difficult time, too."

"Same. Thank you for sharing." Zora hadn't expected anyone at

Bricksbury to know her or her work by memory. It was the first time it had ever happened. Nor had she anticipated the brief, albeit welcomed, trauma dump. But more so, Zora did not dream she would walk into Bricksbury's library and find one of her favorite TikTokers behind the reference desk in trouble for being on his phone. "Are you LamontTheeLibrarian?"

He struck a pose, his earlier sadness dismissed. As he moved, Zora further appreciated his complicated mix of aromas that included... *something mossy and... orange-y?*

"Here and accounted for," he announced before grabbing a Rare Books card, which looked like an ordinary library card, but instead of the school's logo on the front, there was an open book with glowing crimson pages. Zora attentively watched Lamont's process of swiping the card and then typing the barcode into the system.

"Here's the card. Sorry, again, about Mrs. Redmond. On your way out, come see me. We can exchange numbers before ya go!"

"Absolutely," Zora said gently. *Fuck yeah*, she thought. *Another friend. In the library!* Fuck the past. She was killing it.

Chapter Twelve

"I humbly call on God, my ancestors, spirit guides, angels, and other loved ones. I know your strength. Please protect me from the evil I can see and the evil I cannot. In Jesus's name, amen."

As Zora descended the stairs, her whispered prayer echoed against thick stone. The sound of her own words helped to center her, grounding her in the moment. The stairs were made entirely from cold rock slabs and didn't offer a railing, so Zora ran her hands across the rutted walls as she descended. Each tread was narrow and tall, and there was a hard drop every time she stepped down. *No one thought to put a rail here after all these years?*

A single candle flickered at the base of the winding staircase, casting shadows that danced along the dusty walls. Zora's lips were pulled back into a wide smile. History lived here. She giggled with her excitement, which she'd only done once before, at Boston's African Meeting House. Now she stepped into the warm glow of the candlelight, her heart steadying as she inhaled deeply, savoring the moment. Unfazed by the whiffs of acrid smoke, Zora was locked the fuck in.

The light fluttering across the walls emerged from the gaping mouth of a statue, its carved features shadowed. Zora watched its eyes, hollow and unblinking. For a moment, she was certain it would blink once, like the owl from the woods after Conjure Night. But no, the statue was still, its thick lips mirroring wide-opened eyes. A long forehead disappeared behind stone chiseled into tight curls: 4...B? Nah, definitely 4C.

The flame was teardrop-sized, but Zora's senses told her a modern, flameless candle would have sufficed. Was this the place where fire codes went to die? Awfully risky, wasn't it, having an open flame this close to irreplaceable volumes?

Here, though, the air felt...different. Zora herself felt different. Not changed, but as if she'd entered a place that could change her if she wasn't careful. She touched the mojo bag in her backpack, glad to have it. But there was something strange down here. Something was off.

The door to the Rare Books Room was carved wood like all the other original doors on campus, but this one looked far older. The wood wasn't warped so much as it angled outward, avoiding the secrets it held within. It was over twelve feet tall, twice as tall as Zora. Constructed from reddish-brown mahogany, it resembled the lengthy doorways built by small-town frontiersmen in the region at the end of the eighteenth century. Its higher cost suggested to onlookers either wealth or piety. On all sides were fixtures of wrought iron, including an ornate kickplate with lightly rusted hammered edges. This would have been an extravagant addition. *Definitely piety*, Zora decided. The owner of this door was trying to impress onlookers far before the Rare Books Room existed. Before Bricksbury, altogether.

In *An Exhaustive History*, there was mention of a church on the grounds before the school. Maybe this was the original entrance; though, from the description, Zora thought it'd be in the woods. Supposedly, the tiny eighteenth-century church was the only Black church for miles. It was unconfirmed, though widely speculated, that the founders of Bricksbury were members there, and the pastor gave his blessing to use the land for academics in exchange for enough money for him and his parishioners to move closer to downtown.

If this wasn't the church itself, maybe it was an off-site cellar? A subbasement for meetings between the minister and people he didn't want to be seen with? Or was this built for Bricksbury, a place where they could have meetings away from prying, envious eyes? Maybe it was both.

Zora stepped forward to get a closer look at the antique door knocker. Unlike the door's latches, hinges, and straps, the knocker wasn't wrought iron. It was bronze. Oil-rubbed, if she wasn't mistaken. A honeybee stared up at the door with four metal wings open, prepared for flight. Even by candlelight, she inspected the jagged strips of metal that were hairs on its legs and the numerous deep grooves within its wings. *Don't touch. Don't touch.*

The metal was cold and slick with oil. If she squinted, Zora could make out her fingerprints. She rubbed them away.

There was something unique here, which meant Zora had no choice but to pull out her phone and take copious pictures and videos. Perhaps there was a deeper meaning for the honeybee and the woman with fire blazing out of her mouth. Zora would research it later.

Three heaves of the cold knob finally opened the door, and Zora was inundated by her favorite scent in the world: lignin. A relative to vanillin, it was present in all wood-based paper, emitting a sweet, rich scent as the books aged.

An attendant sat at a desk. Her long pink-and-green box braids fell around her body, encircling her. She wore an Alpha Kappa Alpha–branded hoodie and had impeccably soft, natural makeup. Zora watched as she seemed oblivious to both Zora and the extraordinary knowledge around her. How could you not be giddy beside all these treasures?

How far-reaching were AKAs and other societies on campus? Could they reach behind antique doors and a woman spitting fire? Dr. Grant must be aware of them but might not be exceptionally knowledgeable. Or, perhaps, he was just unwilling to share. But why be so secretive? Perhaps he considered the societies a distraction. Maybe her thesis advisor required his mentees to lead a monastic life in the service of "knowledge" or "discipline."

Zora scoffed. She was no monk, so good luck with that.

The attendant, whose name tag said ERIKA, click-clacked stiletto nails against the wood while reading a textbook. Zora would've said something, but even she could hear the raucous drums coming from Erika's headphones, so she settled for a light wave and a brandish of the Rare Books card. Erika glanced at Zora and immediately back down at her reading with no change in expression.

Zora could only go a few more steps before putting on the jacket wrapped around her hips. She shivered as she considered the long shadows cast by the bookshelves. The basement might as well be Dr. Grant's office for how frigid it was, but at least here, she didn't have to worry about anyone seeing her nipples standing at attention through her binder. She only had to deal with the discomfort.

Her steps had led her underneath a miniature version of the chandelier upstairs. Everything was the same except the crystals. Nine thousand clear glass pieces made the foyer shimmer with its pure grandiosity. But down here, the wide, teardrop-shaped glass had been dipped in crimson, casting a faint red glow on the room. Zora paused. As she looked from one room to the other, she found it odd that the school had chosen such tricky lighting in this vital space. It was almost as if they wanted to discourage students from coming down there.

She followed her gut to the far side of the room and down a few more steps, off wide-planked wood and onto thinly carpeted stone. There was another miniature chandelier in the even tinier room. This one also had crimson crystals enshrouding the space in a dark red haze. It reminded Zora of a dream she'd had once, or more accurately, a nightmare.

Zora licked her lips and continued to trust her instincts, moving behind a dusty grayish-brown table in the far corner. She craned her head but couldn't see Erika from this spot, and knew Erika couldn't hear her, so she pulled out her phone and pressed record.

Zora: Recording. My name is Zora Robinson, and today I'm in the Rare Books Room of the library, in the back room, in a corner not far but unseen from the front desk.
My instincts led me to a book. It's bound in a thick black canvas. The canvas has a wax finish with a slightly floral scent, though that could be from the tea I just finished...
[nails click-clacking]
Noting a fore-edge painting of a sunny, cloudless day. A single red apple falls from a weeping willow. Below the tree, a woman with dark coily hair lies on her stomach, gripping her decapitated head in both hands. The apple is directly above her open mouth.
Brushstrokes indicate fan brush. Fore-edge marbling method indicates manufactured prior to 1850s. The apple could be biblical, but the weeping willow may indicate different. Research later.
It's strange, or serendipitous, how similar this is to the fore-edge painting on Esther Fisherman's diary.
The book is titled *The Living Crypt: How Conjure and Sacrifice Shaped Nineteenth-Century Jonesborough*, and no author is named on the binding.

Hmm. Strange. So... if this book covers the
entirety of the nineteenth century and was
written after that time, how could it feature a fore-edge method so old?
[nails click-clacking]
There's a silver lock dangling from the book.
It's not as old or oil-rubbed as the door
knocker on the entrance to the Rare Books
Room. And the silver looks matte or... at
least, I think it's silver. Could be bronze.
The redness from the chandelier is making it
difficult to see clearly in here. There aren't
any markings or letters to help identify it,
but for some reason, it does look familiar.
I... uh... am definitely not picking the lock
with a paperclip. [lock clicks open]
The spine is worn and silent as I open it.
Publication year is listed as 1927, and this
is the second edition. First edition was
1877. Hmm. Weird. Author is listed as Zor—
Wait a second. Zora Robinson? [gasp] How?
[pages flip] This is my research! Written in
my handwriting! I don't underst—

Esther Fisherman's Diary
September 23, 1927
Jonesborough, Tennessee
Bricksbury Mountain College—Staff Housing

My mother used to tell me, "Esther, the sky ain't fallin' just 'cause you feel rain on your face." This always felt equal parts condescending and profound, which sums up my mother. Betty Toussaint never had time for how her daughter's mind twirled in on itself, weaving and unweaving ancient folktales, commanding scripture, and fantastical poetry. My mother used to get so frustrated when I babbled to myself and didn't care when I explained all the diverging roads my mind had taken me on. "Your mind can't take you places you don't wanna go," she said once. I stand by my disagreement with that.

The godly Mrs. Toussaint took a switch across my behind when I pretended I could fly, flapping my arms like the inky-black ravens above me. I was five and had always been jealous of their freedom. My mother's face reddened when she spotted me running in circles, eyes closed, caw-cawing, imagining, dreaming. She took me inside and beat me with a thin hibiscus branch. Girls—colored girls, especially—weren't to behave like this. For safety, we weren't allowed to fly. I never flapped my arms or smiled with the wind rushing across my face again. My mother stilled me.

Looking back, I don't blame her. It took my entire life to know me and find ways to make life easier for someone who can't stop babbling or descending deep into obscure subjects. With effort, I can bring myself back to the surface. This is what I told Hezekiah during our first meeting. He needed to find ways, and I didn't care what they were, to bring himself back to the surface and not float in the waters of worry. We sat in silence for a few minutes as he thought. Then he took out a bright violet pocket square. Stitched into the textured linen corner, his initials, H. L. The enchanting tale of how his grandmother gifted it to him brought a sense of grounding and warmth.

It was the end of the day when the library was slow, and only those still lost in a book or studying late were there. These students were more invested in their college library experience and, therefore, may be more receptive to a quick conversation as they left.

By my lead, Hezekiah and I approached a few students and asked them how their studying went. Three said they were too busy or tired to talk with us, one ignored us entirely, and the last two students wanted assistance finding another book for their coursework. Hezekiah had already memorized the library's layout and volunteered, albeit shyly, to assist. I stood back and watched them walk away together, proud.

After congratulating Hezekiah on a successful day, we said our goodbyes. I walked quickly back to my room, eagerly awaiting the chicken pudding in my unit's cold closet. The aroma of simmering celery, crisp carrots, and fragrant onions filled my mind before I'd even arrived, making my mouth water with anticipation. As my mind turned toward the Last Supper and food Jesus actually could have eaten, two men in wool suits approached. One, I recognized.

"Good evening Mrs. Fisherman," President Williams said. His smile reached his eyes, but barely. "Are you all right?"

I frowned, affronted he'd suggest I couldn't walk the campus by myself, as if I hadn't been doing so since before he was born.

"I'm just leaving the library," I explained, still frowning. I gestured to the silent man beside him. "What's this about?"

The two men glanced at each other, which didn't inspire trust in whatever they were about to say.

"I'm Officer Holston, ma'am, and Bricksbury Mountain College is under lockdown," the man finally spoke.

"First I've heard," I responded; though, when I looked around, I noticed there weren't other students or faculty outside. It was just me and my thoughts about savory chicken pudding and somehow connecting that to the Last Supper. I had been lost in my thoughts for so long that I failed to realize the campus had fallen silent around me. I scolded myself. Although Bricksbury is the most peaceful place I've ever been, I should be more aware of my surroundings.

President Williams scratched the back of his neck before speaking. "We're under lockdown after a student has been reported missing by her roommates. It's probably nothing, but we're being careful and patrolling more at night. Curfew begins at seven p.m. and ends at five a.m."

Officer Holston's rough hands grabbed my arm and easily turned my body in one motion. Breath left my lungs, too, and I gasped to refill them.

"Is this your building, Mrs. Fisherman? Here, I'll walk you inside."

I took two full steps back from the patronizing officer to ensure my arm was out of his and marched to my room by myself. Part of me was angry about their pushiness, and the other was angry that I didn't know about the missing student. Who were they? I'd have to ask Patricia tomorrow; she'd know.

I must return to the book.

I ate the chicken pudding, but it wasn't as tasty as I'd imagined.

———

September 30, 1927

This last Tuesday, as I was sorting through a cluttered desk at the back of the library, I stumbled upon a delicate violet pocket square. The soft linen was a shock of cold. It was Hezekiah's gift from his beloved grandmother that he used to ground himself in challenging circumstances. Holding the cool fabric in my hands, pangs of concern sent my heart racing. He carried it on his person at all times and would not have left it behind. More troubling, Hezekiah has missed three of our regular meetings now, and his absence is starting to weigh heavily on my mind.

There have been several additional missing persons, save Hezekiah, since the last time I wrote. I believe three, but it's difficult to keep track of because the administration (namely President William) isn't being longwinded in their explanations and is downplaying any concerns I bring. I said I bring them, because I don't believe others are concerned, at least not as concerned as I am. The other librarians, who have all seen the flyers around campus alerting students and faculty to the missing people, just aren't as worried as I am. In fact, they aren't worried at all. When I bring it up, they tilt their heads and look at me as if I've said something else, something mildly amusing but not worth responding to. Strange things are happening at Bricksbury.

Yesterday morning, I took Hezekiah's pocket square to the front office. I initially reported it missing, to which the clerk behind the desk raised her eyebrows. "You want me to keep a pocket square in here in case the boy comes lookin' for it? I'll do it, but I just don't find that likely, Mrs. Fisherman." I understood her skepticism.

When I asked the clerk for Hezekiah's room number so I could personally deliver it to him, she huffed and went to a back room. I waited for twenty minutes, listening as she opened and closed drawers, searching for the correct papers.

"You said Hezekiah Lee?" She returned empty-handed, lips pursed.

"Yes, he's a sophomore in the librarianship program."

"You see, Mrs. Fisherman"—she'd gone from annoyed to concerned by this time—"Bricksbury doesn't have a student by that name. We have a Henry Lee, Humberto Lee, and Humphrey Lee, but no Hezekiah."

I stared at her, not knowing what to say, for longer than I should have. "You're sure?" I asked when I found my voice.

"Very certain," she assured me.

And I had heard her clanging around there for a long time. I'd thought she was just searching for Hezekiah's room arrangements, but she had started there and then gone searching that there actually was a Hezekiah at the school. And she came up empty? How can that be?

"But I have his pocket square. His grandmother gave it to him," I insisted.

"I'm…sorry, Mrs. Fisherman. Are you possibly thinking of another student?"

But no, I couldn't be. I'd seen his school badge multiple times. I'd taught him how to read others' by using his as a model. I was certain: Hezekiah Lee is a Bricksbury student. No matter what *happens, I cannot forget that. Because, Lord, someone or something is erasing him from existence.*

October 1, 1927

I see the campus, and Jonesborough, differently now.

I've read all the tales in the book. I worry there's truth to be found there. But which bit? Was the Beast a force for good or the town's undoing?

One of the stories mentions the "Keepers," a word spoken often by President Williams in his nightly meetings, which are troublingly increasing in participants.

I would prefer not to have discovered any of this. I'd prefer to read about romance or notable women in history. I'd prefer to return to living in obliviousness, where my mind knows nothing but peace. Have I not earned that?

But no, I've been cursed with clarity.

Hezekiah is gone. I know it. I feel it. I'm cursed with the weight of it.

It only makes me search harder and think for longer hours into the night. I now suspect this is connected to the revolving groups of men standing guard at the woods' entrance. Are these men believers of the "Beast in the woods" folktale that Dr. Jones told me about?

October 2, 1927

I went to the Bricksbury Press newspaper yesterday, or perhaps it was a few days ago. I asked the first working person I saw—an opinion editor, I later learned—about the missing students article. They had no idea what I was talking about and referred me to the editor-in-chief, who knows each story from the paper intimately. However, upon speaking with the editor-in-chief, a kind but curt person named Melody Holston, it became evident that my search had ended before I even arrived at the paper. Because, diary, Melody Holston assured me they had never written about missing students, and that there were no such students. And when I lifted my paper to attest that they indeed had, the article was gone. Vanished. Replaced by one about repaving the highway leading to Bricksbury's land.

I write down these words with the knowledge that no one else will ever know of these deaths. These students will be written off by someone and forgotten by history and their families. My eyes ache from having cried myself to sleep every night and weeping when I wake in the morning and remember the villainy I'm forced to endure. How can this be real? I scream into my pillow, begging God to make it all imaginary. I'm just an old, crazy woman who's lost her senses. I beg Him to allow me escape.

Apologies, I got off track.

Later that evening, or perhaps several evenings later, I cannot be sure; my body urged me to leave my warm bed and enter the night's darkness. As you know, I've never been one to obscure the physical world. I've never intentionally turned a light off until I could see the next one. And yet, even when my eyes are open, and the room is bright, I seek out the shadows. There, inside the murkiness, is where it happens, Jesus. I can't think on it too much—the unnatural sound, the smell of burned parchment and rotting animal carcass. The realization that I've been staring, unblinking, at nothing at all for God knows how long, as if nothing else exists but my endless spiral of fear and wonder. The source of the terrible cries is a feral, weeping thing. Not entirely demon, but too evil for humanity.

What's more, I'm missing time. Not much—seconds between eyeblinks and lost snippets of daydreams—but enough to concern me. Enough to realize the times I'm missing are directly after hearing this Beast in the night.

What wickedness clutches me? Which sin have I not repented for? Am I not a cleansed and purified child of He Who Is True and Faithful?[10] Will He not save me again?

My knees ache with how long I've begged the Lord to forgive this atrocity I must have committed. As soon as my work is done for the day, I return to my room, fall on my knees, and only budge for biologicals. Speaking of blood, it pools on the wood floors with me, the bruises only deepening. I allow it gladly and will enter the woods this evening.

May God see the sacrifice I'm willing to make to only exist in His holy light.

"I beseech you therefore, brethren, by the mercies of God, that ye present your bodies a living sacrifice, holy, acceptable unto God, which is your reasonable service."

Graciously,
Esther Ophelia Fisherman

---

10 Revelation 19:11—And I saw heaven opened, and behold a white horse; and he that sat upon him was called Faithful and True, and in righteousness he doth judge and make war.

Esther Fisherman's Diary
September 10, 1927
Jonesborough, Tennessee
Bricksbury Mountain College—Staff Housing

I, Esther Ophelia Fisherman, of Jonesborough, Tennessee, being of somewhat sound mind and memory, do hereby make and publish this, my last will, testament, and anything else I decide it will be.

First: I must apologize to my daughters, Josie A. McMannon and Amandla F. Gilbert, my grandchildren, and my great-grandchildren for the gruesome manner in which my body will be found. To my babies, I am terribly sorry it came to this. I can only hope, one day, you will see there are things more significant than you and I.

Second: After the settling of my burial and debts, I hereby will and bequeath any and all properties and monies of which I possess in equal measure to my children.

Third: President Mercer Williams and Vice President Zachary Daniel of Bricksbury Mountain College are hiding multiple deaths that occurred on campus. I heard them discuss this firsthand. They mentioned Hosanna's Crypt, beneath the "old church," was where their bodies were found, and I assume this is where mine will be found. I urge the Jonesborough Police

Department to have compassion and bury their respect for Mr. Williams and Mr. Daniel in a robust investigation into these men and their activities.

<u>Fourth</u>: My mission today is to find Hosanna's Crypt and any other information I can in the woods. I have brought weapons but am under no illusions. I am an old woman, and while I expect to die today, I hope my death will be the catalyst for the truth and justice owed to the colored citizens of Jonesborough and the students and staff of Bricksbury, my home for almost six decades, and the land on which I gladly die. For my people. For Jonesborough. For Bricksbury.

For even the Son of man came not to be ministered unto, but to minister, and to give his life a ransom for many.
Mark 10:45

All my love to my precious family.
We will see each other again at heaven's gates.

Esther Ophelia Fisherman

Chapter Thirteen

Zora's mouth opened as the library and the impossible book in her hands faded away to nothing, replaced by cold shadows and unfamiliar smells. Panic burst to life in her heart as all the muscles in her body clenched hard enough to completely freeze her in place, making her nothing more than a statue in the dark. As the moments passed, her sight started coming back to her, but only certain things—a terra-cotta floor, the shadows of two people somewhere ahead of her—were visible. Concentrating hard, she held her breath tight in her chest and slowly, deliberately, blinked her own eyes. Good. Control was coming back, at least to a point.

"And as Moses lifted up the serpent in the wilderness, even so must the Son of man be lifted up." An elderly woman's voice was resolute in dim candlelight.

Holy shit, Zora thought. *This is a vision. A motherfucking vision!* Had it been prompted by the book? Something in the library?

The mojo bag in her pocket grew warm through the fabric of her pants. If this really was a vision, and she wasn't physically there, it still didn't matter. Her ancestors would be with her, no matter where she was or wasn't.

It was time to excavate the truth like she'd always wanted to do. Zora shifted her focus to take in as many details about her surroundings as she could.

Each shaky step in the direction of the voices wore her out. Sweat snaked down Zora's cheek and gathered where her lips met. The salt was welcome. It was a reminder that she controlled her senses. And that she was having this vision for a reason. Something could be learned from being here.

She focused on the man first. Sunken wrinkles surrounded greedy eyes, partially covered by his wide-brimmed, crimson hat. Thin wool. Itchy. He wore matching robes so long they glided against the floor as he moved. Stalked. *Hunted.*

A chill barreled through Zora's body, lurching her forward toward his hungry eyes. The abrupt temperature change was unnatural and unnerving. She couldn't stop herself. She marched to him on numb legs, stopping a breath away. Did he somehow know she was there? Up close, his beady eyes twinkled with the candles, the rich browns overwhelmed by fire. Were Zora's eyes the same? Could he see the candlelight flicker across her body like she could his? Could he hear her heart roar like she could? Could he judge how her spine shivered in the sudden cold?

Who are you? Zora wondered but spoke no words.

The man sighed at the other person in the room, an older woman with a stiff spine. His teeth stabbed into his peeling bottom lip. They were so dry it must have been painful. He drew blood and left it drying there. Rough hands disappeared into his clipped afro while agitation tugged his eyebrows together. He suddenly grabbed his hair and pulled sharply to the right, cracking his neck so he faced Zora but kept his eyes on his prey.

Zora instinctively flinched away from him, a gasp escaping her throat.

"I am sorry for striking you," the man said. "But you wouldn't come willingly. Willingly. Willfully...hmm...Will Lee...mm-hmm...Billy...he didn't get a lick of credit for the war."

He laughed after he spoke, and while it was a kind sound,

madness overran the edges. He giggled to himself, whispered nonsense, and giggled more.

The old woman ignored him at first, continued on with the verse
she'd been reciting. *"That whosoever believeth in him should not perish
but have eternal life."*

"Ya know, another person of my heart picked the Book of Ezra
when it was her time. But you? No, not you. There's something
much…classier about John, isn't there? You're so lovely, and did I
already say classy? Well, doubly—"

"Is this your pride?" The old woman's voice lifted at the end, her
interest genuine. "Stealing people in the shame of night? Using your
immortality to do Satan's bidding?"

Zora's stomach dropped. Although this was a vision, vomit crept
up her throat. Was this man going to hurt the old woman? Was
he under the impression that doing so would allow him to live forever? The man's face fell, wrinkles slumped, and he looked right into
Zora's eyes for the first time, seeing her clearly and pulling another
silent gasp from her throat.

"Do you see how I am rewarded for my responsibility?" It was as
though he was speaking to her directly. Was such a thing possible?

"Responsibility?" Zora's shock moved her lips, though her
thoughts weren't spoken aloud.

He nodded as if he could hear her before turning to the old
woman. "God's war will never cease."

"This is not the war God would want you to fight," she said. "Our
God is love."

"I will indulge your ignorance, though it does not suit you." The
man's sigh was world-weary; it was heavier than it sounded, somehow pushing reality away and bringing the uncanny closer to him as
it descended. "There are some things that must be done, some ugly
things. But there is ugliness in the *world*. I'm not creating it, merely
killing it from the inside."

The old woman's voice was fierce. "Where are the students? Families are waiting for explanations."

"You gotta die," he answered, somberness coating every word.

"What?" Zora demanded, push-push-pushing the sounds past her lips enough to be heard.

"She must be fed," he said.

"For Bricksbury," the old woman said, not somber: certain. "*For God so loved the world, that He gave His only begotten Son, that whosoever believeth in Him should not perish, but have everlasting life.*"

"Amen," the man whispered. He bowed his head in silence for a moment. When he looked up again, his eyes were softer.

"Will it be quick?" she asked.

"Why does it have to *be* at all?" Zora asked, trusting her voice the more the seconds ticked by.

The man sighed warm breath.

"It's better if you don't know."

"That's not an answer," the old woman and Zora said at once.

Silence.

Until she spoke.

"Will my death protect Bricksbury?" she wanted to know. "Jonesborough? My family? Promise me! Promise me you aren't just some madman who deals in witchcraft!"

"Witchcraft? No, my sweet, this is the closest to God's love you'll ever get in your earthly life. What do we exalt Jesus for?"

"My family—"

"For giving His life. So must I. And now so must you."

Despite his words, the man spoke as casually as seeing a neighbor at the mailbox. The old woman spent no time contemplating his words; she had her own to finish.

"*For God sent not His Son into the world to condemn the world; but that the world through Him might be saved,*" she said.

A ragged sob filled the room. Zora gladly looked away from the others, searching for the source. Long pillar candles sat in rusted wrought iron, throwing off light like a warning. The terra-cotta floors were uneven slabs, but the workmanship couldn't be denied. Where was she? *When* was she? What was happening at Bricksbury during this time? Could she save the woman? No. This had already happened.

Zora froze when she realized *she* was the one crying.

She leaned against the wall momentarily, catching her breath, trying to make sense of the vision. Stone walls stung her with their iciness, and her gasp filled the room. Zora's mind raced once more.

"For Bricksbury," the old woman whispered.

"For Bricksbury," the man agreed. "Prepare yourself."

Zora held her breath as a tall figure burst through a previously unseen doorway, sprinting into the room with a screech of excitement that reminded Zora of the owl in the woods flapping its wings, causing her flesh to erupt into goose bumps.

At first, Zora wasn't sure what she was seeing. The figure was see-through, save its blue, blood-splattered dress and its eyes, which glowed with something Zora could only describe as hellfire.

"Here she is," the man said, his voice heavy and still wavering in its madness, swinging hard between awe and a deepest level of grief.

The woman's screams overtook Zora's sobs. Before Zora had time to process what was happening, the thing in the dress thrust its arms forward, its hands wrapping themselves around the old woman's throat. The screams were replaced by a rush of wet gurgling noises as the translucent hands tightened more and more, draining the old woman's life force until she was nothing more than a slumped, broken husk.

The fire in the screeching thing's eyes only burned brighter as it fell to its knees before the old woman's corpse, panting from the fatigue of what it'd just done, turning its unnatural face to the ceiling as it raised its arms and went completely silent. "Different," it rasped, its mouth pulling into the widest, most impossible grin. "His Blessings awash my soul in the words of the wise, oooh, how good it feels, it's a feeling you'll never know—"

"What's happening?" the man interrupted, overtaken by curiosity, his eyes wide, his hands trembling. "Why is it different? Is it... is it because I... loved her?"

Instead of answering, the thing in the dress transformed while it howled in ecstasy. Its skin darkened to a muddled gray, leaking crumpled paper covered with scrawls of ink over its surface. The words raced across its body in a chaotic rhythm, dancing to one limb before sprinting, black streaks careening, to another. Ink leaked from its smile while bright orange fire burned in its eyes.

Eyes that looked as though they were filled with embers.

Zora stopped wondering if she was witnessing a real event from the past and started instead questioning if someone else had constructed this vision specifically to scare her. Because, upsettingly, the more that Zora took in this inky papered creature, the more she realized where she'd seen something like it before. The woods after Conjure Night. The embers. The smell of burning paper and decomposition, the same smell that choked her now, causing her to cough into the back of her arm.

"Glory be to God," the man said, tears streaming down his cheeks.

Suddenly the room started disappearing around Zora, bringing her back to the place of cold shadows before she felt a new ground forming below her feet, the ground of a different place, the ground of the library. The vision was ending. She could already feel herself coming back into her body at Bricksbury.

To: Bricksbury Mountain College Students
From: Dr. Yolanda Darlene Jenkins, Bricksbury Mountain College President
Date: Sunday, September 12, 2027 09:17:02 EDT
Subject: CURFEW—EXTERNAL THREAT

Dear Students,

Due to a current investigation regarding the disappearance of student Toni Anderson, Bricksbury Mountain College is initiating a 6 p.m. curfew. Students, faculty, and staff must **remain on campus from 6 p.m. to 4 a.m.** and **inside their residences from 10 p.m. to 3 a.m.** Campus security has been notified.

I understand these situations can be stressful. Beginning tonight, the Inez Beverly Prosser Student Health Center will have **virtual expanded hours** and additional counselors.

Thank you,
Dr. Yolanda Darlene Jenkins

Chapter Fourteen

Zora groaned as her bones shook. Thumped. Throbbed wildly to an unknown, staccato rhythm. Spice, cedar, and amber coated her tongue and slid down her throat, overtaking the stench of the thing in the vision and choking her with its bright warmth. Zora thought this was a new way to be trapped—a new way of burning, strangling scents churning, of being enrapt.

Lamont's saffron-scented perfume and gentle prodding of Zora's shoulders further helped to bring her back. The scent of moss calmed her hammering heart while tart orange blossom stung her, flung her eyes open, ensuring she semi-waked with a start.

"Zora?" Lamont asked in a smooth, though concerned, tone. "You good? D'ya need some water? Here."

"What?" Zora's voice echoed in her mind, bouncing off to-do lists and the unexplained ominous energy at the entrance to the Rare Books Room. Crimson flooded her eyesight and didn't clear away as she blinked.

"I said, are you good? You look like a haint just passed through your window."

"Huh? I'm...sorry?"

Zora was only partially in the present. Part of her, a part she wished she could photocopy or otherwise record for later viewing, was still in her vision. She clung to it, but it was already receding, slipping from her grasp like a dream half-remembered.

She held a plastic water bottle she had no memory of Lamont giving her but downed the entire thing anyway to cool her throat's sudden dryness. Was that a consequence of having a vision? A vision. *I had a vision!* Excitement tugged at Zora's full lips, stretching them into a smile. But even Zora knew the joy didn't make it to her eyes.

Her first claimed vision. It was violent and horrifying and left her with an endless amount of questions. But the ask at the top of her list: What did the vision mean?

Zora looked at Lamont with returned, albeit spotty, eyesight. Lamont's eyebrows were still lifted in concern. *The Living Crypt: How Conjure and Sacrifice Shaped Nineteenth-Century Jonesborough* was cradled in his arms.

Sacrifice. Like the eerie dancers in orange on her first day. Like what she'd just seen take place with the old woman. Her hands went cold: What if everything she'd seen in the vision had actually happened?

"Hold on," Lamont said, disappearing with the book.

Zora took a moment to straighten her things and compose herself, allowing her phone to continue recording, though she didn't know why she bothered; Lamont must think she'd completely lost her goddamn mind.

Lamont returned, along with his saffron perfume, with yet another water bottle that Zora drank in two gulps. He stood patiently as Zora caught her breath.

"Sorry." Zora wiped her chin on the soft sleeve of her jacket.

"You already said that, an' it wasn't necessary the first time. Now, are ya sure you're good, honey? What's goin' on?"

"I…"

"Nahhh," Lamont snapped, slicing his hand below his throat to cut Zora off. His eyebrows turned downward in unruly seriousness. "Be straight with me. Should I be callin' an ambulance or somethin'?

I'm not great in an emergency an' don't know CPR, AED, or any other acronym!"

Zora swallowed. A medical emergency wasn't an unreasonable assumption, but no, that was the last thing she wanted. Still, she couldn't think quick enough to dodge that, not so soon after...

"I had a vision," Zora heard herself say too late to stop her traitorous tongue.

"You had a vision?"

"Yes?"

"You aren't sure?"

"I had a vision. There. I said it. Are you fuckin' happy?"

"Am I happy you didn't lie? Yes."

"You...believe me?"

"Ya know, if you took a second not to come at people just askin' genuine questions—"

"Okay, why do you believe me, though?"

Lamont's warm, auburn-dyed locs cascaded down his body as he crossed his arms.

"Zora Robinson."

He spoke to Zora as if they'd long been best friends, not met an hour ago. Despite the overwhelming circumstances, Zora tried to keep up.

"If you were *really* part of my audience, you would know I took a break last year after burnin' out."

"Oh..." Zora began, but he waved away her belated condolences.

"Durin' my tech fast, I got into tarot journalin', then I went to New Orleans for Essence Fest, an' while I was there, my boyfriend at the time, who was Haitian, was dead serious about Vodou."

Zora didn't interrupt his pause this time.

"He was draggin' me all over creation to these itty shops. Thank God to-go drinks are everywhere in that city. Now, some were clearly tourist traps, but others, I could *feel* the power in that buildin', ya know? It just got me thinkin' about my own ancestry, an' so I started researchin' my great-grandmother's family. Hoodoo fell into place after I started havin' conversations with her an' other ancestors. I mean, you get it, right? You said in your speech that you practice, don't you?"

"Yes," Zora said hurriedly, now it was safe to speak. "I get it. I—"

Zora's watch buzzed, and she jumped at the opportunity for distraction.

BRICKSBURY CAMPUS SECURITY: Security concern in the Woodlands. Avoid the vicinity. Report suspicious activity to (423) 423-4234. Stay tuned for more information.

"What the fuck does 'security concern' mean?" Zora asked.

"My question exactly." Lamont was frowning down at his phone. "And 'stay tuned' sounds like they're cuttin' to a commercial break at the Emmys."

Zora couldn't help but chuckle. "It really does."

"This could have somethin' to do with that missin' student, Toni Anderson. Did ya see the email about it? We were actually room-mates a few years back, had a few of the same classes. I wonder what happened to her."

Zora felt like she'd never heard the name in her life, but to be fair, her mind was still spinning from the vision. It was so strange to be sitting here, talking to Lamont in the library. The contrast of the two situations reminded her of leaving a dark movie theater in the middle of the day after seeing a harrowing film.

"Let's get out of here." Zora sighed, relenting at last to the pull of reality. She bit her lip. *Go for it.* "Also, drinks tomorrow night?"

Lamont didn't pause. "Hmm. Let's go to the Cornbread Lounge. You aren't vegan, are ya? I've been dyin' for some country-fried fish!"

Zora laughed. "I'll drive."

"My treat—so long as you spill everythin' about the vision."

"And you tell me about the ex who had you drunk as hell conjure-shop-hopping around N'awlins," Zora said, wagging her eyebrow and butchering a Cajun accent.

"*Oh*, I'm down."

MISSING LIBRARIAN

Esther Fisherman

Any information concerning **Esther Fisherman** should be given at once to Bricksbury Mountain College administration officials or the Jonesborough Police Department. Esther disappeared from staff housing the night of October 2, 1927, and has not been seen since.

Amias Crawfoot
December 16, 1927
Jonesborough, Tennessee
Bricksbury Mountain College—The Woodlands

Esther Fisherman could have been the closest thing to a soulmate Amias had. Knowing it could never be, he'd planned a quiet life with her on campus. Amias had pined for her as if he were in line for another life. But her death put those thoughts to rest. In their place, a gloomy overcast fogged his mind. Who was he now that she was dead? How had he not seen how important she was to him? Could he have explained his immortality sooner? Could he have changed anything? *No, I couldn't,* he thought as he strolled up to the Jonesboro African Baptist Church. It was the one building on campus he forbade others to enter, and therefore made sense to be his prison.

The ivy-infested structure stood far from Bricksbury Mountain College, hidden in the whispering woods that encased the school with haunted histories and honeysuckle-tinted leaf mold. Forgotten to time, only remembered by the one cursed not to forget. Amias still bent knees beneath the lonely, aged wrought iron steeple.

As if God, King of all Kings, would set foot in these charnel woods.

Amias craned his neck and glared at the cross lording above

scarlet oaks. It was unnerving how a thing created for His children could harbor someone made both of scripture and hellfire. Amias could not reckon it. For whom was the holy text written and the church meant to inspire?

Few entered the woods where Hosanna waned in bygone pews and played instruments barefoot on the forest floor, lyrics spewing from crimson lipsticked scowls, awaiting the next opportunity for depravity. Despite looking different ever since killing Esther, the evil in her had now roamed Tennessee for over a century. So long that locals, humans and otherwise, birthed legends to protect their young. Fireside nightmares for children, tales of how vicious and indiscriminate the "Beast in the Woods" was.

Haints whispered up and down the mountains in clipped tones, warning, begging, beseeching one another to haunt earth in pairs, lest the Beast somehow learn to cannibalize their noncorporeal bodies. Even ghosts had limits.

And yet, Amias always returned, stopping her from taking it too far. He'd shout her name, then His, when she'd gotten thirsty at the stench of blood. To her, it had taken on a sweeter note. Blood had become something she'd look forward to when protecting the school. There were times Amias wasn't certain someone's death was warranted, but Hosanna turned her amber-gold eyes on him, and he'd decided this wouldn't be the hill he'd die on. There'd be more dangerous times coming, he knew. This was his curse, and it was evolving.

That "more dangerous time" happened not long after. Hosanna had a fascination with fighting animals. Their bleating huffs excited her. She found stags heavily breathing, warring over territory, or a deer in heat. Amias watched Hosanna as her bloodlust rooted and blossomed until she approached the losing stag and shoved her fist into the deep red severed muscle, then brought out her hand to lick her fingers. Her fiery eyes closed in what was unmistakably...bliss.

This was it; she was no longer Hosanna, nor was she Esther. Amias had held out for a long while, but he had to agree with the locals: The creature was a Beast.

He had lost and couldn't keep any of them entirely within God's light, which he admitted was a fool's mission. But why were he and Hosanna gifted the demon to protect Bricksbury if they were so forsaken? Wouldn't He have known this would happen? This was the plan, wasn't it? And if it were, couldn't He have saved Esther? The questions spiraled inside Amias as he bent his knees at the Jonesboro African Baptist Church altar. Esther's sturdy laugh haunted him in his sleepless nights and across all the Beast's bloodthirsty days.

Amias witnessed the wickedness and spoke no words of contempt. There was no hesitation in how he plucked his banjo, beat the organ keys, or hummed while gospel drumming. There was only a swelling rhythm he couldn't/wouldn't shake, with a tempo free-flowing in his bones. What spell had the Beast placed on him to— No.

No.

He would swallow the thorns of accountability even as they clawed up his bloodied throat. It's not like he didn't know. He had killed for this.

Chapter Fifteen

Speakers in the courtyard blared Kendrick Lamar's "squabble up," a favorite of Zora's. It wasn't the song she minded; it was its volume. Bricksbury students were taking full advantage of the curfew over Toni Anderson's disappearance, and it sounded like they were *all* doing it outside Zora's door. It was nearing ten, and the volume was in reckless disregard of the "Neighborhood's" After-hours Policy. The RAs happily ignored the rules and often joined in the festivities. Zora forgot how motherfucking loud college was. She felt the thumping of the beat like an earthquake in her bones. Overstimulation was imminent. The only thing more deafening than the writhing bass line was the shouts of the people dancing along with the beat. Zora's jaw began to tremble, so she pressed her rows of teeth together. How much pressure did it take for teeth to break?

She eyed her copy of *Brown Girl in the Ring* on her suitcase, with its worn pages and a rip she accidentally made a couple of years ago. Maybe she could distract herself with that. But no, the music was too loud for her to truly enjoy a reread, and besides, Zora had plenty of work to do. She sat on her squeaky futon, the gentle glow of the lamp illuminating Esther's soft leather diary. Zora struggled to block out the cacophony outside her room, so she relented, gave victory to the revelers, and finally inserted her earplugs. Then she sighed in the comfortable silence. Back to Esther.

Zora's watch buzzed—she could *feel* the frustrated sigh of Esther's diary.

LAMONT WATERS: have u heard any more about the curfew? just learned my roommate is a conspiracy theorist & i wanna put my head thru a wall

For the second time that day, Zora was shocked by her laughter. It was a sudden and bright joy. Henry Louis stirred briefly in her lap as her belly rolled with giggles. She tried to hold on to that featherlight feeling. She'd been so determined, so focused on her career that she'd forsaken friendship. Zora wouldn't've changed it, but then again, she hated how foreign joy felt to her.

ZORA: Lol, no sorry. I'll keep an ear out, though. And I'll pray for you.
LAMONT: ugh thanks. i'm gonna need it

Between the unsettling curfew and the criminal noise-level racket out her door, Zora was more than happy to tune everything out and focus on Esther's diary. She understood why Dr. Grant insisted she read this specific book. The first-person account was rare and invaluable, but as she read further, her thoughts grew darker. Esther's ominous accounts weren't that of an average college librarian. She talked about things that were starting to feel uncomfortably close to home, especially in the wake of the incident at Conjure Night and what happened in her vision. Smells of burnt parchment and rot. With a pen in hand, Zora took numerous notes while she examined Esther's diary entries, gathering her own thoughts as she read Esther's. The two of them fell into Zora's favorite type of conversation: one with the dead.

There was more talk of the Beast from the local folktale, but that was nothing new to Zora, only to Esther. Still, Zora scribbled a line about it down, along with "Hezekiah Lee," the name of the unfortunate missing student that was Esther's protégé. She stared at the word "Hezekiah" until it didn't look like a word anymore. Then she clicked back over to her personal email, where current Bricksbury President Jenkins had said there was an investigation happening for a missing student. Of course, Dr. Jenkins offered no helpful details. Instinct told Zora to pay attention. A quick Google search yielded nothing for Hezekiah, but "The Beast in the Woods" had a lengthy history. After scrolling through numerous write-ups about different takes on the piece of folklore, Zora stumbled on a phrase that piqued her interest—the "Keepers of the Beast." She hastily pasted the phrase into the search bar and was floored by the amount of results.

National news articles warned about "Appalachia's Black Cult," the "Questions This HBCU Does Not Want You Asking," and "Secret Society, Religion, or Cult." What sensational and tongue-in-cheek titles to introduce their readers to such weighty topics as decades of missing Black students. *Oughta be ashamed.*

The articles discussed the rumored members of the so-called Keepers dropping out and leaving the country with their families, never returning to America. The former students refused to participate in interviews, even after relocating to a new country. They consistently ignored emails and phone calls, and one individual went to dire lengths by jumping off his high-rise porch when a journalist attempted to approach him.

Zora unclenched her jaw and guzzled lukewarm water. Esther's diary was the treasure Dr. Grant knew it'd be, even if her findings disturbed her. Although the diary had borne fruit, Zora's skin was crawling. These missing people had had no justice. This was a difficult part of her research: finding pain, especially the often unresolved pain specific to the Black and Black Appalachian subjects of her studies. Sometimes, it was like the horrors of the past soaked into her skin until she *knew* what it felt like. She didn't have kids, but she'd read enough firsthand accounts of 1919's Red Summer to feel like she'd lost her own children. Uncovering and preserving these stories wasn't just her job, it was her purpose. She knew it. So, she kept reading.

Since the sixties, seven students had gone missing, each a rumored member of one society: the Keepers of the Beast. Zora raked her hand through her braids. She was onto something.

The curious thing about each case was that the correlation between the student and the society was only mentioned twenty years after the disappearance. Until then, papers across the country, Jonesborough, and even the *Bricksbury Daily News* reported a "missing student." No explanation, no leads, and no talks with their roommates or family. Nothing. Until two decades later, some unseen embargo lifts, and one or two amateur sources make the connection. All the new knowledge combined with the current curfew unsettled Zora, sending a chill up her spine.

And speaking of strange, Zora thought of her experiences with *The Living Crypt: How Conjure and Sacrifice Shaped Nineteenth-Century Jonesborough*. She wished she had more time with it. How could it've had her notes? In her handwriting?! A thought crossed Zora's mind about Jonesborough rootworkers and their uncanny abilities, but the thought wasn't clear enough to draw a hard connection. She had half a granola bar, not even pretending to eat something more substantial. There wasn't time. Instead, she listened to her (frustratingly unhelpful) canvassing recordings, reread the (unnervingly shallow) notes she'd taken the last few times in the library, and fell asleep while listening to herself describing *The Living Crypt*, aka the impossible book. The Impossible Book. The... Impos... sible... Bo... ok...

She was underground, though she could see rough, curved stone walls that were exactly the same as the ones in the Rare Books Room. They were peppered with protruding, saw-toothed edges that bit into Zora's hands like teeth. Their sharpness, Zora knew, was a warning.

Screams rang out ahead of her, but she couldn't investigate. Just like in the vision from before, it was extremely difficult to control her own body. With monumental effort, Zora turned her head toward an altar overrun with tapered candles. *Anguish. Strangulation. Desire.*

Warmth and smoke blew in her direction while shrill voices shrieked warnings. Some told Zora by name to stay away. Underneath, in lower tones, others bellowed and roared. The noise rang in Zora's ears till she was nauseous. What was this place? Was it the same as her last vision? If so, where were the old woman and the man from before? Her vision blurred and then disappeared. *Grief. Trembling. Shame.*

She moved, but Zora felt like she was walking through cloudy mush, unaware of her surroundings and ultimately unaware of her*self*. Her body was doing and saying things, but she couldn't perceive them fully. Zora swayed dangerously and was devoured by murky shadows, gasping, before she lurched in the opposite direction, unable to find her footing. As if she'd never had a firm grasp on lucidity. And Zora was powerless to resist.

"Zora," someone called gently.

———

Zora woke up with a gasp, startled by awareness—sound and touch and all the other senses—and her growing ability to control her movements. She wobbled to her feet, her legs feeling weak and rubbery beneath her. Blinking against the haze that clouded her vision, she took a tentative step forward. Suddenly, her thigh collided with the sharp laminate edge of the kitchen counter, sending a jolt of pain coursing down her leg. She gasped and cursed the kitchen, the counter, and the nap from hell. At Zora's frustrated voice, Henry Louis stood up from the futon and shook his burly body. The sharp jangle of his collar pierced Zora's ears as if she had never heard it before. Her hands went to either ear as she groaned. The sound was *so* harsh. Why was it so sharp? It was as if the metal were scraping the sides of her mind. She stood still, biting her lip and cringing as the sound echoed painfully within her. It was some time before it faded. By then, tears were slick on Zora's warm cheeks.

She pulled the fridge door three times before it opened, and afterward, her hands trembled as she drank a chocolate protein shake. Zora wished she'd chosen something else as the cold sludge slid down her throat. It was heavy in her belly. Her watch told her it was just past midnight. The music and laughter from outside could still be clearly heard in her apartment, but the air conditioner's clunking noise helped ground her inside. *Be with me, ancestors. Be with me.*

When her heart calmed and her head cleared enough, Zora wrote down her nightmare in aching detail. Aching because it was terrifying, yes, but also because of a yearning she'd felt when she'd seen the fiery altar. Zora had *hungered* for it. Lusted for the bergamot, usually fruity and floral, but in the nightmare, it was concentrated on the tart undertones until acid lay bare on her tongue. That's what Zora craved: the uncomfortable combinations of scents and tastes encircling, overwhelming her trapped body.

And now she craved never to forget it.

A feeling crept upon her, saying that she needed to keep alert, saying danger was closer than she thought. Now was not the time to ignore her intuition. She tugged at the collar of her sleep shirt, the warm fabric suddenly constricting her sweaty skin. Zora whipped the shirt off and heaved it across the room, but the warning persisted in her deafening heartbeat and the tense clench of her throat.

Danger is coming.

"I'm okay," she gasped, examining her hands in front of her as if to prove it, forcing herself to breathe in and out. "I'm fine, there's nothing wrong." But even to her own ears, she sounded unconvinced. She glanced at the clock. 12:46. Curfew had long begun. There was nowhere to go. No place for her energy.

Her left eye twitched. No, she wasn't trapped; she was sheltered. All she needed was to change her perspective. She went to the broom closet.

Usually, she'd use a bucket, but that wasn't realistic in her tiny studio apartment, so she brought out three clean spray bottles and boiled water on her only burner. She hummed a melody her grandmother had made her memorize after learning of Zora's night terrors. Then, as an extra step to further support the cleansing ritual that was to come, she soaked a chunk of calamus root in the charged water, removing it and letting it cool before hurrying to the door and drawing a hasty outline around the front door with it. Danger could try to come find her all it wanted. It wasn't crossing over *this* threshold.

Zora bit her lip as she continued with the cleansing ritual. The further along in it that she got, the more paranoid her mind became regarding what could possibly be awaiting her once she had to leave this protected space. If only she had someone on campus who she could call in a time like this. Lamont was nice, but still new to her, and it wasn't like she could call Dr. Grant this late to question him on the more recent details she'd uncovered on the way to her thesis. That only left one name in Zora's mind, as much as it pissed her off to consider it. Did she have the strength to dredge up the past? She remembered the screams from her vision, and her body shuddered. Did she have a choice?

Before she could overthink anymore, she pulled out her cell phone and called Jasmine. Yes, things had gone horribly at Conjure Night. Yes, Zora would have preferred to have *anyone* else to reach out to who might even begin to understand. But aside from all that unsavory bullshit, some facts were undeniable: Something was seriously wrong at Bricksbury, and Jasmine was her sister.

Zora's left foot *tap-tapped* wildly on the thin laminate flooring while she waited for Jasmine to pick up, the sound echoing across the room bare of anything save crucial furnishings. The ringing continued. It reminded her of how time moved in her nightmare. Stretched out. Slow passing. Zora kept nervously licking her lips. When her sister's prim voice told her to leave a message, Zora hung up. As always, she would have to rely on herself. Her cheeks warmed once more; she felt foolish to have ever thought there was a chance her sister would answer. At least she could call upon her ancestors, she thought, as she cast a wary look to the frayed, soggy calamus root in her free hand. The living were so terribly unreliable.

Chapter Sixteen

Well, fuck. Nothing to pull you out of a research and nightmare-fueled paranoia spiral like a too-early alarm reminding you that it was time for school. Groggily, Zora hauled herself in to perch in the lofty eleventh row of the lecture hall for her 8:00 a.m. class taught by Dr. Grant. She was at least pleased that her mojo bag had stayed cool and nothing of note had happened when she first stepped out of her apartment. She reminded herself that her ancestors were with her always, letting the knowledge wrap around her like the most comforting hug.

It was an admittedly foolish move, signing up for a slot so early. But she preferred to see foolishness as daring. Calling someone out for being foolish was a less sophisticated way of saying, *This person has too much faith.* Zora had mustard seed faith—and that required some irrationality.

Although thoughts of Esther's diary and the Keepers of the Beast were heavy on Zora's mind, she could admit the Rural Health Projects class was long awaited. She'd done significant research on the lasting impacts of coal mining and prison labor specific to Black Appalachians. Despite working in similar working conditions or being convicted of similar crimes as white people, Black coal miners and prisoners fared far worse on every measurable health metric. Their life expectancies were depressingly low. Literally depressing, as Zora spent the first two years at Dartmouth with her therapist, learning how to cope with the traumatic histories she studied. For all her high-and-mighty Capricorn talk of separating church and state (emotion and profession), Zora was still human. She could not outrun her feelings.

She also couldn't outrun reminders of her sister. Jasmine's spouse sat at the front of the room, facing the class. Evidently, Ngozi was Dr. Grant's TA.

Of course, Zora thought.

Ngozi was positioned near the door. They wore a copper button-up tucked into striped, wide-leg olive-green pants. Zora thought they must have a thing for green, thinking back to the pear-green babydoll dress they wore to Conjure Night. Did Jasmine like them in green? *Shit*, Zora knew so little about their relationship. What television shows did they watch together? Old ones like *Living Single*? Or were they more into investigative documentaries? Had Jasmine, like Zora, ever had a months-long hyperfixation on the building and selling of tiny homes? What restaurants or coffee shops did Jasmine and Ngozi frequent? Hell, how did they take their coffee? What scented candles did they light? How did they live?

While Zora stewed in her isolation, she couldn't help but notice that Dr. Grant was late, *surprise, surprise*. She made awkward eye contact with her sibling-in-law every couple of minutes, confirming for Zora that neither of them was prepared for this. Ngozi hadn't been in the first couple of classes, so Zora had forgotten that Dr. Grant even had a TA to begin with. It wasn't like the class schedules listed who any professor's TA was, or that Dr. Grant would've known to warn Ngozi about Zora. Dr. Grant didn't even know what time his own class was, much less that there was any connection between Zora and Ngozi.

Dr. Grant, however, had his own connections, because unlike the open-windowed rooms surrounding his classroom, the air conditioner in *this* lecture hall functioned. It made strange kicking and clacking sounds as it ran. Zora thought it'd stop eventually, once it got cold enough, but then minutes passed in sputtering, chilled racket, and she realized she was wrong. Ancient as it might have been, the AC was at least efficient. Zora put on the jacket that was wrapped around her waist and glanced at her buzzing phone.

LAMONT: we still on for the cornbread lounge tonight?

Like the last time they'd texted, Zora was struck by the contrast in her emotions. Lamont pulled her toward more lightheartedness than she was used to. And she was having difficulty focusing anyway, what with the curfew and missing student and the like. Zora was stumbling through a flurry of emotions, but one thing she knew for sure? She was damn sure going to the Cornbread Lounge.

ZORA: 💯!! I already looked up the menu. I know what I want lmaooo. Smotherly Love Chicken here I come.
LAMONT: thank god, can't wait to hang
ppl are acting like they don't have any sense after the curfew
just got to work & i am tired
ZORA: Really? What are they doing?
LAMONT: being hardheaded?
someone just walked in, picked up a book, put it on the ref counter in front of me, & then just left?
????
didn't speak to me or anything
someone else has been here since doors opened an hour ago, just standing on the stairs looking down? no headphones in or nothing
ZORA: Wtf???? Just stands there creepily like Michael Myers?

LAMONT: It's giving scarecrow
zora! i deserve some catfish!

Zora smiled. Maybe her entire brain didn't need to be occupied by mysterious disappearances and visions. Maybe she could let herself forget for a moment. Just a moment.

Zora's eyes scanned the yawning students. She perused her criminally expensive textbook, but her eyes wouldn't focus on a single sentence, on a single word! Despite her greatest efforts, her thoughts kept pulling her elsewhere, to Esther and the Keepers of the Beast. She cycled between them, feeling her blood pressure rising.

Dr. Grant grumbled into the room three minutes later, just as the class was considering making a run for it. He donned the same yellow sweater and midnight-blue corduroy pants he had worn during Zora's office visit. He layered the bright sweater over a sharp gray collared shirt. Without hesitation, he began the lesson.

In Zora's ears, Dr. Grant's voice deepened. The words stretched until he droned in a way identical to Charlie Brown's teacher. She only recognized every other word he spoke about an upcoming fifteen- or twenty-page essay. Her mind was too preoccupied. Her mind...was too...occupied? Occupied as in working? Yes, yes, she'd certainly been working, hadn't she? Of course, she was in class. But Zora stared at her pen and notebook, suddenly unsure what she would even write about. Her eyes drifted over to her recorder, which she used religiously. But no, something was wrong. It was like Zora wasn't *supposed* to be able to focus. She swallowed, unsure if this was a lack of sleep or something external. Something nefarious and external.

Her necklace suddenly felt heavier on her neck. The frigid gemstone pressed stronger and stronger against her slick skin. The coldness jolted her to awareness. When she focused on the weight of the tiger's-eye, something inside Zora shifted. The nightmare, the vision, and the memory of what had happened in the woods on Conjure Night incessantly vied for her attention. She pressed her trembling fingers against the stone, trying to still her racing thoughts. *Stop. Stop it!* Not even nearby students shifting in their seats or staring at the steam floating up from her tea could distract Zora from the looming merry-go-round. She tried to force herself to blink, but couldn't. Something had to be causing this. Zora willed herself to push through it.

The chamomile tea in her tumbler sat untouched, but she still smelled the sweet notes of apple and honey. Zora breathed slower as the tension in her back melted away. She sighed heavily, clinging to the sense of calm that chamomile brought. She clung because it wasn't just tension being released from Zora's body; it was magic. Her brain fog had cleared of its fuzzy confusion with an unnatural swiftness. It was her tiger's-eye, her magic protecting her from someone else's. Zora's eyes darted to her classmates, who were taking notes. They were texting or pretending to type on their laptops. How was no one else impacted? Why?

Zora cleared her throat, earning a few curious glances from nearby neighbors, and was pleased to realize that her mind had slowed down enough to feel functional again. She took a sip of tea to cover her anxiety, thinking back on her morning. There hadn't been anything out of the ordinary. She had boiled the water before feeding Henry Louis *and* feeding her ancestor altar, and got to class early as usual. She'd gotten a seat without fuss. No one had bothered her or lingered too close by. Perhaps she was being paranoid. Studying Esther's diary late into the night until she was having nightmares surely wasn't ideal for her mental health.

Zora had climbed the stairs and chosen a seat in the top corner, where she'd be least noticed. She hoped, at least, that no one had observed her brief inability to pick up her pen or recorder. She did now and noted how damp and clammy her fingers were against the curved plastic, despite Dr. Grant's frigid AC. The dewiness unpleasantly stuck her to the rigid seat, and it wasn't until minutes later, when her heart became fully calmed, that Zora felt her skin cool. She peeked at the others, who all sat equidistant from one another, to confirm she still didn't have an audience. When she was certain, she spread her legs comfortably without touching anyone. A quick look around confirmed that her classmates were perched in their seats, giving Dr. Grant their full attention.

How nice, Zora thought, as her mind oscillated from Esther Fisherman's writing about the Keepers to the murderous, monstrous vision in the library before veering back into the classroom. She blinked at the shiny fluorescent lighting.

Her eyes wandered the lecture hall's rustic, coffered ceiling, listening to Dr. Grant's voice but not so much what he was saying. Her mind returned to their meeting the other day, to when he told her she should visit Jonesborough African American Historical Society. Zora had considered calling since he'd given her their phone number, but she'd learned in undergrad how easy it was for people to evade you if you weren't standing directly in front of them, demanding their attention with a friendly smile. Maybe it'd be beneficial to go in person sooner rather than later.

Zora paused at the top of the lecture hall stairs when class ended. The day was young, and she felt she'd already lived seven lives. Hopefully, the next class would go better. As Zora stepped down the stairs, she realized she'd forgotten about Ngozi. Had they been watching her? What would her sibling-in-law report back to Jasmine, if anything? Approaching Ngozi was a terrible idea. Self-sabotage, a brutal masochism. But Zora needed to know if Jasmine had seen her call the night before and chosen not to answer. A masochist indeed.

"Hey," Zora said, uncaring that Ngozi was clearly overwhelmed with the amount of papers in their lap.

"Oh, hi, Zora," Ngozi greeted, their soft-spoken voice mingled with the hesitant silence that hung in the air.

A few papers fluttered to the ground as they stood and shook Zora's hand, but neither of them bent down to pick them up. Behind Zora, the room was hushed. Did Jasmine honestly turn her back like Zora had done in those woods long ago?

She tilted her head up, emphasizing her slight height advantage. "Do you know if Jasmine got my call last night?"

Ngozi looked away, effectively answering Zora's question. The familiar lump swelled in Zora's throat. *Ah fuck.* She vehemently wished she were less of a masochist.

"Okay," Zora said. It would always come back to the incident in the woods when they were children, wouldn't it? Zora would never be redeemed or forgiven, no matter how many years passed. "Thanks."

Ngozi opened their mouth, but it was Dr. Grant who spoke behind Zora.

"Ah! Are you enjoying your Rural Health Projects class, Miss Robinson?" Dr. Grant's booming voice asked.

Zora whirled, plastering as genuine a smile as she could muster. "Of course, Dr. Grant! It's so nice to see you in action."

He smiled gently, then indicated Ngozi. "The meeting of the assistants. Ngozi Okafor, meet Zora Robinson, who was much help to me over the summer at the Beck Cultural Exchange Center."

Ngozi's eyebrows shot up, and Zora's mood lifted slightly with a pang of pride.

"Oh wow, Zora, I didn't know you were working with Dr. Grant."

"Ngozi is my sibling-in-law," Zora explained to a confused-looking Dr. Grant. Would he remember her reluctance to discuss her sister? When a look of caution crossed his eyes, Zora swallowed. This was awkward enough. Now it was too much.

"Anyway," Zora said, picking up the sheets of paper Ngozi

dropped to cover her flushed cheeks. "I'll let y'all finish up here. See you later, Dr. Grant. Ngozi."

Zora turned on her heel without waiting for their response. She returned to her room and walked Henry Louis under gloomy clouds. Though it wasn't forecasted to rain till the evening, the clouds were the dark, threatening kind unique to summer storms. The overcast day soothed Zora's anxiety about someone seeing Henry Louis, even though she trusted the mojo bag she'd refreshed. Henry Louis did his job (being adorable), which only furthered the walk's contentedness.

Zora was grateful to have Lamont and the Cornbread Lounge to look forward to. It was the ideal end to her day. Until then, though, she split her time between the Rural Health Projects paper (twenty pages, it turned out) and her Central Appalachian Literature assignment. Thoughts of Esther Fisherman and the possible magic from class crept in every once in a while, but Zora was determined to focus.

She found a comfortable rhythm of switching from one topic to the next if she got frustrated or bored, or if the darker thoughts lurked too close for comfort. An extended break included groaning through stretches with her favorite YouTube yoga instructor, Jessamyn Stanley, to try to strengthen the connection between her mind and her body.

Later, after microwaving her beloved creamy chicken-flavored instant noodles, Zora cracked open a Bud Light Lime. It was a sour habit she'd picked up from Victoria. And, for better or worse, they were by far the most-stocked beer in Jonesborough's country grocery store.

Looking over her apartment, Zora sighed. The place was a chaotic jumble of textbooks, tarot decks, tampon boxes, dirty clothes, extra Florida water for spur-of-the-moment offerings, an oscillating fan, clean clothes, and chafing gel bottles. They were all strewn

across the floor, futon, bed, and kitchen counters. To say nothing of
Henry Louis. He had a nasty habit of collapsing atop Zora's clean
clothes and slobbering in his adorable sleep. As he lay on the futon,
chest grumbling, he made his laissez-faire intentions for life at
Bricksbury clear.

Zora gave herself over to a pulsing workflow, keeping rhythm
with the acoustic guitar that strummed from the speaker that was
deftly wedged between the sink's faucet and the outdated tile back-
splash. She hummed with one hand wrapped around the soft beer
cozy she'd bought years ago. It was the summer between sophomore
and junior year, and she'd let her friends drag her to P-Town for
Pride. She'd fallen in love a thousand times that week on the beach
with a thousand different people. As Zora had stood on the ocean's
edge, she reveled in the taste of the salty water on their lips and then
on hers. Each moment glistened.

She was far from that carefree bliss now. Far from bliss in general.

Zora bit down on a bitter pencil eraser while she read a line in
Effie Waller Smith's *Rhymes from the Cumberland*. The poetry book
was a poignant ode to a childhood living in the Eastern Kentucky
Mountains. Zora almost wept for joy upon discovering that it was
a required reading in the Central Appalachian Literature rubric. It
rightfully sat in the top ten of her favorite poetry books. Top five,
even. According to her neatly designed Adult Poetry spreadsheet,
her "homework" was squished between James Weldon Johnson's
God's Trombones and *Don't Call Us Dead* by Danez Smith.

Zora first read *Rhymes from the Cumberland* in its entirety at age
twelve and then reread it as part of her annual summer read-a-thon
during her seasonal-aesthetic-obsessed teenage years. The book was
the whole reason she started read-a-thons.

One of Zora's favorite poems in the book was called "Beauties of
the Cumberland." The opening stanza mentioned folklore, but the
poem itself did not evoke wistful nostalgia. It had all the hallmarks

of it—a yearning to go elsewhere, a remembered, rural refuge from the city, where one must always perform. But this poem wasn't a homesick elegy like the others. It had no innocent ending. It was duty or die.

Zora's protection amulet rattled in the corner opposite where she sat in bed. The clamor of the cowrie shells momentarily distracted her, freezing her in place hunched over the book. For one... two... three... heartbeats, she couldn't help but fixate on the smooth shells' cream color, marveling as though it were the only detail that mattered, wishing with her entire heart that it was. But when Henry Louis's head shot up from his sleep, Zora broke out of the trance, springing into action. She leaped out of bed, her heart pounding in her chest. The smell of burned paper and decomposing flesh filled her nostrils. Where was it coming from?

Danger was coming. And it was more than a feeling this time. The shells clinked together once again in a sturdily physical tremor, as though some invisible fist had struck them. Her eyes shot a look of betrayal at the calamus-rooted door, only to realize that the pocket window in her kitchen space was wide open.

Shit.

She hurried to shove the window shut before scrambling over the room's mess, shoving aside a stack of spiral notebooks to drop hard to her knees at her altar. It was an antiques shop buy; Zora had hollowed a bulky open-shelf bookcase by removing the shelves, then sanded and stained it a cherry red oak color. She touched her grandfather's hunting knife, recently sharpened, and the obituary program for her great-aunt Ramona before lunging for the extra bottle of Florida water. *Ancestors, be with me.* She unscrewed the bottle's cap and dabbed some on the altar's awaiting saucer. She followed suit on her forehead, behind her neck, and on both wrists.

As she sat with Henry Louis at the altar, a sudden energy shift caused him to turn away and let out a low growl toward the door.

The cowrie shells continued to rattle in the corner, and the acoustic guitar still strummed from her speaker above the sink. Coupled with her heart's heavy thuds, the room vibrated with an ancestral war cry. Zora rose from her altar with a Bible in one hand and Grandpa's hunting knife in the other and approached her front door. Even if whatever force was trying to push its way through wouldn't ever make it inside, Zora was not okay with the idea of it just lingering right outside the door, waiting for her. This was *her* space.

It was as important as ever to remember that she wasn't alone. Even in this apartment, in this town where no one gave a fuck about her, Zora wasn't alone. Henry Louis's growls only emphasized this. She tucked the Bible underneath her arm to free up the hand that wasn't holding the knife.

As soon as she gripped the doorknob, the presence receded.

Unease trickled down her back as she glanced through the peephole. The scattered groups of people revealed no specific intentions toward Zora. No one even looked in her apartment's direction. But she knew what she'd felt. And she'd known the mojo bags warned her. She licked her lips and put Henry Louis in a sit-stay beside the door, able to jump in and protect her if need be.

A couple in the courtyard turned when Zora opened her door, but they immediately resumed making out when she looked back at them. No one else noticed her.

Zora jumped at the vibrations of her text notification.

LAMONT: sis r u readyyy? 😊🐾🔪
ZORA: Meet at my room? I'll walk us to my car

Chapter Seventeen

Zora had found her new happy place in Jonesborough at the Cornbread Lounge. She sank into her cozy mustard-colored armchair, letting out a contented sigh, while a half-finished glass of cabernet franc sat before her. Her belly was full of smotherly love chicken, collard greens, and sweet, buttery cornbread. Zora's eyes were fixed on the waitress as she carefully refilled Lamont's glass with another frozen lime daiquiri. He savored a long sip and sighed, satisfied, before mirroring Zora's actions and slumping into his seat in exhaustion.

Lamont tipped his head back and stared at the brushed-tin ceiling. "This is the type of gluttony they discussed in the Bible."

"I don't think He mentioned anything about catfish dinners and fried okra." Zora shut her eyes and willed a food coma to grant her a much-needed mental escape.

"You forgot the candied yams."

"I don't think He mentioned those, either."

"Well, definitely not the candied kind."

Zora grabbed her stomach as she laughed. They'd been chatting and giggling for over an hour, and now that Zora had satisfied her physical hunger, her mind had turned back to Esther's diary and the Keepers of the Beast. She'd been craving understanding. But now things were only getting more complicated, and the cowrie shells kept jangling in her mind, casting her thoughts in an even darker tone. Zora had studied fictional villains in folklore, but the Beast in the Woods felt more complicated than wives' tales or a real-life wild animal blown out of proportion. Her gut told her there was something of substance here. Something real. She thought of the screeching demon from her first vision, how its skin had become something like crumpled paper scrawled over with ink, how its eyes had glowed with the embers that Zora had recognized.

"So, what are you thinkin' so hard about?" Lamont asked in the first serious note Zora had heard from him that night.

Zora looked up at him. Maybe she wouldn't be able to tell him everything she'd seen, but at the very least, she figured he could handle the basics. "Have you heard of Esther Fisherman?"

Lamont's eyebrows shot up. "Did you bring me to the Cornbread Lounge to discuss my work?"

"*Your* work?" Zora frowned. She pulled Esther's diary from the backpack beside her seat, showing him the worn leather and slaughtered lamb fore-edge painting. "I've been studying her diary."

Lamont didn't reach for the book Zora handed to him. His eyes went through several emotions, widening and scrunching as he oscillated between them. Finally, he looked at Zora and shuddered.

"How. The fuck. Did you get that book, Zora?"

Shit. Dr. Grant had all but told her he had stolen this book from the Rare Books Room. Holy shit. Was this expulsion worthy? Zora was confident it'd be Henry Louis's nighttime barks or an eruption of her relationship with Jasmine that would get her to leave Bricksbury. But Zora Robinson never would have considered that she would be discovered having broken library rules. Library rules? Zora loooved the library! It was her only safe space as a child. The only place her parents allowed her and her freedom to go unchecked. There wasn't a secular place on earth Zora respected more than a library. But Zora knew, rather elementarily, that her actions spoke louder than her words. She hoped she hadn't fucked this friendship with Lamont before it got started.

"My thesis advisor gave it to me," Zora said hurriedly. She wouldn't be taking the fall for Dr. Grant. "I got the feeling when he gave it to me that maybe he shouldn't have it, though." She laughed, but it wasn't the full-chested laughter of a moment ago. This was a thin, nervous trill that said, *Please don't judge me. I need a friend.*

Lamont frowned at the book, then finally reached out and took it. "Ya know, I've never touched it. Usually, it's in the basement with the oldest antiques."

Zora bit her tongue from saying, *I know.*

"Esther Fisherman was a beloved Bricksbury librarian, but more than that, she was a trailblazer for library science an' was involved in printin' at some point, I think. They named the quad after her and everythin'."

Zora considered Esther's words about Bricksbury's president and vice president from the twenties. Esther had stalked them for years, waiting for them to whisper in the Occultism section and writing her findings in her diary. She had been so concerned about the school and its future. She had no idea her name would live on here for eternity.

"Do you know if she was close to any of the other librarians or professors at the time?"

Lamont shook his head. "Are you kiddin'? She was a notorious asshole. In fact, 'Esther Fish Her, Man' is carved into a chair on the library's fourth floor under 'Frigid Fisherman' and 'Mrs. Fisherswisher.'"

Zora laughed so loudly the couple beside them turned to see what the commotion was. She relaxed once more into her seat. It'd been so long since she'd had a night out. A *real* night out without the pressures of a formal date.

"Is Dr. Grant your thesis advisor?" Lamont asked suddenly.

"How did you know?"

"Makes sense why Mrs. Redmond was havin' a fit with you," he answered. "I think those two used to be a thing or somethin'. Every time he comes in, she gets all riled up."

Zora sat back in her seat. Lamont's initial hesitation had disappeared now that he knew she hadn't maliciously stolen Esther's diary from the library. Not only was Zora not to blame, but this was a prime opportunity for tea-spilling.

"Does it take much to get Mrs. Redmond riled up?" Zora asked a softball question, vague enough to allow Lamont to hold forth but specific enough that he wouldn't veer off and start bitching again about BookTok's latest algorithm change.

"More than you'd think. She's an old-school librarian—next to nothin' ruffles her. But there's somethin' about Dr. Grant that does it." Lamont looked down at his empty plate for a moment. Esther's diary lay forgotten in his hands. "He's always been nice to me— well, the one or two times I've come over to try an' break up him an' Mrs. Redmond, he was nice to me."

"Yeah, Dr. Grant is cool."

"'Cool' as in steals books from the library?" Lamont asked. "I get why Mrs. Redmond is wary, in that case."

"'Cool' as in he encouraged me to apply to Bricksbury after not getting in for undergrad," Zora admitted. Lamont nodded for her to continue. "Dr. Grant heads the Beck Cultural Exchange Center in Knoxville, where I worked until this summer. Even though he's a highly accomplished academic, researcher, et cetera, when discussing my interests, I could tell he just wanted me to learn. He's the kind of professor—maybe old-school like Mrs. Redmond—where he wants me to do an enormous job, and he's willing to do a bit of upfront help, but largely, he wants me to do it on my own. He pushes me constantly but is still hands-off."

Zora stopped herself before she began rambling. She wasn't

proud that the things she'd uncovered so far were affecting her real life in such a way. She doubted Dr. Grant would know what to do if she ever spilled everything that had followed their meeting on that first day anyway. She quashed the troll-brain insinuation that suggested she might not be able to handle all the knowledge that awaited her. That she wasn't as capable as Dr. Grant clearly believed she was. But she told herself she wasn't like most other students. Her personal abilities were blurring the lines more and more each day.

"Why Bricksbury?" Lamont asked.

"When I didn't get in for undergrad, I went to Dartmouth." Zora sighed. "I did well, but...my grandfather went here, and my sister goes here, so Dartmouth was...I never felt like I was fully there. I always felt called here. Like I fucked up by not getting in, and I was cursed to never forget this school exists and that I'm not in it. But this is my legacy, regardless of what Jasmine says. I belong here."

Lamont was quiet for a long moment before saying, "You absolutely belong here, Zora."

Zora smiled. She'd needed to hear it more than she liked to admit. "Thanks."

"So, Jasmine is your sister?"

"Yes." Zora cut off his next question. "We aren't close. She... didn't even want me to come here, actually."

"Damn," Lamont said, letting the heaviness of sibling estrangement hang in the air. "I'm sorry, Zora. That fuckin' sucks."

Don't you dare fucking cry. "Thanks, it's old news, really. What about you?"

"I want to revolutionize Bricksbury."

Zora was glad to discuss someone else. "What do you mean?"

"Everythin' about this place is outdated. The infrastructure. The lesson plans. The *professors.*" He wagged an eyebrow. "It's time for radical change. An' social media is part of the foundation for that change. Did you know the library didn't even have an Instagram account before I got there this summer?"

"No," Zora said, though Lamont didn't wait for vocal validation; he was on a roll.

"I mean, it's ridiculous. How are they expectin' the librarians to get grants or advertise for events? How are students supposed to know about anythin' goin' on at the library? They are not readin' those lame-ass flyers."

Zora laughed. "So you've spent the summer doing some basic modernizing?"

"Ugh. You have no idea. I've had zero social life for the last five months."

"Does that mean you've had zero communication with a certain Haitian ex of yours?"

Lamont giggled and snapped his fingers. "Sneaky, sneaky. Okay, I did promise to spill."

Zora nestled into her dark yellow chair, allowing herself rest even at the center of the restaurant's busyness. The mingling spicy scents and laughter danced around her, yet her gaze was drawn, magnetically, to a bedazzled cowboy hat glinting in the corner of her eye. The hat perched on the back of an unused chair, its vibrant sequins shimmering like captured starlight. Khadijah filled the air with her laughter, a melodic joy that rang louder than Zora's own moments of mirth. Immanuel and Shawna were each cradling a different colorful drink. They wiped away tears of laughter.

Zora's heart quickened as she stole glances at Khadijah, remembering the faint thrill that tinged their last interaction—a brush of fingers that sent warm ripples through her. That was it; nothing more, but somehow it was so much more intimate than that. Zora's mind pondered, no, *wandered* as the memory replayed. Thick, sweet honeysuckle in the air. Khadijah's flushed skin. Would she taste like honey, or like the salt from the sweat on her lip? Zora hoped for some sorta fusion of the two, something that would send her to her knees, tongue ready for—

All at once, the scarier details of that night emerged through the bliss of Khadijah. The crunching of leaves and the snapping of twigs as she was followed. The owl turning its head sideways as it spotted something Zora couldn't see, somewhere in the darkness of the woods. The disgusting odor, unmistakable to anyone who'd smelled a dead animal, sickly sweet and deeply meaty. The distant glimmer of what might have been embers. Real or not, she'd needed a protective spell to make it back home. The memory came to an abrupt end, and Zora roused as Khadijah's laughter echoed.

"Who is that?" Lamont asked, his body already twisting in his seat to openly stare in the direction where Zora's gaze was pointing. The dim lighting of the bar flickered over the two of them, casting playful shadows on their faces.

"Don't look!" Zora hissed, her eyes wide.

Lamont quickly turned back around, his curiosity palpable, and grabbed his near-empty drink, swirling it around as if it might reveal some hidden secret. He settled back in his seat. "Your turn. Spill," he insisted, leaning forward with an expectant grin.

Zora groaned softly, but in truth, she was happy as hell to have someone to discuss this with. "Not much has happened yet. And I'm not looking for anything serious, but I don't know, every time I see her, it's like nothing else exists." Her voice softened, revealing a trace of vulnerability beneath her confident facade.

"The one with the blond wolf cut and bangs?" Lamont's eyes sparkled with mischief, ready to dissect the full story.

Zora shook her head. "No, that's Shawna. Khadijah is the one who keeps inspecting her cowboy hat."

"Ah," Lamont said, glancing over his shoulder as inconspicuously as he could manage, which wasn't at all subtle. The low chatter and the clinking of glasses surrounding them created marginal cover.

"Why aren't you lookin' for anythin' serious?" Lamont asked.

Zora hesitated for a moment, then took a deliberate sip of her wine, letting the richness of the flavor buy her some time to think. "I'm not going to give a relationship the attention it deserves right now. I don't want to, and I doubt I have the time it needs."

Lamont nodded in understanding and spoke gently, "Then there's that other reason..."

Zora smiled despite herself. "I've been caught."

"Red wine handed," Lamont said with a smile.

"The truth is...I have abandonment issues. I've fucked up a few relationships, and I don't wanna go there again. I'd rather..."

"Yearn from across the Cornbread Lounge?"

Zora rolled her eyes. "You're being dramatic."

"Mm-hmm. Well, her friend is cute. Do you know his name?" Lamont asked.

Zora looked up at the ceiling for a moment, as if the answer might be scribbled there. "Immanuel. Both he and Khadijah are jazz majors. Shawna is ethnomusicology? Is that how you say it? I don't think I've ever said it out loud."

"Jazz," Lamont said, his eyes gleaming with interest. "I've never dated a musician before."

Zora frowned playfully, shaking her head at his romantic daydreaming. "I hate to state the obvious, but you aren't dating a musician," she said, her tone teasing.

"Not yet," Lamont retorted, wagging his eyebrows mischievously.

"Dating *anyone* during a curfew sounds difficult enough," Zora said. "I wonder if they know any more about that missing student."

"Who?" Lamont raised an eyebrow as he took another sip from his drink. "Missing student?"

Zora reflected his own confused expression right back at him, the alcohol making her feel pleasantly warm. "Yeah, Toni Anderson."

She laughed uneasily at his blank expression. "Didn't you say she was an old roommate of yours? How could you forget that?"

Zora could practically see the gears in Lamont's head struggling to turn. "Toni Anderson?" he repeated slowly. "No, I don't think I know anyone with that name."

It struck Zora as odd. Had she somehow misheard him yesterday? The waitress appeared out of nowhere, setting another frozen lime daiquiri in front of Lamont. He thanked her graciously before he started going off about how he'd always wanted to date a musician. The drinks. Maybe they'd gone to Lamont's head. Or hers.

Zora shook off the feeling in her gut, enjoying at least half a bottle more of vanilla- and oak-tinged cabernet franc, the exact amount slipping her mind.

Amias Crawfoot
June 9, 1947
Jonesborough, Tennessee
Bricksbury Mountain College—The
Woodlands

Amias would never forget the first time the Beast asked him to kill for its pleasure. He had been playing music in the cemetery. Hellfire eyes turned on him—not asking, but demanding—before she spoke the unredeemable.

He'd been playing "The Gospel Train," had decided on its importance and wanted to saturate the woods with its sounds. It was guesswork. He wouldn't even call it a theory, but it didn't matter. He stroked the banjo strings, eyes closed, reveling in the *bum-ditty bum-ditty*. Bliss.

A dear friend (the only friend he had in his regular life) had called him Craw-hammer, a combination of his name and "clawhammer," the style in which he played.

The world thought Amias had been dead for seventy years now.

The foxes listened to the music with interest. They'd grown to accept him and the thing that used to be his sister and no longer ran away at their smell. Perhaps they were Amias's friends in *this* life.

Between the choruses, the Beast turned and asked him to snap one of the fox's necks, said something deep inside it was yearning for the last gasps of life. It was unnatural, as was he, but Amias didn't consider that. Then all he thought was *It is no longer my sister, it is a monster.*

He lost it.

"How dare you?" he asked, fingers swinging in the wind, the banjo forgotten.

Amias stormed the Beast with his anger, spewing the loathing he felt for himself at it. He knew the hunger in its eyes when the Beast looked at stags or foxes, knew this was just the beginning. The thing's appetite had grown, as had his apathy.

"Amias," it wept between words, "I can't help who I've become. I yearn to rip them apart, to bring about the smell of their bodies rotting away into nothing, to watch the maggots reclaim their materials while I continue to burn on the inside. It keeps me happy between sacrifices. A little treat."

Speaking of the sacrifices, there would soon be a new round of them. His control over the Beast was slipping daily. He required help—someone who understood the magic used to cover Bricksbury in the blood of Jesus. Someone whose family was from the area, so they'd have as strong a connection to the land and people as Amias. It would take time and prayer, but Amias would find them.

In the meantime, he knew that he could not refuse the Beast's command. With a lump in his throat and tears in his eyes, he gently set down the banjo and grabbed the nearest curious fox, crying out in despair as he felt its delicate neck bones break between his hands. The Beast watched through glowing eyes, licking its ink-smeared lips as the blood ran from the animal's snout.

He needed to find the perfect helper as soon as he could. He wasn't sure how much longer he could take this.

Chapter Eighteen

Most weekend mornings, Zora spent a half hour cuddling and "who's a good boy-ing" with Henry Louis. This morning, she then spent another half hour reviewing the notes she'd taken during Conjure Night. It was weeks ago now, and the next Conjure Night approached. Lamont would go with her this time, partially because of his interest in conjure and partially because of his interest in Immanuel.

Zora licked her lips at the memory of Khadijah in the woods after she'd run after Zora. They'd shared a tiny touch—too brief. Zora had been hoping for a run-in, leaving their apartments, but no matter how long she lingered with her keys, one never materialized. It was time for Zora to put herself out there more in the dating department. There was "it's been a while," and there was "this vibrator can only do so much." Still, she was glad Lamont would be with her for the next Conjure Night.

Zora was doubly glad for an excuse to get off campus. Jonesborough African American Historical Society was the other ask of Dr. Grant, after Esther's diary. And since the diary was more promising than she could have imagined, Zora was happy for the trip into town. She kissed Henry Louis's head and marched toward the door, glancing at the amulet pouches hanging in the room's four corners, assuring herself they were working before leaving.

Outside, Zora spotted Khadijah immediately—she donned a

snug, ash-gray sundress and a studded cowboy hat one shade darker, mirroring the storm clouds looming overhead. With her vibrant red banjo case carelessly slung over her shoulder, she crouched down, her back facing Zora. Khadijah was completely focused on Dr. Ncuti, her tabby cat, who twirled gracefully on the laminate flooring like a fluffy gray acrobat. He welcomed her home with shrill *meows*. At the sight of Khadijah, Zora froze. Her mind returned to the Cornbread Lounge, not just where Khadijah had been, but where Zora had been vulnerable with Lamont about her past with Jasmine and not getting into Bricksbury for undergrad. She'd been brave. And now it was time to be brave again.

When Khadijah began closing her door, her widening eyes swept up to Zora's. They shared a smile across the courtyard, and Khadijah abandoned Dr. Ncuti. Zora's heart slowed further.

"Hey..." The word disappeared from her into the muggy air as she approached Zora.

Khadijah's bangles chimed and clinked with each step she took, a sharp symphony that swept away the surrounding energy. Zora's mind cleared of anything but Khadijah's violet lipstick and how her rich brown eyes made everything unnecessary disappear. *Has she thought of me, too?*

"Hey." Zora cleared her throat. "I'm on my way to the Conjure Shoppe." *Am I?* "After my appointment at the Historical Society, I mean."

"Oh?" Khadijah strolled over. "I'm working later today."

Zora spoke without thinking. "Well, thank fuck for that."

Khadijah reached up and tucked a few micros behind her ear, pausing to touch the silver hoops dangling near her shoulder. Her smile was shy at first, but when Zora refused to look away, allowing the truth of her statement to lay between them, Khadijah's full lips spread into something stunning Zora wanted to quantify but couldn't.

"I gotta go, but do you wanna go to homecoming together?" Zora asked quickly, the words tumbling out close together.

Khadijah's eyes widened in time with her smile. "Yeah. I mean, yes. I do."

They exchanged numbers and social media handles, and then Zora stepped away.

"My shift starts at two," Khadijah said, reaching up to place a firm kiss on Zora's cheek.

Zora felt like it was only meant to be a quick peck, but the energy between them as they stood so close together shocked them both into still, charged silence. After a moment of electricity, Zora slid her hand up Khadijah's back and pulled her close, their mouths meeting in a perfect, pillowy kiss. Zora blissfully let the world slip away, intoxicated by how good Khadijah felt, their tongues pressing against each other with equal, thrilling pressure. Just when Zora thought she might gladly miss her appointment at the Historical Society, Khadijah pulled back, dark eyes twinkling with silent but wicked promises of what—and, God willing, *who*—would come later.

"See you later," Khadijah said with a smile, her eyes closer to Zora's than they'd ever been. They weren't just a rich brown, but there were swirls of bright copper, and several darker, ruddier dots at random. "I look forward to homecoming."

Zora returned Khadijah's smile and nodded, then ducked out of the way of the banjo case when Khadijah suddenly twirled around and walked away. The sound of her bangles clanging echoed with a sharp sense of finality. It was as if they closed the hazy, horny loop they wrought.

Zora stood stunned at the sheer intimacy of what had just occurred. She swallowed, eyes staring at the place where Dr. Ncuti had twirled on the floor. After a minute, she remembered why she'd left her room in the first place: Dr. Grant and the Historical Society. A quick glance at her watch told her if she planned it well, she could swing by Mallory's early enough in the afternoon to see Khadijah, hopefully before other students woke up and craved a productivity tincture or something more powerful.

Zora parked to the sound of an anthemic Tanner Adell track, then flicked off the car engine. Humidity had already soaked her shirt before she even opened the door. No pulling or rearranging made it more comfortable, so she grimaced until the cool brick interior of the eighteenth-century buildings of downtown Jonesborough made her forget her discomfort.

The Historical Society was at ground level, two blocks from the Conjure Shoppe. Across the street was the Washington County Courthouse, a building punctuated with four dramatic Greek-inspired columns. Brick steps seamlessly gave way to brick pavers. The American and all-red Tennessee flags hung still in the dense air. Planted in the courthouse underbrush, the Confederate flags stood out, vulgar and deluded even from across the street. Each flag stood resolute among the bright yellow evening primrose ground cover. Zora begged herself to look away, to spare herself unnecessary pain. They weren't planted in any official capacity. It was probably done by some incel dude-bro one step away from a dip-induced coma. Still, Zora had to admit it hurt to see.

She turned away from the hate and toward Jonesborough Antiques & Artisans, a charming store with massive glass windows that stretched from floor to ceiling. The kind from which the phrase "window-shopping" was coined. Zora had never window-shopped personally, but she'd seen it in nineties movies like *B.A.P.S.* The antique store was an adequate buffer between actual evil and Zora's quest for information.

Jonesborough African American Historical Society's wooden circular sign was a light brown pine. When Zora stepped closer, she noticed a zigzag pattern carved into the edges. Art Deco or maybe something, anything more interesting. *Sigils?*

The metal plaque affixed to the brick building read:

JONESBOROUGH AFRICAN AMERICAN HISTORICAL SOCIETY ESTABLISHED 1872

THIS ORGANIZATION IS COMMITTED TO PRESERVING REGIONAL PRE-REVOLUTIONARY AFRICAN HISTORY AND BRINGING TO LIFE THREE CENTURIES OF VIBRANT HISTORICAL ACTIVITIES OF AFRICAN AMERICANS IN THE JONESBOROUGH AREA.

IT ALSO SEEKS TO IDENTIFY LOCAL AFRICAN AMERICAN ARTIFACTS, PICTURES, PHOTOS, AND OTHER OBJECTS OF VARYING DEGREES OF POWER CONNECTED WITH ANY AFRICAN TRADITIONAL RELIGION OR AFRICAN DIASPORIC RELIGION AND/ OR SPIRITUALITY WITHOUT EXCEPTION.

"Without exception," Zora said, wiping sweat from her forehead as she tried to determine if the words sounded more normal aloud. They didn't, not really.

The jingle of cast iron doorbells above the entrance echoed as Zora pushed open the front door, cascading across the semigloss emerald walls and ceiling. The doors and trim were contrasted in a darker green. *Bold for a historical society.* As she stepped out of the doorway, her ears perked up at the sound of a distinct *crunch* beneath her feet. Zora leaned in to inspect the crumpled remnants of painted gloss and long-ago chevron wallpaper. She stifled a sneeze, the musty air thick with dust swirling around her like a forgotten memory.

"Oh," she said, turning to the sunny cramped room. Oh. Much, much smaller than she'd thought. Had she thought? *My apartment is bigger than this.* It could barely accommodate two executive desks, a modern printer, and the row of weathered black metal filing cabinets lining one wall. Besides, there was no need to alert an employee, since Mallory sat behind a desk, eyes already on Zora.

Zora blinked rapidly, squinting at Mallory and trying to make sense of them being there.

"Oh…Mallory?"

The person behind the desk shook their head. "Ya've met Mallory? I'm Charlene, Mallory's cousin, an' I'm the director here. Zora, right? Dr. Grant called ahead."

Zora's mouth hung open as she gazed into eyes identical to Mallory's. Zora pressed her lips together. Suddenly, her heart was in her throat. A tingling sensation surged at the center of Zora's chest. She clenched her jaw, fighting the impulse to scratch herself as she licked her parched lips. Salty sweat mixed with the gritty taste of dust, a reminder of the sweltering heat outside that blew inside with her. Why would Mallory pretend to be someone else?

She supposed they *could* be cousins, but they looked far more like twins—the identical kind. Zora stammered something unintelligible when Charlene stood. They were the same shortish height and had the same furrowed bushy eyebrows. But the locs had been replaced (covered?) by a highlighted, toffee-colored lace front. As Charlene approached, Zora smelled a sharp mint scent mixed with something woodsy and citrusy: eucalyptus. It reminded her of Mallory's apothecary.

"Is this…a joke?" Zora asked, looking at a person who *had* to be Mallory.

"Is what a joke?" Charlene asked, a clipped tone overtaking their voice. "I don' take kindly to wasted time."

Zora swallowed. She had to get it together. Maybe it was the lack of sleep catching up to her at last, all that bottled-up paranoia that she'd been feeling since reading Esther's diary. She'd worry it was some sort of conjure-based trickery, but her mojo bag was cool to the touch, and the only thing this Charlene person seemed interested in was getting on with the conversation.

"I apologize," Zora began, falling back into a canvassing role where she could get a healthy distance from herself. "My name is Zora, and I'm an Appalachian studies graduate student at Bricksbury Mountain College. I'm researching for my thesis, which will center around the religious and spiritual cultures of Black Appalachians."

Charlene rested on their heels and listened, but Zora remembered when she'd explained the exact thing to Mallory that first morning in the apothecary, and then again in the clearing before Conjure Night. They'd been interested in Zora's research and, it seemed, her well-being. Zora maintained a gentle smile. Friendly, without performing.

"I'm hoping you'll have information about secret societies at Bricksbury, especially religious/spiritually based ones."

"Yes, I see why Dr. Grant sent ya here."

Zora purposely avoided looking at the stained ceiling, where darker patches signaled enduring moisture damage. Charlene led her back to their desk and waited for Zora to sit before following suit.

"I don't understand."

"Believe it or not, we don't get asked many questions 'bout Bricksbury, an' 'bout secret societies even less so. When I looked it up, there wasn't much in our files."

Charlene handed Zora a manila folder with photocopies of various texts and documents.

One began:

The Keepers of the Beast (c. 1877) is a secret society started by Bricksbury's founders, siblings Amias and Hosanna Crawfoot.

Despite the abolitionist leanings of the area, when the school opened, they were subject to a great deal of white violence. White townspeople weren't happy with the influx of free Black people to the area. Although there weren't many enslaved people in the region, there were enough to worry their owners about an uprising if they saw free people—or worse, got some education of their own. The racist assaults and threats didn't stop after the Civil War; in fact, they continued for over two decades afterward (see attached newspaper clippings, police reports, student protest flyers, etc.).

To protect Bricksbury and Jonesborough's Black population, Amias and Hosanna Crawfoot worked not only with God, but with His Hoodoo magic.

The Crawfoots. The cofounders of Bricksbury. Hoodoo magic. God's magic. The room blurred at the edges of Zora's vision; all she could hear was her hammering heart. Excitement tingled at her fingertips. Although Zora still couldn't see the complete picture, a puzzle piece clicked into place.

Charlene's sharp voice made Zora jump.

"Did ya have any other questions, sweetie pie? Dr. Grant wasn't sure what else ya might need?"

How much of this does Dr. Grant know? Zora clearly needed to schedule a meeting with her advisor.

"Oh...yeah, actually. Do you know any stories about...the woods? Specifically, the Woodlands outside Bricksbury."

Charlene chuckled, warmth bubbling up through their laughter. "Do I ever! Okay, this'll be quick."

Zora laughed along with Charlene as she stealthily began recording on her phone.

"All right. This was an old Jonesborough legend told by grandparents to their grandchil'ren when they turned 'bout eight or so. The ritual fell outta style in the early eighties recession an' it began in the mid to late 1800s. Can't narrow it down much further 'an that, I'm afraid."

Zora nodded, ready.

"It began at sundown when the grandparents took the child to the woods' edge, where they each stood with hands full of hyssop. There are many versions, but they generally focus on a mountain town where strange cries are comin' from the woods. What made it different from other stories was that not everyone could hear the cries. Only a handful could: the Ones Who Heard." They paused, their voice lingering on the last word.

Like Mallory, Charlene had a mesmerizing way of speaking, capturing Zora's attention with every subtle change in tone and pace. The legend's heaviness hung in the dusty air between them, swollen and aching as it demanded all the attention. Zora found herself leaning forward involuntarily, her body instinctively reaching for the intense emotion. She craved to analyze and understand it. Where did the Crawfoots land in Zora's revolving series of questions? Where did Esther?

While Zora frowned, Charlene observed her with unsettling focus. Their eyes followed Zora's every flicker of movement as if studying her, trying to decipher her thoughts. Zora shifted, wincing as the rusting metal in her seat screeched in the silence.

"Eventually, the Ones Who Heard went to the woods," Charlene said.

Don't go into the woods, Esther.

"They said they needed to sacrifice themselves to the Beast."

Sacrifice. Zora thought of Eliza Deadbody and the vision she had in the library.

Zora licked her lips, certain she was dancing with fire. Still, she was unable to stop herself. "Do you know what 'the Beast' could be referring to?"

Charlene's eyes narrowed at Zora's question, but their lips

widened into a smile. Zora felt a shiver across her shoulder blades at the contradictory sight. *In fact*, Zora thought, *Charlene's entire presence is contradictory.*

"There are many legends about the Beast," Charlene said, straightening their back.

Zora sat up in her seat, ready to sprint out the door. She was highly aware that her racing heart must be audible by now, especially with how closely Charlene was monitoring her.

"That wasn't really my question." Zora laughed faintly.

Charlene didn't laugh.

"The Beast was a gift from God."

Zora looked back down at the ripped beige newspaper article.

To protect Bricksbury and Jonesborough's Black population, Amias and Hosanna Crawfoot worked not only with God but with His Hoodoo magic.

She frowned again, flipping the article over in case something was useful on the underside. Was Charlene simply relaying what the newspaper said, or was this personal? Zora thought to ease into that line of questioning. She didn't want Charlene to become... what, guarded? They were already guarded, but Zora had to start somewhere.

Zora's neck *cracked* as she turned toward a sudden, light scratching sound to her left. But there was nothing odd about the dark green walls, other than it being a strange color choice in an already dark space, as if it were chosen to make the room feel *more* cramped.

"Do you know if the Crawfoots practiced Hoodoo themselves? The article says the Keepers of the Beast began in 1877, but if Bricksbury opened in the 1820s, wouldn't the Crawfoots have been elderly by then? Was Hosanna still alive at that time?"

Charlene smiled, which should have been comforting or encouraging. It should have indicated that Zora was on the right path: A Good Thing. Instead, when Charlene smiled at Zora, her tiger's-eye necklace suddenly burned hot against her skin, and Zora yelped in surprise. *Get the hell out of here, now!* Zora stood suddenly, and Charlene's smile didn't move.

"I'm sorry, I have to go." Zora indicated the stacks of papers Charlene had given her. "Can I keep these?"

"Of course," Charlene said calmly. "Let me know if ya have any other questions."

Any other questions? There were so, so many of them, but just now, Zora thought she may have found a fragment of an answer. She needed to look into the Crawfoots.

Chapter Nineteen

A train roared in the distance as Zora opened the door to Jonesborough Conjure Shoppe. The rumbling wheels grew closer, and the rhythmic chugging tugged at something inside her. This was serious business. The fierce burn of her tiger's-eye necklace signified danger was near. She touched the now-cool spot on her skin, remembering how it'd burned before. It meant the spirits had blown past all the relatively passive signs like repeating numbers or instinctual feelings, and also through the more straightforward signs, like dead animals in your path or a plague on your land. But was Zora stepping into a past of evil or an evil with a long past?

Three people hung an *Old-Fashioned Hootenanny and Tarot Readings* flyer at the top of the stairs.

"Hey," Zora said. She shouldn't be surprised to see Shawna, Immanuel, and Khadijah on the landing—after all, they worked there. And she'd known she'd see Khadijah after their encounter in the courtyard earlier, but that was before the bizarre meeting with Charlene at the Historical Society. Zora felt a frown begin on her face as she remembered the way Charlene's eyes traced Zora's movements. Why had they been...inspecting? Investigating? Observing her reaction to the Keepers, and the Beast being a "gift from God"? It had been Zora who arrived with boundless curiosity, but Charlene's strange resemblance to Mallory had thrown Zora off from the beginning of their meeting.

"Hey," Immanuel called out, playfully nudging his hip into Khadijah's side.

Khadijah turned to give Immanuel a fierce glare, her eyes narrowing as they locked on to his mischievous grin. Instead of backing down, however, Immanuel's smile only widened, as if he thrived on her fiery reaction. Meanwhile, Shawna stood back, giggling at the two of them. Her curly blond bangs framed her face, sultry and accentuated by lips painted a vibrant raspberry red.

While Zora was considering Charlene's intentions, part of her found Shawna, Immanuel, and Khadijah's playful friendship enviable. Immanuel had traded his Nina Simone shirt for one featuring Eddie Murphy from his "Party All the Time" music video while Khadijah wore the same snug gray dress as earlier. Zora wanted badly to focus on Immanuel, or Khadijah, or Khadijah in that fucking dress, but her mind kept returning to Charlene's keen eyes.

Zora cleared her throat. *Be present. You like this woman. She seems to like you. Don't fuckin' blow it now in front of her friends.*

"Are you okay?" Khadijah stepped forward, a concerned look on her face. Zora realized that she must not have been able to shake off all the weirdness from what happened at the Historical Society. Despite it, she couldn't help but feel warmed that Khadijah was able to tell something was wrong at all.

"What? Yes, I'm fine. I'm good. Still coming down from my meeting, that's all." She hoped she sounded convincing.

"Oh, right," Khadijah said. "How did it go?"

"It was…" Zora had a thought. "Do y'all know Charlene? The society's director?"

Immanuel let out a frustrated groan. Meanwhile, Shawna and Khadijah burst into laughter.

"Oh yeah, we know them." Immanuel raked a hand through his curly afro. "How much you wanna know?"

Now it was Khadijah's turn to groan, the leftover smile from her laugh fading quick. "Don't start."

"Let it go, Manny," Shawna agreed, her voice rising.

"I'm not starting it! *They're* the one who started it! I know how to do my job—just because they like their ritual baths made with grapefruit and rosemary, it doesn't make that way the *correct* way. It's just *their* way."

"Are you done?" Shawna asked. "I doubt Zora cares how Charlene likes their ritual baths."

"Hardly." Immanuel sighed but took out his phone, turning away from Khadijah and Zora to give them some privacy. Shawna followed suit and the two of them tittered with each other.

"Sorry about that." Khadijah laughed faintly. "Charlene has always annoyed Immanuel to no end. Are you really okay, though? You look...I don't know, worried."

Zora swallowed. *Don't fuck this up.* "Nah, it just takes me a minute to get out of my head while I'm working. Is it like that for you when you're playing?" She hoped a change in conversation would go better for them both.

Khadijah tilted her head, her eyes sparkling with a hint of excitement as she absorbed Zora's words. "You know what? You're right! I get so lost in the music, in the rhythm of it all. It's like the world fades away, and I just want to drown in that feeling forever, ya know?"

Zora chuckled, a warm smile spreading across her face. "Absolutely! There's something magical about those moments, right?"

Khadijah nodded enthusiastically, and Zora realized this was the first time she had seen her without a cowboy hat. Her long black micros swung freely in the air as she spoke with her hands, causing the bracelets on her wrists to jangle even more. "It's pure bliss! Just me, the music, and nothing else."

Zora leaned closer, her curiosity piqued. "What's your favorite song to lose yourself in?"

"I don't think anyone has ever asked me that." Khadijah fell silent again, considering Zora's words.

Zora smiled faintly but remained silent, wanting Khadijah to answer without distraction. God, it was hard not to kiss her and continue what they'd started in the courtyard.

"When playing the banjo, honestly, I fall back on what I played in church as a kid," Khadijah said. "So, usually old hymns and spirituals. They'll always be comfort songs for me. And when I'm playing the piano?" She smiled, her mind inside a faraway memory. "It's anything by Herbie Hancock, but especially when I'm playing while listening to *Head Hunters*, which I believe is his best album because of what it did for jazz fusion."

Zora had more questions, like what the emotional difference was between playing the banjo and playing the piano, but she was cut off from asking by Immanuel's booming voice.

"Okay, important question," he began as if they'd been mid-conversation. "Who is your favorite *Drag Race* winner?"

Zora opened her mouth to answer but first registered Immanuel's raised eyebrows above narrowed eyelids. There were correct and incorrect answers here.

She opted for honesty. "Bob the Drag Queen."

Immanuel's face smoothed as Zora apparently passed some kinda queer media test with unspoken rules and consequences.

"Ooh, have you read their latest book?" Shawna looked up from her phone with a frown, her mind halfway still inside Instagram.

"Let's not get off track here. I'm having a *Drag Race* watch party the weekend after homecoming," Immanuel said, stepping forward. "You've gotta come."

"Yeah, bring a friend," Shawna said with a knowing smile.

Ah, they've definitely discussed me and Khadijah.

Zora turned to Khadijah. "Are you going?"

"She'll be there," Shawna said easily as Zora descended the stairs.

"And so will you, right?"

Zora laughed as Khadijah glared at her friends once again. "See y'all down there."

She waited a beat before exhaling and climbing downward. Zora followed. Invisible wisps of incense nudged Zora's shoulders down as she descended. Zora inhaled the same earthy lemongrass incense as the others in the basement apothecary. Some customers walked around plucking candles and dark brown oil bottles off the marked tables. A larger, louder group stood along the back of the herb wall, pointing and taking pictures with their phones. The gentle plucking of an acoustic guitar was barely audible over the lively chatter of the crowd. Amid the bustling excitement, Mallory moved gracefully from one group to another. Their denim overalls had been replaced with a stunning beaded coral maxi dress that trailed behind them with every step. Pink pearl earrings dangled from each ear and were neatly mirrored in the pearl bracelets on each wrist.

Zora stood at the bottom of the steps and watched as Mallory introduced themself to a group of young students. There was no way Charlene could've gotten here before her, was there?

"Here ya go," Mallory said, all business.

Baby-blue eyeshadow adorned their eyelids and, oddly, the apples of their cheeks. Surprisingly, it worked, showcasing impressive makeup skills. Mallory pointed to the heart-shaped jar resting in their open palm, and tried to hand it to a lanky figure, even taller than Zora. His long, pointed beard tapered into his fleur-de-lis cardigan. He hesitated briefly before finally reaching for the glass.

"This is exactly what I was looking for. How did you know?" he asked, lifting the honey jar to accentuate his words.

Mallory's head tipped back as they laughed good-naturedly. "Oh, honey, I've been doin' this for a long while."

"Well... thank you," the man said, ducking his head with a smile.

"Yes, thank you," one of his friends said.

"Follow the instructions," Mallory said, holding the man's gaze. "This ain't a one-time fix. This spell only works as part of a larger love altar. D'ya hear me?"

"Yes, Mx. Holston." He nodded.

Mallory scoffed so loudly the other groups in the apothecary glanced over. "Please, just Mallory. Nothin' as formal as all that."

The man nodded again, and then he and his friends pivoted to the altar cloths. Zora contemplated an organic opening in conversation.

"I *know* you ain't here keepin' an eye on me, child." Mallory turned around, a sly smile playing on their glossed lips revealing that they'd known Zora was there the whole time.

"No." Zora shook her head. She breathed in the lemongrass incense and allowed it to rest her shoulders. "Of course not."

"Good," Mallory said. "'Cause I don't take kindly to bein' watched."

Zora's reply was on her tongue, but she suddenly remembered the last time she'd seen Mallory when she felt like *she* was being watched in the woods after Conjure Night. She'd lost time staring into the woods. A presence had been in the trees, eyes zeroed on her. She knew it.

"Zora?" Mallory placed a hand on her shoulder.

"Sorry." Zora smiled thinly. "Can we talk privately for a moment?"

With a look of intrigue, Mallory arched an eyebrow as she led them to a secluded corner. It was a step back in time. The antique cash register crowded the counter, flanked by twinkling pillar candles and a granite mortar and pestle. A fluffy scarf draped on a wooden rocking chair brought Zora back to a forgotten childhood memory at her grandparents' house. *How can alpaca fur be so soft?* Zora yearned for a chance to unwind in the snug corner and leave behind the pressures of campus.

"I'm looking for information about the Keepers?" Zora whispered as soon as they were out of earshot of the others. "I just found out a little about them from your cousin, Charlene, but I thought that maybe you'd—"

She stopped talking when Mallory's broad jawline clenched.

Their eyes narrowed, and their nostrils flared. Zora swallowed so loudly that she was confident the others across the room could hear. She didn't know why Mallory would be pissed off by the question, but regardless of the answer, Zora knew that she didn't want to piss Mallory off. The last thing you should do is piss off a powerful practitioner, and if the shop's scent wisps were any indication, Mallory was incredibly powerful. The wisps suddenly pressed hard on Zora's shoulders, and when that didn't work, they moved up to her neck and down her back.

"Return to this shop when you need something we provide."

Their tone was so chilly that Zora shivered. She was suddenly struck by all the odd things that had been happening lately. Had they been the work of a practitioner, it would have had to be someone powerful. Was it possible Mallory was behind it in some way?

"I didn't mean to offend you." Zora laughed faintly, but she knew that no matter her intentions, the smile didn't reach her eyes. Knowing that this was likely the last time she'd be in the position to question Mallory, she pivoted from the Keepers to ask another burning question. "How about the Crawfoots? Amias and Hosanna Crawfoot, specifically. I'd be incredibly grateful for any information you could give me."

Mallory's chest expanded as their shoulders pulled back, making them look wider and more pissed off. It didn't matter that they were shorter than Zora, because the look they gave her was absolute: Mallory didn't fuck around. *Neither do I,* Zora reminded herself.

"Are you Charlene?" she blurted the question before she could stop herself. "Have you been watching me?"

Mallory's face didn't move. "Return to this shop when you need something we provide."

Zora stood frozen, her eyes wide as she struggled to find the right words. Mallory's tightly pressed lips and rigid stance sent a clear message. With a heavy heart, she silently turned away and left.

Chapter Twenty

Zora navigated through Jonesborough's rugged backstreets, back toward Bricksbury, her Subaru Outback gently humming over the hilly terrain. Somewhere in the recesses of her mind, she was grateful she'd chosen a used all-wheel-drive car that could hold its own against the upcoming winter. As she drove, she extended her hand out the window. A finger twirled absentmindedly as she savored the sensation of the hot breeze against her skin. The wind had gained momentum, sending ripples through the saplings and causing the brush to sway in a mesmerizing dance. She wished she had more time for a scenic drive but knew she needed to return to campus immediately. Zora's outing had been equal parts helpful and disturbing, with a brief brightness when she remembered Khadijah's smile.

It was written down in sparse words across her notes, but now it needed to be actualized. "Charlene" had helped, but Mallory hadn't been accommodating. They were definitely hiding *something*, right? Strange, Zora would have thought her brief prior relationship with Mallory would have tipped the scales in their direction, but it was Charlene who pointed Zora in the direction of the Crawfoots. The siblings had cofounded Bricksbury, but what else had they been up to, and for how long? Was their relationship less complicated than her and Jasmine's, or was sibling drama one of those things that surpassed time?

Zora still found it hard to believe elderly siblings in the 1870s were busy creating and maintaining divinely blessed groups while also working at the school. It wasn't impossible, just unlikely. There had to be more context here, nuances, and players that Zora hadn't found yet.

She thought again of Esther Fisherman. Esther would have been at the school in the 1870s, but she would have been young. Did Esther know Amias or Hosanna? Were they contemporaries?

Zora glanced up from her internal musings to find she'd driven to a residential neighborhood to the campus's north. The front doors were inches from the sidewalk, with gaping cracks in the wood like mouths screaming open. The 1820s-era homes, whether they were wooden farmhouses with oversized country porches or shockingly square and golden brick, were more than just architectural marvels. Transported, Zora drooled at the characteristic gabled roofs and large, symmetrical windows. She wished she had time to stop and consider the decorative eaves and intricate cornice work. It was such delicate artwork. These houses were designed primarily for convenience and secondarily for beauty, but they also entombed a treasure trove of untold stories. What secrets were held inside? What was hidden above the high ceilings in the parlor and inside the ornate mantels of one of the seven fireplaces? History was there. People unknowingly walked among ghosts all day.

Bricksbury Mountain College Road was over a mile long and lined with dense thickets of pine trees. They were the only pine trees on campus, having been the favorite of a past university president's wife. Over seventy years later, they welcomed students with fat pine cones and narrow needles. The needles' lengths ranged from a few inches to more than a foot, prompting many students to hike up from their dorms and have a literal dick-measuring contest with the trees at the end of every school year. It was a tradition ignored and, therefore, encouraged by every administration.

Homecoming was almost a week away, and still the drive back to school was filled with intermittent stops and starts as visiting vehicles navigated the roads with as much direction as Zora had exhibited moments before. She inhaled sharply as she pulled into her designated parking spot, bracing herself for the chaotic symphony of sounds before opening her door.

As expected, more people than usual idled on the uneven pavers. Each corner was congested with excited, cackling people, selfies, and good-smelling cocoa butter lotion. Zora ground her teeth as she squeezed between groups of alumna aunties performing rival step shows. Her eyes scanned the area, searching for a place of peace to stop, but there was no reprieve.

She recoiled as she passed a group of theater majors doing an impromptu show on the lawn. The earlier show, "Sacrifice," still danced in her mind, as did the vision that had her seeing a sacrifice up close and personal. Who had those people been? Keepers of the Beast?

Zora shook her head and forcefully swallowed as bile crept up her throat. Her anxieties were far too specific for her liking. She put on her headphones; Zora needed to cut the fog of sound. The music enveloped her as she pressed play on her favorite Doechii song. She turned up the volume and let the catchy beat carry her away, closing her eyes and surrendering to the melody. The raspy delivery was caught somewhere between punk and hip-hop, allowing her to flow effortlessly from one genre to the next. Feeding her desire to live in the in-between. She didn't want this or that. She wanted it all.

The journey to the "Neighborhood" felt interminably long, with the oppressive mugginess of late September hanging in the air. Each step required more energy than the last. Zora kept wiping her forehead and upper lip, but still, salty sweat crept into her mouth. The bitter taste brought her back to Conjure Night, where the sensation of being watched made her sweat through her favorite dress shirt.

Unfortunately, Zora wasn't under the stars in a moderately quiet woodland clearing. She shuddered every time someone's feverish shoulder pressed into her. Although she'd had plans, Zora suddenly changed her mind as she stood in the Esther Fisherman Quad. She checked her watch to confirm Dr. Grant's office hours were still in effect. Now was the ideal time for a check-in with him, while meeting Charlene and Mallory was still fresh on her mind.

Zora had to make a quick detour to Bricksbury's general store. Remembering Dr. Grant's sweet tooth, she thought that bringing him a treat would help her plan. Inside the store, she found the usual convenience items, but it was the bright bakery and the chocolate pastry that caught her eye. *Perfect.*

———

"Zora Robinson." Dr. Grant smiled as he looked up. "It's so nice to see you."

Zora grinned as she zipped up her jacket, feeling the chill of Dr. Grant's room. She handed him the chocolate pastry she had picked up at the general store and settled into the deeply cushioned armchair, accepting its comfort.

"A chocolate hazelnut puff pastry?" Every word Dr. Grant spoke was louder than the last.

Zora stifled a laugh. *Success.*

"I know our check-in is scheduled for a couple of days from now," Zora began speaking as Dr. Grant started eating, "but I was close by and figured, what the hell?" She ensured her laugh was soft and her eyes were the picture of spontaneity. Dr. Grant didn't need to know that she'd considered coming by every day for the past week, but she'd wanted to wait until she'd gone to the Historical Society so the two would have more to discuss.

"I just got back from seeing Charlene at the Historical Society, and our conversation is fresh on my mind," Zora said. She didn't pause to allow Dr. Grant to speak as he only gave her half his attention anyway; the other half was fervently on his pastry. "You sent me there to talk about older Bricksbury societies? Well, they told me about the Keepers of the Beast, which could have been started by Hosanna and Amias Crawfoot—the founders."

Dr. Grant savored the last crumbs of his pastry. For a frustrating moment, Zora thought he was completely oblivious to her presence until he finally broke the silence.

"And how will the Keepers of the Beast be helpful to your thesis?" Dr. Grant took a long swig from his coffee mug after speaking.

Zora took out the notes from her phone, the additional summaries she'd written in a notebook, and Esther's diary from her backpack. Dr. Grant nodded, seemingly impressed. Oh, he didn't think she came prepared? Zora stayed ready.

"I actually wanted to ask about the Crawfoots first," Zora said. She'd started with the Keepers of the Beast to Mallory, so perhaps starting at the Crawfoots was a smarter plan of action. Or it could blow up in her face. Either was possible. The Crawfoots were revered. Their legacy wasn't something to play with or question when it came to Bricksbury. She'd have to be careful.

"Are you familiar with the siblings or the history of their family?" She started out light.

Dr. Grant shook his head. "The only thing I remember learning about the Crawfoots that interested me was Amias's banjo playing. He'd made a bit of a name for himself in the area. You might find luck in the school's newspaper archives."

"Ooh, thank you," Zora said. She wrote down his suggestion as if googling him hadn't been her plan as soon as she walked through her door. It didn't matter; Dr. Grant needed to think he'd gifted her with invaluable information.

"Okay, next question. After cross-referencing my visit to the Historical Society with Esther Fisherman's diary, my theory is that

Amias and Hosanna Crawfoot started the Keepers at the school with some sort of religious ceremony. Now, assuming they were Protestants, and taking into account the open practicing of Hoodoo on campus—"

Dr. Grant frowned. "Open practice?"

"I would classify Conjure Night as openly practicing Hoodoo," Zora said. "And I believe its long-standing meetings only further prove my point. It's a part of the culture here."

"Okay..." Dr. Grant said.

Get to the point. "I'm still researching, but I've read that the Crawfoots practiced Hoodoo and that they used it to protect Bricksbury. Then I read that the Keepers of the Beast began in the 1870s, which would have been at the same time Esther Fisherman was a student. In her diary, Esther *also* talks about feeling unsafe on campus, and wishing she could protect people, like her apprentice, before they both disappeared. The thing is, Esther's diary is from the late 1920s, well after Amias and Hosanna would've died. So, I'm still trying to find the connection between the jumps in time. But there's something there, I know it."

Zora pointed to Esther's corresponding entry. "'Hosanna's Crypt' here may reference the old church on the school's original grounds. Given that the Keepers began with God and"—she pointed to a newspaper clipping—"'Hoodoo magic,' I believe this seamlessly ties in with my work. I have enough to dig through here to make my thesis, *The Spiritual History of Affrilachia*, into *Eighteenth-Century Affrilachian Secret Societies*. What do you think?"

Dr. Grant gazed at Zora with a fondness that filled the lines of his face, causing his wrinkles to soften and Zora to smile.

"I'm proud of you, Zora. This was well thought out and researched, even in its beginning stages."

Zora beamed. She was closing in on the final pieces that would form both the resolution of mysteries long since passed and a perfect thesis. If she could pull this off, she'd be lauded for unveiling the school's darkest secrets, kicking off a ton of further opportunities for discussion and study. She just had to hang in there, refuse to let outside forces throw her off the right path. Justice was coming for those who never got it, Zora promised herself. Even if someone out there wanted the truth to stay hidden.

"Thanks, Dr. Grant," she said coolly, turning to leave. "I'll be back to report my full findings soon enough."

Amias Crawfoot
September 1, 1977
Jonesborough, Tennessee
Bricksbury Mountain College—Jonesboro
African Baptist Church

A hundred years after Hosanna's death and fifty after Esther Fisherman's, God's bargain still demanded five additional sacrifices. Despite being on the lookout for decades, Amias hadn't found someone he deemed spiritually strong enough to help him keep the Beast calm and in God's light in the thirty years since deciding it was necessary. The greatest problem was that there were fewer religious students with each passing semester. Agnosticism, willful indifference, and excessive drug use reigned, though it was predominantly the spiritually anemic walking the halls. Amias would know; he'd perfected the ability to move around Bricksbury undetected.

Every building had false walls and hidden attics. There were abandoned basements full of vintage furniture and art from Esther's time and a few older ones from Amias's natural life. They should be regularly cleaned and displayed with awe from the students, but instead, they were neglected. Various insects had long hollowed the carved wood. The canvas oil paintings, at least one by Robert S. Duncanson, were in poor condition, with long, frayed rips caused by being repeatedly jostled to the back of the storage area. They'd been beautiful once. The vibrant colors of the artwork were dulled by water damage, making it difficult to discern each piece's original details and beauty. That didn't matter, really, because everything sat under heavy layers of mold spores and dust.

Amias maneuvered around the crowds of antique pieces without thought. He'd done it for decades, listening to conversations above him with middling interest. He was more interested in the students being safe than hearing their thoughts on "*Night Driver* versus *Sea Wolf*" and anything regarding Billy Dee Williams. Still, he was glad they could emotionally rest. There were students in previous generations who spent their entire first semester with knives under their pillows lest the notorious slave catchers storm Jonesborough as they'd done back home. They were supernaturally in tune with their surroundings. They used God and His magic to warn them of danger, from weather to nearby policemen. The students and the magic were just more powerful back then.

Perhaps, Amias mused, *their reliance on magic strengthened their bond with God. Present-day students should invest in a stronger relationship with Him.* These students had valid concerns, but they were lessened compared to those of their elder alums. Thus, their awareness of their surroundings became less important. Their certainty that no harm could come to them on campus made them lazy, never considering checking their surroundings, rarely closing their curtains or locking their doors. It was both heartwarming and terrifying how little they worried. And their shameless vulnerabilities drove Amias's determination to protect them even more. Jim Crow laws had been abolished, but all it did was force white people to mold their hatred and segregation into more convoluted shapes.

To the current students, it had been fifty years since five mysterious campus disappearances. The deaths had become a hushed ghost story with missing details and new, more salacious ones added depending upon the storyteller. Amias's beloved Esther had become a half-remembered icon. They'd named the quad after her, but few on campus remembered, only persistent local historians. Many people who'd been around during her time had died. Amias tried not to think about everyone he'd known during his natural life. They were dead. All of them. Many of their bloodlines had ended, but some of their descendants still worked at Bricksbury as third- and fourth-generation professors.

Amias had promised not to mark one of *those* professors to be sacrificed by the Beast. It was a frail morality but one he intended on clutching forevermore. Instead, he'd choose people who were newer to the school, who he didn't have any connection to. After Esther, he couldn't fathom falling in love with another sacrifice. It had to be a stranger, but still one he wished wouldn't die. Amias only hoped God accepted this balance.

The first person he marked to be sacrificed for the current cycle was a botany student named Charlene. They called themself a conjurer and even started a Conjurer Club on campus for others wanting to gather to discuss ancestor veneration and magic as spirit work. Amias hid behind walls in Crawfoot Hall during their meetings, fascinated by how Charlene merged God and magic. It was perfectly balanced. They were educating others while being a Bricksbury student. Like Esther, Charlene was the personification of Amias's dreams for an all-Black school. They were the perfect sacrifice. He didn't think much more of it at first.

But when it came time for the deed to be done, Charlene did something Amias never could have expected. Instead of willingly allowing themself to be taken by the Beast—something they definitely had the understanding and dedication to be capable of—Charlene asked Amias to spare them.

"I can help," they said, and that was when Amias understood that God had sent Charlene directly to him for an entirely different reason than he originally thought. *Of course.* He'd mistaken the bright-eyed botany student for the perfect sacrifice, when in reality, they were who he'd been searching for over the last thirty years.

Amias accepted their offer with hardly a second thought, and just like that, Charlene became a Keeper of the Beast, one like there had never been before. As a sign of devotion to their cause, Charlene marked their body. He watched them grit their teeth while the tattoo needle emblazoned the image of a honeybee on their rib cage; God would gift Charlene immortality, too, enabling them to help keep the Beast at bay for as long as He deemed necessary.

There was only one thing left to do. After the tattoo was bandaged up and they were on their way, Amias told Charlene what their first order of business would be.

There were still sacrifices to be identified and carried out. And now, Amias realized with a selfish surge of happiness, he wouldn't have to do it alone.

Chapter Twenty-One

On the morning of homecoming, Zora's walk with Henry Louis consisted of searching for the closest unoccupied patch of grass. It was more challenging than it should have been because every available square inch was full of bustling alumni. By the time they returned, Zora had cursed out two separate groups of tailgaters who'd run into her. One group of six stood in a circle around a sizzling grill, each absorbed in their phones, while another group teetered in precariously high heels as they danced, indulging in the wine spritzers.

Afterward, Zora showered and changed into clothes—an outfit that said she was open-minded...but aware. College-aged...but grad. Horny...but tasteful. She felt the balance in khaki shorts and a plain white tee, perhaps a bit too bright. She picked up a crimson Bricksbury-branded snapback, but considered the heat and thought better of it. Instead, she slid on a crimson, gold, and silver bracelet. It wasn't much, but Zora wasn't one for uniforms of any kind. As she gelled down her baby hair, she couldn't help but laugh at herself in the mirror. She looked exactly like a twentysomething masc from Knoxville would look.

Her smile faded as she thought of Jasmine. Would she be there with Ngozi? Zora's sister was almost done with her PhD, but Jasmine had gone to Bricksbury for her undergrad, grad, and doctorate. The school's crest was tattooed on the small of her back like the most embarrassing collegiate tramp stamp in existence. It was funny till Zora thought about it too long. It was after Jasmine came to Bricksbury that everything fell apart. She became less and less connected to Zora and more and more attached to this place. Sometimes, it was like Jasmine had sold her soul.

Zora jumped when a knock sounded on her door. Despite nothing out of the ordinary happening since the night she went to the Cornbread Lounge with Lamont, her eyes immediately went to the amulets in the corner, but the cowrie shells weren't rattling. The pouches were immobile, hanging happily in the air, protecting Zora from, apparently, *not* Khadijah. The ChapStick in her hand smeared sharply to the right, and she took her index finger and smudged it away. She glanced down at her phone to find Khadijah was two minutes early, which was absolutely unreasonable.

"This is absolutely unreasonable," Zora said as she opened the door to Khadijah's lovely, albeit confused face. The courtyard pulsed with laughter and shimmering homecoming attire, yet Zora remained fixated on Khadijah's every move.

Zora's date wore a crimson halter bodysuit paired with pale, high-waisted denim jeans. Her cowboy hat was Bricksbury colors, but instead of the usual crimson, it was matte gold with crimson thread lining the letters. It was a special and expensive edition. *How expensive, I wonder.* Zora's frown deepened as she realized how little she knew about Khadijah.

"What?" Khadijah boldly searched Zora's eyes for answers. "We agreed to meet at your place."

"No, I mean, you're two minutes early. That's waaayyyy too early to think I'd be ready."

Khadijah's laugh bounced around Zora's doorstep with more life than she'd encountered in days. She didn't know what to do with ringing joy, so she stood and absorbed it. Zora hadn't known how lonely she'd been till coming to Bricksbury. How starved for the experience of just existing with someone else. She'd gotten so used to the emptiness that she'd convinced herself that was all she wanted. All she needed. Khadijah's arresting energy was determined to prove her wrong, as did Lamont. Proved as Zora laughed at a text from him.

LAMONT: Where r u?
i need u to take some pics of my outfit lol
it's RENAISSANCE themed
can't wait for u to see the tambourine

"Let's get going," Zora said. "I gotta meet up with a friend for a minute."

"Ooh, I'm meeting the friends already?" Khadijah cooed sweetly.

Zora burst into laughter and, riding a wave of confidence, reached out to grab Khadijah's hand as they exited the bustling courtyard. The "Neighborhood" sat at the top of a hill, in the least convenient location for walking to class but most convenient for attending football games. It was across the street from the stadium, which meant a ruckus some Saturdays, but it was the only collection of buildings on this side of campus. It was mostly quiet. Peaceful. Which Zora missed as she and Khadijah walked toward the Stokes-Pickett Sports Complex with throngs of others.

The distant echoes of the marching band grew louder, each booming beat resonating like the battle drums of an ancient army. Zora worried that she had overestimated her ability to handle loud noises. She swallowed, promising herself she would stay for as long as she could endure it.

Rat-a-tat.

"Zora."

Zora turned, releasing Khadijah's hand in the crowd, and was surprised to come face-to-face with a fidgeting Jasmine bouncing her weight from one toned leg to the other. She scratched and grabbed a forearm while Ngozi managed the pleasantries.

"It's so nice to see you out of class, Zora. Which building are you in? We're 17A in Yards if you ever wanna—"

"Oh, am I even allowed to come over?" Zora spoke directly to her sister. "Would that mean you'd have to publicly claim me?"

Jasmine picked at her glittery crimson nails. Zora grew more infuriated as her sister's gaze remained cast downward. However, it was the distinct frankincense bracelet adorning Jasmine's wrist that caught Zora's attention the most. Its brushed orange beads were traditionally burned. The smoke was used as an ancestral offering or psychoactive incense. But which was Jasmine using it for?

"Of course," Jasmine said. "I mean . . ."

"Ugh, Zora, there you are," Khadijah said as she stepped up between them. When she saw Jasmine, her smile died a swift death. "Oh."

"Khadijah?" Jasmine frowned, yet sounded surer than when she was addressing her own sister.

"Y'all know each other?" Zora asked. Jasmine and Khadijah stared at each other, wordlessly passing information. Zora's hands were on her hips when she spoke again. "I said, 'Y'all know each other?'"

"Khadijah's been helpful to Jasmine at the Conjure Shoppe," Ngozi spoke up, their voice two octaves higher than before.

Zora frowned. "Oh, right. I forgot."

"Anyway, have fun, y'all!" Ngozi said, clutching Jasmine's wrist around the bracelet of frankincense and urging her into the mass of people.

Jasmine pulled away for a quick moment, moving unexpectedly close to Zora in order to whisper in her ear. "Stay away from Khadijah. For real. Trust me when I say—"

"Oh, so *now* you give a shit about what I'm doing with my life?" Zora felt her cheeks warm in anger. "You can't be bothered to check up on me after I tried to call you in the middle of the night, but you feel okay telling me who I can and cannot see? Fuck off, Jasmine."

She had to admit, it felt good to be the one to leave her sister behind for once. She savored the look of upset on her sister's face as she turned back to Khadijah and took her hand.

By the time they'd reached the top of the nearest hill, Zora's thighs ached, but she perked up when she smelled tailgate food. She looked over at Khadijah, whose legs didn't seem to be crying with each step like Zora's did. How annoying.

"Zora!"

Zora turned in a circle, giggling the whole time, trying to find Lamont. Finally, he strutted over between two revelers who looked up at him and blinked as if looking at the sun. Lamont wore a shattered-glass cat suit that shimmered—glared, really—in the sunlight. Zora opened her jaw in astonishment at the snug fit and neatly placed accessories.

"Lamont!" The two ran to each other, but Zora pulled back at the last second, afraid of upsetting the delicately stitched suit, or getting hurt by it.

"Nah, c'mere." Lamont pulled Zora in for a warm, saffron-scented hug.

Zora breathed deeply for a moment before saying, "You look so fuckin' hot!"

Lamont laughed, and when they pulled away, he struck a pose. "I won't tell you how many hours this took. Okay, since you're beggin', it took forty hours! Look at my hands!"

Zora laughed at the reddened indentations and bruises from his hard work. "Battle scars. You killed the game, though. I wanna introduce you to someone; this is Khadijah."

Zora took a step back so Lamont and Khadijah could shake hands.

Khadijah took Lamont in. "Zora's right! Is this look from Beyoncé's Milan show?"

"No," Lamont said, stepping closer to a fellow BeyHive member, "it was the Amsterdam show. My version, of course. Inspired by the one LaQuan Smith did for her."

Zora snapped repeatedly, admiring her friend's beautiful artwork. "Body? Tea. Sewing skills? Tea. Glass shard earrings?"

"Tea!" Zora and Khadijah snapped in time.

Lamont looked near tears; he was cheesing so hard.

"Okay, let's get some pictures of you so you can post this ASAP," Zora said.

They spent twenty minutes with Lamont posing in various positions, directing Zora once the sunlight changed or he wanted a more flattering angle. After reviewing the photos, they agreed to meet up later. Zora took Khadijah's hand again as they passed a group of giggling friends taking shots in pickup truck beds. Zora couldn't help but laugh along with the group when a bearded man among them couldn't handle it and hacked the shot back up all over his beard and his shirt. Amid the blaring music, some people were yelling in a ridiculous attempt to converse in the chaos.

"To Hosanna! To Amias Crawfoot!" shouted a group of middle-aged women who, Zora noticed, all *could* take shots.

All incoming undergrads were enrolled in African American Tennessee History, which extensively explored the Crawfoots' role in establishing the area. The class was the one thing every Bricksbury student had in common, nurturing a communal respect for the cofounders within the student body, which was particularly palpable during the homecoming festivities. Their names reverberated through the crowd, and their statues across campus were adorned with interlocking hemlock branches painted in the school's colors. Even Khadijah yelled "To Hosanna!" with the next group they passed.

They fell in step with the crowd headed for the bleachers. Sweaty bodies pressed against Zora. They jostled her in conflicting directions yet invited her to move 'n' groove with them, heave on their downbeat, become a one-two-step extension of the crowd. All while Zora salivated at the smell of barbecued meat. It was mixed with the smells of lemonade, fresh nail polish, and cocoa butter. Home.

Rat-a-tat.

Khadijah led the way, twisting and weaving around friend groups taking pictures and couples dancing to the beat of the encroaching *rat-a-tat, rat-a-tat* of the marching band's drums.

A sound boom crashed into Zora as the band turned the corner into the crowded parking lot. They'd marched from the school's entrance to a procession of cheering onlookers. Everyone knew the song the band played—including Zora. She stopped short, knowing Khadijah would turn back to investigate. With an open-mouthed smile that was entirely genuine, Zora hollered the lyrics and finally threw it back.

"To Hosanna!" someone yelled.

Tangy barbecue made the air syrupy. *Dance with me.* Dampness clung to Zora's khakis. *Breathe with me.* Khadijah gripped Zora's hips, and they became a swaying thing. *Exist with me*: heavy breaths, bodies coiling.

One of the best things about Bricksbury was the vibes. You couldn't get those vibes anywhere else. Certainly not at a PWI. You couldn't enter a parking lot and fall into rhythm with a near stranger, each of you rapping along, not missing a beat. Not like at Bricksbury. It was magic.

But also, it was sensory overload.

After a quiet summer, Zora forgot how motherfucking loud college was. She felt the drumbeat thump like an earthquake in her bones. Her jaw trembled, so she pressed her rows of teeth together and breathed through it.

Inhale. Count to ten while exhaling. Inhale. Count to RAT-A-TAT *five while exhaling. Inhale. Fix your face so no one suspects your social veiling. Repeat.*

"Aye." Khadijah stopped and grabbed Zora's hand. "Are you good?"

Zora nodded, though it was an instinctual response rather than a truthful one. "It's just been a while since I've gone to a football game, and—"

"Yo, Dijah!" someone behind Zora shouted.

Khadijah's face broke into a smile, and she dabbed up Immanuel. "Yo!"

Immanuel's hair was braided down and disappeared behind a crimson cowboy hat. His right arm was covered in a vivid rosary tattoo. Each bead was a different colored gemstone. Zora made out black onyx, rose quartz, and...was that emerald or serpentine? Instead of a Nina Simone or Eddie Murphy shirt, his was matte gold like Khadijah's hat. The fabric looked expensive. Zora stepped back, and *RAT-A-TAT* watched as they greeted each other.

"To Amias!" someone yelled.

"How y'all doin'?" he asked, giving Zora a friendly smile. Square diamond earrings winked in the sunlight. "Excited for my *Drag Race* party?"

"Immanuel"—Khadijah's voice raised in warning—"don't embarrass me."

"Honestly, how dare you." Immanuel feigned hurt by putting a hand over his heart and frowning. He had a baby face. The soft, rounded kind that made mothers melt and grown adults ignore their instincts.

Khadijah rolled her eyes. "We're going in. See you later?"

"Yes, later." Immanuel shook his head. "Meanwhile, I've spent all morning convincing Khadijah to wear something lacy under this bodysuit. Matter of fact, while I have you, totally unrelated, do you prefer the colors gold or dark green?"

"Ignore him," Khadijah said, grabbing Zora's hand and leading them to the bleachers.

But before Zora could fully turn around, a *wide* smile on her face, Immanuel took ahold of her other hand, squeezing tightly.

"Ow!" Zora shouted. She tried to pull her hand away but got nowhere with Immanuel's larger frame and toned muscles.

"Don't go into the woods, child," Immanuel whispered several octaves higher than mere moments before.

RAT-A-TAT

Ice froze Zora's feet.

"Wh...at?"

RAT-A-TAT

"Don't go in—"

"Yo, what the *fuck*, Immanuel?" Khadijah barreled past Zora in a *whoosh*, pulling Immanuel off immediately. She seized her friend by the collar and shook him to punctuate every furious word she spoke. "Are. You. Fuckin'. High? Don't. You. Ever. Put. Your. Goddamn. Hands—"

RAT-A-TAT

The crowd swallowed them. Zora reached for them but couldn't make her legs move. She shouted, but *RAT-A-TAT* no sound left her lips. *Don't go into the woods, child.* That wasn't Immanuel. That wasn't his voice, and while she didn't know him, she'd wager he wouldn't ordinarily call her "child." No, this was someone else. Someone older.

"To Hosanna!" someone yelled.

Bile slid up Zora's throat. Salt water seeped from her eyes. Her body twitched and overflowed.

Inhale. Count to ten while exhaling. Inhale. Count to five while exhaling. Inhale. Fix your face so no one suspects your social veiling. Repeat.

There. She controlled her breaths. Well, she was breathing, and that was what mattered. Barbecue was thick in her mouth, turned from tangy to fiery. Swallowing didn't make it go away. Only made it turn sour. She swung her neck around but couldn't see Khadijah or Immanuel in the shifting horde. Zora's feet were heavy. She would fall over if she didn't—

She caught herself on someone's shoulder. Thankfully, she didn't bring them down with her. The person turned around, and Zora finally fell to scorching concrete when Mallory Holston faced her. The same kindness swam in their eyes as when Zora met them at Jonesborough Conjure Shoppe.

Mallory offered Zora a hand, which was an unsettling surprise in light of their last interaction. But when they pulled her up, they looked into Zora's eyes and said, "Don't go into the woods, child. Don't go into the woods." Not Mallory's voice. Someone else's.

Someone else repeated the words behind Zora. On numb legs, she turned to find that everyone sang the words to the song's beat.

Another hand grabbed her.

When she turned this time, it was Khadijah.

Her deep frown rattled Zora. *Not you too*, Zora thought desperately, tears welling up in her eyes. Who was causing this?

"Don't..." Zora said, yanking her hand out of Khadijah's grasp. "Please stop, don't say it. Don't say it." She covered her ears and then yelped as her body heaved, deceived. "Stop. Stop. Stop."

But as Zora bit her lip hard enough to draw blood, Khadijah put her hands up in surrender and said, "Don't go into the woo—"

Zora screamed. Kept goin' when her head began to ring. Ran-an'-ran, ran-an'-ran toward the "Neighborhood," outrunnin' falsehoods. Couldn't feel her feet. Couldn't listen, only breathe.

RAT-A-TAT

The drums echoed again and again behind her.

Chapter Twenty-Two

Halfway to the "Neighborhood," Khadijah's voice caught up with Zora. "Hey! Are you okay? Oh my God, did Immanuel hurt you? I'm...fuck you're runnin' fast...I'm an EMT if that helps!"

It, in fact, did not help. Nor did it stop Zora from rushing into her apartment and slamming the door behind her to stop Khadijah from following. Henry Louis awoke with a startled bark. The lock's sharp click brought no relief. No resolve. Khadijah banged on the door, causing Zora to yelp. She scurried backward. She turned and grimaced at familiar surroundings, scrunching her nose and forehead, untrusting of the sudden quiet. *Protection. I need protection.*

Khadijah stopped knocking. Zora doubted that any of the people who'd spoken under the influence of whatever spell that was would remember it after, which meant that Khadijah must have thought Zora was unhinged for running off like that. No matter. She'd take care of that later. Now was the time to help herself.

Zora flew to her closet, searching for the jewelry she'd worn only the day before. When Zora found the tiger's-eye necklace, she put it on and held the icy gemstone above her heart with both trembling hands. She low, low, lowered herself to the ground and shoved a random garment under her head. Fingers trembled. Zora closed her eyes. Sighed. *Be with me, ancestors. Be with me.* She couldn't force sound up her frozen throat. So, she repeated the words in her mind.

Tears still fell, and she'd begun hiccupping, but her heart slowed the longer she held the gemstone there.

Inhale. Count to ten while exhaling. Inhale. Count to five while exhaling. Inhale. Cry if you need to. Inhale. Relax your jaw. Repeat.

She lay there for
hours, staring into her closet like it was
an
e   n   d   l   e   s   s
void.

Zora had no idea when she walked to the stove, but she took it as a sign from the ancestors, who didn't often opt for subtlety, she thought as respectfully as possible before thanking them. She pulled out her pot and started boiling water. She undressed while she waited and refused to look at herself in the mirror after using the bathroom. Her house shoes offered comforting softness. The familiarity warmed her, but she still swung a robe over her cotton pj's and chilled skin.

She pulled out her container of homemade Florida water and added a few drops to a clean spray bottle. Zora frowned at her collection of herbs inside glass bottles. Only a tiny drop of cinnamon oil was left, but it was enough. The extra boost of protection was crucial for her peace of mind, if nothing else. When everything was mixed, Zora stood in the back corner of the room, hands clutching the washcloth she wrapped around the scalding water bottle. Normally, she would've waited for the water to cool. That was what her grandmother had taught her to do. She'd said patience was part of the ritual. But Zora didn't have time for patience; she had to protect her space from...whatever was out there. Whoever was trying to scare her.

One hand on the washcloth, and the other on the trigger, Zora spoke her intentions: "Protect this space from evil seen and unseen." She repeated the phrase as she meticulously sprayed the air, extra on all four corners, until she saturated the room in the sweet scent of Florida water. It further comforted her, and when she looked around, she felt safe. Finally.

Safety was first on the list. The second: chill.

This time, Zora boiled water for her beloved sesame-oil-flavored instant noodles. She swallowed a whole edible, which was double her usual intake. *This is an emergency.* She willed the THC to work overtime and allow her what reprieve it could.

Zora burrowed into her thin futon, Henry Louis half on top of her. He was fulfilling his duty as a snoring weighted blanket. Zora's body was warming, helped by the steaming bowl of noodles she cradled against her chest. She slurped slowly, examining the meticulously protected room around her, taking in the well-fed amulets on the walls and the name papers on her ancestor altar, finding pure comfort in their presence. The room's stillness stretched gently. And Zora just breathed.

The tiger's-eye rested against her chest, its warm weight anchoring Zora in the moment. With a deep breath, she felt its energy pulse through her, igniting a spark of determination. It was time to focus, to craft a plan that would lead her forward.

Zora thought quietly, chewing her food and considering her options. There were puzzle pieces, but they didn't make sense together. None of them were the same shade, and their shapes were too similar to differentiate when inspected. What story were they telling? And how could she translate it into something she understood? The Crawfoots. Bricksbury. Esther Fisherman. The visions. Mallory.

Did the Beast in the Woods actually exist? Or did someone (or some spirit) just want her to believe it did?

Amias Crawfoot
September 30, 1977
Jonesborough, Tennessee
Bricksbury Mountain College—
Hemlock Chapel

In every way, Bricksbury's Hemlock Chapel was offensive. Like the crystal chandeliers in the library, it relied on its grandiosity and ornate details for its value rather than its intended purpose. It was another thing diluted by time. Churches used to be spaces to commune with God. Now they were social occasions.

Reverend Thunder was the best thing about Hemlock Chapel by far. He had an oval face with deep, golden-brown skin. His wide, shiny forehead and bold cheekbones rounded gently into his jaw. The reverend was soft-looking. It sometimes ached to see him, though Amias welcomed the pangs of soreness in his chest. Pain reminded him he was alive, or the closest he could come to life. Amias hid in the basement, watching through an air vent. He never missed one of Reverend Thunder's sermons.

"Good Sunday mornin', Bricksbury! God is good, what?" the reverend's voice bellowed.

The congregants didn't skip a beat. "All the time!"

"An' all the time?" Reverend Thunder leaned back and spread his long arms, a wide smile stretching his soft face.

"God is good!"

"Amen, church!" the reverend clapped.

"Why are we here again?" Charlene asked, voice shaking slightly.

Amias hadn't realized how hard he had been smiling, so when he turned away from the air vent and found Charlene Holston, it was shocking how quickly his face dropped into a frown. He swore the wrinkled folds bounced back slightly if only to humble him.

Amias and Charlene had spent hours praying together already, ever since he'd decided against marking them as one of the next five sacrifices and accepting their bargain to become a Keeper of the Beast. The first thing he'd done was take them to the woods, a move he'd avoid in the future, given how traumatic it was for each of them. The road to eternal life wasn't one paved with gold and honey. It required pain. Anguish. Charlene struggled to walk it as the situation became more real. And when the time finally came for them to see the Beast itself, terror overtook everything, even if briefly.

It was a delicate situation for Amias, too. The Beast couldn't know that he had lost control of it and that only God's Hoodoo magic had the chance of taming it. It needed to keep thinking Amias was confident and sure of his decisions, even if that decision was adding another person to their plans. While Charlene gaped at the curious Beast in fascinated horror, Amias explained the Klan attack, the catalyst for Hosanna's death, and the demon's merging, making sure to do so in a way that only left the Beast feeling honored. Charlene had never heard of violence on campus, which Amias found relieving, a sign that maybe it'd all been worth the trouble after all. It was another shock to them. Nothing violent ever happened at Bricksbury. As for the trauma of the trial required to seal Charlene in as an active moving piece, Amias likened it to baptism by fire. If they were going to help keep the Beast tamed, a strong stomach and countenance was needed.

He'd kept Charlene in the unused gym's basement for weeks now. They'd needed time to adjust to their new reality somewhere that was nearby but not close enough that someone might stumble in. Amias didn't need to push for time. Their deadline for the five sacrifices was the winter solstice, and they had more than two months till then. After explaining his immortality for the umpteenth time and that, yes, God would still grant them the same if they officially joined in their mission to protect Bricksbury, Charlene had calmed. Amias would be sure to use it in the future for others who might help him. Immortality was the great equalizer.

Reverend Thunder's powerful voice echoed through the lower room, weaving a melody that intertwined with Amias's thoughts. It felt like the reverend was specifically made for Amias, and he could have been, right? Perhaps God wanted to remind Amias of beauty before demanding he give Him death.

"Let's give our lovely choir another round of applause! Mmhmm... *Good Lord, show me the way... O mourner, let's go down...*"

Amias listened in awe as the reverend effortlessly flowed from his speaking voice, rich with warmth and authority, into a sweet tenor that verged dangerously into romantic.

Reverend Thunder hummed to himself before saying, "What y'all know about 'studyin' 'bout that good old way'?"

The crowd erupted in cheers, their voices writhing, then rising in unison as they belted out one of Amias's favorite songs. Society called them "Negro spirituals" now, which Amias largely felt neutral about, so long as they kept singing them. Charlene sang these songs. Amias had watched them carefully. They came to church, sat near the front, and remained engaged throughout the entire service. Unlike the others, Charlene didn't chat with their friends or doodle in their Bible. They were there to commune with God. Charlene was perfect.

Once Charlene was ready to begin their work, Amias took them out at night to study his movements. Even nearing midnight, the campus bustled with students hurrying to and from dorm parties and arcades. At the same time, some stayed late at the library—a habit Amias appreciated, but it saddened him and reminded him too much of Esther. He and Charlene stood in the shadow of one of the campus's food trucks.

The truck was called Slice on Wheels, and it never moved. It was Amias's favorite spot to stand and stare at the library, remembering Esther. The air was charged with a mix of excitement and distraction, making it a perfect environment for their task. Amias taught Charlene the art of moving unnoticed through campus. He showed them the false walls leading to hidden hallways and taught them to time their movements to the rhythms of the crowd. With each step, Amias emphasized the need for subtlety and awareness. Charlene would need to replicate his methods on their own in the future.

"Mr. Crawfoot?" Charlene shook Amias out of his thoughts. "Why are we here? What does this have to do with the Beast?"

Amias sighed, turning back to the slits in the floor that barricaded him from the reverend's beauty. He could explain without missing the reverend's face...er, voice? Sermon. Amias wouldn't miss the reverend's sermon.

"Listen to the reverend's words, Charlene," Amias said slowly.

"I can't listen to anything else now, can I," they huffed.

Amias ignored them.

"All right, all right," Reverend Thunder was saying. "Please bow your heads. Father God, I ask that you ensure this word falls on open hearts an' clear minds, Lord. May these words nourish your people. In Jesus's name..."

The crowd and Amias said together, "Amen."

Reverend Thunder cleared his throat. "If you have Bibles, please open them up to the book of 2 Corinthians, specifically 2 Corinthians 7:7—*And not by his coming only, but by the consolation wherewith he was comforted in you, when he told us your earnest desire, your mourning, your fervent mind toward me; so that I rejoiced the more.*"

The reverend closed his Bible, removed his glasses, and looked seriously at the crowd. "Bricksbury, today, I'm talkin' about repentin'. That's right. Yes, I said it."

The crowd laughed. Charlene laughed. Amias did not.

"Ain't no use in bein' shy, Darrel Whitefield. Uh-uh, nor you, Roberta Owens. Mm-hmm. This is a message for alluh y'all because we must *all* repent at some time. Everyone."

Amias swallowed. Was this sermon from God about him?

"Now, it don't matter what it is that brought you to repentance. It don't. It don't matter if you lied, cheated, stole from your father, and then pinned it on your mother."

Charlene laughed with the crowd. Visions of Hosanna in a pale blue dress swirled in Amias's mind. She'd been on Jonesboro African Baptist Church's floors, covered in his blood, and he'd shoved a knife into her body because God demanded a sacrifice. But...who was meant to be sacrificed? Hosanna? So she would become banished into the woods and renamed a Beast? Or was God...challenging Amias to make the ultimate sacrifice? Had He given Amias the test of his life and death, and Amias failed?

Reverend Thunder clapped suddenly, startling Amias and making him jump beside Charlene. They looked at Amias curiously.

The reverend continued, "For all have sinned and?"

This time Amias and Charlene spoke together, "Fallen short of the glory of God."

"We're here," Amias began, "to mark the first sacrifice."

Charlene turned to him with interest. They looked down at their hands, as if wishing for something to write with. Amias hadn't considered another person's needs for some time, and he would need to get used to it.

CURFEW LOCKDOWN

ATTENTION:

STUDENTS, FACULTY, AND STAFF

Due to concerning events on campus, President Jenkins is expanding the campus-wide curfew and instituting lockdown from 7 p.m. to 5 a.m. daily beginning September 25, 2027.

No student, faculty, or staff member may leave their housing during this time.

No exceptions will be given.

Chapter Twenty-Three

Zora glared at her door, or rather, at the knocking at her door. It reminded her too much of the *RAT-A-TAT* from homecoming on Friday. Her watch told her it was 7:00 p.m.—prime "I'm Not Leaving My Room" time, the start of the school-mandated curfew. She ignored her door and returned to *Rhymes of the Cumberland*. Effie Waller Smith had been a teacher, working in both Kentucky and Tennessee in her lifetime before moving to Wisconsin. How many other Black professionals did the South lose and the North gain by way of the Great Migration?

"Zora!" Lamont's voice rang over Zora's Central Appalachian Literature homework. "Get your ass out here, loca. We're goin' to that *Drag Race* party whether your Type-A ass is ready to leave or not! Curfew be damned!"

Zora sighed and looked down at her phone and the messages she'd been ignoring. Since homecoming, she found herself caught in a bizarre cycle, alternating between the chilling sensation of cold, clammy skin (when she remembered what happened) and the embrace of her warm covers during bed meditation. Cold, then a shock of heat before cooling comfortably. Back and, unfortunately, forth. To Lamont, oblivious to the turmoil within her, it probably felt like she had vanished. Ghosted him.

Days had slipped by since she'd last ventured out, aside from the occasional walks with Henry Louis that barely coaxed her into the light. Although the terror that clung to her felt less sharp in the aftermath of homecoming, it transformed from a tangible threat into something more nebulous—a fierce anxiety that constantly gnawed at her.

Regardless, she liked Lamont. She didn't want to fuck up the friendship.

She opened the door to Lamont's frowning face and his unmissable saffron perfume. The scent was bittersweet, and she'd come to describe it as half woody leather, half honey. Why did he only wear this scent? Not that she was complaining, but he was a Sagittarius, and she'd seen his endless travel vlogs and his trying new foods, music, and fashion. Zora wouldn't've guessed that the man behind LamontTheeLibrarian didn't fix things that weren't broken. He did, however, insist on the occasional party.

"I don't wanna to hear excuses. I wanna to hear Rico Nasty in your car on the way to Immanuel's." Lamont crossed his arms expectedly, then uncrossed them when his eyes landed on Henry Louis. "Oh my fuckin' God, who is that?"

Zora grabbed Lamont by his mesh tank top and pulled him inside her room, lest Henry Louis get any funny idea about leaving.

Immanuel. The party was at his house. He'd been the one to begin the *Don't go into the woods* chorus at homecoming. While she reminded herself that he wasn't to blame for what happened, the haunting lullaby still lingered in her mind, its eerie melody echoing in whispers. What would he remember out of what happened? What would any of them remember?

Esther had written in her diary that she felt she was "cursed with clarity," a phrase that had felt melodramatic at the time, but Zora was starting to understand its meaning. How do you even talk to others knowing their memories have been altered? Zora was already struggling with Lamont, because the most important question she had been avoiding was one she didn't want to confront—she feared its real, human impact. Now, as she stared into her friend's playfully angry face, all she could think was: *Who is altering the memories of Bricksbury students, and how many other students have had their memories changed?* What was real? She thought about Lamont not remembering Toni Anderson at the Cornbread Lounge, how strange Zora had thought it was. Turned out she was right to be suspicious.

"I assume this adorable beast of war is here low-key?" Lamont asked, gazing down at Henry Louis with a forced smile.

"He's actually—" Zora began, mind already wandering back to Immanuel.

"Don't tell me, he's a teddy bear." Lamont looked unconvinced, but he still reached out to let Henry Louis sniff his hand.

"Lamont, this is Henry Louis; Henry Louis, this is the Big Bad Librarian dragging me away from you." Zora laughed for the first time that day. For the first time in a couple days, actually.

"Yes, well, his mama is in desperate need of fresh air," Lamont said, eyes trained on Henry Louis's eager paws.

Before her mind could wander again, Zora asked, "So, what's with the Baccarat Rouge?"

Lamont's eyebrows raised in surprise, and a smile spread across his face. "You've noticed?"

"Noticed? It's literally saffron, cedar, and honey. Those ain't exactly the most subtle scents."

He let out a soft chuckle but remained close to the door, maintaining a safe distance from an exuberant Henry Louis. "Baccarat Rouge 540 is simply my favorite. It makes me feel..." He lifted his arm and sniffed the inside of his elbow, still laughing. "I feel powerful. Now, don't think this is gonna distract me from the party we are *definitely both going to.*"

Zora waited momentarily for Henry Louis to properly greet Lamont with violent tail whips and slobbering kisses. While Lamont was busy, she freshened up in the bathroom, her mind again returning to Immanuel and the frantic look in his warm brown eyes when he grabbed her. Would the panic he'd inflicted on her ever be forgotten? How did this work? The lights in the mirror only flickered twice, but each time made Zora wince. She wasn't so much on edge as she *was* the edge.

RAT-A-TAT still pounded in Zora's head, reminding her of homecoming and running for her life, or at least, feeling like she was running for her life.

In the reflection, her eyes appeared bloodshot and filled with an untamed intensity, unaffected by the soothing relief of eye drops. Zora hurriedly donned loose-fitting denim shorts that softened her tall frame, paired with a snug, plum-colored crop top. Her smile didn't reach her eyes, but how could it? Maybe Lamont was offering something she needed. A night out? *Drag Race?* Khadijah was even supposed to be there—maybe it was a chance to make things right after homecoming. *This should be fun. I can be fun.*

Zora's windows were heavily tinted, so the winding Appalachian roads had a sepia tone in the dusk light—like Khadijah's Instagram grid. Tierra Whack's electrifying beats pulsed through the speakers, setting the ideal pre-party tone. There were no streetlights in the countryside like in Jonesborough, only fields with golden wheat ready for harvest, swaying gently in the warm evening breeze. In the distance, the silhouette of an old barn stood against the horizon, its wooden beams shrouded by the encroaching night. It was too dark to see far into the fields, but the rustle of leaves and the occasional flutter of a night bird hinted at the lively world hidden in the shadows. Zora knew never be out here on her own, streetlights or not. Growing up in Knoxville, there were always places Zora knew not to go. And they weren't all alleyways or busy downtown streets before a UT game. They were places outside the city. Rural towns and country stores. Churches that looked like they'd nourish all current and past KKK members with a Bible verse about rage or punishment or homosexuality. Churches round there thrived off that shit. And they always had.

"This is the sticks, all right," Zora whispered as they made a right down a long driveway with three hay bales beside the mailbox.

"Tell me about this Khadijah," Lamont said to Zora as his torso twisted away from her. "She must be somethin' special to have you out here in the boondocks." He peered down the edge of a cliff as they rounded a perilously tight hill.

"She works at the Conjure Shoppe downtown *and* lives across the courtyard from me."

"You're datin' someone across the courtyard?" Lamont suddenly turned to her, his face grief-stricken.

"We aren't dating! Does this *seem* like a date to you? Almost driving off a cliff with you and SZA?"

Lamont was unconvinced. "This is date-adjacent. Besides, you are the one who invited me to this, remember?"

"Oh yeah," Zora said. "I forgot."

"Well, I have a favor in return. I need a ride to my endocrinologist. He's holdin' my T hostage till I get bloodwork done."

"How's tomorrow?" Zora asked after mentally going through her schedule. "It needs to be fasting, right?"

"Yeah." Lamont had a smile in his voice. "Thanks. Now, back to Khadijah. This is date-adjacent. An' since this isn't a formal thing with Khadijah, that means you're free to be with anyone, right? D'ya want a condom?"

Zora shook her head, laughing.

"What?" Lamont asked, already laughing alongside her.

"I'm realizing no one has ever asked me that. Everyone just... assumes I would never need it, ya know?"

"What's the logic there? You could never be masc4masc?"

Lamont's shrill laughter reinvigorated Zora's. "Back to my point, Khadijah's friend—"

"Immanuel," Zora corrected, cringing as she said the name, remembering his grip on her. "Immanuel set this up knowin' you'd both be there. So, take that into consideration. Ugh! You have all the fuckin' luck. I've asked out every twink an' vers on my floor, an' they're all taken! How the fuck am I supposed to find—"

The driveway snaked endlessly, and Zora tuned Lamont out to focus. Pavement ended, and the crushed pea gravel began. The road wound so sharply that they leaned over with the car every thirty seconds. Zora couldn't see fields anymore, only thick woods. She suddenly remembered her name being called on her way to Conjure Night and the warnings Esther received about not going into the woods and being followed on her way back. Then, of course, there was homecoming.

The dense trees enveloped Zora like a thick, suffocating blanket, their shadows stretching and twisting around her, whether she was physically within their grasp or not. She could feel the weight of the ancient Appalachian trees bearing down on her, their gnarled branches reaching out like skeletal fingers, brushing against the metallic shell of her Subaru with a screeching insistence. Each scrape of the thorns seemed a reminder from the forest, that she was never free of it.

Zora felt the cloying heat of claustrophobia rise in her chest, making her more and more unnerved. The fading sunlight struggled to filter through the thick canopy, casting dappled patterns of light and darkness that danced across the dashboard. The scent of damp earth and decaying leaves flooded her senses. It mingled with the engine's faint hum. She remembered the smell of decomposition that had choked her after Conjure Night, mixed with the singe of paper, and frowned.

Zora tightened her grip on the steering wheel, her knuckles near cracking as she fought the rising tide of anxiety. The woods, with their silent watch, breathed alongside her, wrapping her in a turbulent embrace that made her heart race and her thoughts scatter.

She stopped the car behind a long line of vehicles and inwardly sighed. *Stop thinking about homecoming. I can do this. I can be fun.*

"Ready?" Zora asked, rubbing her hands together, asking herself more than Lamont.

"Ready," Lamont said.

Zora stepped around her car and adjusted her noise-canceling earbuds. The vibrant emerald-green lawn was alive with a dozen people, all vying to be heard over one another's voices, while a speaker blasted the same song Lamont had on repeat during their journey. Zora instantly picked up on the pulsating bassline of Tems's "Love Me JeJe."

"Have you been here before?" Lamont asked.

"I already told you, no." Balloons flew over the crowd, bopped left and right by the revelers. Zora dodged an inflatable unicorn aimed at her and whipped around to glare at the unknown assailant who had already disappeared into the crowd.

Lamont dodged an entirely different inflatable. He grabbed it out of the air, looked at it, and turned it toward Zora. Another unicorn, this one conspicuously well hung.

"What?" Lamont asked after a beat.

"No," Zora said, knocking the mylar out of his hand with a *thunk.* Together they walked up the creaking front porch steps. The screen door squeaked like the steps had, and Zora hated how fucking noisy this house was already.

As she opened the door, a babbling roar rushed over her. Zora gritted her teeth against sensory hell. The smell of buttery popcorn and fresh nail polish wafted in the air, and Zora was anonymous in a crowd of bodies thrashing to the beat. Guests swayed their shoulders with the music, and Zora found herself slowly relaxing, too. Zora shimmied to the beat alongside Lamont, mouthing the words as they sang together. The more she moved her body, the calmer she felt. It had always been that way for her. Zora needed movement to manage her panic and anxiety, as well as to maintain emotional balance. It had been ages since she had attended a house party, and it would be (long-awaited) fun. She was determined to make it so.

Down the shag-carpeted stairs, Monét X Change and the Vixen were prancing silently on-screen. A couple on the couch were half making out, half gagging at Miss Vanjie's signature voice and strut down the runway. Zora was just happy to see one of her favorites— Asia O'Hara—on-screen. This season was in Zora's top five.

Megan Thee Stallion transitioned to Flo Milli in the speakers. Everyone knew this song—including Zora. They raised their cups, hollered the lyrics, and finally, *finally*, Zora could swing her hips.

"I'm gonna get us drinks," Lamont screamed into Zora's ear.

Zora nodded but knew it'd be a while till they found each other again. The beat dropped and "Wipe Me Down" began playing. Zora had 0.25 seconds to prepare before elbows started swinging, and "Move! Move!" foretold a mass scramble as others began dancing. She retreated to the foyer to text Khadijah.

ZORA: Hey, I'm here. Where are you?
KHADIJAH: in the kitchen. cum find me 😊

Apparently, Khadijah wasn't mad about homecoming. *Thank God.* Zora nearly fell over her feet as she marched toward the kitchen, the suffocating party noise tumbling to the back of her mind with each step. The speakers shifted to a slower song. The one that could be rapped to, fucked to, or used to soothe you to sleep. Zora harmonized her contralto with "Bad Habit" as she waded through the crowd, careful not to bump into any outstretched hands holding plastic cups. She stopped in a hallway, unsure whether to turn left or right, when a woman approached, her cup's rim resting against her crimson-painted lips.

Zora boldly stared at Khadijah's bubblegum-pink bralette and faded jean shorts. There was a tattoo of a honeybee on her rib cage that Zora had never seen before, reminding her briefly of the one on the door of the Rare Books Room. Aside from the sexy, tattoo-showing outfit, there was her hair...Admittedly, Zora had a thing for Bantu knots. Khadijah's were perfectly spiraled with crisp sections. Her baby hairs were skillfully swept into place on her reddish-brown skin. Her heavy thighs caught the light when she shifted her stance. She peered directly at Zora, who didn't need an engraved invitation to get the hint.

"It's good to see you again," Zora said. She kept an easy smile on her face. "You look good as fuck, by the way."

"Same." Khadijah maintained eye contact. She reached up and trailed a finger down Zora's broad shoulder blade, then wove her fingers together with Zora's. "An athlete?"

Zora stared at Khadijah, her brain trying to make sense of the woman's boldness. Was she not even going to mention what happened at homecoming? "Yoga," she said, but the sound turned up at the end like a question. She'd gone to twice-weekly free classes at her local YMCA. Yoga *had* made her biceps more defined, though she didn't know if other people could tell. Well, now she knew.

People brushed against Zora's back as they passed by; their laughter and singing quieted to a buzz as she drowned them out. The overhead lights were turned off in favor of the oil lamps dotting the walls. The hallway took on a dim haziness that made everything feel slightly *off*, slightly unreal. Though she was sober, Zora suddenly felt drunk with the way Khadijah's chest rose and fell. The arrogant look in her almond-colored eyes. The warmth of her skin as Zora grabbed her waist. How she shivered when Zora ran her hand over the honeybee tattoo. She must've anticipated Zora's next thoughts because Khadijah let her head fall back onto the wall, giving Zora a perfect view of her asymmetrical C cups, maybe small D cups. They were lovely. Zora was ready to have them fill her hands; for a thrilling moment, she pictured them bouncing in her face.

The smell of Jack Daniel's and Cherry Coke rising from Khadijah's cup was sweetly familiar. It smelled like Bricksbury, like home. Khadijah took a sip and handed the cup to Zora, who downed the entire drink to make a point. She wouldn't be strung along tonight.

"You wanna get outta here?" Zora asked, surprising herself *and* Khadijah by how her mouth fell open.

She frowned for a moment, just a moment, but long enough for Zora to catch it.

"Is this the part where you tell me not to get attached?" Khadijah's voice lifted at the end, but not like a question, more like an anticipation of the plummet.

Zora opened her mouth, but the vulnerability in Khadijah's eyes stopped the lighthearted U-Haul joke on her tongue. Something aching hung in the air. A wound too soft for Zora to touch but alive enough to see in the slight tremble of Khadijah's swollen lips. They weren't going there. Instead, she crowded Khadijah against the wall, leaned forward, and whispered, "Point me to the nearest door, behind which I will tongue fuck you till you stop askin' me questions. How about that?"

Khadijah's crimson lips *finally* parted with a bright smile, revealing flawless teeth. She licked her lips to show off the curved barbells in her tongue piercing. "Let's fucking go."

Chapter Twenty-Four

Zora smiled when Khadijah's warm thighs shook on either side of her face. It'd been too long since she'd tasted musk and Jack Daniel's together. They danced across her tongue even while it was buried inside Khadijah. Zora paused to build the suspense and fill her nose with the heady scents before starting again. When she moaned, the vibrations made a keening sound escape Khadijah's throat, and the quaking in her thighs became more pronounced.

The heavy bass of the house music downstairs made for perfect background noise. They could be as noisy as they wanted up here. This would go down as one of the best quickies of Zora's life.

One hand was wrapped around Khadijah's legs to help keep her upright, a necessity that broadened Zora's smile even more. Her other hand placed sloppy swipes on Khadijah's clit in time with her tongue. She reveled in the slick sounds only they could hear. Khadijah's back was against the door, and her hands gripped Zora's head. She guided Zora to a quick rhythm that had already driven Khadijah over the edge once, and now threatened to do so once more.

"There," Khadijah breathed, her voice and fingers trembling. "Right...fuck, right there." She took a hand from Zora's head to tweak a nipple.

Zora grunted in approval and watched from her knees, enthralled. At the risk of Khadijah falling on her ass, Zora took the hand that helped hold her up and used it to rub her own clit. She knew her body and could tell she was close. Seconds, not minutes. Another rumbling moan and they each faltered in their movements. Zora was lost to a pressure building in her belly and the smell of throbbing lust.

When Khadijah warned her, Zora swirled her tongue and swiped hard, elated to hear that sweet, melodic voice break mid-cry, just as her own did.

———

There were three different types of bottled water in Immanuel's textured black mini fridge. Zora unscrewed the cap off a Voss container after using the bathroom and washing her hands. Her eyes were low in the mirror, heavy with satisfaction. The brightness of her phone screen was jarring, but she was glad it was only nine o'clock. Curfew had started two hours ago, but apparently nobody was planning on honoring it. There was still plenty of time in the night, and she'd only been away from Lamont for an hour or so. She'd used her index finger to brush her teeth with cinnamon-flavored toothpaste before gargling with the water.

"Thanks for the hydration." She laughed as she opened the en suite door and thought of what to say to avoid ending on an awkward note. Khadijah wasn't in the bedroom. "Oh."

The hall buzzed with lively conversation, but as Zora scanned the groups, a sense of embarrassment crept in. No matter how hard she looked, she couldn't spot Khadijah anywhere amid the laughter.

Zora frowned, returning to the quiet bedroom. Maybe Khadijah was grabbing food or something. *She's not*, a voice said that Zora studiously ignored. She cast her gaze on the hutches and walls in Immanuel's bedroom. It was fully decorated with fairy lights and crimson peel-and-stick wallpaper. His posters were cheesy, if endearing. The poster for the original 1975 *The Stepford Wives* was directly above his bed. With a cracking porcelain face and a dainty and fragile severed hand, it was the perfect embodiment of the movie. Zora refused to acknowledge the 2004 sham of a remake. The original was delightfully pretentious (she was learning more about Immanuel than she'd thought) and effective in its critique of the horrors of sexism. But was Immanuel a horror movie lover or a lover of media designed for women? As Zora's not-girlfriend's friend, Zora hoped the former.

ZORA: Hey, where'd you go?

She sent the quick text to Khadijah before leaving Immanuel's room, hoping she'd get an instant reply with a joke about needing a smoke break or something. But the minutes...passed...and Zora had to admit that Khadijah wasn't returning. A new type of embarrassment (*shame?*) had been unlocked for her. *Fuck, I shouldn't've started by going down on her. We should've just...How did I not see this coming?*

Weed overpowered the burnt popcorn and Cherry Coke smells; it sailed across the hallway and down the stairs. Zora searched the couches for Lamont. Friend groups chatted, excitedly showing one another pictures on their phones. *Pokémon GO* players made bets over boxed wine and a shared bowl of hot Cheez-Its. Someone with pink-and-green boho braids—another AKA?—twerked to a Ceechynaa song. Someone on skates did a line of something bright and powdery off the round ass of the twerking AKA. Not to be outdone, a Delta with dark red fringe cowboy boots screamed in elation as someone dropped to their knees and buried their face up her denim skirt. Zora watched, fascinated—horny? An inflatable unicorn glided across the crowd, the bright white a shock to Zora's eyes. She gladly returned to the cowboy boots, which reminded her of Khadijah, and that she'd ghosted after Zora had given her at least two orgasms. Zora sighed. *It was fun, but at what cost?* A few couples made out in shadowed corners as if to throw Zora's shame in her face.

ZORA: Are you okay?

Finally, Zora found Lamont. Apparently, she hadn't been the only one looking for him. Immanuel was perched on her friend's lap, his arms wrapped around Lamont's neck to bring him closer. Lamont wasn't fighting him off. Rather, he broke off the kiss to trail his lips over to Immanuel's ear. He whispered something that made Immanuel grind on top of him. *And that's my cue to leave*, Zora thought.

She sprinted down the hall, avoiding the place where she'd met up with Khadijah.

ZORA: At this point, I just wanna be sure you're good. You don't have to talk to my face, but can you at least let me know that you're okay?

Then Zora turned and collided with someone... and their plastic cup full of sour brown liquor.

"Fuck!" Zora yelped and stepped back as the drink sloshed onto her, dampening her loose crop top, and making the material cling to her. When she looked up, she glared into impenetrable amber eyes.

"I just refilled that," the woman whined, peering into her cup.

"Excuse me. You covered me in Henny," Zora said, waving at her front.

The woman glanced up from her cup at Zora as if she had just realized she was there. Her flat-ironed hair had been straightened to within an inch of its charred life. It was pulled back into a loose, half-up, half-down ponytail that she touched to ensure it was still in place. It was ombre shades of indigo and sapphire and smelled newly dyed. Her over-lined lips were painted such a deep orange they were well past burnt. She looked at Zora's oversized denim shorts and Nike shoes, then her eyes shot to Zora's furious ones.

"You're Jasmine's sister, right?" It was not the time to be thinking of her sister. *Stay away from Khadijah*, Jasmine's words echoed in Zora's head. And now Khadijah had apparently ditched her. Dread weighed heavy in Zora's stomach.

"*My* name is Zora." She spoke louder than necessary to ensure she'd be heard over the music. A light tapping on her outer thigh made her look down. It was her. Usually, she didn't notice stimming. She supposed this was a special occasion. And was Jasmine really so popular that people remembered Zora just by association?

"Right, right…Zora…" The woman rolled the name on her tongue, then shrugged like it was too bland to be remembered. "I saw you and Jasmine at Conjure Night. I'm Imani."

She paused. Zora put both hands on her hips.

Imani sighed. "Imani Brown?"

"You're talking as if I should know you."

Zora spoke more to herself than to Imani.

"Jasmine hasn't mentioned me? She's been running my African Diasporic Religion Book Club for years. I changed my major to biblical studies because of her. She's a fucking genius."

Zora stared blankly at Imani. *Ah. This is someone I would know if Jasmine and I were close.*

"Jasmine literally officiated my wedding and Ngozi played the organ. Has she honestly never mentioned me?" Imani's voice rose in frustration.

Zora swallowed. Her eyes swung wildly around, hunting for an excuse to escape. The Hennessy on her shirt had turned from sour to nutty sour, which was considerably worse.

"Anyway, now that my drink is on the floor, I might as well head to the party across town." Imani turned away, dismissing Zora. "Good luck this year!"

Watching her go, Zora's heart skipped a beat. There, on the back of Imani's neck, was a tattoo of a honeybee. A couple people turned their heads to see her as she went by, then their eyes swung to Zora. She stared each of them down till they turned away, but already, she knew an episode was imminent. What was with the honeybee tattoos?

Stay away from Khadijah.

Zora's sudden lightheadedness mixed with the nausea from the wet fabric clinging to her body, and she knew she was in no state to drive. She needed quiet.

She doubled back and shielded her eyes from Lamont and Immanuel on the couch. She took the steps two at a time, returning to the room where she had her tongue in Khadijah's sweet— Zora stormed into Immanuel's clammy en suite. The fight left her shoulders when she crossed the threshold and exhaled with a whimper. The sweltering air in the hallway had been too much. Slick bodies were greasy from cocoa butter and languid from alcohol. But now it was quiet.

She kept the light off. Closed her eyes. She turned up the brown noise in her earbuds. Breathed.

She didn't know how long she stood there. Why was she standing? She sat on the cold faux tile. Didn't know how long she sat there. Didn't matter. Nothing mattered right now. Nothing. Nothing but breathing.

Eventually, she focused on the freshly painted wall behind her head. Then the way her chest moved. And finally, each of her limbs, one by one; she felt her body, and it didn't make her wanna scream. It didn't make her feel anything except sore from sitting for so long. Zora scrunched her nose when she got a sour wave of Hennessy from her shirt.

The music thumped quietly behind her earbuds. She was grateful she'd found the perfect low-frequency sound to ease her overstimulation. Pink noise was too flat. White noise was too broad. Brown noise, a heavy roar in her ears to keep her grounded, was just right.

Her phone told her she'd spent two hours on the floor, which accounted for her aching joints and need to stretch before walking further. It was barely past eleven. She had one missed text.

LAMONT: stayin the nite dont wait on me luv u bye

Zora couldn't help but laugh.

ZORA: Happy for you. Be safe!

The few people still out in the hallway were slow-dancing to Syd and Kehlani—the vibe had changed. Zora had seen enough and now longed for her quiet dorm room and Henry Louis's slobber. She'd been foolish to think that coming would be a good idea.

The front lawn lay deserted, save for three colorful inflatables swaying gently in the breeze. Despite the tranquil scene outside, the muffled thud of music from inside the house continued to reverberate through the air. With her mind pinging back and forth all over the place, Zora suddenly remembered the missed opportunity to attend a Kehlani concert a few years back, regretting not seeing one of her favorite artists perform live.

As Zora strolled toward her car, the distant echoes of pulsating music and alluring whispers faded behind her. A sudden surge of intuition compelled her to halt on the gravel. *Danger.* Zora activated the flashlight on her phone, noting the time—11:23 p.m.—as she retrieved her protective luck mojo bag from the depths of her backpack. She spoke the spell without hesitation, the spirits acknowledging her as warmth burst through her body, up all four limbs and settling in her lips: *"Though I walk in the midst of trouble, thou wilt revive me: Thou shalt stretch forth thine hand against the wrath of mine enemies, and thy right hand shall save me."* She repeated it twice more. Warmth pulsed in her body. Zora saw stars.

Ancestors, please protect my steps from evil.

Zora stood still, night air heavy in her lungs as she held on to the warm pouch. She closed her eyes for a moment, seeking comfort in the gentle heat. Suddenly, a faint noise to her right shattered the peaceful moment. Before she could react, something soft and cottony was wrapped around her head, disorienting her. In the chaos, her phone slipped from her grasp, and before she could comprehend what was happening, multiple hands seized her. They forced Zora into the back seat of a sedan, muffling her desperate cries for help.

Chapter Twenty-Five

Zora sat in the sedan's back seat, her head shaking with disbelief at the events unfolding and her body shaking from the careless way her abductors drove/tumbled down the hill. Did that mean they were familiar with its sharp twists and turns? Or were they just in a hurry? Questions ricocheted in her mind. Was this how all the students went missing, one by one, swallowed up by the shadows lurking in their "safe" college town? The weight of that realization settled heavily on her chest, as did the burn of her tiger's-eye. *Lord save me—Esther was right.* Dangers lurked that she had dismissed, chalking them up to mere paranoia or the overdramatic actions of some disgruntled practitioner who didn't want her digging through history. But now, heart thumping wildly and clarity rushing in, Zora was no longer disillusioned. Bricksbury wasn't, and perhaps never was, safe—in the past *or* in the present. Zora was terrified, but another fiery emotion also thundered through her: righteous fury.

"Whoever the fuck you are," Zora screamed into the thick pillowcase covering her face. The driver must have been able to hear her, though they were silent as she let them have it. "As soon as I get outta here, my ancestors and I will drag your sorry ass across every painful dimension and parallel plane until your soul is battered; then I'm gonna bring your consciousness back so I can personally whoop your ass with my bare fuckin' hands. D'ya understand me? You will—"

"How 'bout you shut the fuck up till we get to where we're goin'," a man said.

Zora didn't recognize his voice, but he sounded to be around her age, if not a bit younger.

"Who are you?" Zora asked, ignoring his words. He kept quiet, so Zora changed tactics. "Who are you working for?" Esther's diary flashed across Zora's closed eyes. She'd been so worried about being watched. And had concerns someone would attack her... This was painful proof of Esther's valid fears. Zora was a believer. The puzzle pieces may be blurry, but they were there and unmistakable.

"Are you the Keepers of the Beast?" Zora asked.

"Shut. Up," a different person, a woman, whispered in the passenger seat.

Zora immediately recognized Imani's voice. She swallowed. *Holy fuck.* Imani, one of Jasmine's disciples, was kidnapping her? She thought about the honeybee tattoos again. Was the whole party a trap? Were... What about Khadijah? And Lamont? Zora had brought him into this twisted circle, and now he wasn't safe.

And if the party was a trap, who laid it? The Keepers?

Zora remained silent the rest of the drive.

Esther. Poor Esther. What actually happened to her?

Nothing would keep Zora from the truth. This was what she had trained for, to excavate reality from the noise. If Esther had run afoul of someone, Zora would find out who, and why. If the Keepers were real, Zora would be the one to unearth them.

The car stopped, and Zora's heart quickened. Esther had observed a rotating guard of men stationed at the entrance to the Woodlands. Was that where she was being taken? Had those men been Keepers? She licked her parched, cracking lips, readying herself until a thought stopped her. *Don't go into the woods, Zora. Don't go into the woods.* It was lyrical, the last dregs of a soliloquy. And it reminded her of the first words in Esther's diary, in tight letters: *Esther's belief in the beast in the woods, and her unholy domain, endures.*

Her domain. It indicated a femme Beast.

Both entries were written in the nineteenth century. It was a time Zora knew well, which was heartening, but the century spanned the moral, ethical, religious, and societal spectrums. A Beast in the Woods could have just as easily been a misinterpreted wolf howl or a metaphor for temptation as something sinister in the spirit realm. There was no way to draw airtight conclusions from the information she had, but the more things had been piling up, the worse it all looked.

Her door clicked open, and the pillowcase that was on her face was ripped off.

Zora blinked at Bricksbury's manicured lawn and entrance to the Woodlands' path. Her backpack lay on the ground in front of her. She leaped on it, searching for her trusty bear spray that sat snugly in her backpack's outer pocket. Once she had it engaged, she swept it upward to find a group of masked people in crimson robes, all facing her.

Zora tipped her neck backward and squinted at the familiar welcome sign.

BRICKSBURY MOUNTAIN COLLEGE WOODLANDS

THIS 300-ACRE TRACT WAS ONCE THE WOODLOT OF JONESBORO AFRICAN BAPTIST CHURCH (C. 1796). IT WILL BE LEFT UNDISTURBED FOR PRESENT AND FUTURE GENERATIONS. REMAIN ON THE PATH.

Zora squared her shoulders among the chirping birds and squirrels scurrying between moonlight-dappled branches. She'd fucked around, digging into the Keepers, but she wasn't weak. Zora was never powerless. She searched her backpack again and found her phone and protective luck mojo bag.

Wait. Why would they let her have these things? If they meant to take her somewhere against her will, these items would complicate their plans. Another quick glance revealed they hadn't confiscated her spy camera, either, useful in canvassing for research, cleverly hidden inside an ordinary-looking pen. Yes. She had them now.

Zora cleared her throat, the sound covering the click of the pen, its recorder engaged. She looked back at the group with renewed interest. If they weren't planning to kill her, what did they want? Her returned phone told her it was 12:03 a.m. She held it in the air, displaying it to her kidnappers.

"What's stopping me from calling the police and reporting you for abducting me?"

"Zora Robinson," one of the robed members said, ignoring her question. "You have business with the Keepers. Enter the Woodlands and find the church. There you will discover the answers you seek."

Zora glanced back at the bright lights of the Esther Fisherman Quad. She could run. She could.

Another robed person laughed softly and spoke loud enough for the others to hear. "She's not very good under pressure, is she?"

"Get on the trail." The leader spoke directly to Zora, stepping between her and the open quad. "Move. I think you know by now that there's nowhere for you to hide."

Zora wasn't about to hurry. She looked around her and considered her options. There were at least a dozen robed people of varying heights and builds. Zora thought she could hold her own against one, maybe two, but anything more than that was fantasy. Letting out an anguished sigh of defeat, she swung her backpack on.

"Fuck," Zora said as the heavy weight hit her back. *It wasn't this heavy earlier.*

Her eyes still examined the others, memorizing what little she could. "Fine! Get the fuck outta my way, then."

Chapter Twenty-Six

When she finished crying and ensuring that she'd walked far enough ahead of the robed group who'd kidnapped her, Zora pulled out her spy camera pen and clumsily tucked it into her hair, wanting to ensure that everything that could possibly be recorded was. If the Keepers were not only real, but still active in the present day, it could mean a whole lot of disturbing things. Namely, that the Beast was real, at least to them. But how could they feel so empowered to engage in so much kidnapping and... Zora gulped...murder? Did they go as far as to murder the students they took? No, right? That would be too wild. Elements of what she'd discovered so far repeated themselves in her head. Missing students. Missing Esther. Altered memories. The vision. *Sacrifice.* Eliza Deadbody's shrill voice, then her hard face, flashed in Zora's mind, far too real for comfort. Zora could *see* the bright hallway fluorescents in the sweat beads slithering down Eliza's face. Zora shook her head. Her next thought was about what she'd read on the Crawfoots at the Historical Society, about how they'd used Hoodoo magic to protect Jonesborough and Bricksbury's Black population. They'd used *His* magic. She thought about how people had been shouting Amias and Hosanna Crawfoot's names at homecoming just before the incident occurred.

"No fucking way," Zora whispered as she pushed ahead on the trail, holding the flashlight she'd found in her bag, alongside granola bars and water. These people really believed that they were killing in the name of something important. When all signs pointed to the fact that they were in a cult. Cults were dangerous in their own right, but when certain members possessed ancient knowledge of rootwork and rituals, it only served to magnify the intensity of potential consequences for anyone that learned the truth.

Zora cleared her throat, ensuring once again that the camera was sufficiently hidden. Her braids were loose enough to accept it but tight enough to pull painfully as she adjusted the plastic. It didn't matter. It would be worth it.

She stayed on the path as the night waned, her nose full of pine, her skin damp with forest fog, and anxiety-induced sweat. What awaited her at the old church?

Zora limited her sips from her water bottle, intent on conserving it since she didn't know how long she'd be out there. She checked her phone to see if she was still within range of internet. At 1:00 a.m., she was. At 1:33, 1:35, and 1:41 a.m., she was. By 2:00, she was well and truly in the woods, cut off from any potential help. Good, she thought wildly. Let Lamont stay as far away from this mess as possible. She knew that if she'd tried to text him about what was going on, it'd only fill him with confusion and worry. And she knew that if she'd tried to call Jasmine, she'd only get sent to voicemail. Like with every other situation she'd found herself embroiled in while at Bricksbury, Zora knew she was going to have to face this alone.

Her calf muscles screamed in alarm; the shock radiated downward to Zora's heels and upward till heat pulsed at each of her hips. Even though she'd strolled, the climb was rougher than expected. Not that she'd expected anything or thought to consider elevation *at all* or—

There'd been nothing to see between entering the woods and now. Little mercies, though this was something she *had* expected.

The Keepers had gone to a lotta trouble to prevent people from going into the woods, and yet, they'd forced Zora directly into them.

A stick snapped to Zora's left, deep in the woods. She held her breath. Her eyes went wide with fear as she was reminded of the other time she was followed in the woods after Conjure Night. That time, she'd been so much closer to safety. Here, there was none. Panic flooded Zora's system, and she immediately grabbed her bear spray, whirling around to point it at the sound. Was there someone there? The Beast in the Woods? No, she scolded herself, pushing the thought away. Regardless of how the Keepers treated the folklore as though it was actual history, Zora knew there was no way there was a real Beast. How could there be, after all these years?

She stood silently for several long minutes. Zora tried to think of anything her therapists had ever taught her, but her mind was empty of everything but fear. The bear spray and her mojo bag were her only weapons against whatever lived out in these woods.

"Let's go," she said out loud at 2:27 a.m. "Maybe it was a rabbit or something."

Zora had finished two (Keeper-provided) protein bars and three-quarters of her water (which she began to regret) and wished nine times that she'd had another edible. This shit was not for the faint of heart.

The cool leather of her protection mojo bag hanging above her heart calmed her. She palmed it.

Let's pray that it'll work.

Chapter Twenty-Seven

Eventually, Zora heard a rise of soft, murmuring whispers around her, a halting mumbling that continued long after she came to a stop. The whispers grew louder by the moment. Heart racing, she felt the weight of unseen eyes upon her, and the whispers took on a sharper edge, as if the very shadows around her were alive. Not only alive, but were they...singing?

Oh no. A chill crept down her spine, leaving a distinct feeling that she was not alone in this spinning madness. The whispers, now urgent, pressed in on her from all sides as if heralding something they couldn't yet comprehend.

What the hell is going on? Zora swallowed as the pine on her tongue turned bitter, combining with the scent of wood rot and skunk. *This is it. This is it? This is it.* She dared not close her dry eyes, even knowing the humid forest air would soothe them. She remembered the snapping twig from minutes before and tried not to consider she was being followed, stalked by the Keepers who brought her here. But for what? Her shaking grip was firm on the flashlight. She didn't care if the thick plastic dug into her hands. If anything, it reminded her what was real and what wasn't. What was imagined and what wasn't.

I'm listening. Her face fell into a frown when the voices led her off the path. She swung the flashlight toward the sounds and found bowed branches. They formed a misshapen semicircle above a smaller, forgotten path. Broken and shaped long ago, the branches were covered in twisting vines that hung above the path leading toward horrors and/or collectible research unknown. Zora huffed. It wasn't enough to come all the way out here?

But now wasn't the time to ignore her instincts. Zora followed the voices, clutching the mojo bag with one hand.

Be with me, ancestors. Be with me, spirit guides. Be with me. Her steps were careful. Slow. Twigs were silent even as her tennis shoes broke them. It hurt to hold her breath for so long, but she was terrified of the sound of her existence. Terrified the noise would alert a wild animal or, worse, bring her to her senses.

An iron sign was buried in the underbrush, forgotten in the shadows of twisting branches. Copper rust plagued the wrought iron, and gnarled vines encircled it. This far into the woods, everything was corroded.

Zora stopped. Was this what the Keepers wanted her to see— er…was this what *she* wanted to see? She pulled out her phone and snapped pictures.

"It's officially time to document," she explained.

JONESBORO AFRICAN BAPTIST CHURCH
& CEMETERY
EST. 1796

Questions seized Zora's mind as she crept toward the cross that presided, hauntingly, above the tree line. Wait…was she…forgetting something?

Her phone's light quivered more than the flashlight had. Luckily, as she turned away from the sign, the cemetery and church beyond came in focus across an empty field.

…*She was def…initely forgetting something*…

It was 3:03, and the moon soared in the cloudless sky. The night's deep blue was soft to Zora's eyes. Despite the situation, she had to admire nature's quiet beauty.

Thwump. Thwump. Thwump.

She remembered now. Churches meant graveyards. Graveyards changed things. They were resting places for spirits, sites for spell-casting...among other dealings. And it meant she needed to pay her respects before setting foot on consecrated ground.

Looking for an offering, Zora dug at the bottom of her backpack and came out with four dimes and a quarter.

It wasn't much, but it would do.

Zora lifted them all above her head in one swift movement, braving exposure in the blaring moonlight before turning clockwise to display her offering and reverence.

After placing it on the ground, Zora swung on her jacket, careful that the hood entirely covered her head. Protection. Self-warding. And she needed safety as she walked into the clearing. It felt ten degrees cooler than in Bricksbury's valley, hissing with crisp air. A sudden chill sent Zora's neck cracking to the left as she shuddered. *Keep it together, for fuck's sake.*

The field's path had been beaten recently. She crouched down, zooming the camera onto the blades of switchgrass, bent in a pattern.

"This must be one of the Keepers' spots," she said out loud for the recorder, sweeping the flashlight across the graveyard. What sort of rituals did they practice? Did they use the graveyard's power, or was whatever they'd deemed the "Beast" a power source? Either way, she was onto something. She had learned the Crawfoots had used Hoodoo and God. A graveyard and an old church made perfect sense.

Shoulders back. Elbows in tight. Eyes cunning, sharp behind glasses as she gazed at the site. Past the disorganized rows of tilting gravestones, the church's door was open. This place was...old. The chilled air and honeysuckle swirled around her body like restless ghosts. How...many...ghosts...?

How many people had worked, lived, worshipped, and been buried here? How many lives were changed? Saved? What did this place—and its power, which Zora felt as palpably as the cold—make possible for them?

Chapter Twenty-Eight

Unlike her childhood house of worship, there was no vestibule at Jonesboro African Baptist Church. No cozy, welcoming foyer. No double doors. When wood creaked on ancient hinges, Zora immediately stepped between thin pews. Inhaling dust. Sneezing on dense air, blinking against moonlight spilling through fractured stained glass. She surrendered to the stench of rot on her tongue. Yet, still, there was beauty. She marveled at the speckled orange-and-navy light cast through the windowpanes as they danced across her hands and the rough-sawn planks. Enduring.

The downward draft hummed with buried life. They sang spirituals between these walls. Caught the Holy Spirit. Saved and sanctified God's children right where Zora stood. *Jesus, the lives lived here. The stories lost.*

Without thinking, she bowed her head. It felt right, just for a moment, to pay additional respects inside the spiderweb-stippled house of God. The Keepers, and whatever evil they did, couldn't change the fact that this was His house.

Like the door, the floors creaked beneath her with each cautious step down the aisle. Zora swung her eyes from her phone's screen to the scene before her, ensuring she covered everything. No Bricksbury—she paused to consider the bent grass outside—few Bricksbury students would ever see this. But the Keepers, they'd seen this. They'd been here. And now they'd sent her here. Why?

The slanted roofline looked familiar, at least. Most mountain churches—all buildings in the area—were built this way to accommodate the snowy season. Zora racked her brain, trying to remember the area's weather patterns in the late eighteenth century. She didn't think there'd been a storm severe enough to put this place to ruin, at least nothing large enough to make the papers. A placard on the front pew read:

THIS PEW IS DEDICATED TO OUR
STEADFAST SHEPHERD,
AMIAS CRAWFOOT

So, Amias Crawfoot was not only the cofounder of Bricksbury, but also a pastor here at this church? Zora snapped a picture of the placard, thoughts racing to make sense of it. This certainly hadn't been in any of the reference books, not even *An Exhaustive History of Bricksbury Mountain College*. Although it wasn't strange that a pastor would be educated and go on to start a school, it was contrary to the official history, which had said both Crawfoots were in the printing industry prior to Bricksbury. Nothing in the history had ever mentioned ministry.

A wooden altar commanded all the attention at the end of the aisle. It ran the width of the building, leaving narrow cutouts on either side for the clergy and choir. Water stains created pale splotches like polka dots. Overall, though, the structure of the dais held up. And was it...cleaner than other parts of the church? In front of the altar, Zora found a symbol burned on the wooden floor.

It was a honeybee.

Shit, shit, shit. The same one from the Rare Books Room in the library. The same one she'd seen tattooed on Imani and Khadijah. Zora couldn't know for sure, but she would have bet money that

Mallory had that same tattoo somewhere, too.

Something shuffled on the ground only a few feet away, pulling Zora from her frozen shock. It could have been a rat or something, but the gasp that followed was irrefutably human. Young and human. Zora's left knee protested as she hunched over a few pews away from the origin of the sound.

"Hello?" She spoke louder to convince the others she was less afraid than she was. They didn't need to know she'd already pissed herself a little, and the longer this went on, the more likely that "little" would turn into something more.

Zora coughed on dusty air while she waited and stared at the echoes of the stained glass scattered across the floor. She had a mind to sprint out of the building, scrambling down the cursed mountain till she found safety on her familiar futon. Instead, she gripped her phone and her tiger's-eye while trying to stay balanced on tired feet. The flashlight on her phone couldn't reach around the church pew; it was flooded in darkness.

"Who's there?" Zora didn't even whisper loud enough for her ears to hear, still the voice across the floor replied immediately.

"Toni," a shaking voice said from somewhere in front of Zora. Dark eyes and wild red hair stretched around a pew, pinning Zora with their coldness. "M-m-my name is Toni. Toni An-Ander..."

"Toni Anderson?" The missing student! The one who used to be Lamont's roommate, before some spell made him forget.

Only Toni's eyes moved as Zora stood, tracking her movements but seeming unable to untangle herself from the fetal position. Hooded eyelids drooped forward and away from her body unnaturally. But still, Toni watched.

Zora tried to swallow but her dry throat felt strained and shriveled as she spoke. "Toni...?"

"The time has finally come," Toni said, a frown sinking her eyeballs further. "I'm ready to be sacrificed."

"You're ready to what?" Zora's eyes bulged outward, but when she heard another sound, this time behind her, she wasn't quick enough to turn around. The last thing she saw was a scowl on wide lips before a hard blow to the head knocked Zora out cold.

Chapter Twenty-Nine

Z ora's gaze swept over the frantic scene before her, but it was not she who turned her eyes. She was a prisoner in her own body, trapped and unable to move, a sensation all too familiar during her other visions. But this wasn't like the other visions she'd had. This time, someone else was controlling her body, as though she'd been claimed for this vision rather than stumbling across it. But why?

Someone else blinked Zora's eyes. Heavy lids lifted and collapsed several times as her puppeteer perfected their bodily intrusions— rather, their bodily crimes. Searing tears escaped the foulness, eagerly evaporating on clay floors. She'd been left for dead, abandoned, trembling inside her corpse. In a blinking, seized thing. She wondered again who this vision was for and if they got off on her suffering.

"I ain't got nothin' to fear cause I'm keepin' my eyes on You, Jesus. Stayin' my mind on You," a man's low voice somehow rang in the grim darkness.

"I believe in God,
the Father Almighty,
maker of heaven an' earth."

The man laughed after he spoke, and while it was a kind sound, madness overran the edges. He giggled to himself, whispered nonsense, and giggled more.

"I gotta die," he said eventually, somberness wilting his hysteria.

What? Zora thought. She'd meant to speak, but the intruder controlled her tongue. Her feet, too, or she'd've turned sharply to her left to avoid the man's warm breath on her shoulder.

"Yes," another man said, not somber, but shameful. "As much as this...distresses me, you must die, Reverend." *Wait a second*, Zora thought. *I've heard that voice before.* It was the man from her first vision, she was sure of it. This time he was with another man instead of the old woman.

"Reverend Dr. Junis Thunder," the voice corrected, lucidity suddenly sharpening his speech. "What's your name? You an angel?"

The other man sighed quietly. "You can't know the bliss it would bring me to have you know me, Reverend. Nevertheless, it's best if you don't."

Zora couldn't help but wonder if what she was witnessing took place before or after the vision where the old woman was killed by the ember-eyed demon. With everything that had happened since dreaming up that horrifying scene, Zora was chilled to consider that the demon in the vision might not have been a reflection of interpretation or a straight-up illusion after all. Could there have been some impossible truth in the thing with the ink-and-paper skin and the fiery eyes? Maybe it had represented some real presence, a spirit, that the Keepers were able to sense? Maybe that was who they were sacrificing the missing students for?

"That ain't an answer," the reverend replied. "If you gon' watch me die, the least you can do is tell me your name."

Silence.

"An' in Jesus Christ His only Son, our Lord;
who was conceived by the Holy Spirit,
born of the Virgin Mary,

> *suffered under Pontius Pilate,*
> *was crucified, dead, an' buried"*

While she waited for the man's response, Zora tried to move her fingers and then her jaw. When even the Kegels didn't work, she gave up entirely. Whoever controlled this vision clearly didn't want her to move or even breathe on her own.

Reverend Thunder swallowed loud enough for Zora to feel sympathy for this man she didn't know and whose death she'd be forced to witness. Well, be forced to hear.

> *"the third day, He rose from the dead;*
> *He ascended into heaven,*
> *an' sitteth at the right hand of God*
> *the Father Almighty;*
> *from thence He shall come to judge*
> *the quick an' the dead . . . the dead*
> *the poor, poor dead"*

"When this is over . . . will people remember me? Will the congregation, the students, remember me?" Reverend Thunder sobbed.

When what is over?

"Ah, don't want your favorites to forget you, huh? Do you need them to ensure your legacy is heralded in your absence? Do you need to be revered? Would you like a throne and crown as well?"

Despite his words, the man whose voice Zora recognized from the other vision didn't raise his voice or speak with a sliver of an attitude. He berated Reverend Thunder for his professional and moral failures, and yet sounded like the perpetrator himself. The guilt was palpable, wrapping and trapping the words in its misplaced anguish.

"The pastor should offer a holy escape on a college campus

obsessed with material achievement. Playing them against each other, though?" He tsked as if the reverend (or himself) were a naughty schoolchild, then gruffly quoted scripture. *"For the pastors are become brutish."*[11]

Keening breath left Reverend Thunder to blow against Zora's shoulder. It'd gone from warm to fiery, searing like the tears still escaping her eyes. The reverend, though, seemed to have complete control of his body because Zora heard his knees crack against stone as he begged.

"Not that...don't...you can't use it against me."

"I can't use the Bible against a reverend?"

"That's not what I..."

"For the pastors are become brutish and have not sought the Lord: Therefore, they shall not prosper, and..."

> *"I believe in the Holy Spirit,*
> *the holy universal church,*
> *the communion of saints,*
> *the forgiveness of sins*
> *the forgiveness of sins*
> *the forgiveness of sins*
> *the resurrection of the body"*

"I surrender," Reverend Thunder said, finality clear in his voice. "An' it don't matter what you say." He sniffed. "I loved my congregation."

"I was one of your flock—there ev'ry Sunday! But, thanks to this *listen* mojo bag, I've heard your thoughts, an' you're unfit to be Bricksbury's shepherd." The voice belonged to an unseen third

---

11 Jeremiah 10:21—For the pastors are become brutish, and have not sought the Lord: Therefore they shall not prosper, and their flocks shall be scattered.

person, someone who Zora also recognized, but it didn't make sense. "I'm not sayin' He won't forgive ya, Reverend Thunder. But you are a prideful, greedy man. You love your congregation, but ya love *leadin'* 'em more. Your love is tainted."

Why the hell was Charlene here? Charlene knew the murderous man from the impossible first vision? Zora's mind spun. The reverend didn't refute Charlene's words, and from Zora's perspective, that was smart.

"They won't remember," the other man finally spoke. "Their memories will be...altered."

That's who's been doing it, Zora thought wildly. *Charlene has been the one altering memories of the students on campus, potentially with the help of whoever this other murderer is.* Was Mallory involved as well? What was it with those two?

"How d'you live with this?" Reverend Thunder asked.

"I don't," the man said. "Or, I guess now we don't."

The reverend took a breath to speak but was cut off by muffled screams. Growls. A keening sound like the one he'd let out when faced with his sins. This was it. Just like with the old woman, the other man wouldn't kill the reverend himself. Like Zora, he was a witness.

A strange sensation started awakening in Zora then, a hard press on the back of her body, as though she was lying down on the hard ground instead of standing up. With every ounce of strength she could muster, she tried as hard as she could to simply make a fist. While her hand in the vision showed no motion, Zora could feel it happening in some background part of her mind, in the same place that registered the feeling of the floor beneath her. *I'm coming back to my real body*, she realized, trying to remember what had happened after she found Toni Anderson in the dark church, muttering about being sacrificed.

"Ain't you gonna ask me for my last rites?" the reverend wanted to know.

"I would," the man said slowly, "but I'd rather not hear them. I made that mistake the first time."

"You...the first time?"

"I still haven't gotten over it," the man whispered as a creature's nails scraped on the ground, heading for them, and even though Zora couldn't see the thing, she could certainly guess what it looked like, or at least, what its eyes looked like, the only thing that seemed the same about it, its eyes and its pretty blue dress all ruined with blood. "Prepare yourself."

"an' the life everlastin'.
Amen."

Chapter Thirty

Zora awoke aching. Tiny spasms ricocheted up her thigh, past her abdomen, and down each arm, lingering echoes of the awful vision about the reverend's death. Each groan resonated within her chest, an unsettling vibration that mocked her attempts to regain control of her own body. When she tried to open her eyes, it felt as if they were glued shut—an absurd notion, but one that clung to her. Most confusingly, the smell of whatever room she was in matched not those of the dark, dusty church, but of her own apartment back at Bricksbury.

Panic set in as she strained against the unseen force that held her hands still, resting unnaturally by her side, placed there by someone else's design. Impatience made waves of anger wash over her—the vision was over, she should have been able to move by now. The room around her was eerily quiet. If she *was* at home, how had she gotten there? Where was Henry Louis? She should at least be able to hear his snores or his playing with his toys. That dog was never silent. Why couldn't she hear him? A chilled sweat trickled down the side of her neck, merging with the deep, throbbing ache that pulsed through her limbs, blurring the line between pain and something far more sinister. She couldn't think. Slumber welcomed... er, forced her into its drowsy warmth. It seemed to be the only choice she had, for now.

Later, Henry Louis whimpered. His warm tongue swiped back and forth across Zora's face until she gently turned her head. The spasms throughout her body had calmed, now concentrated in her tender calves. Light painfully filtered through her eyelashes, and she sought shelter under the warm covers. She stretched her limbs, drowsy, beneath her beloved olive-green linen sheets. They were titans against her night sweats. As she stirred, she instinctively reached to the back of her head and found a slight discomfort from resting on her pillow in an awkward position. Zora massaged the tender area. She kept massaging, applying gentle, then moderate pressure to the dull ache.

Suddenly, she swore, the pain more intense than she'd expected. As she shook her head in disbelief, she slowly rose from the bed and then stumbled back, collapsing onto the soft linen as her eyes fixed on the bloodstains on her hands. *No. No. No. No.*

The scenes from Jonesboro African Baptist Church trickled into her memory, one flimsy, dust-covered recollection lining up after the next, further distorted by a pounding headache. She tripped over the pile of notebooks she'd bulldozed through when...when was that? Was it yesterday? Searing pain shot up and down her leg as her knee slammed into the sharp wooden edge of her ancestor altar. She'd hiked. That was why she'd awoken so, so, *so* sore, and why falling had only made the discomfort worse.

Zora's heart sank as she remembered what had come before the church. The party. The shaking noise of laughter that vibrated within her. She could still taste Jack Daniel's at the back of her throat. Could still feel the jarring coldness of the bathroom's tile. Khadijah had been so soft and vulnerable, then brazenly told Zora where to slide her tongue next. The night hadn't returned to her in the correct order, but she knew she'd gone with Lamont. Zora immediately called him, but it went to voicemail.

ZORA: UH ANSWER YOUR PHONE!!!
SOS
CONFIRM YOU'RE ALIVE, PLEASE!

If anything had happened to Lamont, she would never be able to forgive herself. Still cursing on the cluttered floor, she looked over to find her mud-caked tennis shoes thrown on the futon's clean clothes. *What the fuck?* She spent a few more minutes cursing and waiting for the pain in her leg to subside until she remembered that she didn't need to rely solely on her memories. It was Research 101: *You can be your least reliable source.*

She'd recorded everything. She sighed and pulled out the camera that was still tucked into her hair. Her thoughtful, admittedly obsessive planning was coming in more handy than she ever would have imagined. She raced from her position on the floor, finding, then shoving a USB into the camera's port before putting the other end in the laptop. While it loaded, she texted Lamont again, willing him to answer her already.

ZORA: HELLO?!

Zora pushed PLAY and fast-forwarded through her midnight hike in the Woodlands, finding the cemetery, and then Jonesboro African Baptist Church. She stopped when the spy camera hidden in her cornrows collapsed with her body.

Zora took a second before pressing PLAY again. This could either be the most traumatic thing she'd ever witnessed, or the most enlightening. She sat on the floor to prepare, focusing on her breathing. *Inhale. Count to ten while exhaling. Inhale. Count to five while exhaling. Inhale. Cry if you need to. Inhale. Relax your jaw. Repeat.*

When she was ready, she pressed PLAY.

A woman's delicate fingers reached forward, and the camera angle shifted back and forth. Her face was unclear, though Zora's stomach dropped when glittery crimson nail polish entered the frame. They looked familiar. Hadn't Jasmine had nails like that at homecoming? Still, it'd been a minute since then, and it wasn't as

if she were the only one. There had to have been others. Jasmine…
Jasmine couldn't have been the only one. Just statistically.

Frankincense bracelets, though, especially when paired with glittery nail polish? That was a fact Zora couldn't explain away, along with the fact that she knew she heard Imani in the car after she was kidnapped. She slid backward till she leaned against her bed, laptop angled awkwardly in her lap as fresh tears rolled down her cheeks. Her own sister was a part of whatever had happened to her last night.

Zora could have stopped the recording, but instead, she just scratched Henry Louis behind the ear as she watched.

The church solidified in Zora's memory as she watched it onscreen. She remembered the fetid, rotten floorboards and how the multicolored stained glass lit the abandoned—or, not so abandoned—sanctuary.

The camera swung wildly around the space, and Zora caught sight of the woman who'd introduced herself as Toni Anderson. She was limp and in the fetal position between pews.

"Jesus Christ," Jasmine said.

Zora wasn't a purist but found it interesting Jasmine had no problem taking the Lord's name in vain *in a church*.

Jasmine shook Zora's body so violently that the camera jostled and repositioned at a higher angle, but not before panning across Imani's face. *Wow, you really love Jasmine, huh?* Zora thought bitterly.

Jasmine, meanwhile, was solely focused on Zora. "What in the hell were all of you thinking? How dare you try to pull something like this behind my back?"

"Step away from Zora." She was not in frame, but Khadijah's shaking voice rang through Zora's laptop speaker.

Zora felt as though her breath had been taken. She sat, hiccupping through her tears on her apartment floor.

In front of the camera, maybe six or seven other people surrounded

Jasmine. The robed people who'd taken Zora from the party and sent her into the woods. These were Jasmine's friends? Khadijah's? *They're Keepers. I was always surrounded.* Zora's sister looked incredulous, eyebrows raised, round lips upturned in a wicked scowl.

"Excuse me?" Jasmine asked. Her voice had been frantic when handling Zora's body, but now lowered dangerously in a different direction.

Khadijah scoffed in the background. "Would you like me to count how many fuckin' violations this is, at this moment? Or would you like me to list the ones I'm gonna commit if you don't step away from the woman you just assaulted?"

Assaulted. Zora paused the video.

She touched the back of her head, where the blood had mostly dried. Some of it, though, was still wet and gummy. Zora supposed the wound hadn't scabbed over yet. Jasmine had done this. Henry Louis followed Zora back up to her bed, licking away some of her tears and leaning against her body. His instinct to care only made Zora cry more. But this wasn't something she'd shy away from. She never hid from the truth and wouldn't stop now.

Zora rewound a bit, then pressed PLAY.

Khadijah's sharp voice again: "...would you like me to list the ones I'm gonna commit if you don't step away from the woman you just assaulted?"

Zora's thoughts swirled. How long had Khadijah been there? Had she been in the car that took Zora to the woods? On the recording now, was she rescuing Zora? From what exactly? And why?

Now Jasmine scoffed. "Listen, Khadijah, the fact that you thought she'd come all this way after being kidnapped and just happily go along with whatever you asked only goes to show—"

"You're not the one who gets to decide." Khadijah's voice grew closer, and then she came into frame. She was shorter than Jasmine but didn't seem to care. She stepped to Zora's sister, eyes livid.

Jasmine finally looked at the people surrounding her. She swallowed loud enough for the camera to pick up the sound. "I've only ever done what was required of me. I ask a favor—for you to leave my sister out of all this—and I'm just ignored? Why? Because you want to hook up with Zora?"

Khadijah's eyes narrowed. "Careful," she warned. "You're already on thin ice, Jasmine. You tried to warn Zora to stay away from me, didn't you? And she chose to ignore you. Just like you've chosen to ignore her all these years."

"That is not fair," Jasmine countered, her voice rising. "Listen, I can still help you find someone if you're looking—"

Khadijah snapped, "I don't need help, thanks. You've already done enough to ruin tonight. Zora was *right there*. We were just about to give her the choice to join of her own accord. Now, instead, this was all for nothin'. The bloody knot on the back of her goddamn *head* is for nothin'. This is all your fault."

"I've said it once, and I'll say it again." Jasmine's voice was so quietly enraged that it made Zora shiver. "Leave. My sister. Alone. I'll take it up with *him*, if need be. *She is off-limits.*"

"Step away from Zora," Khadijah responded. "I need to make sure she gets home safely, after, you know, bein' knocked the fuck out."

Jasmine glanced down at Zora one last time before finally backing away, her eyes misted over with angry tears.

"What do we do with Toni?" someone asked.

"Don't fuckin' touch her. You know the rules," another hissed.

Khadijah spoke up. "At least five of y'all, please follow Jasmine back to her dorm to make sure she doesn't try to pull anything else."

Khadijah crouched beside Zora's body and cradled her head. Finally, the camera pointed at her. She wore a crimson shirt—was it a robe? It was difficult to tell from the angle. The honeybee and hemlock branches around the collar were the same ones from the floor in the church she stood in on camera. The very same one tattooed on her rib cage.

Khadijah whispered close to the camera, "I'm so sorry, Zora. I'll make this right."

Like fuck you will.

On Khadijah's meticulous instructions, the group moved Zora's body out of the church. They placed something under her nose when she stirred by the cemetery, ensuring she stayed out. Off the trail, there was a four-wheeler, which Khadijah used to hold Zora's body as they returned to campus. Was she having the vision by this point?

"What are we supposed to do now?" one of the Keepers asked. "She never got to make her choice."

"We have time. The Beast will wait. Y'all need to stop worryin'," Khadijah said, matter-of-fact, before kissing Zora's forehead. "She's smart enough to understand the importance of what we do. Soon enough, she'll be one of us."

Amias Crawfoot
Present Day
Jonesborough, Tennessee
Bricksbury Mountain College—Edward C. Williams Library

Amias watched with interest as Zora Robinson entered the library. A trail of burnt-orange energy lingered behind her. Tiger's-eye. The fire-like protection energy hovered in the air long after Zora had walked away, covering her path from potential harm. It crackled so loudly, surely it was all Zora could hear. Not only did she know how to use tiger's-eye, but she'd enhanced its properties by connecting them to her ancestors. Amias eagerly twisted his neck, feeling a tension release as a satisfying crack echoed in the air. The faint sound sent a shiver down his spine and made him grin. He hadn't seen such a powerful conjurer in many years, perhaps since finding Charlene in the seventies.

She was the perfect choice for a new Keeper.

The present-day Zora marched beneath the library's ostentatious chandelier with even strides, but even from behind an aisle on the fourth floor, Amias could see Zora's pulse thrumming in her neck. Along with his immortality, God had gifted him enhanced senses that Amias had spent years honing with Charlene. The structure of their rootwork had been immensely helpful. Amias had never been interested in botany, though he understood the benefits. Now he was an expert in all things roots, herbs, and conjure. Enough of an expert to see Zora and know immediately she was different.

She approached the counter and chatted with the librarian, Lamont, with an easy smile on her face. Amias often gazed at them walking arm in arm around campus, sometimes giggling and other times focused intently on a book. Their friendship embodied everything Amias had hoped for among the Bricksbury students: two intellectuals connecting over their shared love of knowledge. It was a shame it'd all come to an end soon.

Chapter Thirty-One

Zora stood in front of Lamont's dorm door in the Robert Robinson Taylor building, her knuckles rapping against the weathered wood for what felt like an eternity—fifteen minutes to be precise. As each knock reverberated down the long, empty hallway, the sharp taps turned deeper, more like thumps, more like a beating heart. The dim overhead lights flickered intermittently, casting Zora's muted shadow against the grayed wood. She shifted her weight from one foot to the other, glancing at her watch and terrified as to why Lamont wasn't answering. Zora's mind went straight to the worst-case scenario, as was its usual undertaking.

Each unanswered knock deepened her impatience as she contemplated the Keepers, Jasmine, and Khadijah. They'd all played a part in Zora's abduction from the party. They'd also all *played* Zora. She'd had no idea they were working together, even if under duress, given the tension between Khadijah and Jasmine in the spy video Zora took. Jasmine had tried to warn Zora at homecoming. Now she knew why. More important to Zora was where she lay in their current plans. Would they still try to convince her to join the Keepers of the Beast? Or would Jasmine have her way by getting Zora officially labeled as "off-limits"?

At last, Lamont's door swung open with a grating creak, unleashing a flood of brilliant light into the hallway. His roommate stumbled into view. Emir's bobbed box braids were tousled. The dark circles under his eyes told a different story—less of sleepiness and more of relentless nights spent battling exhaustion. Emir looked utterly spent, a casualty of chronic sleep deprivation common at Bricksbury. Though it seemed a bit extreme so early in the semester.

"He's gone," Emir said, his voice flat and devoid of emotion. "Left for work this morning."

The initial wave of relief was enormous, but after it passed, Zora still felt like something was off. Lamont never left her hanging after a text; he was always quick to respond. And he loved to text during work! In fact, he texted her more at work than at any other time. Were his memories altered somehow? Would he even remember going to the party? Did Immanuel try to pull anything with him like Khadijah had done to her?

Zora breathed in sharply, knowing her perception of reality had begun to blur. The silence of the hallway closed in on her, making her skin crawl. Doubts and shadows danced at the edges of her mind, merging the line between what was real and what was imagined.

"I tried to reach him," Zora insisted, her voice sharper than she intended. Emir merely shrugged, the faint flicker of a smile playing on his lips that didn't reach his eyes.

"Yeah, sometimes he just... disappears."

As he said this, a shadow flickered in the corner of her vision, but when she turned, there was nothing there—just the worn posters lining the dorm walls and the distracting sound of her own heavy breathing.

With a swift *whoosh*, Lamont's door shut tight. For a second, Zora thought someone's wrinkled hands reached for her. She yelped, instinctively leaping back, breathless, only to remind herself that it was just her imagination playing tricks. But she wasn't being silly. Zora wasn't a woman gone mad; rather, she was listening to instincts that had kept her safe and alive up till now. And that counted for something.

Zora couldn't shake the feeling that something was wrong. The air felt thick with unspoken words, and she was left standing there, an unsettling mix of anger and dread swirling in her chest. Maybe she was just still wound up from last night and watching the recording. She tried to rationalize it: At least Lamont was alive. But the more she thought about it, the more furious she became, both at Lamont for his silence and at the oppressive sense of something lurking just beyond her perception. Her library trip would be one stone for two birds.

———

Zora entered the library with her chin pointed at the twinkling chandelier and her shoulders squared. All she heard was the *thwump* of her heartbeat. She studied the room in seconds. A Very Alive Lamont was sorting papers at the front desk. Mrs. Redmond *(come hell)* plus two other librarians *(or high water)* were stationed on the upper floors, giving a group of high schoolers a tour. The students stretched their necks at the library's vastness. LED light dappled across soft, youthful awe.

More librarians were scattered across the ground floor, slowly putting books away and typing on computers without expression in their dead eyes locked behind blue light–blocking glasses. Monotone voices and still feet. Dark circles like bruises drooped under their eyes. Zora might've considered it more if she weren't in the middle of an undertaking. As it was, she didn't have the time.

She marched to the front desk. Chapped lips pricked her tongue. She also didn't have the time to hydrate.

"The name is Zora Robinson. I need to go to the Rare Books Room," she said icily as she approached the desk.

Lamont looked up in surprise. "Oh my God, Zora!"

"Where the hell have you been?" Zora leaned over the desk, voice low in hurt and concern. "I've been texting and calling."

"New rules. No phones on the floor. An' I was in such a hurry this mornin'." Lamont raked a hand through his long auburn locs, lips wide in a silent groan. "Last night was crazy."

"Yeah, we need to talk." Zora peered around the library as if someone was watching. Maybe the Keepers were. It was possible. She didn't know their habits, but given the missing students, stalking people on campus was beyond believable. "My place. Whenever you get off."

"It's been far too long since I've gotten off," Lamont said under his breath.

You didn't get off last night with Immanuel? Hmm. Weird. Wait, wait, there isn't time to think about this.

"This isn't the time!" Zora said, exasperated. "I've got some serious shit to unload on you."

"Okay, but not your place. You said you'd take me to get bloodwork, remember? My shift ends at two."

"Right," Zora said. "Okay then. Two."

Lamont swiped a card and typed its number. Zora's fingers shook when taking it from him. He frowned, but she waved away his concern.

"I'm just cold," she explained. She took off the jacket wrapped around her waist and put it on to display how cold she was. "Much better."

"D'ya really think I believe that?" Lamont asked, stone-faced.

Zora shrugged. "It was worth a try."

Lamont came out from behind the desk and wrapped his arms around Zora. He was so warm, and the saffron was so leathery. How was he so comforting?

"Whatever it is," he whispered in her ear, "we'll figure it out together, all right?"

Zora smiled, but her hands still shook as she turned away. Lamont was an incredible friend, but he couldn't make her forget the footage she'd watched. How Jasmine had knocked her out to stop her from hearing or seeing anything else, how Khadijah had gotten angry, giving orders like she was in charge.

Zora needed answers.

She entered the basement door. Cold stone greeted her as she spiraled down the stairs. When she got to the entrance to the Rare Books Room, it was just her and the woman spitting fire; even she was more company than Zora sought.

She zipped up her jacket and rubbed her hands together to generate warmth. The ancient door's knob stung her with its iciness, and her eyes narrowed at the damned honeybee that was still there, mocking her with its presence. Her gasp at the sudden cold ricocheted in the stairwell, echoing the pain of her sore muscles back to her. Zora swallowed. Clenched her teeth. This was it.

She would find *The Living Crypt*, and she'd get some real goddamn answers. It was the book she'd held when she triggered the first vision. But was it the book that had given her the vision, or was it some presence using the book?

Erika's *clickety-clacks* were…slow? Not so much *clickety*, more so *cl-cl-cl*. Zora showed her Rare Books Room card, but Erika didn't look up from her phone. Not when Zora stepped closer, concerned because she'd realized Erika wasn't blinking, and not when Zora slid the card on the counter till it was beside the phone. Still… no…blinking. Zora's eyebrows drew together, and a dull throb in her forehead reminded her of the headache she was ignoring. Wasn't staring into space something that Esther had reported during the times when people were going missing? She suddenly remembered Lamont's text from weeks ago, when he'd spotted a random person in the library staring at nothing like Michael Myers. *No time*, she reminded herself. There was no time to rehash that stuff now. She left Erika behind in the chilling, unblinking state.

The crimson chandelier shimmered with something *other* than grandiosity or mystery this time. The light felt murkier, more ominous—a warning. Zora stepped under the light, forcing her body away from another bafflement.

She focused on the thin jacquard carpet as she walked to the back room. Her steps were sure, and her memory was even better. Zora knew precisely where *The Living Crypt* would be and managed not to shout with excitement when proven correct. She put three powerful mojo bags in her backpack, with enough *see me not* privacy to ensure no one would see her leaving (stealing from) the library.

Finally, her hands remained steady as she worked. The coppery diced leather smelled of birch, just like last time. The bloody fore-edge painting split as she opened the book. Zora readied herself for another vision. But it didn't come. Neither did the pages have her research or handwriting. Instead, it was just a page, a correct page, in the correct book.

*The Living Crypt: How Conjure and Sacrifice
Shaped Nineteenth-Century Jonesborough*

Chapter Four
The Keepers of the Beast

The Keepers of the Beast (the Keepers) is a spiritual secret society at Bricksbury Mountain College started by the school's founders, Hosanna and Amias Crawfoot. The Keepers are labeled as spiritual because of the group's use of conjure (Hoodoo), ancestral veneration, and other rituals historically carried out by African Americans.

Siblings and business partners, the Crawfoots created the society at the school's inception in 1827. Until 1877,* the Crawfoots spoke openly about the group, claiming its mission was to uphold and preserve both Bricksbury Mountain College and the Black community of Jonesborough. However, they refused to elaborate on their

---

* Hosanna Crawfoot (1801–1877) died of influenza at her Bricksbury Mountain College housing accommodations on September 1, 1877. Her brother, Amias Crawfoot (1803), was with her when she died. Thousands attended the funeral, hosted by the school, on November 18 to give attendees time to travel to the rural school. Amias was reportedly too devastated to attend the services. He would never again publicly discuss the Keepers of the Beast, nor would he be seen in public past March 1881.

methods and activities for doing so. Students publicly discussed their membership and often went on to achieve unparalleled success in their fields.

One such member, Caldonia "Cal" Fackler Johnson, class of 1865, was born into slavery in Knoxville and became the town's first African American millionaire. Another member, Edmonia "The Grand Monia" Littlejohn, class of 1872, went on to study painting at Beaux-Arts de Paris. She was an apprentice to Henry Ossawa Tanner, had commissions from two sitting presidents and eleven international royal families, and had a lifelong annual commission from Henrietta Vinton Davis.

Beginning in the late 1870s, there were reports by Jonesborough townspeople of strange, musical sounds coming from the woods. Reports of the melodies heard ran from classical to religious music to vaudeville. Students at Bricksbury reported the same. A lack of evidence meant the noise was up for interpretation, giving way to myths as the people in the area tried to make sense of the phenomenon. Eventually, the Keepers were linked to the music when an unknown group of Bricksbury students painted the Keepers' crest across the Music Department's front door.

Historians continue to debate the origins of the formal name, as no member or ex-member has ever come forward with any official information. As to the shortened name, a bee is emblazoned on the crest, a reference, some say, to the area's historic reliance on honeybees. Under the bee, the church on the hill is believed to reference Jonesboro African Baptist Church, the first Black church not only in Jonesborough but in Tennessee, and whose land was sold to the Crawfoots for Bricksbury.

Chapter Thirty-Two

Zora tightened her hold on the steering wheel while maneuvering through the twisting backroads leading to the lab on Jonesborough's outskirts. It was the only lab in the area that Lamont's health insurance would cover, but Zora didn't mind the drive, especially because it provided ample time for her to fill Lamont in on everything she'd learned up until now.

Inside the car, a palpable fear hung in the air as she answered Lamont's many questions and gave him time to review the harrowing footage from the previous night at the church.

"Who in the *fuck* are these creepy assholes?" Lamont snapped, his fingers trembling as he pointed at the screen that played the recording. His soft face transformed from shock to rage. "They've been lyin' to you this whole time! Followin' you! Were they even 'accidentally' at the Cornbread Lounge that night, or were they just there to get your briefs hot?" he asked, indignation flaring his wide nostrils as he yanked his locs into a bun.

Zora was too overwhelmed to be offended. She hadn't considered that, but he was probably right. Zora was the perfect victim for Khadijah. She'd made herself the right amount of available to ensure Zora pined from afar. And then, when she batted those eyelashes just enough, Zora could think of nothing but making her cum on her tongue. She'd seemed... soft. Safe, because Khadijah hadn't asked Zora for more than she could give. Maybe that was what killed Zora the most about it. Khadijah had been the exact opposite of the safe option. But Zora couldn't have imagined this— much less planned for it.

She glanced over at the screen periodically, heart aching at the flashing images of familiar faces. Her own sister. It hurt even more than their previous level of estrangement ever had. Sure, Jasmine had tried to protect her, but not hard enough.

"They've been followin' us, haven't they?" Lamont quietly asked sometime later.

Zora sighed. "I don't know. I mean...I have felt like someone was watching me."

"What? When?" Lamont turned in his seat to face her.

Zora considered. "Well, a few times. At Conjure Night. In my apartment. Then I told you about what happened at homecoming. Also, there was something weird when I went to go see you this morning. Emir answered and said you'd gone to work—"

"Emir answered the door?" Lamont's brown eyes widened. "Didn't think he got up before noon."

"I was...insistent," Zora said, remembering how long she'd stood in the empty hallway knocking.

"Damn, you really wanted to see me, huh?" Lamont laughed softly.

Zora killed what could have been a lighthearted turn in conversation. "Yeah, I mean...I thought you might be in serious danger."

"Oh, right."

"Anyway, I was standing in the hallway and felt like someone was watching me. I can't prove it, and I never saw anyone. It was just a feeling."

"'Just a feelin'' is never just a feelin' when it comes from a conjurer," Lamont said.

Zora's eyebrows shot up. "Damn, how wise."

"Why are you actin' surprised?" Lamont feigned hurt. "But

seriously, think about it. They said Amias and Hosanna used 'God's Hoodoo magic' to protect Bricksbury, someone you met at *Conjure Night* was already in the church last night, and on the day that we met, you got a vision in the Rare Books Room. I don't think we're dealin' with anythin' ordinary here. How 'bout you lock into your Hoodoo instead of feelin' sorry for yourself?"

"Excuse me?" Zora was only halfway hurt.

"You know I'm right. Hoodoo is the common denominator here, an' I'm still an amateur! You've been practicin' your entire life, Zora."

Her throat clenched in anxiety.

"I'm sorry this is happenin', but someone has got to tell it to ya like it is," Lamont continued.

Zora nodded in agreement. Her mind had already turned to her childhood learning conjure in her grandparents' woods. Zora's elders had created a locked coffer reinforced with protective charms, amulets, and all sorts of other spells that Zora didn't know about. There, she'd learned the bounds of magic and knelt before God and her ancestors, promising to use her gifts to enhance and tamper as her conscience saw fit. But God hadn't taught her what to do when assaulted by her sister in His house. He'd known this was coming anyway, hadn't He? God knew Zora would end up here, and while not entirely comforting, He knew how this would all end.

Outside the lab, Lamont and Zora sat in silence for a moment. Lamont was breathing heavily, his anger and fear pulsating through his body. Zora felt as if she were holding her breath. She didn't think this was over yet.

Lamont headed inside for his tests, leaving Zora alone. As she waited, she looked back at the footage. Toni had said she was ready to be sacrificed. She wasn't crawling on the dusty church floor against her will. There was a sick need (obligation?) in her voice, a desperate desire for...death. What had happened between the time she went missing and the moment she decided she would willingly sacrifice herself? Zora thought of the old woman from her first vision, how she'd ultimately done the same.

Zora rubbed her temples and breathed deeply, going through the steps to calm her body. A panic attack wasn't necessarily imminent, but it lurked nearby, waiting for the next anxiety spike. When her heartbeat had sufficiently lowered, Zora glanced up, spotting Charlene across the street at a busy farm stand, the sight jarring Zora from her thoughts. Their toffee-colored wig was laid perfectly, and they walked unhurriedly, waving to the people rocking on the wide front porch. The townies lingered outside the country store, their lips wrapped around ashen cigarettes and their eyes darting toward Zora's car, the obvious outsider. Zora's jaw tensed, and her stomach swirled as a wave of dread rushed through her.

Even though she wasn't certain of Charlene and Mallory's connection, she *was* certain they were involved. Her vision about the reverend had revealed that much. She didn't know anyone, not really, Zora realized. Her instinct screamed at her to follow Charlene, to uncover whatever secret threads tied them to Mallory. However, before she could act, Charlene emerged, arms laden with colorful fruits and vegetables, oblivious to Zora's tensed muscles. *What else are you hiding?* she wondered. *Who was the man you were working with? Are you working with him still?*

She suddenly remembered something Jasmine had said on the recording. *Leave. My sister. Alone. I'll take it up with him, if need be.* Who was the "him" she'd been speaking of? Was it possible it was the same man who—

Zora's passenger door suddenly opened, and Lamont sat heavily beside her, apologizing for how long the draw took. Zora couldn't help but smile a bit, realizing she had at least one true friend at Bricksbury. Yet, the urgency of their task quickly overshadowed the comfort this brought her.

"Okay, so as I was sittin' in the chair, thinkin' about anythin' other than them stickin' needles in me, I had a thought. You should meet with Dr. Grant," he said, the weight of their mission settling heavily between them. "He's our only...what? Ally?"

Encouraged by his use of "our," Zora nodded.

"You're right." She'd avoided bringing anything outside of the purely academic on this research journey to Dr. Grant to avoid being seen as incapable of focusing on the "right" details, but things had gone far enough now. Dr. Grant had known about all the pieces— Esther, the Keepers, even the Crawfoots—but to him, they were all just bits of history. Zora, however, saw the ripple effects of all those pieces were splashing against the reality of today. She saw them, and they pained her.

———

"Thank you for meeting with me on such short notice, Dr. Grant." Zora spoke as slowly as possible, but she heard the increased pace and hoped her thesis advisor didn't catch the tremble in her voice. There was no time now to process trauma—that was what therapy and marijuana were for—she was in Dr. Grant's office for an entirely different reason.

"Of course, Miss Robinson," Dr. Grant said. His soft smile met his knowing eyes. "But, Zora?" he asked.

"Yes?"

"Are you okay?"

The question was simple. The answer, less so.

When she didn't answer immediately, Dr. Grant sat back in his chair, frowning. "Are you being safe on campus? I assume you've heard about the missing student. Toni Anderson."

Oh, if only he knew how close he was to Zora's anxiety.

"I'm staying safe, yes. Keeping in constant touch with friends and such. But, Dr. Grant, I was hoping you could help me with my thesis." Zora dodged the question and tried not to think about dodging the Keepers. They had to be watching her, right? Did they know where she was now? Would they hurt Dr. Grant for getting too close? Suddenly, being there felt foolish, or at least, more hurtful than helpful. *The faster I get outta here, the less danger Dr. Grant will face.* Zora spoke with renewed speed.

"Esther's diary has been incredibly helpful. It's sent me in many other directions," Zora began, "but I believe the Keepers of the Beast is a currently operating secret society at Bricksbury." Dr. Grant opened his mouth, but Zora rushed to finish. This was difficult as it was, and she didn't know when she'd have the courage to suggest this to Dr. Grant again. "I also learned that Amias Crawfoot founded the Keepers and was pastor of Jonesboro African Baptist Church. I believe he and his sister, Hosanna, were conjurers or maybe working with conjurers. This connects the Crawfoots to the church, Bricksbury, and the Keepers of the Beast. I'm onto something here. They are functioning as though the Beast is real."

Dr. Grant steepled his fingers and closed his eyes. "How much writing have you gotten done? I'd love to see a proposal with this new direction. It's all a little more specific than what I was initially picturing, but I know how these projects can run away from us."

If only he fucking knew. "I haven't gotten much writing done, actually," she said. "I've been focusing on compiling the sources and—"

Dr. Grant frowned. "Zora, I don't want you to get caught up in the minutiae. You could research these topics for years. I don't need to tell you that the mark of a great historian is the ability to hone one's intensity, do I?"

Despite Dr. Grant's belief that it wasn't a practical use of her time, Zora knew differently. Her life might have even been on the line. He didn't fully understand because he had no idea about just how much had happened since he first sent her off to interview

Mallory. The Keepers couldn't get away with what they had been doing. Even if her revenge was limited to exposure, Zora was determined to have it. She would uncover the truth and make it known to others—they were sacrificing people and forcing others to turn their heads away.

She thought of what Lamont had said to her in the car, about taking matters into her own hands, with her own powers. Some old, frail professor wasn't going to be able to offer her anything better than that. It was highly unlikely he'd believe her about half of this shit anyway. She shouldn't have even come here, she realized now. It was time to face the problem head-on. Zora wasn't about to let the Keepers snatch it away from her. Come Lucifer; come His song.

Chapter Thirty-Three

D r. Grant was about as much help as any boomer is during a crisis!" Lamont fumed the next day through the phone.

Zora let out a muffled sound of agreement while balancing the phone in one hand and Henry Louis's leash in the other, feeling as though she was doing a dozen things at once. The morning sun beat down on her, causing her ribbed tank top and cotton shorts to gather damp sweat in uncomfortable areas. Zora trudged through the dewy grass, looking for a clear and inconspicuous area for Henry Louis to relieve himself. As far as she could tell, nobody was following her, or if they were, they were keeping well hidden. Good. Let them underestimate her, like they'd been doing all along.

"Okay, we need to regroup." Lamont was also huffing. He'd woken up late, as was usual. "I'm closing tonight, so I'll be out of the library around . . . maybe eight or eight thirty. Until then, follow the Hoodoo. Try to figure out just how the Keepers are using it."

Zora pulled out a thin, crinkled bag as Henry Louis circled a grassy spot. "I'm on it," she said. "First place I'm headed is Jasmine's."

Half an hour later, Henry Louis was gobbling breakfast when Zora left, eyeing the still cowrie shells in the corner as she went. Grandpa's hunting knife was in her pocket, while her bear spray was in her backpack. She would carry it with her everywhere now. Lamont had been right; they needed to be careful.

She made her way to William F. Yardley Hall, or "Yards," a relic composed of apartments like the "Neighborhood," except they had more bedrooms and square footage than everyone else. They were used primarily for families and married couples, but grad students could sneak in sometimes—not Zora, unfortunately.

One would expect such housing to be updated, or at least in acceptable condition. Instead, the long fluorescent lights above Zora's head either flickered or had died long ago. Insect bodies darkened yellowing plastic. Roaches. Shiny wasps.

The building's condition notwithstanding, Yards was a Gothic-revival mansion made of pointed arches, steeply pitched roofs, and stone, and thus was magnificent. Thin pavers were cracked like all others on campus and periodically filled in with resin. The fissures only exaggerated the colors, turning them into ash-gray and olive slivers. Broken, yet stunning. It was as if the building continued to survive despite all the reasons not to.

Uniform black iron welded onto the wall held a single unlit bees-wax pillar, reminding Zora of the woman spitting fire outside the Rare Books Room. Her neck snapped to the right as déjà vu gripped her. The dust coating the crimson stained glass reminded her of Jonesboro African Baptist Church. The feeling of witnessing dead history. Knowing Jasmine had knocked her out.

Ah. Back to the mission. Today, she would face Jasmine and force her to talk—about what she'd done to Zora, and how she came to join the Keepers. If they were using Hoodoo, then Zora wasn't the only Robinson with expert-level knowledge. She was following the conjure, just as she promised Lamont. And it had told her that the person with whom she'd learned conjure should be her first stop.

She was at her sister's door, but no one answered when she knocked. Five, ten, fifteen minutes passed, and she knocked peri-odically, but nothing changed. Zora had no problem standing in the hallway till her sister or sibling-in-law woke their asses up, just like she'd done outside Lamont's door yesterday.

"Yo." A man across the hallway opened his door. A baby's screech hurtled through the air. He had a pacifier and a stuffed giraffe in one hand. "They ain't home. Stop knockin'."

"Sorry...uh, do you know them?"

"No," he said, crossing thin arms.

Zora chewed her bottom lip for a moment before turning and pretending to leave. She made a show of sighing loudly when she turned the corner. The baby's screams followed her down the hall like punishment.

Zora ascended two carpeted flights of stairs, flinching at the sudden noises that reverberated behind the closed dorm doors. They sounded louder than they should, a touch sharper and harsher, too. A chilling sensation crept down her spine; it felt as if unseen eyes were tracking her movements. Zora spun around abruptly, convinced she sensed someone breathing on her neck. She unsheathed Grandpa's hunting knife, turning to aim it at her stalker. However, her eyes revealed no one else in the hallway. The crimson stained-glass windows glared at her like pools of blood, and the unlit beeswax now resembled long, bony fingers grasping toward the ceiling. The sounds behind the doors gave way to Zora's roaring heart as she sprinted back down to the opposite side of the building. She hung a *see me not* mojo bag around her neck. *Protect me, Jesus.*

She peeked around Jasmine's hallway, quiet from the infant's cries. Blessedly, the man had left, and no one else was there, as it should have been. Jasmine wasn't there, but now was time for plan B. Zora went for a hair clip, because she didn't know where to start looking to steal a crowbar and didn't want to know where to purchase one.

Her hands were steady as she broke into her sister's apartment. Cracked wood gave way with a yawning creak when she applied pressure. Half of her wished Jasmine had been there so Zora could confront her; the other half wanted to investigate without cutting eyes and without her sibling-in-law.

Darkness spilled out of the room. Zora warily swept her phone's light across the main living area to confirm no one was in the room with her. Her shoulders deflated when she got confirmation. She scratched the back of her neck in disbelief at her luck.

"Thank God," she whispered. She placed each foot slowly on the ground as she walked, not wanting to cause any more creaking than necessary. It was difficult. The rich walnut floors were far older than the cheap laminate in Zora's apartment. This was natural wood. Real *old* wood.

The room was cluttered, but in an organized way. Rumpled blankets were gathered in a pile on the thin baby-blue couch. Converses, black pumps, and leather boots cluttered the floor in front of the empty shoe rack. The kitchen counter was tiny and covered in unopened mail and opened textbooks. The scent of basil tomato sauce lingered in the air.

Focus. Zora gripped her tiger's-eye necklace, willing it to calm her heartbeat. It didn't work, but focusing on something else momentarily helped ground her. She didn't have much time. After another quick sweep of the large bedroom and bathroom to ensure she was alone, Zora went searching.

She rifled through thick paperbacks with bold words like "chemical equilibriums" and "Bayesian statistics," two (unrelated?) things Zora had no interest scrutinizing. The mail was uniformly bills, mostly credit card and medical. Nothing that clued her in to Jasmine's current doings within the Keepers.

A writing desk was wedged between the couch and the kitchen counter, wrapped in marbleized contact vinyl. Zora opened the desk's drawer, releasing pungent oils into the air. Sweet licorice dissolved into damp grass. Zora sneezed. Why did Jasmine have hyssop and vetiver oils? The dark amber glass bottles had measured droppers—and there were more. Cinnamon bark and black pepper. Condition oil labeled *Protection from Evil*, handwritten in tight cursive on parchment.

No alluring locked boxes were hidden in the chaotic bookshelf or under their sagging boxsprings. Zora didn't see a single letter written in mysterious code. She didn't see anything that offered anything new. Hot tears fell from Zora's eyes as she circled the room again. Trembling fingers wiped them away. There had to be something there. Anything. She'd take any-fucking-thing.

Then she found something. A golden necklace hung from a slender, elegant red glass perfume bottle in the bathroom. There was something etched into it, but Zora's eyesight blurred the harder she looked. As she reached for it, her eyes fixated on the ordinary face serum on the counter behind it. Necklace forgotten, Zora picked up the serum bottle, considering it. The longer she stared, the more ordinary the strawberry-scented salicylic acid remained. *Wait... why am I looking at this?* She shook her head and returned to the necklace. It hung from crimson and was far more interesting than the serum, but Zora couldn't stop her neck from turning away.

Zora sucked in air as she, once again, picked up the serum. The necklace must have been spelled. It wouldn't be so difficult to pick it up otherwise. She checked the time.

Without thinking, Zora closed her eyes. She wrapped both hands around the *see me not* mojo bag around her neck. This wasn't its intended purpose, but it held power—and she captured it. The warmth shot up her hands, neck, and jaw to settle on her lips. Her voice was steady as she spoke the spell.

"He giveth power to the faint; and to them that have no might He increaseth strength."[12]

---

12 Isaiah 40:29—He giveth power to the faint; and to them that have no might he increaseth strength.

Her hands grew looser on the mojo bag each time Zora repeated the Bible verse. She spoke rapidly, spittle flying as she pushed a hand toward the perfume bottle. *Please give me strength, ancestors.* Zora would need all the help she could get.

Her hand wrapped around the cold metal. She opened her eyes to find the Keepers of the Beast's crest, honeybee and all.

"Holy fuck..." Zora's voice shook. She'd finally found something, even if it didn't offer new information. Just seeing objective proof of the connections she'd made after watching the footage made her feel more sure of herself and what she was doing.

The sound of the front door opening on the other side of the apartment caused Zora's heart to skip a beat. She set the necklace down and carefully peeked out from the crack between the bathroom door and its frame—it was Jasmine. Just Jasmine, thank God.

Zora would get to have her confrontation after all.

"Hey, sis," she called as she stepped into the hallway. Jasmine screamed, dropping the canvas grocery bags that had been balanced in her arms. "Time for you to answer some questions for me."

Chapter Thirty-Four

Jasmine didn't react after her initial scream, instead watching Zora as she made her way closer. She would have her answers, and she would have them right fucking now.

"You hit me," Zora said, not asked.

Her sister fully closed her eyes and turned to the left, full cheeks trembling as if Zora had struck her.

"You hit me over the head in a church in the middle of the woods and then left my body with a bunch of cult members."

Jasmine opened red eyes, spilling what Zora hoped was shame. Her tears made no difference; actually, they made it all worse. What right did she have to feel sad? What great grief did she hold that would ever justify what she'd done? Zora felt Grandpa's heavy knife in her pocket and, for a wild moment, considered showing Jasmine what actual pain felt like.

"Well, maybe you should have heeded the *blatant* warning I created for you at homecoming," Jasmine finally said, her eyes trained on the ground. "And they aren't cult members."

"It would sure appear that way."

"They aren't."

"Who are they, then?"

Silence.

"Huh? You're so fuckin' sure I was safe with them? Why the hell are they doin' this, Jasmine? Why would you ever join a group like that? Why would you use your powers to hurt people?"

Jasmine shook her head. Zora was about to scream in frustration when, suddenly, everything became achingly clear.

"This is why we stopped talkin', isn't it?" Zora took a step back without realizing it and backed into the pile of shoes. "Because you wanted to join this . . . this murder cult!"

"It's not like that," Jasmine spat.

"Yeah, okay," Zora said with a soulless chuckle. She tilted her head to look at her sister differently as the last decade twisted to reveal itself in the light. "If you think I'm gonna let y'all get away with this—"

Jasmine's jaw clenched. "Don't be stupid. The Keepers are dangerous, Zora, if you hadn't already figured that one out."

"Why did you leave me in the church with them, then? Do you just fully not give a shit if I live or die?"

"Okay, first of all, I . . . I had to leave you. It would've been worse if I hadn't done what the Cardinal said. Besides, you two are a thing; I knew she would protect you."

Zora shook her head, her body rejecting this explanation, wounded heart rejecting Khadijah's mention. "And why did you hit me to begin with? What was the point of that?"

"I didn't want you to see any more. Hear any more. I didn't want you drawn in. Zora, I only wanted to protect you so you wouldn't be near this world. This place." She threw her hands outward, indicating the space around her. "You are a practiced, powerful conjurer, Zora. You showed as much on that first Conjure Night. What was I supposed to do? Once they decide they want somebody, that's it. Nobody else's opinion matters."

Jasmine closed her eyes again and swallowed loud enough for Zora to hear.

"Why did they bring me there in the first place, then?" Zora demanded. "What did they hope was going to happen?"

When Jasmine predictably didn't answer, Zora said, "Fine. You won't tell me? Then show me."

"What?" Jasmine frowned.

"I said, show me what y'all were doing in that church." Zora's voice had taken on a strange, menacing tone. She knew what would get Jasmine's attention, and after the confirmation that her sister was indeed one of the Keepers, Zora had it in her to fuck some shit up.

"Zora." Breath left Jasmine's lungs in hesitant gusts like it was afraid of what it might find. "I can't do that. You have no idea what you're getting into. This is . . . vital work. It's important and complicated. More complicated than you can imagine. But you do not want to be involved. You could leave, right now. Leave this behind and never look back."

Jasmine must have forgotten who her little sister was, what she was or wasn't capable of. There was no way she'd leave Lamont and all the other students vulnerable to whatever the hell the Keepers thought they were doing for the school.

"You take me to that church and explain everything, or I will publish all my research, including the part where the Keepers are connected to missing and murdered Bricksbury students going back centuries, plural! Centuries!" This was a dangerous bluff, yet one that Zora was ready to execute. She certainly didn't have that evidence, but Jasmine was unaware of the depth of Zora's research, and Zora planned to leverage that to her benefit.

Jasmine's body grew tense against the counter, and her eyes cut into Zora's. *I fucking got you*, Zora thought. Jasmine's voice was lower than it'd been during the entire conversation, as if she, too, had made a realization.

"You can't do that." Jasmine spoke to Zora as if she were half her age. "There are things you don't under—"

Zora took the blade out from her pocket, unsheathing it, absorbing its weight in her palm. She didn't have time to consider how she'd gotten here. Jasmine could surely call her society friends to stop Zora and make all the evidence disappear if she wanted. This was her moment. If she was gonna get the full information from Jasmine, it was this second and only under these circumstances. No more waiting.

"Are you serious?" Jasmine's eyes bounced from the metal's gleam to Zora's glare.

"Move," Zora said, stepping out of the way to sweep her arms toward the door.

"You cannot be fucking serious."

"I had a camera hidden on my body when I went to the church, Jasmine. I have multiple recordings scheduled to go out into the world, showing you assaulting me, then Khadijah and other Keepers surrounding you and making you go away."

"You...recorded..."

"And then they loaded my unconscious body into a four-wheeler and dumped me in my dorm. Do you have any idea what it was like to watch that back? I am traumatized."

Jasmine shot forward, arms reaching frantically for Zora. She stopped short when Zora lifted her weapon.

"I will kill you." Zora pulled her shoulders back and locked eyes with her sister. "Because you're right. This is vital. This is centuries of murders vital. I interviewed someone whose father wouldn't let them attend Bricksbury after the 1920s disappearances! This is a *known* thing. Y'all are not even bein' subtle! And I'm not gonna sit back and let y'all get away with this. You are a criminal. You do understand that, right? A crime committed under the guise of a noble reason is still a crime."

"Says who?"

"Says the person with the knife in their hands and bear spray in their backpack."

"Jesus, Zora."

"Walk, Jasmine."

Amias Crawfoot
Present Day
Jonesborough, Tennessee
Jonesborough Conjure Shoppe

Charlene steeped water in silence while Amias wandered around their shop. They'd kept it how their family had for generations with little change; even the carpet hadn't changed since the seventies when Amias and Charlene first met. Now they went by their middle name, Mallory. They'd been an only child, so when "Charlene" disappeared, it was a tragedy for the family. But when "Mallory" arrived months later, looking eerily like Charlene, the family asked few questions. Especially since Charlene and Amias had been secretly spelling them for weeks, stripping their protective amulets from the corners of their house and replacing them with ones that made them susceptible to Charlene and Amias's magic. It only took one generation before the others accepted it without question. An unknown cousin was hard to turn away, especially given the likeness.

Charlene's shop was thick with lemongrass incense, balanced between sweetness and tartness. Amias resisted the strands of smoke, which insisted he lower his shoulders. Amias wasn't calm and wouldn't be magicked into being so. He passed a table of gemstones. Bright orange and russet-brown tiger's-eye made him pause.

"What do you make of her?" Amias asked aloud. It was the first time he'd spoken since entering the shoppe. Charlene had closed an hour before and it was nearing two in the morning, which was the height of Amias's day.

"Who?" Charlene asked. They kept their eyes on the kettle.

Amias picked up a tiger's-eye bracelet, staring at the orange, remembering seeing Zora in the library. The trail of power she left in her wake could only be divinely given. Who was God to Zora?

"Is this sarcasm?" Amias asked, bored with wherever Charlene's intentions would lead this conversation.

"Why are you obsessed with her? Is it like Reverend Thunder an' Esther Fisherman? Are you 'in love'?"

Amias wasn't looking at them, but he nevertheless heard the air quotations in Charlene's tone. He regretted being honest with them about Esther. No one needed to know the extent of his tangled emotions. No one but Him, at least.

"Are the Keepers in line? How's my Cardinal doing?" Amias had more pressing concerns than Charlene's questions.

"Cardinal" was the term he'd come up with for the member of the Keepers who was still an active student on campus and who would work directly with Charlene to ensure the Beast's boundary in the woods held. Amias had chosen Khadijah himself. She'd impressed him enough by her third semester. She'd been one of the few con-jurers who used music in their magic. It was a perfect fit given the Beast's passion for playing instruments and singing folk songs among the oak trees. Khadijah used music offensively, planting flowers and herbs around the perimeter that dampened and warped sound.

With help from the other Keepers, Khadijah planted the same flowers nearer the center of the Beast's territory. These not only amplified sound, but the hidden amulets sent the Beast an urge to remain close. It'd been decided that the urge would be grounded by white willow bark, making the Beast more susceptible to their magic, and hops, which further calmed her.

"Khadijah's doin' fine. You know, actually, I was reminded recently that this shop used to have live music an' food. Khadijah an' her friends would love that. Maybe she could stay here after a new student becomes the Cardinal."

Amias cut through the fat of Charlene's words to get to what mattered. "Zora reminded you of that."

Charlene sucked her teeth. "You were listenin'? Amias, I told you... I don't *love* when you do that here, in my shop."

"Do you love immortality?"

The threat that Amias would rescind Charlene's immortality was insinuated but present nonetheless. The kettle sang a shrill song, reminding Amias of something older than Zora, Charlene, and even Esther. Kettles were one of the few things that functionally hadn't changed over time. They were a comfort in a time overrun with discomfort.

Charlene cleared their throat. "Yes, the Keepers are goin' strong. They're usin' a combination of holy water an' Rose of Jericho in the woods' air droplets an' they've finally made peace with the spirits in the graveyard. Your Cardinal did the final negotiations via fiddle."

Charlene removed the kettle from the heat and poured water into the awaiting teacups. Mint for Amias and spiced apple for them.

"Oh, really?" Amias finally turned to Charlene to take his cup, thinking of how much the Beast loved the fiddle. "That took Khadijah longer than I would have liked."

The spirits resting in Jonesboro African Baptist Church's graveyard were fickle. They had conflicting opinions on the Beast, and so rarely helped Amias in his magic. Now that he and Charlene had assembled a group of powerful conjurers called the Keepers to keep the Beast calm and in God's light, the spirits were more amenable. They'd even begun allowing the Keepers to use their land as an energy source to solidify the Beast's boundaries. Keeping her within the woods but outside of Bricksbury's campus was difficult but easier with their help.

Amias drank his tea silently with the tiger's-eye bracelet fastened to his wrist. Something would have to be done to clean up this mess that was forming around Zora Robinson. If she wouldn't join them willingly, he decided, he'd happily resort to something more drastic.

Chapter Thirty-Five

Zora watched her sister go through all the stages of grief in real time. Being this close to her felt like touching fire—a searing pain she foresaw yet reached for anyway. She had planned versions of this confrontation for her entire life, had written it down in journals, and talked endlessly about it in therapy. Zora had convinced herself she had processed being abandoned by Jasmine. Thought she'd successfully moved on and placed her focus entirely on conjure's stability and her burgeoning career. But looking into Jasmine's teary eyes now told a desperately different story, one of repressed anger and hopelessness. Zora hadn't known how desperate she'd be for the truth. She was so desperate and, now, sure of nefariousness that she held Jasmine's gaze without blinking.

Jasmine licked her lips with fists on her hips. Her body was frozen, but her eyes were in constant motion. They swung from Grandpa's blade to Zora's eyes to the front door to the ceiling and back again in a frantic loop. Her face rose and fell with denial, rage, and the full spectrum of depression. Aching expressions. Shaking hands clung to cornrows. Finally, Jasmine put her phone in Zora's empty, outstretched hand, eyes leery of the knife in the other.

"Z..." Jasmine began.

Zora's chest panged—she hadn't heard that in such a long time.

"They won't like this," Jasmine said, though she opened the door and walked outside. "Our leader won't like this. And I swear to

God, Zora, you don't want to piss him off. *I* do not want to piss him off. Okay? So be quiet, don't do any conjure. He feels it every time you do it."

Zora tried not to show the level of interest that was piqued at the mention of the mysterious leader. She didn't want to come off as overeager and spook the deer. "Is he the one who has been casting things against me? Trying to scare me? Showing me the visions?"

Jasmine didn't answer, which was fine because Zora was done asking questions. It was time to discover the answers face-to-face. She pointed her head down the hallway, silently telling her sister to stop stalling. She kept the distance she instinctively knew she'd need as she followed. Zora could feel her mind racing, so she violently wrung out her hands to distract her body. It worked. She kept the weapon in her pocket, though she and Jasmine were aware of its presence. Jasmine huffed while walking in front of Zora, who looked around frantically for the other faces from her recorded footage. She was bold in front of her sister, which she was proud of. But out here? There were too many unknowns. Too many lies floating around and liars available to dispense them.

Eventually, they reached the far side of campus. Far enough away from anyone who didn't plan on going for a hike. Zora was glad for the quiet after the campus bustle they'd marched through. She also looked up at the sign. Could there be some hidden meaning or code among the words? Possibly, but her rushing adrenaline didn't allow time to consider it.

BRICKSBURY MOUNTAIN COLLEGE WOODLANDS

THIS 300-ACRE TRACT WAS ONCE THE WOODLOT OF JONESBORO
AFRICAN BAPTIST CHURCH (C. 1796). IT WILL BE LEFT
UNDISTURBED FOR PRESENT AND FUTURE GENERATIONS.
REMAIN ON THE PATH.

"Up for the trek?" Jasmine asked, a low warning in her voice as they entered the woods under an emerald, fluttering canopy. "Y'know there are...mountain lions and copperheads. Did you know that? And gray wolves! Some of them have rabies."

"Stop stalling," Zora said, unamused. "If you think those are enough to scare me after everything I've seen around here, you're just as crazy as I thought you were for joining the Keepers."

Zora had worn comfy sneakers and was confident she could reach the church and back without a map or snapped ankle. Her oversized water bottle sat happily in her backpack, as did a mini flashlight. Besides, there was still plenty of sunlight. It peeked at her every few seconds, reminding her that something besides her sister's betrayal existed. Besides the empty pit she'd left in Zora's life. She'd taken her whole self away and given it to the Keepers. The Keepers who murdered people.

"What happened to your friend—Toni Anderson?" Zora asked.

"She wasn't my friend."

"Oh, I'm sorry. What happened to your coconspirator that you left for sacrifice in the church?"

"She was marked," Jasmine answered sadly. "There was nothing any of us—"

"Marked? What does that mean?"

Jasmine didn't respond. Zora sighed, and they walked in silence as she pondered the meaning of being "marked." Was that different from being sacrificed or a natural progression from it? It sounded involuntary, so why had Toni been so willing? Desperate, even?

"How is your group 'keeping' the Beast? How does that work? What is it?" Zora was following a thread in her mind.

"Hoodoo is how it works," Jasmine said as she kept walking. "And the Beast is real. Physically real, not just a force or spirit."

"Bullshit," Zora said, although she wasn't so sure anymore. "That's not possible."

Jasmine stopped and turned around, immediately finding Zora's eyes. Then she stepped back when Zora brandished her knife. Zora wasn't taking any chances. It was daytime, but there were still plenty of shadows around them. Pollen suffocated the air, giving everything a slight sepia tone and causing Zora to sneeze every few minutes. She wiped her sweaty palms against cotton shorts to maintain a good grip on the knife's slip-slippery wooden handle. She knew what Jasmine was capable of and had to be capable of more to best her.

"You know too much already, Zora." Jasmine turned with a fingertip caught between her teeth. "You were always good at figuring shit out, I guess."

"If you'd texted in the last decade, you would know a single thing about me, including that I—"

"Got the *Dartmouth* to include a permanent history section in the paper? Became the associate editor, and then the editor of it? Spent years of your life in Knoxville repairing old pictures and maps? Gave a moving speech called 'Deconstructing the Centuries-Long Respectability Politics Plaguing the Black Church' at the Southern Black Historical Convention that's now being used in at least three college courses in the country?"

Zora opened her mouth, hoping words would emerge. When they didn't, she panicked and squeezed her lips together, but the sudden blunt, brunt of pressure was painful, and she ended up with her mouth wide open again; how it should have been this whole time if Zora were nakedly honest with herself, which she only did on special occasions.

"Breathe, Zora," Jasmine spoke softly.

She'd come closer as Zora's mind raced and distracted her. Of course, Zora panicked at the abrupt physical closeness with her sister. It was too much. Too soon. And Zora was now literally on a mission. She was so close to the truth that she could taste it mixed in with the sweetly floral pollen.

Zora cleared her throat. "Some crazy, long-dead siblings from the 1800s decided that Hoodoo and murder were necessary to keep Bricksbury running, and now you and dozens of other students have been doing their bidding ever since? Abandoning your families? Allowing—*assisting* the murder of students. Does that about cover it?"

"No," Jasmine said.

"Not really," someone said from behind Zora.

Zora turned slowly. They locked stares, and Zora took a beat for confusion to clear. Khadijah's eyes were red-rimmed, and purpling bruises covered her body. Her jaw trembled as she looked at Zora. What happened to her? Why was she covered in bruises like that?

"Let's be fair," a man's voice said from somewhere out of sight.

Zora spun back around, knife held high, to find none other than Dr. Grant standing there. Zora's brain blanked for a moment, and all she heard was a soft breeze so rhythmic like a gentle melody. Zora wanted badly to give herself to it, to fall into the forest's depths of pine and honeysuckle, anything that would allow her to escape this terrible moment. This could not be happening.

"Let's be fair," Dr. Grant repeated. "Neither I nor my sister were crazy, at first anyway. And indeed, both of us are still very much alive. Lawd, are we."

Zora blinked in her shock. "I'm sorry?" she asked. "Dr. Grant... you don't really believe that you're Amias Crawfoot, do you?" Dr. Grant, the one who encouraged her to apply to Bricksbury, the one who first gave her Esther's diary. Dr. Grant, who only ever encouraged Zora to continue the research that brought her here. He was the leader of the Keepers all along?

"It's true, Zora," Khadijah tried to explain. "He *is* Amias. He was given the gift of immortality by God in order to continue his cause. *Our* cause. We are the reason that Bricksbury is safe."

"Safe?" Zora demanded, a mad giggle escaping. "There have been people, innocent people, who were killed by…" Her words drifted off as she realized something. Zora's head started spinning a million miles per minute. "The man in my visions," she said, turning to Dr. Grant. "It was you."

"Yes, indeed," he said with a weak smile. "I've been keeping the Beast at bay since I helped to create her. My sister, Hosanna, the first human sacrifice, and arguably the most important."

Dr. Grant—Amias—stood on the other side of Jasmine; hands clasped together behind his back. His eyes weren't the same as they were in the visions. There, they were covered in heavy wrinkles. They were small. Beady. Now the round orbs dominated his face unnaturally, relegating his nose and mouth down several inches. They were brown, just as Dr. Grant's had always been, but somehow more than color. Pointy shards of amber and swirling bright honey made up the murky depths, giving rise and textures to an otherwise flat surface.

They should have been stunning—and maybe they were. Perhaps they were the most alluring, aesthetically pleasing pair of eyes. But before they could be anything else, they were terrifying.

The fire-eyed thing from the vision had been Hosanna Craw-foot. That paper-skinned demon with the ink dripping from its lips. Hosanna Crawfoot was the Beast.

And he'd just said that she was still alive to this day. It hadn't been a spell that caused Zora to see the embers in the woods after Conjure Night. It had been the Beast, watching her. Just as it had been the Beast who called her name from the depths of the trees earlier that same night.

"Yes, Hosanna is alive," Amias hissed as though he could read her mind. "And she needs us. Now."

Chapter Thirty-Six

Amias blinked. Zora's breath caught in her chest as she tripped backward, crashing hard on wrists that were already sore. She might have been on the forest floor, but in that moment she could've been anywhere. Anyone. Nothing made sense anymore. Khadijah rushed forward to help her, and Zora was too dazed to object.

"It'll be okay," Khadijah whispered in her ear. "I promise."

Khadijah's voice shook like Zora's knees. Amias smiled like he could hear them from where he stood.

"Zora Candace Robinson doesn't know the full story—she only thinks she does."

Amias's voice sailed through the air, bellowing against the wind. Like an unholy godsend, the baritone sounded halfway between a church bell and a funeral toll.

"Furthermore," Amias continued, "she has an important decision to make, but I'll get to that later."

Zora accepted Khadijah's strong hold on her hips, keeping her upright while Zora processed her new findings. Amias Crawfoot was alive. He was alive, and he stood in front of her. He was alive, stood in front of her, and looked to be threatening her in some way? *What do I do? What do I do?* She grabbed her tiger's-eye necklace and averted her gaze from his while she gathered renewed strength from her ancestors.

After blinking to clear the stinging wetness from her eyes, Zora looked back into Amias's. His gaze, though, was riveted on her necklace.

"Do you use it when you're afraid?" he asked, walking toward her. His head tilted to the side inquisitively while his hands remained behind his back. "Or just when presented with new... findings?"

His steps were fluid even though he went down a rugged mountain trail. Amias walked over exposed roots and rogue sticks with ease, without looking down once.

Zora had half a mind to lower her gaze and confirm he was actually walking on legs and not just floating like the ghost he was. But her instincts were clear: *Do not move. Don't you dare fuckin' move.*

Before Amias reached Zora, Jasmine stepped in front of her younger sister. One of Jasmine's hands grabbed Zora's sweaty shirt, and the other thrust in front of her, begging words that weren't coming out of her mouth, maintaining additional distance between Zora and Amias.

Zora was shocked anew by Jasmine. Who was this person, and why didn't she fit into the vault in Zora's mind? It was custom. Jasmine should fit. But she was... someone different now. Someone determined to protect her.

While Zora continued trying to process, she was thrust behind Khadijah, who walked up to Amias with a deferential, lowered head. All the while, Amias's eyes hadn't left Zora's necklace.

"Amias." Khadijah spoke loud enough for everyone to hear. "Zora may have meant harm initially because she was searching for the truth, but she will keep our secret. She's a legacy, after all."

Khadijah indicated Jasmine, who used the hand holding Zora's shirt to push her back even farther. Zora took the hint and backed away slowly, ignoring the dampness pooling under her bra and down her entire back. For the first time, she noticed the rest of the Keepers were there as well, standing with arms folded on the side of the trail. They must not have deemed Zora worthy of a confrontation with Amias, which she didn't take personally.

Jasmine stepped forward, though slightly behind Khadijah. "Zora won't be a problem once she leaves here today. You know that."

Amias kept his gaze on the tiger's-eye as he spoke. "I do, now?"

"Well…" Jasmine began.

But Zora had heard enough. She'd seen enough visions and read enough of Esther's diary and *The Living Crypt*. Not all of it. She certainly didn't understand everything and could admit that, but she knew enough. Zora filled her lungs to their pollen capacity and marched to Amias, stopping beside Khadijah. She looked into Amias's dark pupils, because, although they were oversized, they didn't shift and flow like the other sections. His pupils were still.

"The old woman in my first vision," she said. "That was Esther Fisherman, wasn't it?"

The corners of his mouth flicked up to the most subtle smile. "I have to admit, I thought you might realize that a bit sooner."

Poor Esther. It'd been clear from her troubled diary entries that whatever happened to her couldn't have been good, but never did Zora imagine that she would have been drained of her life force by an actual, real-life demon. She'd always allowed herself to ponder other scenarios—getting lost in the woods and dying of exposure, getting fed up with all the drama before leaving Bricksbury behind forever, or maybe in the worst case, attacked by one of the men she'd seen guarding the campus. But her vision hadn't been symbolic or metaphorical. Esther's last moments had been of pure, unnatural terror and pain. It angered Zora to no end.

"To answer your question from before," Zora continued, refusing to engage with Amias any further on Esther, as it seemed like a bad idea to lose her temper on an immortal man. "It's twofold. My necklace is a tool used to connect with my ancestors. I've cleansed and prayed over it. But also"—she cleared her throat midsentence— "tiger's-eye helps my…mental clarity."

Amias still focused on the gemstone, but he blinked once and nodded when Zora finished. What did that mean?

"What made you choose this, though? There are so many other options. Lapis lazuli as a tether. Clear quartz for cleansing negativity. Iolite for clairvoyance. But you chose tiger's-eye, the one that shields you from psychic attacks, and you did so before learning about the Keepers or the Beast and wore it consistently, even while bathing. Why?"

"I . . . well . . ." Zora looked down as she searched her mind for the origins of choosing the necklace. *Wait. While bathing?*

"Let it go." Khadijah spoke urgently. Her hand nudged Zora's. "Right now. Please, Zora."

She heard the distress in Khadijah's voice. A kinder person would have taken pity.

"I was looking at my gemstone collection and wanted something to protect myself. *Instinct* told me to choose this one," Zora said, speaking the truth as it came to her.

Amias's gaze moved up Zora's pulsing throat and settled on her eyes. Zora was dizzyingly close to hyperventilation. His breath smelled of nothing. It might as well have been the wind the way it caught the honeysuckle and damp grass. Still, all Zora could think about was that he'd been in her apartment. He had to have been. And he'd been there when she was there. Otherwise, how would he know she showered with the necklace on?

"Do you even know of your namesake? The biblical Zorah? Do you know who was born there?"

"Sorry, but as you know, Dr. Grant"—Zora's voice came out in whisps; she winced and chastised herself for something she hadn't said yet—"I'm not a theology major."

"Fuck," Khadijah groaned, finally grabbing Zora's hand. Zora wished she could tell Khadijah not to bother. She could never undo the damage she'd already done to Zora.

"Here is your offer, Zora Candace Robinson." Amias's eyes returned to her necklace, his only genuine interest. "Join the Keepers of the Beast in our duty to protect Bricksbury and the Black citizens of Jonesborough. You would be an asset as a powerful conjurer. I have witnessed your God-given rootworking. I have memorized the intensity and the tenderness with which you construct your system mojo bags. Join us, Zora, and see everything God and the universe have to offer—or die."

Chapter Thirty-Seven

W hich do you choose?" Amias asked, frustration raising his ringing voice. He spoke...unhurriedly, hands loose behind his back, shoulders relaxed. Words...rose and fell, uttered by someone...unworried about being ignored or interrupted. "Are you a sanctimonious martyr? Or are you willing to admit that freedom requires sacrifice? Hmmmm? Without help from anyone here! Without additional research or cross-referencing the handbook stolen from the library. Who are you?"

Zora looked frantically at Khadijah and then Jasmine, but they only stared back with blank, unreadable faces. Was this another thing Amias just knew? How long had he been stalking her? Lamont? How long had Zora been entangled in this without even knowing?

She couldn't believe she was worried about a fucking thesis proposal when she first arrived at Bricksbury. It was weeks ago, but it felt like a lifetime. A different life. A life without knowing about murders going back centuries or how her sister...well, she still wasn't sure about Jasmine. But, candidly, in her mind, Zora could see it hadn't been blissful ignorance. It was hollow, a belly full of fluff and air. Now she could see everything in new, horrifying ways. Horrifying but truthful—and that had always been Zora's intention: to excavate truths.

"Do I learn the whole truth?" Zora asked. She risked nausea as she looked into his swirling eyes. The bands of bright honey glowed up close. Their cosmic size stunned Zora into silence.

"Leave us," Amias said, looking at Khadijah for the first time. "Prepare quickly. Miss Robinson is in a hurry."

Zora studied the ground as everyone left. There was nothing a supportive glance could've given her, and she had nothing to offer these people.

"I said *leave usss.*"

Jasmine's sigh was heavy as her steps retreated. Zora considered glancing up at Amias but waited until the others had marched forward. A pool of dampness slid down her back, causing Zora's body to recoil—neck snapping to the left and shoulders rolling involuntarily. Inhaling had become more and more challenging the farther up they moved. She didn't remember having as difficult a time the last time she was here.

"Don't worry, it'll be a short walk. You'd gotten your sister most of the way, but we waited for you."

"How did you know we'd be here?"

"I heard you whissssspering in her room. I can't hear everything, you know. Just chit-chit-chit-chittering most of the time. But you'd just come out of a vision, and the conjure was strong, so I could hear clearly from afar. Have you considered, Zora"—he swept his arms up the trail, and they strolled side by side—"your belief that you can know all truths, or take them by force, coincides with the Keepers' mission seamlessly?"

"And what is that mission...exactly?"

"First, hand me the camera."

"What do you mean?"

"I've graciously allowed you to keep it this long, haven't I? I know I have. Because I believe that you won't want to publish what you've learned by this end. You'll help us keep it a secret."

Zora couldn't fathom a justification for keeping their secret. And even if she could... all those murdered people deserved justice. She wasn't an investigative journalist, but even she knew abandoning this would be (kindly) cowardice or (more accurately) complicity. Still, Amias had mentioned death, so she handed him the camera hidden in her hair, which launched a different memory.

"Did you see what happened to me in the church?"

Amias sighed. "I hope you can forgive your sister, eventually. Severing... tethering?... no, definitely severing your relationship was incredibly difficult for her. That night could have been beautiful for everyone involved, but Jasmine's reluctance to accept you as a potential Keeper ruined everything."

They walked silently for a minute while Zora calmed and then controlled her breaths. She looked over to find Amias gazing at the leafy branches bent over the trail. Enveloping, containing. He seemed fascinated, enchanted, like he could hear or see something Zora couldn't and wouldn't look away till he located and devoured it. If a squirrel or flecked butterfly got in his eyesight, he'd follow it till his neck bent unnaturally, drawing heavy nausea in Zora.

"You may want to find a new lover," he added, out of nowhere. "Best to keep your mind and heart clear of entangling emotions such as lust."

Zora stopped, though Amias kept walking. His neck didn't turn to look at her, which she was grateful for. She picked up the pace to catch back up with him. Sweat rolled into her eye, stinging it and drawing her curses. Amias was silent.

"You didn't... watch Khadijah and me together?"

"Do you honestly think I could watch every time that happens on this campus? I love you as siblings in Christ, but you are entirely guided by your sexual desires."

"Mm-hmm. I think you had time to stalk me; why pick and choose the circumstances?"

Amias laughed, and the ringing in his voice turned harsher—from a bell to a horn. He'd unsettled a group of birds, whose storm of flapping wings paused the conversation long enough for Zora to see they'd arrived.

JONESBORO AFRICAN BAPTIST CHURCH
& CEMETERY
EST. 1796

"The church used to be surrounded by a quiet neighborhood. A few families. Widows. Some who'd been freed, others who'd run, and we'd shielded them until they moved on." He looked down as his lips tugged upward. "Quiet but full of life, especially at the market, which I'd always considered too disorganized to be called that. It never looked the same from day to day and both the quality and quantity were dubious. My wife...she sold honey from our hives and was a better businessperson than I'll ever be."

Zora accepted the distraction, even knowing it was chosen because it aligned with her interests. This was, unfortunately, her shit.

"Some structures are still around if you go off the trail. I found the old hives crumpled at the bottom of a notch last year, pushed downhill over time by rains. Like they'd never lived."

"You didn't sell the honey with your wife?" Zora asked, zeroing in on what was said between the vague memories.

"I enjoy you," Amias said, a smile growing incrementally. "But you already knew that."

"Thank you?"

"I helped build, then taught up at the schoolhouse." He pointed behind himself, to dark woods. "One room. After my parents, the schoolhouse was the main inspiration for Bricksbury. There was such a need for it. And fervent desire. We all knew a place like Bricksbury must exist. It's *needed*, Zora. Nowhere else can offer this refuge, however expensive, selective, or any of the other extensive, ungrateful complaints you hiss as you walk the pavement. Hosanna and I were thinking on a large scale and not for modern times, certainly—and yet, Bricksbury's existence remains needed."

Zora held her tongue on a question about Hosanna. He wouldn't answer anyway, so it'd only piss him off. No, she should ask something he'd be more willing to answer. Something that showed her interest and hinted at respect. Zora was familiar with the tone from all the canvassing and public education classes she taught as part of her job in Knoxville.

The sun had moved from overhead, but Zora still felt it on her neck, glaring at her. She licked her lips. Pollen and salt. Trouble.

"Were you also the preacher?"

"For a time, yes. But that had never been my calling. I wasn't meant to be behind the altar. Not naturally, anyway."

"What does that mean?"

"I'm only behind it now by divine intervention."

Zora took a beat to absorb that, then decided she didn't have enough time, so she packed it away in her mind for later.

"That was over two hundred years ago."

"Mmm."

"How are you still alive?"

Amias inhaled. *"He giveth power to the faint; and to them that have no might He increaseth strength."*

Zora flinched away from his words. Isaiah 40:29—she knew it well. So well, she'd just used it to help show her the necklace in Jasmine's room. Amias, formerly and currently Dr. Grant, did not flinch from his words nor look away for Zora's ego or to soothe her quivering fear.

"The bread of the Father," he said, tilting his head toward the church. "The blood of His covenant."

She'd been so focused on Amias that Zora hadn't noticed Jasmine walking toward them. She carried a crimson ceramic platter with patterned edges. Gold and silver swirls glittered even in the setting sun. Matching dishes sat on top. A stemless wineglass and a dish that was a miniature version of the platter both sat full. The wine was dark; the soda crackers looked stale. Jasmine's gentle but encouraging smile gave Zora no comfort. The point of no return had been long since passed.

Chapter Thirty-Eight

Feeling like she didn't have any other option, Zora took one of the crackers from the tray Jasmine offered and chewed it slowly before willing herself to swallow. Amias closely watched her eat, his breath still tinted with honeysuckle. The oppressive heat made it impossible for Zora to find any comfort, and things only got worse when the sharp edges of the platter pricked her skin. As she reached for her wineglass, she found it to be heavier than expected, and the wine was too sour to be pleasant.

"Bow your head," Amias said.

Zora followed instructions, holding her breath as a bead of sweat slid off her forehead. She'd never felt so exposed, so utterly vulnerable in her life. Somehow, Amias managed to be both terrifying and angelic. Hearing him hurt, and it was made worse when he prayed because his voice turned soft. Like he was humming a forbidden lullaby.

"Lord God, hear our prayer. Protect Zora Robinson's soul as she journeys through life and joins the Keepers of the Beast. Let her remain in Your light, Lord. In Jesus's name."

"Amen," they all said.

Although Zora spoke, it was more instinctive than intentional. Her mind had begun a foggy dance, where she didn't understand everything but smelled too much. The leaf mold was pungent. The wood's musk was sickly sweet, then tart and vinegary.

After the prayer, Zora didn't trust her legs. They wobbled with each of her steps, and although Jasmine spoke to her, Zora was too busy remaining upright to carry on a conversation. Finally, Jasmine steadied Zora with a firm hand wrapped around her waist. She helped as the group walked Zora into the Jonesboro African Baptist Church.

The Keepers stood in reverent silence in the pews, gazing toward the ornately decorated altar, offering Zora the space and time she needed. No, it wasn't a physical entrapment. It was something worse. Maybe it was the crimson. There was too much of it roving the walls, turning the church into a throbbing womb. She didn't know if she could endure that.

They'd lit candles inside glass jars, which threw crimson light onto the rotted rafters. So much effort was put into an abandoned place. By then, Zora's dizziness was accompanied by acid-swirling nausea made worse by Amias gripping her hand. He walked Zora slowly down the aisle of the church. Zora held on to his arm tightly, excitement and repulsion fighting each other in her mind. When they reached the altar, Amias placed Zora's hand on the altar, and she felt calm.

Zora turned her head to see Khadijah had found an empty pew and stood there quietly, opening the Bible with reverence. The congregation was deeply engrossed in their Bibles, reading and reflecting. Their lips were still, but they turned the page occasionally, reading at their own pace.

"Haggai," Amais said. "They're reading the book. It's about rebuilding His temple and is what they read at initiations."

He'd taken his place behind the altar and flipped up the headpiece on his robes, obscuring his cosmic face.

"The entire book?" Zora asked. As soon as she had finished speaking, she felt a sudden wave of regret as an uncomfortable amount of saliva pooled in her mouth.

Amias shrugged. "It's a short one. They repeat it until we're finished."

The room swerved suddenly, but no...no it was all in Zora's head. She hoped it was.

"Do you promise to put Bricksbury's needs ahead of your own?"

Easy. Bricksbury was an extension (the heart?) of Affrilachia, as were the students that attended it. "Mm-hmm."

"Jesus sacrificed, and so must we. Do you agree to this without exception?"

"What?" Zora asked, those words sparking something in her.

"Do you promise to sacrifice as all God's children must do?"

She mumbled her answer, her words soft around the edges. The questions went on for a while, as did the extended blurs in Zora's vision. The leaf mold from the outside had been replaced by rotten floorboards. Zora eventually found herself on top of the altar. She was definitely under the influence of something stronger than that sour wine. All those candles, all that crimson...

The wood of the altar was sturdier than it looked, and Amias kept his meandering speaking pace as he tied her down to it and explained that while the others were reading Haggai, her initiation was reading something else.

Then she would have to face the Beast.

When that moment came and the thing in the blue dress came bursting into the church, eyes alight with fury and hunger, words raced across its flesh, the same way that they did ever since Esther Fisherman was killed. The words moved too quickly to make out, and Zora couldn't discern them any more now than she could when she saw the Beast in the vision. All she knew was that when she looked into what used to be Hosanna Crawfoot's eyes, and smelled the pungent odor of rot and burned paper radiating from her body, she was witnessing something that no human was ever meant to see.

"All the Glory to God," Amias whispered, hardly able to contain his excitement. "Welcome, Zora Robinson. Welcome to the Keepers of the Beast."

As if she'd ever had a real choice. Zora promised herself that this wasn't over. Nothing could bind her to a life she refused to live. At the very least, her initiation would buy her some time to figure out what her next move would be.

Amias Crawfoot
Present Day
Jonesborough, Tennessee
Bricksbury Mountain College—The
Woodlands

Before Zora found herself tied to the altar of the church, Amias was still processing his thoughts on her, still searching his mind for the spark before the smoldering explosion. How did other people do it? Ruminate. He heard them discussing their emotions as if they were laid out for them by a master architect, explaining the blueprints in traumatic detail. His never revealed themselves in such a way. Was this part of what made him broken? Was it the source?

Khadijah had summoned him. It was the first time she'd ever done that. Her self-sufficiency was why he'd chosen her to work directly with Charlene as Cardinal. That was the one characteristic of all the Cardinals, from Khadijah to Gerald, who in 1994 became the first Cardinal of the Keepers, once the Beast had calmed enough for it. Bless Gerald. A resilient soul. All this to say, he was surprised when Khadijah called upon him.

"I saw you in the library," she said, voice steady but heartbeat wild.

His first shock was that he'd been caught, and the second was that she would confront him with this. Where did she find the nerve? Khadijah must have taken his silence for something other than fury, because she continued speaking.

"Somethin' happened at homecoming…I'm not sure what, exactly, but Zora literally *ran* away." A purple cowboy hat was clutched in her hand as she spoke. "I'd like to ask that Zora isn't marked as a sacrifice. I know she's mad powerful, but that's exactly why she'd be a better asset alive. Look, I'll even help you find a better sacrifice. Her friend Lamont would be way better for what you're looking for."

Amias always chose the ones who were marked for the Beast. Khadijah didn't have a say. Still, sadness overtook him as he explained that Zora wasn't the one who would be marked, but she.

Amias smiled as brightly as he could manage. He quoted from scripture, "*I beseech you therefore, brethren, by the mercies of God, that ye present your bodies a living sacrifice, holy, acceptable unto God, which is your reasonable service.*"

Chapter Thirty-Nine

After the initiation was complete, Amias allowed Zora to be taken back to her dorm by Khadijah, while Jasmine had to stay behind "for a word." As angry as Zora was at her sister for making so many choices that all directly led to this moment, she couldn't help but worry at the tone in Amias's voice when he asked Jasmine to stay behind.

Jasmine had pleaded with Zora to run, to refuse joining the Keepers. If what Amias said was accurate, he would have probably overheard that. Would Jasmine be punished for it? How?

"It'll be okay," Khadijah said as they made their way through the woods, away from the church and the cemetery and the Beast, as though she knew exactly what Zora was thinking about. "Jasmine always fulfilled her duties without issue until you were in the mix. He'll grant her mercy. He has a soft spot for her. He'll swear to the ends of the earth that he doesn't choose favorites, but I think we all know that isn't true."

"That's good." Zora didn't even know why she said it. None of this was good, not even a little bit. "Hey, good job on tricking me from day one. You, Mallory, and Immanuel. Never woulda suspected that you were all secretly trying to ruin my life. I should have run screaming as soon as I saw that honeybee tattoo on your ribs."

"It wasn't like that, Zora." Khadijah let out a prolonged exhale of frustration. "Despite the circumstances, my feelings for you were real. As is my belief that once you wrap your head around all this, you'll thrive as a Keeper—a protector of Bricksbury. Hell, you may even discover that you can trust both Mallory *and* Immanuel."

"Until it's time to, you know, *choose someone to be fucking murdered.*" Zora couldn't contain her disgust. "Do you even hear yourself, Khadijah? You're allowing innocent people to be killed! This isn't fate, or God's will. It's the product of one man's ego and refusal to accept reality. Full stop."

"Every proper sacrifice goes willingly in the end." Khadijah's voice softened unexpectedly, like she was holding something back. "I guess you'll learn that soon enough."

"What do you mean?"

Khadijah's pace slowed, and she let out a sharp bark of a laugh. "You want to know what's wild? When I realized that Amias was paying special attention to you, I thought he was going to mark you for sacrifice. I actually summoned him for a meeting—which, by the way, nobody had ever done—and asked him not to."

Zora frowned. Before she knew he was Amias, Dr. Grant had always seemed genuinely invested in helping Zora to become the best she could possibly be, always encouraging her ambitions for the future. Why would he have gone through that only to mark her for death? "Yeah? What did he say?"

Khadijah turned to look at Zora now, her beautiful eyes meeting Zora's and holding them like they did when they first met. "He said that it wasn't you who was being marked for sacrifice. It was going to be me all along."

Zora bit her lip, unable to tell if Khadijah was messing with her or not. "Excuse me?"

"Yeah." Khadijah nodded, her smile forced. "Who would have guessed that's how our story was gonna end, right? I should have known it, honestly. We—Mallory and I—think that you remind him of Esther Fisherman. He was in love with her, I guess, and regretted marking her for sacrifice. So of course he wouldn't mark you."

Silence bloomed between them as they kept walking. In the distance, Zora heard the strangled cry of some bird. Now that she knew what was waiting out there, the woods didn't scare her as much as they made her angry. This was all *so* fucked.

"It's not going to happen." Zora finally broke the silence. "I'm not going to let that thing near you."

Khadijah's laugh was real this time. "It's cute that you think you can stop it. On multiple levels. I'm here to let you know that it's impossible."

They fell into silence again, Zora huffing as she willed her body to push on. Her bed and Henry Louis awaited her, if she could just find the strength to keep going. A proper night's sleep would offer much in the way of formulating a solid plan. Khadijah adjusted her pace to fall more into place with Zora's, tenderly holding her arm for support whenever Zora needed a minute to breathe.

Let her think it's impossible to save her, Zora decided as she leaned on Khadijah's frame for a second before continuing on. *I'll show her just how stubborn Zora Robinson is when she wants to be.*

And then what? Where could she possibly go, what could she possibly do with her life, without her mind always coming back to Bricksbury at the end of the day? If the way Khadijah was talking was any indication, she believed in the purpose the Keepers prided themselves on protecting. Maybe she'd change her tune when she got a new lease on life. That was all Zora could hope for at this point.

What was Jasmine doing right now? Or Amias? Listening in? Just in case, Zora realized she'd better shut up about her intentions to save Khadijah. She didn't want to give Amias any reason to try to insert himself into her life any more than he already had.

After what felt like an eternity, Zora was able to make out the outline of Bricksbury's housing units in the distance. Her body was getting more used to this hike after being forced to make it so many times.

"I know today was a lot," Khadijah said as they entered the courtyard.

It was unfathomable that, after this dark spectacle, they would simply retreat to their dorms and carry on as though the Beast were nothing more than fleeting shadows and the church in the woods was merely a church, and not a sanctuary for protection poisoned. Zora shook her head, overwhelmed with sadness. People's ability to disregard the haunting nightmares that encircled them stood as a cruel mockery of the human spirit. Yet it wasn't a human spirit haunting the Woodlands; that was something else entirely.

Khadijah wiped her hands on her shirt, then cursed at the streak of thick church pew dust. "Just try to take it day by day. And, hey... I appreciate your willingness to fight for me, but I want to reiterate that it isn't worth the trouble it'd cause, okay? You'd fail in the end and you'd only succeed in pissing Amias off."

Zora bit her tongue to stop herself from telling Khadijah that she didn't give a shit about pissing Amias off. Maybe that had always been a part of the problem, that people were afraid of him. For the first time, she allowed her mind to consider the measures taken to put a stop to him, permanently. The magic that had allowed him to live and thrive for hundreds of years would have to be powerful, stronger than anything Zora had ever seen before or even read about. But aside from Amias, there was the other element to consider: the Beast. She had no idea where to even begin when it came to untangling the complexities of the demon's existence.

Zora realized that Khadijah was studying her curiously, waiting for her response. "All right," she finally conceded, nodding toward Khadijah's door. "Dr. Ncuti is probably wondering where you are."

Khadijah's shoulders relaxed at the mention of her cat. "Yeah, it's been one helluva day, hasn't it?"

"It has," Zora said. "I'll see you tomorrow, Khadijah." She paused for a moment. "Count on it."

Khadijah frowned. "Zora, please don't—"

But Zora was already on her way to her own door, envisioning the comfort that her safe space would bring. Shower, food, sleep. She'd figure out the rest later.

Chapter Forty

Zora had to give it to Khadijah—she was nothing if not dedicated. But Zora was even *more* dedicated. She had been ready and waiting when her lover tried to sneak through the courtyard undetected the following morning. The air still held a crisp chill, tinged with the earthy scent of dew-kissed grass, as tiny droplets sparkled in the early light. The sun hadn't crested the hemlock trees, but the faint glow of dawn cast long, soft shadows that danced on the gray pavers. Zora spotted Khadijah as she moved stealthily, her silhouette in stark contrast to the pale sky and lingering fog.

Birds chirped softly, their songs jarring amid such grim surroundings. Though how was anyone ever to know? The worst of it was hidden; Amias had ensured that. *This isn't about him. Focus.* Zora kept her distance when gravel eventually crunched softly beneath her feet. She had to remain unseen until the... right... moment...

Zora was patient. She had to be. Eventually, she took a deep breath, grateful for the cool air filling her lungs. *I can do this.* That was when she whispered the incantation she had toiled over all night. The thick words rolled off her tongue like honey. The spell glided through the air, curling around Khadijah, casting a shimmering veil of foggy confusion over her mind. The magic tasted sharp. It was electrifying as it took hold, enveloping them both in its stillness. When Khadijah stumbled, then froze in place, looking around as though she didn't know where she was, Zora swooped in.

She linked her arm around Khadijah's as though they were headed to class together, and pulled her into Hemlock Chapel.

A holy place was as good as any for something like this. Hopefully, it would offer some level of protection while they waited the sacrifice window out, or until she could convince Khadijah to run away from Bricksbury and never look back. As she went about securing Khadijah, she noticed a crimson mark on the skin that was visible beneath the short hem of her shirt. When Zora lifted the shirt up, she was met with the same symbol she'd seen burned into the pulpit at Amias's church.

The mark of the Beast. It filled Zora with disgust. She refused to entertain it as something so concrete. This mark couldn't be a death sentence. She wouldn't let it.

"You were really gonna scurry off to get killed without even saying goodbye, huh?" Zora asked as she tightened the camping rope around Khadijah's ankle and a choir stall leg in Hemlock Chapel's upper level. "I would have at least expected a kiss or something."

She was lightheaded, but her body felt heavy. The army-green rope she'd swiped from a custodian closet earlier that morning kept her steady while she swayed. *I should've prayed.* The braided nylon she clutched was riddled with plastic slivers, piercing into her skin, but she held on, her knees sinking into soft carpet flooring. When she found the strength, she transferred trembling fingers from the rope to her necklace, accepting renewed mental clarity from her ancestors' protection. Their comfort. And Lord willing, forgiveness for her behavior.

When the veil of confusion finally dissolved, Khadijah cried. She didn't try to stop Zora, but didn't help, either. It was as if she'd accepted the loss of control, which Zora thought was a good start.

"I wasn't going to prolong it any more than necessary. It would have only hurt you to say goodbye." Khadijah sniffled. "But I guess you were ready for that, weren't you?"

"It's like I said on the hike home yesterday," Zora said. "Not. Gonna. Happen."

When the ropes were finally secure, Zora stood. Beeswax candles scented the church with musky honey, still too sweet for Zora, who grabbed her belly before it turned. She looked out onto the sanctuary with weary eyes. Was Amias watching? He wouldn't try to come pull something here, would he? This wasn't his territory; this wasn't his church. He had no authority here... right?

"Zora," Khadijah said.

Her croaky, pity-laced voice dragged Zora out of another spiral, crashing her into the present. Khadijah tried to sit but couldn't lift her shoulders off the ground due to the ropes tying her down.

"It won't work, Zora." Khadijah cleared her throat. "I don't *want* to evade sacrifice. You're still new, but once Amias and the others teach you, you'll see. We can't stop. Bricksbury needs us."

"Bricksbury? What about the people you're mining for medieval sacrifices?"

"You should know better than that," Khadijah said. "This is the Jacksonian era."

Zora took the bait. Couldn't help it.

"Yeah, but shouldn't it be Reconstruction? That's when Amias killed Hosanna, right? The first sacrifice in 1877?"

Khadijah smiled and disarmed Zora with the sudden lucidity in her eyes. "I wish you and I could have... I bet we woulda been happy."

Zora died inside. She felt it. *Knew* it. One way or the other, this plan wasn't going to work how she hoped. She shook her head as if denying Khadijah's words would make them obsolete. As if she could delete this entire reality and make one where she got to grab ahold of happiness, and it actually stayed.

"Don't say that," she whispered, too low, she was sure, for Khadijah to hear.

"Okay, since you wanna bring it up, how do you think, after 1877, Bricksbury never experienced violence on campus?"

"What does that have to do with this?"

"How do you think it has the lowest rate for *all* on-campus crimes? The highest graduation rate in the country? Think, Zora!"

"Well? I mean, they say it's the homogeneousness and...the mountain atmosphere." She whispered the last words. She knew what Khadijah was getting at. As messed up as this entire sacrifice business was, it actually worked. It was real. But that still didn't make it right!

"Mountain atmosphere?" Khadijah laughed, but the soft sound was hollow. "It doesn't matter. You can't stop this; it's too important. Nah, look at me. *Look at me!* I have to die. I am so sorry, but I have to. The Beast must be fed."

Zora fought through tears and snotty hiccups. Her hands went behind her head, and her crop top rose, exposing soft skin to the church's cool air. It was refreshing at first, and then so cold that she lowered her arms. "No, there must be a different way. No one's dying. Y'all just haven't looked for an alternative. But I am! And I'll find it. Just hold on, okay? Can you at least do that for me?"

"This is surprising," Amias said below in the sanctuary.

Zora squeezed her eyes shut before turning and facing him. Shoulders stiffened. Khadijah shifted on the carpet but otherwise remained silent. She'd accepted her fate.

"Hello, Zora." Amias sat forward in his pew. "I sincerely hope you've had a fulfilling day so far. Have you come to your senses yet?" His hands intertwined on the seat in front of him as he looked up at Zora with his mouth open. Eyes wide, teeth bared in a grin. He must have snuck in like a snake in tall grass while she was tying up Khadijah.

"Go to hell."

"How quickly you show your ignorance—I *am* in hell. This is my punishment. Can't you see? Or are you too busy trying to save someone who doesn't want to be saved? Ignorance twofold."

Zora gripped the railing and then, in a wild moment, imagined herself killing Amias. Her shoulders loosened as she felt his warm blood splatter on her face and watched his robed body collapse backward. Zora heard his ringing voice screaming, then cut *short*. *Shh. Shh.* Wetness pooled on her tongue. Amias bounded up from his seat, emotion lifting his voice until Zora thought it was a piano chord, and not him, that had hit a sharp note.

"We've built a rapport by now, haven't we, Zora? So, please, speak freely. I want to know what you're thinking."

Zora lingered in her envisioned justice. It felt so close. So grabbable. But the illusion melted before her as Amias stepped into the aisle. If he was immortal, it was unlikely she'd be able to beat him in a brawl.

"I'm impressed by your strategy of denying Khadijah entrance into the woods," he said. "That was clever. You were always so, so clever, but it won't make a difference here, darling."

"Call me darling again."

Amias opened his mouth as a man in black robes opened a side door. He was humming and had at least one headphone in his ear. His balding head was shiny even in the dimly lit sanctuary. And when he looked up at the collection of people in the chapel, his jaw went slack.

"Wha—what's goin' on here?" he said.

Yes! Zora thought. *Someone who can help!*

"Ah, Pastor Wilburn, how are you?" Amias's robes swept the floor as he greeted the frazzled clergy member.

"I'll be better once you explain what's going on." Pastor Wilburn's eyes swung frantically from Amias to Zora.

Zora frowned at the pastor's robes. They whipped through the air quicker than Amias's. The lighter material hung to the floor, but Zora was zeroed in on his chest, where the symbol burned before the pulpit in Jonesboro African Baptist Church was stitched with crimson threads. *That can't be there. It doesn't make sense.* Even though she knew it did.

"This is a Bricksbury student, not one of your flock, I'm afraid; she hasn't stepped foot in this chapel before. She is holding a sacrifice hostage."

"She's what?" The pastor took a complete step backward.

Zora's mouth hung open as the pastor looked back at her with equal shock. He...knew? How many others knew? Was this built into the foundation of Bricksbury?

"I don't know you," Pastor Wilburn said, newly confident eyes staring down Zora from the sanctuary below. "But, uh...that necklace looks like tiger's-eye. Do you practice conjure? If so, you must understand that you cannot get in the way of God's plan."

Amias took a step back with folded arms and watched Pastor Wilburn take over the conversation with Zora.

"You are my sister in Christ. I want you to..."

Pastor Wilburn's voice faded out, first slowing, then quieting altogether. One of his hands was in midair; the other bunched on his hip. He stood frozen as the symbol on his chest glowed bright crimson light, eventually becoming blinding. Zora blinked, and when the light receded and she was able to see again, the Beast stood on Hemlock Chapel's carpet in front of Pastor Wilburn, summoned to the sacrifice.

"No!" Zora screamed. "No, you can't have her! You can't..."

The Beast's eyes were hellfire. Flames leaped from her face to lick the wax-scented air before she fell to all fours, bounding with terrifying speed to the upper level, screeching with excitement as the familiar smell of burned paper and the rotting dead filled Zora's lungs.

Hardly thinking, she turned,
Thwump.
    threw herself on Khadijah,
    Thwump.
        and winced at a burst of orange.
        Thwump.
Zora wrapped her body around Khadijah's. A grotesque paper hand covered with moving words—"*I urge you,*" "*living sacrifice,*" "*pleasing to God*"—seized Khadijah's throat. Her body twitched against Zora's. A sickening *crack* echoed through the air.

Zora screamed, and the Beast taunted her by mimicking the scream exactly. That was when Zora's spirit broke.

All the while, Amias sang an upbeat spiritual beautifully...

"The Gospel train's a'comin'
I hear it just at hand
I hear the car wheel rumblin'
And rollin' thro' the land
Get on board, little children..."

Chapter Forty-One

*B*lood *is not red.*

 Zora walked without seeing. It was midmorning, maybe afternoon. Could've been Christmas for all she cared. Her soles hurt from constant use. They still hadn't forgiven her for the sudden obsession with trail hiking, nor had her calves or thighs. Would she grow new muscles? But Khadijah...Khadijah would never see them, or her, or anything ever again. She was just...gone.

Did anyone know? And if not, who would...

Gone, gone, gone...

Zora wasn't aware one could feel both overwhelmed and empty, full of vampiric emotion, sucking away her own...

Blood is not red.

This was all Amias's fault. He started the Keepers, killed his sister, forced a cult of students to shield her from outside view, and *then* either murdered them or allowed them to become some twisted indentured servants their whole lives.

Zora frowned as her mind teetered in a dark, nightmarish direction before sliding off the cliff. She once again imagined bashing Amias's head against cool altar wood. Not stopping until his body was limp and the blood pooled on the soft carpet. That was important because she wanted the last thing he saw before righteous death took him to be defeat. Zora would stare, too, and think how blood was not red. It was brightly scarlet, tender rose, muddy mahogany—rich in its darkness and warm as it slid off Amias's body and splattered to the ground.

Oh my God. She cleared her throat and felt the sun sting in her eyes. Nausea bubbled within her. The preceding acid had already climbed up her throat. Zora swallowed, but the burning remained as she roamed on campus, seeing nothing, feeling sick. She tried to calm her racing heart, but it still drummed in her chest.

Khadijah is dead. She's dead.

Khadijah had begged Zora to accept it. She certainly had. Zora was the only one in the room with a problem. It was just... Khadijah was so calm, lying there motionless as she'd waited to die. Could she have really been ready for it? How?

She'd been so insistent on reminding Zora of the facts. *How do you think, after 1877, Bricksbury never experienced outside violence on campus?* Khadijah had said. *Lowest rate for all on-campus crimes...* But why, why, why, why, why, why, why, why, why, why, why, why, why, why, why, why was this the cost for peace?

The sun's glare shocked Zora out of her thoughts. She shuffled onward until she was on the grass of the courtyard once again. Once she was inside her apartment, she lay on the floor and sobbed until she fell into a disturbed sleep where all she could see was the life leaving Khadijah's eyes, and the only sound she could hear was the Beast's earsplitting impression of Zora's guttural scream.

MISSING STUDENT

KHADIJAH MARQUEZ

Any information concerning **Khadijah Marquez** should be given at once to Bricksbury Mountain College administration officials or the Jonesborough Police Department. Khadijah disappeared from her dorm the morning of September 29, 2027, and has not been seen since.

Description of **Khadijah Marquez**:

Black. Age 26 (twenty-six) years. Brown eyes. Has micros and was wearing a green dress and blue sandals.

Chapter Forty-Two

Someone pounded on Zora's door, each thud causing Henry Louis to bark anxiously. Inside, Zora lay curled in her bed, shivering despite her skin being slick with a sheen of sweat that clung to her, sticking her to the mattress. The shock coursing through her veins held her captive, blending fear of Amias and the memory of Khadijah's eyes into a numbing haze. She strained her ears, catching the faint sound of scraping at the lock, and glanced up at the cowrie shells adorning her wall. They remained still, unmoving— silent sentinels that offered no forewarning of danger. But their lack of movement did little to calm her. With a resigned sigh, Zora pressed her head back against the rumpled linen of her pillowcase.

Finally, Lamont entered, the door's creaking echoing through the clutter in her apartment. Zora heard the rush of water in the kitchen, a mundane sound among the chaos of her thoughts. Then he crossed the room with an air of gentle determination, his presence filling the space with a warmth Zora desperately craved and gratefully accepted.

Lamont made no mention of the tornado of clutter surrounding them as the bed dipped behind her. He placed a cool washcloth atop her fevered forehead. The gesture was tender, yet it felt unbearably heavy with unspoken words. Wrapping his arms around her, he pulled her close, a saffron sanctuary. As Zora's eyelids grew heavier, surrendering to the quietude of his embrace, she couldn't shake the emptiness, even in this moment of solace. In Lamont's arms, Zora drifted off again.

When she awoke the next morning, Lamont and Henry Louis lay on her futon. Gentle orange sunlight streamed inside, so tranquil and pure, in defiance of Zora's reality. Henry Louis was snoring on Lamont's lap while Lamont looked gravely down at his phone. The sound of Zora stirring in bed caught both of their attention. Four brown eyes looked up at her, and Zora almost smiled.

"You've been asleep for ten hours. Feelin' better?" Lamont asked.

Zora considered lying but shook her head. There was no point anymore. "No."

Lamont nodded, then breathed deeply. "Khadijah is missin', Zora. There are flyers around campus an' I just reposted about it from the library's account."

He stood and showed her the phone, but Zora didn't even look at it.

"Khadijah is dead."

Lamont froze, arm still outstretched toward Zora. *"What?"*

Zora stammered. "I . . . I tried to save her. I got her to the church, and I tied her down! But then Amias brought the Beast—"

"Amias? Amias Crawfoot?" His voice lowered in concern. "Come on, Zora, what are you even sayin'?"

Zora tearfully told Lamont about everything that'd happened since she went to confront Jasmine at her apartment. The revelation about Dr. Grant, the power that kept him alive after all this time. It all sounded like folklore at this point. She could hardly believe that he listened seriously.

After a while, Henry Louis stood and shook himself. The sharp sound of clashing metal from his collar reminded Zora of Khadijah's bangle bracelets.

Zora finally stood and explained her failure to save Khadijah from the Beast.

"Fuck," Lamont said when she'd finished.

Zora went to the kitchen and got herself a glass of water. The cool liquid slid down her throat, but Zora barely registered it. Her mind was elsewhere.

"Fuck!" Lamont said again, louder and causing Henry Louis to jump. Lamont raked a hand through his locs and pinned Zora with a look. "We gotta get outta here, Zora."

Zora opened her mouth to explain why she couldn't, but Lamont didn't let her speak.

"Look, I know this is your family legacy. I get that. I know you love an' miss your sister. I know y'all have a complicated relationship that has only gotten more complicated, but, Zora. You *have* to leave. Or you're gonna end up like Khadijah."

Lamont paced the room, his anxiety rolling off him and crashing into Zora, amplifying her own. She knew there was nothing she could say to make this easier for him. He had been a good friend and stayed longer than most would have, and the last thing Zora wanted was to hand Amias someone else she cared for.

"You have to go," Zora said in a firm voice. "You are in way more danger than I am. Trust me when I say I know this to be true. There's something I have to do first, and then I'll be right behind you. I promise."

Lamont suddenly turned to her, tears streaking down his face. Instead of surprise, resignation lowered his jaw. *He's thought of this already*, Zora thought. Good. One of them needed to bend to their survival instincts. One of them needed to save themselves.

"Zora..." Lamont began, but his voice trailed off, and his pained eyes pierced Zora's.

"C'mere," Zora said, opening up her arms.

After crying together for a while, Lamont finally stepped back. "I'm givin' you one day, Zora. One day to figure this shit out somehow, then I'm callin' the police."

"What are the police gonna do against rootworkers?"

"That's the police's job to figure out."

———

Once Lamont was gone and safe, Zora broke into her sister's apartment for the second time. Her cheeks were flushed from running. Cold sweat dampened her underarms and plenty of other places she didn't have time to assess. After what happened with Khadijah, Zora knew that it wasn't possible to fight this. They couldn't fight Amias or the Beast. The only choice they had was to run.

"Ngozi?" she yelled. Zora didn't know or care where her sibling-in-law was, but they needed to help get her and Jasmine out, immediately. Zora yelled again, uncaring how loud she was or if she woke up the neighbor's baby. "Jasmine? Where the fuck are you?" If Jasmine ever loved her, this was the moment to show it. This was when Jasmine stood up to Amias, with Zora's help, and refused to continue this method of saving people. This was when Jasmine shed the shell of her new "family" and came back to Zora forever.

As she turned the corner from the kitchen/living/dining room into the bedroom, Zora froze. Jasmine lay at the foot of her bed in the fetal position, gasping for breath. That would've been upsetting enough, but when Zora's eyes scanned her body, Jasmine's skin was covered in the mark Zora found burned into the floor of Jonesborough African Baptist Church. It was the same symbol on the pastor's robes, the ones the Beast traveled through.

The same one that had been emblazoned on Khadijah's belly before she died.

"What?" Zora asked when she finally unstuck her feet from the floor. She wrapped her arms around her sister's sticky, hot skin. "How?"

Jasmine's teeth rattled as she turned to Zora, surprise evident in her raised eyebrows. "Z-Z-Zora?"

"This isn't right," Zora said, shaking hands covering her mouth. "How is this possible? How do you have the Beast's marks?"

Now it was Jasmine's turn to shake her head. "Don't worry, lil sis. I fixed it."

"You what?" Zora scowled. "What does that mean?"

"When I heard what happened with Khadijah, I made a trade with Amias. Went...went to the church and offered myself instead. He didn't...He likes you, I think. It wasn't hard to convince him."

"No, no, no. This can't be." Zora heaved. Her body violently folded over as a rush of new emotion overwhelmed her. "You can't do this. This isn't supposed to happen. We were supposed to leave, show him that he can't have us whenever he wants. He says the Beast has the final say, but it's him, it's always been *him*..."

"It's done, Zora. Listen...listen. I want to say I'm sorry. I'm so sorry for abandoning you."

"Hold on, where is Ngozi?" Zora asked, looking around suddenly.

"Dr. Grant—er...Amias sent them to Knoxville, to the Beck Cultural Exchange Center, on some wild goose chase. Didn't...I didn't, couldn't tell them. Amias bought me time to sacrifice myself alone, with dignity, not tied to a church pew."

Zora flinched. She hadn't considered...She'd wanted to prevent Khadijah's death. Instead, she'd taken away her choice of where she wanted to die and on her terms. Zora had meant well, though. That mattered, right?

Jasmine sat up but seemed too weak to stand on her own. Zora collapsed on the floor in front of her, grabbing Jasmine's hands and sobbing alongside her. Grieving her sister anew.

"What are these bruises?" Zora whispered. She'd long wanted to know, but now that she was this close to the truth, she was afraid of it, knowing it would break her heart. She reached out with shaking fingers to feel Jasmine's thin skin, softer...papery.

"It's her mark. The Beast's. My body is breaking down to accept our merge."

"Our...your..." Zora hiccupped as she remembered seeing Khadijah disappear into the papery skin with ink racing across it. Of course. It wasn't just a sacrifice of life, but of one's physical body. Which meant...the sacrifices were immortalized somewhere inside the Beast. Their bodies, at least. Their souls, God willing, were elsewhere.

"Tonight, I'm going to the woods," Jasmine said. "Amias told me...he said specifically that you can't stop me. There were two sacrifices before you arrived, then Toni Anderson, then...Khadijah, then me. I'm the last of the sacrifices for this round, Zora. There won't be another death for fifty years. Let me go, or someone else will have to die."

Behind Jasmine's tears and red veins growing darker, Zora finally found her sister. More sobs racked Zora's body as she realized she'd lost Jasmine all over again. Zora held her. She crushed their bodies together like turning them into one person would make them invisible. Invincible. Inventing their world.

"But I love you." Zora shuddered.

"I love you, too. But the Beast must be fed."

"I know. Are there any clean metal pots in this apartment, or are they all moldy?"

Jasmine's frail laugh made Zora turn her head away. She got up and helped Jasmine to her feet.

"Bitch. Can't you see I've been busy? Why?"

Zora sighed. "You *would* make me do dishes at a time like this. Here, let's get you to the couch. Take a long nap. Rest. We can talk more when you wake up. We'll figure this out, Jasmine, I promise."

For hours, Zora washed dishes. While Jasmine slept, she cleaned the kitchen counters and tidied the living/dining room. Discovered the stinking fridge was full of condiments and old take-out containers. The freezer food was freezer burned. Ice blanketed the ground beef, opened edamame bag, and the bottom of the freezer itself. Zora saw a job that needed doing, and that could clear her mind.

She didn't think about sacrifices as she swept and mopped the floors. All that coated her mind was how much she loved Jasmine and how much she loved Bricksbury. Zora changed damp sheets, wiped down the bathroom counters, cried, cried, cried, and swiped a fingerprint-riddled mirror. She took one trip back to her apartment for a couple extra supplies, and four trips from Jasmine's to the dumpster that necessitated a shower, wherein she also cleaned the shower. At 4:00 p.m., Jasmine woke up.

Zora put a pot to boil, helped her to the bathroom and, afterward, into a wobbly dining room chair.

"Stay here," Zora said. She took the boiling pot off the heat to cool on a clean, spiraled eye.

"As if I could go anywhere." Jasmine's cracked lips smiled, but it didn't reach her soft cheekbones.

"Very funny."

Zora had a collection of things she found around the apartment. From behind the closet door, a neatly organized suitcase with seeds, flower oils, and fine powders. Thrice as much as Zora had in her minuscule kit back at her place.

Zora prayed Psalms 1[13] and 2[14] over a shot glass of olive oil and then poured it into the water.

---

13 Psalm 1 1–3—Blessed is the man that walketh not in the counsel of the ungodly, nor standeth in the way of sinners, nor sitteth in the seat of the scornful. But his delight is in the law of the Lord; and in his law doth he meditate day and night. And he shall be like a tree planted by the rivers of water, that bringeth forth his fruit in his season; his leaf also shall not wither; and whatsoever he doeth shall prosper.

14 Psalm 2 8–12—Ask of me, and I shall give thee the heathen for thine inheritance, and the uttermost parts of the earth for thy possession. Thou shalt break

Like a warning, the Florida water bottle stung Zora's hand with its chill, the cold seeping into her skin like a sharp bite of winter amid the kitchen's warmth. As she shook a few drops into the pot, the delicate, earthy fragrance of agrimony began to weave through the air, mingling with the sweetness of angelica root. The sage was bright and fresh, while the hyssop added a subtle hint of bitterness: a reminder that this wasn't a casual sister hangout, but something just as gentle and revolutionary.

The bottle's cold sting was no match for Zora's unwavering determination. Her resolve burned brighter than any discomfort. She watched with unwavering focus as the vibrant colors of the herbs swirled in the steaming water, creating a tapestry of green and gold, before patiently bringing the pot to Jasmine.

"What you know about old-school foot washing?" Jasmine wheezed. A teasing glare sparkled in her eyes.

"Given the circumstances, I'm gonna ignore that you said that," Zora said, though she could admit a smile played on her lips. "But best believe if you weren't dying today, I would whoop your ass."

"I'm glad you'll have Lamont. When I'm gone, I mean," Jasmine said.

Sorrow closed around her heart like a fist. "Mm-hmm."

Zora cleared her throat, but the lump didn't go away no matter how often she coughed. Then her chest hurt. Jasmine grabbed her hands and squeezed. "Lord, I ask that you protect Jasmine's soul and prepare her for what's coming next. I hope... please let her find peace. In Jesus's name, amen."

---

them with a rod of iron; thou shalt dash them in pieces like a potter's vessel. Be wise now therefore, O ye kings: be instructed, ye judges of the earth. Serve the Lord with fear, and rejoice with trembling. Kiss the Son, lest he be angry, and ye perish from the way, when his wrath is kindled but a little. Blessed are all they that put their trust in him.

"What verse are we reciting while you wash? Which did you pick?"

Jasmine spoke in a higher-pitched tone. But Zora *hadn't* forgotten that part of the ritual.

"It's written down behind you, in case you don't have it memorized. I assumed you preferred the version King James mistranslated. It's my favorite, too."

Jasmine looked at Zora with renewed feeling. "You did all this while I was sleeping?"

"Not bad for someone unfamiliar with 'old-school foot washing,' huh?"

Zora laughed, then Jasmine, and they shared a smile that set aside all those forgotten years. Above all else, they were sisters.

A letter written by Zora Robinson
September 30, 2027
Jonesborough, Tennessee
Bricksbury Mountain College—William F. Yardley Hall

Sister,

As I watch you sleep, I realize I don't remember the last time I told you how beautiful you are. Everyone says "beautiful" is an outplayed or ambivalent word, but it's everything you are to me, and that can't be ambivalent. It just can't.

I'm sorry for my angry words. They held no truth.

I'm sorry I don't have time to accept that we were apart for so long. I want you to know that I understand why you made those choices. And I didn't understand it until I saw you on the bedroom floor. Really. It wasn't until that exact moment. All I could think was <u>I'm going to fix this</u>. Well, Jasmine, I fixed it.

I have no regrets, only pride in saving my sister and continuing a functioning, albeit flawed, legacy of sacrifice.

The Beast's marks on your body are fading. So will the pain I'm sure you'll feel when you discover what I've done. You will get through this. Use your strengths. Use your vulnerabilities. And be honest about which one is in the driver's seat.

I love you, my beautiful sister.

PS

Given that both you and Ngozi have cars, I would appreciate it if y'all could help Lamont get to his medical appointments occasionally. Also, <u>give Henry Louis to Lamont</u>, but you'll have to do the <u>sound dampening</u> amulets and <u>see me not</u> mojo bags.

Chapter Forty-Three

Zora said she would accompany Jasmine to the woods' edge. But first, Zora said, she would give Jasmine time to prepare by herself mentally. She reasoned that Jasmine might want to gather herself or look at her things for the last time. Forty-five minutes, they agreed, then fifteen minutes of prayer together. However, Zora closed Jasmine's door . . . and booked it.

Her necklace bounced on her chest, reminding her of her ancestors' presence and, she hoped, their acceptance. Zora careened down the stairs, dancing with danger. When her feet touched the ground floor, and she was certain Jasmine wouldn't hear, Zora made a sound halfway between a wail and a holler. It boomed in her chest, mourning with her and yet pushing Zora toward her destiny.

Grief as she huffed through the Esther Fisherman quad, passing by crimson brick and obliviousness. *Resolve* as her sneakers scuffed against the William F. Yardley water feature. *Anger*—brain blurs— as she almost ate shit on jutting stone. Zora righted herself on a thorny bush, yelped, picked three thorns from her palm, watched the blood swell, and carried on.

Chest: fiery. Legs: liquid. Ankles: cursing.

Zora tore through the scraggly grass between the auditorium and the library. She wasn't a runner, but against any opponent, even time, Zora's shoulders were back, and her elbows were tucked in so mother*fucking* tight.

As she ran, she pictured Jasmine lying on her peeling leather couch. Would she start to feel better immediately? Maybe her fever would go down, and her mind fog would gradually clear. It might even be clear enough for her to realize what Zora had done and find the letter Zora left where the shoes used to be, ensuring Jasmine could only follow barefoot at night. Maybe, but unlikely. Zora was moving too fast. Heavy September air sagged in her lungs, but it didn't matter. Groups of freshmen roamed the lawns with plastic cups in their hands and their heads on a swivel, hoping no one of import would catch them this late. Raccoons and squirrels large enough to be raccoons were hazards as they scurried in zigzag patterns—in Zora's way. She didn't even slow down. Nothing would stop her. Nothing.

She swung her backpack around in one movement and stuck her hand in for the flashlight's loop. She wrapped it around her wrist to secure a grip. Zora ensured her backpack was strapped tight even as she kept running. Its contents were vital.

On the other side of the obscenely large auditorium was a building that Zora would know the name of under ordinary circumstances. Circumstances after which she'd live, that is. Behind that building was a shadowy stone pathway leading upward. The lights were tall and dim, too warm-colored and far away to offer significant assistance.

BRICKSBURY MOUNTAIN COLLEGE WOODLANDS

THIS 300-ACRE TRACT WAS ONCE THE WOODLOT OF JONESBORO AFRICAN BAPTIST CHURCH (C. 1796). IT WILL BE LEFT UNDISTURBED FOR PRESENT AND FUTURE GENERATIONS. REMAIN ON THE PATH.

Zora's left knee protested when she entered the woods, and the path started inclining. She slowed but didn't pause. Night air slicked against her skin. Tired arms still pumped—*forward, forward, more, more.* The dryness in her mouth spread down her throat. Zora's body would've never recovered from this anyway. Her lungs screamed at her. A desert lived in her esophagus.

There was no moonlight. It was just Zora and rustling bushes and hooting owls. It was jumping over exposed roots. It was crying and still going. Still pushing. Still fulfilling her life's mission. It was remembering what it was like to run endlessly through the woods behind their grandparents' house with Jasmine as a kid. *One last run.*

A gentle light spill grew brighter as she rounded a bend and passed the wrought iron gate. It looked ancient, older than before. More knowing, fact instead of folklore. Zora didn't have time to consider it more. Or that the swelling light was a mountain of tapered candles.

Guilt and curiosity twinged in her mind when entering the cemetery. She could be on top of bodies at that moment. She didn't make an offering. Would they ever forgive her? Would He? Would He not accept her because she didn't respect her ancestors?

More candles adorned the outside of the church as well—a harrowing welcome, but a welcome, nonetheless. Zora stopped in front of the jumping flames. She doubled over, one hand on her cramping abdomen and the other limply on a knee. Her glasses slid off her face and landed on the ground before her. She tried to lick her lips but couldn't make her tongue move.

"I...did it." Zora stumbled over her words. Her breath had abandoned her.

Amias barreled toward her, his arms reaching out, grabbing her shirt, and throwing her off the church steps. Zora's skull cracked against packed soil, but it was the sharp pain in her hip that made her scream. She'd landed on something, but her flashlight had flown in a different direction, and its light faced away from Zora.

"What are you doing?" Amias crouched over Zora, hand raised, ready to slap her. He looked at it, then at her as he lowered his arm. His giant eyes, though, remained crazed. "I had you spared! It was settled!"

Even from her position, Zora stared him down. "I'm not going to let you kill my sister."

"She's not being *killed*. She's willingly sacrifi—"

"Yeah, I'm sick of your sales pitch. Here."

Zora gingerly rolled over to hand him the backpack. He frowned and opened it while Zora used a nearby stump to help get back on her feet. She ignored the splinters. They were tiny pricks beside the gaping wounds left from the thorned bush on campus. They wouldn't ache for long.

"What's this?"

"The Impossible Book. Er... *The Living Sacrifice*. Before I went to Jasmine's apartment, I went to the library and took it. I've been studying it, analyzing it, trying to understand what the stories plus my research meant."

"And did you figure it out?"

"When I returned to my apartment to write Jasmine a letter saying goodbye, the book had changed. The lock was gone. And it wasn't just *my* research. There were others: Esther Fisherman and Reverend Dr. Junis Thunder. I googled it. The reverend officially died of a heart attack. There was a coroner's report and everything. But that was just another sacrifice, wasn't it? Another death covered up and balmed away by naming something after them. What are you gonna name after me? The place where you had Khadijah killed and made me watch?"

Amias's tiny mouth shook as liquid leaked from his eyes.

"No? Too soon? How about my home, where you stalked me and invaded my privacy under the illusion of 'protection'? Hmm?"

Amias remained silent.

"I know you didn't think I'd be smart enough to figure out how to transfer the mark from one person to another. But we both know the truth, don't we? That while the Beast accepts the mark as final, it isn't as permanent as you like to let those marked for sacrifice think. That really all it did was use sneaky rootwork to make the person weak, make them more agreeable, make them feel like they didn't have a choice. So, I cleansed Jasmine and transferred *your* symbol on to my own skin. Accepting sacrifice."

"Zora."

Amias's voice whistled through pollen and fireflies. Zora found no comfort but no fear in it. Behind him, the Beast approached, her ember-filled eyes shining eagerly, her ink-black tongue sliding over hungry lips. She could sense the symbol, Zora could tell. The transfer had worked.

"NO," Amias screamed, trying to grab the Beast as it passed him but failing. "WAIT!"

It was too late. Zora took as much comfort in this as she possibly could, knowing that even though Jasmine couldn't be totally saved from this, at least she could go on to protect others at Bricksbury. That was why she'd made her choices, after all. After there was nobody to protect her all those years ago in the woods when they were kids, Jasmine got to be a protector of sorts now. Zora would never agree with the trade-off, but that didn't matter anymore. This was an unmovable mountain, and like Esther Fisherman once said, it was time for Mohammed to come to the mountain. Zora couldn't free her sister completely, but at least she could save her life. And that felt like it was enough.

The Beast pushed past Amias and grabbed Zora's neck with her stinking, ink-stained hands. When the hellfire was all she could see, Zora did not look away.

She kept her eyes open.

Acknowledgments

Before all others are the ancestors. Thank you to those who came before me, including Grace, Willie, Louisa, Annie, Alonzo, and Keivon. I see you every day. I hear you every day. I am grateful to have you walking alongside me. To my literary ancestors, we will never know the pain you endured along your journeys. Thank you for the rich, heartbreaking, bone-shaking gifts you have left us with.

Thank you to Charlie, whose patience and relentless belief in me and my gifts continue to humble me and drive me to push for *more*. Thank you, thank you, thank you for loving me fully, just as I love you. Thank you to my mother; there was a time when your strength was the only thing keeping me alive. Thank you for being the embodiment of love and instilling in me a belief in my inherent strength—also, thanks for my dry sense of humor. Alicia, men and friends really did come and go, huh? But you and I truly are forever. Thank you for being unequivocally yourself and always inspiring me to do the same. I love you. Thank you to Homeschool for teaching me that we choose our family.

Glenn, your horror movie/book recommendations (and the resulting comprehensive discussions about them) were instrumental in the making of this story. Also, on perhaps the most serious note we've ever been: Our long nights playing board games, talking about books, and *being friends* have healed parts of me. Friendship is so powerful, and you helped teach me that. Thank you to my besties, podcast cohosts, and authors extraordinaires, Jill Tew and Chelsea Gayden, for the endless (daily!) support. Thank you for challenging me. Thank you for making me laugh so hard I scare my cats. Who would have thought that three people in three different regions of the country, who don't often write in the same genres and are in different stages of life, would be as close as we are? Y'all are family. Thank you to Shelly Romero. Your friendship, ghoulish humor, and taste in music are impeccable and unmatched. You are forever my fairy gothmother.

Chelsea Hensley, you are part literary agent, part strategic mastermind, all while being effortlessly (seriously, you don't even be trying!) hilarious. I'm so, so grateful for you.

Thank you to Dhonielle Clayton for being both an encouraging shepherd for marginalized authors and an indomitable wolf against an industry designed to reject us. Don't worry—we will flood the market with diverse books, for readers, for us, and in honor of our literary ancestors. Thank you to the Electric Postcard Entertainment and New Leaf Literary & Media teams! This story is years in the making and there was so much work behind the scenes that no one will ever know about. Thank you, Carlyn, Clay, Eve, Haneen, Kristen, Jordan, Jenniea, and Joanna. Thank you to the Orbit/ Run For It team, Angelica, Kelley, Rachel, Tim, Ellen, Natassja, Kayleigh, and Elina. This story is much fuller, bolder, and brighter because of you. Thank you.

Lisa and Mike, the book cover is overwhelmingly badass. Thank you for creating such a striking art piece.

Thank you to Alyea Canada and Nivia Evans for *seeing* this story and my talent. I am forever grateful.

Meet the Author

Charlie Iker

BEATRICE WINIFRED IKER (eye-kurr) (they/them) is a storyteller, hiker, and tarot reader from southern Appalachia. Beatrice is a cohost of the *Afronauts Podcast*, which discusses and uplifts Black speculative fiction. They are a Voodoonauts fellow and a Dwarf Stars, Ignyte, and Rhysling Awards finalist.

RAISING READERS
Books Build Bright Futures

Thank you for reading this book and for being a reader of books in general. We are so grateful to share being part of a community of readers with you, and we hope you will join us in passing our love of books on to the next generation of readers.

Did you know that reading for enjoyment is the single biggest predictor of a child's future happiness and success?

More than family circumstances, parents' educational background, or income, reading impacts a child's future academic performance, emotional well-being, communication skills, economic security, ambition, and happiness.

Studies show that kids reading for enjoyment in the US is in rapid decline:

- In 2012, 53% of 9-year-olds read almost every day. Just 10 years later, in 2022, the number had fallen to 39%.
- In 2012, 27% of 13-year-olds read for fun daily. By 2023, that number was just 14%.

Together, we can commit to **Raising Readers** and change this trend. How?

- Read to children in your life daily.
- Model reading as a fun activity.
- Reduce screen time.
- Start a family, school, or community book club.
- Visit bookstores and libraries regularly.
- Listen to audiobooks.
- Read the book before you see the movie.
- Encourage your child to read aloud to a pet or stuffed animal.
- Give books as gifts.
- Donate books to families and communities in need.

BOB1217

Books build bright futures, and **Raising Readers** is our shared responsibility.

For more information, visit **JoinRaisingReaders.com**

Sources: National Endowment for the Arts, National Assessment of Educational Progress, WorldBookDay.org, Nielsen BookData's 2023 "Understanding the Children's Book Consumer"